GAMES WOMEN PLAY

GAMES WOMEN PLAY

ZAIRE CROWN

KENSINGTON PUBLISHING CORP.
www.kensingtonbooks.com

DAFINA BOOKS are published by

Kensington Publishing Corp.
119 West 40th Street
New York, NY 10018

All Kensington titles, imprints, and distributed lines are available at special quantity discounts for bulk purchases for sales promotion, premiums, fund-raising, and educational or institutional use.

Special book excerpts or customized printings can also be created to fit specific needs. For details, write or phone the office of the Kensington Sales Manager: Kensington Publishing Corp., 119 West 40th Street, New York, NY 10018. Attn. Sales Department. Phone: 1-800-221-2647.

Dafina and the Dafina logo Reg. U.S. Pat. & TM Off.

ISBN-13: 978-1-61773-989-7
ISBN-10: 1-61773-989-8
First Kensington Trade Paperback Printing: December 2015

eISBN-13: 978-1-61773-990-3
eISBN-10: 1-61773-990-1
First Kensington Electronic Edition: December 2015

10 9 8 7 6 5 4 3 2 1

Printed in the United States of America

Chapter One

For most of his life, Tank's luck with women had been all bad. Being six foot three, black as a Michelin tire, a sloppy three hundred forty-five pounds with big bug eyes, he knew that for him, love would always be conditional and very expensive, which was why he hustled so hard. But now, thanks to Simone, even that changed.

He met her six weeks ago at a hand car wash that a lot of ballers hit. One day while he was getting his truck detailed, she pulled up in a G6 and stole his heart.

Tank had never been a sucker-type nigga who believed in love at first sight. Before Simone, women only fell into three categories: those he couldn't fuck, those he wanted to fuck, and those he didn't; but from the first moment he saw that tiny light-skinned angel standing at four foot eleven with the innocent hazel eyes, he didn't just want to fuck her, he wanted to spoil her, to protect her, he wanted to be everything for and to her, and this was before even knowing her name. To Tank, she shined brighter than all the custom paint and polished chrome being washed that day.

Simone was his type without being his type. As far as looks, she was everything he'd ever been attracted to: petite but curvy with a pretty face and tiny feet; but her personality was unlike anyone he'd been with before. She had just enough street smarts but for the most part was a square: she didn't smoke or drink, and spoke so proper that Tank thought it was funny when she tried to curse. She was not spoiled or money-hungry like so many other females of her status—twice Tank had tried to surprise her with gifts, first a Louis bag and then a diamond bracelet, only to have her turn them down. She was always friendly, always smiling, always humble and considerate. She viewed every stranger as a potential friend rather than a threat. She was almost unreal and Tank couldn't believe that a girl this pretty wasn't conceited, wasn't a slut, and wasn't into his big black ugly ass for the money.

He soon came to accept that Simone was simply something special, like some beautiful goddess come straight down from heaven. This was the reason he nicknamed her Tiny Angel.

Although she was pretty close to perfection, the only thing that frustrated the hell out of Tank was Simone's sixty-day rule. Regardless of who it was, any man courting Simone had to endure a two-month waiting period before they could do what she called "the nasty," and the two months did not start at introduction but rather at the first date. Since it took Tank ten days to convince her to go out with him, that meant he still had close to four weeks to go. He was like a child in December counting down the days to Christmas, and as any eager child will tell you, those days move incredibly slowly.

Lately, they were spending almost every day together, having plenty of make-out sessions that always ended with her suddenly pulling back, leaving him all rocked up and begging for more.

On this particular night, luck struck. They were at Tank's loft on his California king–sized bed in the middle of another heated make-out session when she broke their kiss, looked up at him with those sparkling gold eyes and said: "I think I'm ready," even though he technically still had twenty-eight days left on probation.

"You ready now!" he blurted with excitement. She nodded while chewing on her bottom lip and Tank damn near started to cry.

Watching Simone undress was the closest he had ever come to a religious experience. She slipped off her top then ran her fingers through her silky black hair. Tank gazed up at this delicate porcelain doll as she rolled her hips in slow circles. It surprised him that she could dance so sexy.

She unbuttoned her white jean shorts and let them settle at her ankles then playfully kicked them off. The lacy turquoise panties underneath complemented her shape and skin tone. She did a slow turn so that he could see that they were thong; that was when Tank noticed the small devil tattoo on the upper part of her right butt cheek. Apparently his good girl had a bit of a wild side.

She stooped down to mount him and their lips met again. Tank held her against his chest and ran his hungry hands all over her. The kiss was eternal, blissful, but she broke it only to ask: "Why do you still have your clothes on?" Tank had been so mesmerized by her striptease that he forgot to undress himself.

He jumped out the bed and stripped to his boxers while she slipped beneath the covers. With a shyness that he just found too cute, she pulled the sheets up to her neck, unhooked her bra and shimmied out of her panties then tossed the lacy underwear at his feet. When Tank scooped up her panties and sniffed them, Simone giggled like a schoolgirl.

Back in the bed, he rolled on top of her four-foot-eleven-inch frame, using his arms to brace himself so he wouldn't crush Simone under his 345 pounds.

She playfully jiggled the fat rolls on his side and said, "Papa Bear," which was her pet name for him.

He called her "Tiny Angel."

"I love you." The words were spoken so sweetly and meekly that he cried tears of joy for a future filled with promise. A future with Simone. He knew that her words weren't just a confession, they were a plea. Simone was surrendering herself to him while asking only with her eyes: *Take me but don't abuse me!*

Tank kissed his way down her neck until he found her breasts. Simone was a modest B-cup and while he had seen much bigger, none had been more flawless. On mounds of buttercream flesh, her quarter-sized areolas sat like caramel brown peaks. Each was crowned with a fat, stubby nipple that he teased with his tongue before taking both swells into his mouth one after the other.

He sank beneath the covers leaving a trail of kisses down her stomach, past a navel ring he never noticed, and then lower. Tank learned that she was waxed and this relieved him, because he feared that a girl who wasn't heavily into sex might neglect her lady garden. He kissed her lips, opened them, then attacked the clit with a trained tongue. This was where he shined and he had been eager to show off his skills to Simone.

Tank was under the sheets doing what he did best. He wasn't big and couldn't last very long but Tank learned that a female was less likely to complain about a little-dick nigga who couldn't fuck if he could make her cum four or five times by eating it first. She moaned her appreciation and the sound of her ecstasy made him go harder. When Simone grabbed the back of his head and started grinding her crotch into his face, Tank knew he had her.

Then Simone screamed and it was not the pleasure-filled cry of a girl about to bust. There was surprise and terror in that sound. Tank feared that he somehow had hurt her, so he threw the blanket off his head to check on her.

When he saw the gun, he knew that his talented tongue had not been the problem. Two big black guns were pointed directly at his head. They were only rifles but with the barrels only an inch away from his face, they loomed as large and menacing as battleship cannons.

Four of them. Armed. They were all surrounding the bed. They had crept into the room as stealthily as ninjas and were dressed the part. Black from head to toe: combat boots, cargo pants, long-sleeved shirts under Kevlar vests, ski masks, and leather gloves. Their masks were the type made without a mouth hole and only a horizontal viewport along the eyes, but even this small swatch of exposed skin was painted black, revealing nothing of their true complexion. They were shadows.

Tank saw that two of them were standing at the head of the bed, one with a .40-caliber Glock aimed at Simone. The two covering him had AK's in his face.

For a long unnerving moment the four of them stood there silent and motionless. To Tank it was almost like someone had slipped into his loft and set up a display of mannequins as a joke.

After that initial scream Simone had also gone quiet but now she was silently weeping. Tank reached out to comfort her but the fourth one jammed another Glock .40 in his face as a warning.

Tank threw his hands up to surrender. "Look, man, just take whatever the fuck y'all want and go!"

One of the Glock-holders went to the side pocket of his cargo pants and pulled out a device that Tank was scared might be a Taser. When the gunman held it out and pressed the button, it didn't produce electric volts, only words from a tiny hidden speaker: "Thomas Humphries, the four men that have you surrounded have no problem with killing you and your lady friend unless you follow my instructions."

Tank didn't know if it was a recording device or some sort of CB radio but the deep, gravelly voice that came from it frightened him.

"You are about to lose something, Mr. Humphries, but how much is totally up to you. If you obey, these men will only be taking your money and drugs, but if you disobey the cost will be your life. Nod if you understand, Mr. Humphries." He switched it off.

Tank nodded, still trying to figure out how they knew his full name. There wasn't a nigga he had fucked with since tenth grade that knew his whole government.

The second Glock-holder grabbed a fistful of Simone's hair and dragged her off the bed. When she tried to pull the sheets to cover herself, they were snatched away from her. He stood about three feet away from the others holding the tiny naked Simone by the throat with the .40-cal pressed to her temple.

Number one pressed the button again: "Now, Thomas, your

instructions are simple, straightforward, and fairly easy to understand. Step one: You are going to lead these gentlemen to the drop safe that you have hidden in the floor. Step two: You are going to open that safe. Step three: You are going to give them everything inside. Step four: You are going to let them leave without doing anything stupid." He stopped it again.

Tank looked at them wild-eyed. "I don't know what the fuck y'all talkin' 'bout. I ain't got no safe! Now I got 'bout three bands in my pocket and my truck keys on the dresser but ain't no safe. Somebody done fed y'all some wrong information."

Without warning the gunman holding Simone smashed her over the head with the butt of his Glock. She crumbled to the floor in a heap of flesh, cried aloud. The sound pierced Tank as if he'd been struck. Before he could voice a plea, she was snatched up and held by the throat again.

The voice on the recorder said: "Mr. Humphries, any hesitations, denials or stall tactics will be considered disobedience, and disobedience will be punished severely. The assaults on your lady friend will gradually escalate in brutality until it ends with a very gruesome violation then two bullets pumped into her skull. Nod if you understand, Mr. Humphries."

Tank nodded. He didn't finish high school but it didn't take a diploma to understand what "gruesome violation" meant. The raspy voice on the speaker reminded him of Anthony Hopkins when he played Hannibal Lecter. His calm tone and sophistication made him sound like a madman. Only a twisted mind could speak about rape and murder with such eloquence.

The voice said: "Step 1: You are going to lead these gentlemen to the drop safe that you have hidden in the floor." The order was repeated with the same rhythm as the previous time; this made Tank suspect that it was just a recording and not a two-way radio.

Sadly, that tidbit of information gave him no strategic advantage nor made his enemies any less dangerous. None of the masked men had spoken; they did all their communicating via the recorder. The fact that they apparently knew his full name, knew about his safe, and the ease with which they got past a first-rate security system with a seven-digit pen marked them as professionals.

He stared into Simone's glistening eyes and saw the fear in them. Already so tiny, Tank imagined that she shrank until she was as small and fragile as a doll. He knew he had to protect her. It was no stretch to assume that men so disciplined might be equally ruthless. Any threats made against him or Simone had to be treated as serious.

He decided to stop bullshitting with them.

"Please don't hurt her!" He folded with tears in his eyes. "I'll take you to the safe. I'll do whatever you want. Just don't hurt my Tiny Angel!"

Chapter Two

The Bounce House was not one of those inflatable castles parents rented for children's parties. It was a small gentlemen's club set in a strip mall on 7 Mile with a beauty supply store, a rib joint, an outlet that sold men's clothing, and an unleased space that changed hands every few years. In no way was The Bounce House on the same level as some of the more elite clubs in Detroit; with a maximum capacity of two hundred fifty and limited parking, it would never be a threat to The Coliseum, Cheetah's, or any of the big dogs. It wasn't big but it was comfortable, well managed; plus the owner was very selective in choosing the girls so this had earned it a small but loyal patronage.

Tuesday Knight knew that Mr. Scott, her neighbor and owner of Bo's BBQ, would be waiting in the door of his shop the moment her white CTS hit the lot. The old man had a crush on her and always made it his business to be on hand to greet her whenever she pulled in to work.

She frowned when she saw that someone had parked in her spot right in front of The Bounce House. The canary Camaro with the black racing stripes belonged to Brianna, and she was definitely going to check that bitch because she had been warned about that before.

Since all the other slots outside The Bounce, Bo's BBQ, and KiKi's Beauty Supply were taken, she had to park way down in front of the vacant property and she speculated about which business would spring up there next. In the past five years it had been an ice cream parlor, a cell phone shop, and an occult book-store. She wished its next incarnation would be as a lady's shoe out-let that sold Louboutins at a discount.

She shrugged the Louis Vuitton bag onto her shoulder then slid out of the Cadillac.

Up ahead on the promenade Mr. Scott was standing in front of his carry-out spot pretending to sweep the walk but really waiting for her. This was practically a daily ritual for them.

"Hi, Mr. Scott," she said, beaming a smile.

He did an old-school nod and tip of the hat. "Hey, Miss Tues-day, you sho lookin' mighty fine today." He always called her Miss Tuesday even though it was her first name.

"Thank you, Mr. Scott. You lookin' handsome as always."

He removed his straw Dobb's hat and was fanning himself with it even though the afternoon was mild. "Girl, if I was thirty years younger I'd show you somethin'!" Mr. Scott was seventy years old and had always been respectful of her and all the dancers so she didn't mind putting on for him.

"I know you would, Daddy! You have a nice day now, okay."

What The Bounce House lacked in size it attempted to make up for in taste. There was nothing cheap about the place despite being a small independent establishment. The design wasn't unique: a fifteen-foot bar ran against the far right wall; a large horseshoe-shaped stage dominated the center with twenty or so small circular tables surrounding it; booths were lined against the left wall and wrapped around the front, the entrance was where that front wall and right one intersected and the deejay booth was next to it.

Before Tuesday had taken over, the entire place was done in a tacky red because the previous owner thought that it was a sexual color. Tuesday had brought the place into the new millennium with brushed suede booths, a bar with a granite top, more understated flooring, and mirrored walls that gave the illusion of more space. She even gave it a touch of class and masculinity by adding dark woods, brass, and a touch of plant life.

When she came through the door, the first thing that jumped out at her was that the fifth booth hadn't been bused. There were half a dozen double-shot glasses on the table, an ashtray filled with butts and cigar filters, and a white Styrofoam food container that had most likely come from Bo's. She knew that it was her OCD that caused her to immediately zero in on this but before she could start bitching, one of the servers was already headed to clean it up. Everyone who worked there knew their boss had a thing for neatness so she shot the girl a look that said: *Bitch, you know better!*

Things were slow even for a Monday afternoon. There were only three customers at the bar with eleven more scattered throughout the tables and booths. Most of them were entranced by a dancer named Cupcake who was on stage rolling her hips to the latest hot song. Two more girls were on the floor giving table dances.

Whenever Tuesday came in, her first priority was always to check on the bar. The bartender on duty was a brown-skinned cutie named Ebony who had started out as a dancer then learned she had a knack for pouring drinks. She took a couple classes, became a mixologist and has been working at The Bounce since back in the day when Tuesday was just a dancer.

Ebony called out: "Boss Lady!" when she saw her slip behind the bar.

Tuesday pulled her close so she wouldn't have to compete with the music. "Eb, how we lookin for the week?"

From the pocket of her apron Ebony whipped out a small notepad she used for keeping up with the liquor inventory. "What we don't got out here we got in the back. We pretty much straight on everythang, at least as far as makin' it through the week, except we down to our last case of Goose."

Tuesday made a mental note to send Tushie to the distributor.

Ebony asked, "How dat nigga A.D. doin?"

"He all right. Reading every muthafuckin' thang and workin' out. That nigga arms damn near big as Tushie's legs."

"When was the last time you holla'ed at 'em?"

Tuesday scanned the bar, quietly admiring how neat Ebony kept her workstation. "Nigga called the other day on some horny shit. Talkin' 'bout, 'What kinda panties you got on? What color is they?'" She did a comical impersonation of a man's deep voice. "Nigga kept me on the phone for an hour wantin' me to talk dirty to 'em."

Ebony poured a customer a shot of Silver Patrón. "No he didn't!" she said, smiling at Tuesday.

"So I'm tellin' him I'm in a bathtub playin' with my pussy, thinkin' 'bout his big dick. The whole time I'm out at Somerset Mall in Nordstrom's lookin for a new fit."

"TK, you still crazy!" Ebony was laughing so hard that she fell into her. "The funny part is, he probably knew you was lying and just didn't care."

"Hell, yeah, he knew I was lying. A.D. ain't stupid. But when I know that's the type of shit he wanna hear, I always tell 'em somethin' good."

"That nigga been gone for a minute. When he comin' home?"

Tuesday's smile faded a bit. She hated when people asked that question, especially when most of them were already familiar with his situation. A.D. was doing life and a lot of times people asked her when he was coming home just for the sake of gauging her faith and commitment to him. If she said "Soon" she looked stupid when the years stretched on and he didn't show, but if she said "Never!" it looked as if she'd just wrote the nigga off. Her and Ebony had been cool for a long time and she didn't think that the girl was trying to play some type of mind game but the question still bothered her.

As much as she hated being asked about A.D., it happened so often that over the years she had come to patent this perfect response: "He still fighting but that appeal shit takes time." This way she doesn't commit herself to any specific date while still appearing to be optimistic.

Ebony nodded thoughtfully. "Well, next time you holla at 'em, tell that nigga I said keep his head up."

Tuesday left from behind the bar agreeing to relay that message.

She was crossing the room by weaving her way through the maze of tables on the floor when suddenly: *whack!* Somebody smacked her on the ass so hard that it made her flinch.

At first Tuesday thought it was some new customer who didn't yet know who she was, and just as she turned around ready to go H.A.M., she realized that it was her big bouncer DelRay.

DelRay was six foot seven and close to four hundred pounds. He was heavy, but didn't look sloppy because it was stretched out by his height. He also knew how to handle himself, possessing a grace and speed rarely seen in men his size. While he had the skills to deal with unruly customers physically, he had the game to get most of them out the door without making a scene. This was what Tuesday liked most about him.

She said, "Nigga, I was about to flip!"

"We at four!" he yelled over the music. Lil Wayne was playing then.

She shook her head. "Hell, naw, nigga. We at five!"

He used his thick sausage-like fingers to count. "Two Saturday night, one Sunday before you got in your car and one just now." He grinned and rubbed his hands together like a little kid eager for a gift. "I get to smack that fat muthafucka six more times!"

"Fuck you!" she said, but with a smile. Actually, she knew it was only four.

He teased her. "Don't be mad at me, you should be m̶
boy LeBron! When it get down to crunch time he always cho̶

"That's all right, though," she fired back. "I still like Miami to̶
win it all. Yo weak-ass Pistons ain't even gone make the playoffs."

"Give us two more years to draft, we gone be back on top
again!"

Changing the subject, she asked, "I saw Bree's car out front
but is the rest of 'em here?"

DelRay nodded. "Everybody but Tush. Jaye in the locker
room skinnin' them bitches on the poker. Bree and Doll in there
with her."

"Tush will be here in a minute. I already holla'ed at her. But go
tell the rest of them bitches I'm in my office."

"I got you, Boss Lady."

Just as she turned to walk away: *whack!*

She whipped around trying to mug him but DelRay's fat face
made one of those goofy looks that always melted her ice grill.
"I'm sorry, Boss Lady, I couldn't help it. You shouldn't have wore
that True Religion shit today. You in them muthafuckin' jeans!"

She jerked her fist like she was going to punch him. "Now we
at five!"

"You wanna bet back on Miami and Orlando?"

"You ain't said shit, nigga, I ride or die with D. Wade! But if you
win this time, goddammit, I'm just gone pay yo heavy-handed ass."

DelRay lumbered off toward an entryway at the left of the
stage and parted the beaded curtain that hung over it. That hall
had three doors: One for a storage room where all the extra booze
and miscellaneous supplies for the bar were kept; the second was
the locker room where the dancers changed clothes and spent
their downtime in between sets; the third, the door in which the
hall terminated in, was a fire exit that led to the alley behind the
strip mall. DelRay went to the second door, knocked three times,
then waited for permission to enter.

An identical hall ran along the opposite side of the stage, only

...minate in a fire door. It was where the rest-
..., and just beyond them was a door stenciled
... *s Lady*.

... a modest but tidy space that was only fifteen by
... It had a single window with only a view of a
... alley. There was a cheap walnut-veneered desk
holding ... and computer, a small two drawer file cabinet,
two plastic chairs that fronted the desk, and an imitation suede
loveseat given to her by a friend. The most expensive thing in the
office was her chair: a genuine leather high-back office chair er-
gonomically designed for perfect lumbar support, costing more
than fourteen hundred dollars; she had spent more on it than her
computer. The office also came with a wall safe that Tuesday
never kept any cash in. Other than the above-mentioned items,
there was nothing else in the way of furniture or decor. Tuesday
didn't have anything hanging on the walls and no framed photos
were propped on her desk to give it a personal touch. She stepped
into her Spartan little space and closed the door.

Tuesday had spent twenty-one years at The Bounce House—
ten as a dancer, four as a manager, and seven more as owner—but
whenever she came in the office her mind always flashed back to
that first time she stepped into it. She was sixteen years old, ex-
pelled from all Detroit public schools, a runaway crashing at a
different friend's house every night and desperate for money. She
had an older cousin named Shameeka who danced there but at the
time the place was called Smokin' Joe's. Because Tuesday was light-
skinned, pretty with green eyes and a banging body, Shameeka
swore she could earn enough money for her own car and crib in no
time. So led by her favorite cousin, a young and naive Tuesday was
brought in and walked to the door of this office. Shameeka handed
her a condom then pushed her inside like a human sacrifice to a
sixty-two-year-old bony Polish guy, whose name, ironically, was-
n't Joe. There was an eight minute pound session in which he
bent her over the very same desk she still had, then fifteen minutes after that Tuesday's new name was X-Stacy and she was on

the floor giving out lap dances for ten dollars a pop. The old man never asked her age, or anything else, for that matter.

She dropped her bag on the desk and sank into her favorite chair. She thought about what this place had given her, but mostly all that it had taken away.

She was snapped from her reverie when the door swung open. Jaye came in followed by Brianna, and Tuesday immediately cut into her: "Bitch, how many times I got to tell you to stay out my spot?"

Brianna responded with an impudent smirk. "It wasn't like you was using it. Shit, we didn't even know when you was gone get here."

"The point of havin' my own parking space is so that I'll have a place to park *whenever* I pull up at the club. I don't give a fuck if I'm gone three weeks, when I roll through here that spot right in front of the door is me! Every bitch who work here know that shit, even the customers know it."

Brianna took a drag off the Newport she was smoking then flopped down on the loveseat. "Well, you need to put up a sign or somethin'."

"I don't need to put up shit!" Tuesday barked. "The next time I come through and you in my shit I'ma bust every muthafuckin' window you got on that li'l weak-ass Camaro!"

Brianna shrugged nonchalantly and blew out a trail of gray smoke. "And it ain't gone cost me shit if you do. 'Cause like a good neighbor State Farm will be there . . . with some brand new windows."

Tuesday pointed a finger at her. "Keep talkin' shit and see if State Farm be there with a new set of teeth!"

Jaye quietly witnessed the exchange with a smile on her face. She took one of the plastic chairs that fronted the desk.

Just then Tushie came in rubbing her ass with a sour look on her face.

Tuesday laughed. "DelRay got you too, huh? Was it that Miami game?"

She poured herself into the second chair. "Naw, you know fucks wit dat sexy-ass Carmelo Anthony," she said with her heavy southern drawl. "New York let da Celtics blow dem out by twenty."

Tuesday asked, "How many he got left?"

Tushie thought back. "He done got me twice already, he only got three left."

"You only gave that nigga five, he got me for ten! How my shit only worth ten dollars a smack and yours worth twenty?"

Laughing, Jaye said, "Maybe because she got twice as much ass!"

Tuesday shot back at her, "And I still got three times more than you!"

After sharing a laugh she then said, "We can settle up soon as Doll bring her ass on." Tuesday looked to Brianna. "I thought she was with y'all. Where the fuck she at?"

"How the fuck should I know!" Brianna snapped back at her. "Just because the bitch little don't mean I keep her in my pocket!"

Baby Doll came in as if on cue and closed the door. She snatched the cigarette out of Brianna's mouth, dropped onto the loveseat next to her and began to smoke it.

Brianna said, "Ughh, bitch, I could've just got finished suckin' some dick!"

Baby Doll continued to drag the Newport unfazed. "Knowin' yo stankin' ass, you probably did. Besides, my lips done been in waay worse places than yours."

Baby Doll took a few more puffs then tried to offer it back to Brianna, who rolled her eyes and looked away. "Bitch, I wish I would."

Tuesday handed her an ashtray. "Well, now that everybody *finally* here, we can take care of this business."

This was the crew: Tuesday, Brianna, Jaye, Tushie, and Baby Doll. Five hustling-ass dime pieces with top-notch game who was out for the bread. Individually they were good but together they were dangerous. These were the girls who played the players.

Tuesday looked at Baby Doll. "You get yo shit up outta there?"

She butted what was left of the Newport and blew the last of the smoke from her nostrils. "The little bit I had being moved today. I only brought *what* I needed for the lick—just enough to make it look like home. It ain't like him and Simone spent a lot of time chillin' at her crib anyway. We either went out or was chillin' at his loft."

Code name: Baby Doll. She was only four feet eleven inches tall with hips and ass that stood out more because of her short stature. Her buttermilk skin always looked soft even without touching it. Delicate doll-like features had earned her name and made her age hard to place: if Doll told a nigga she was thirteen or thirty, he would believe either one. The type of men who typically went for Doll had low self-esteem and loved the ego boost she gave them; her small size and the helplessness they wrongly perceived in her made them feel bigger and stronger while that childlike *naïveté* she faked so well made them feel smarter. Baby Doll's greatest asset was her bright hazel eyes because she could project an innocence in them that made men want to protect and possess her. It was because of this that, of the five, Baby Doll was second only to Tuesday in having the most niggas propose marriage to her.

Tuesday asked, "What about Tank?"

"He don't think nothin' up," said Doll. "He done spent the last two days blowin' up that phone and leaving texts for Simone. Of course he thinking that li'l situation done scared her off. Same shit every time."

Tuesday nodded. "Good. Text his ass back and break it off. Tell him you thought you could deal with his lifestyle, but after what happened you can't see being with him—"

She cut her off. "TK, I know the routine! I ain't new to this shit."

"Make sure you lose that phone too," Tuesday reminded her. "How did he feel about that loss he took?"

Doll shrugged. "He wasn't really trippin' 'bout the money and he say he got insurance on the truck so he gone get back right off that. He was just so happy that ain't nothin' happen to me."

"That's cause you his Tiny Angel!" Jaye said, teasing her. " 'All right, I'll open the safe. Just don't hurt my Tiny Angel.' " She did a spot-on impression of Tank's pathetic voice that made them all laugh.

Code name: Jaye. She was five foot nine with a medium build. She wasn't that strapped but her face was pretty as hell; she had dark brown eyes, a cocoa complexion, and big full juicy lips that promised pleasure. Jaye was not the stuck-up dime, she was the ultimate fuck buddy. She was that fine-ass homegirl you could hit and still be cool with. Staying laced in Gucci and Prada heels, Jaye was a girly girl but had some special tomboy quality about her that made a nigga want to blow a blunt or chill with her at a Lions game. She was cool, she was funny, and could easily make a mark feel at ease with her sense of humor. Her best asset was her personality but Jaye's secret weapon was her amazing neck game. She sucked dick like a porn star and the same big lips that got her teased in school were now her sexiest feature. Not too many niggas could resist a bad bitch who kept them laughing all day then at night gave them the best head they ever had.

"I know the type of nigga Tank is," said Tuesday. "He gone be suckerstroking real hard about you." She looked at Baby Doll. "Lay low for a while and you might wanna do something different to yo hair. Trust me, this nigga gone be stalkin' you for a minute."

While they spoke Brianna just quietly shook her head with a look of disgust on her face. "I know having to get next to some off-brand niggas is part of the game, but god damn, Doll, you a better bitch than me. That fat, black, greasy-ass nigga with them big bug eyes; I don't think I could've pulled this one off." She jerked forward pretending to dry-heave then put a hand over her mouth. "How could you look that nigga in the eye and say you love him with a straight face? Just thinkin' about that nigga kissing and touching on me got me ready to throw up."

Doll looked at her sideways. "Bitch, like you said, it's part of the game, that's what we do. I'm playin' his muthafuckin' ass the same way you done had to play niggas and every other bitch in this room. I don't give a fuck what a mark look like, I'm about my paper!"

"Church, bitch!" Tushie leaned over so her and Doll could dap each other.

Brianna leaned back on the loveseat and inspected her freshly polished nails. "Well, I guess I just got higher standards than you bitches."

Code name: Brianna. She was six foot one with the long slender build of a runway model except for her huge 36DD's. Bree had that exotic look that came when you mixed black with some sort of Asian. She had a peanut butter complexion and thick lips but had inherited their distinctive eyes. Nobody really knew what Brianna was mixed with—Tuesday didn't even think Brianna knew—but whatever she was, the girl was gorgeous. The type of men who were attracted to her were typically looking for a trophy. They liked rare and beautiful things and had no problem with paying for them. Brianna played the high-maintenance girlfriend so well because acting snotty and spoiled wasn't really a stretch.

Tuesday told the girls that they needed to work on their choreography. She felt that it didn't look real enough the other night when Brianna pretended to hit Baby Doll with the gun. "Y'all timing was off. Bree, you looked like you was just tryin' to give her a love tap. And Doll, you looked like you knew it was comin', you was already going down before she could hit you."

Brianna responded the way she typically did to criticism. "Why is you trippin'? The shit was good enough to fool him."

"I'm trippin', bitch, because we can't afford to make mistakes like that. Small shit like that is what could get us knocked."

"Watch this." Tuesday stood up and came from behind her desk. Tushie rose from her seat knowing that she had a role in the demonstration.

The girls squared off then pretended that they were two hoodrats in the middle of a heated argument: they rolled their necks, put fingers in each other's faces and Tushie improvised some dialogue about Tuesday fucking her man. They pushed each other back and forth, then Tushie gave Tuesday a loud smack that whipped her head around. She held her cheek, looking stunned for a second, then came back with a hard right that dropped Tushie back into her chair.

She fell limp with her head dropped against her chest unconscious but two seconds later she opened her eyes and smiled. "See, bitches, that's how it's done."

Code name: Tushie. This Louisiana stallion was five foot seven, and while she only had mosquito bites for breasts, her tiny twenty-four-inch waist and fifty-six-inch hips meant she was thicker than Serena Williams on steroids. "Tushie" was the only name that had ever fit her because by thirteen the girl was already so donked up that all her pants had to be tailor-made; by fifteen she was causing so many car accidents from just walking down the street that the police in her small town actually labeled her a danger to the community. Her Hershey bar skin and black Barbie doll features made her a dime even without being ridiculously strapped. Despite having an ass like two beach balls, Tushie's best asset was really her mind. Many people had been fooled by her deep southern accent but she only talked slow. Tushie knew how to play on those who thought she was just a dumb country bammer and rocked them to sleep. Any nigga thinking she was all booty and no brains would find out the hard way that southerners ain't slow.

Jaye was impressed by the girls' fight scene. The moves and timing were so perfect that it looked as if they had spent time training with actual Hollywood stunt men. Jaye was only a foot away from the action, and even though she knew it was fake, she still thought that their blows had made contact. "Wait a minute," she said, curious. "I know she ain't really just slap you but I swear I heard that shit."

"What you heard was this." Tuesday clapped her hand against her meaty thigh. She explained: "I'm the one gettin' hit. You lookin at my face and her hand. You ain't watching my hands! Me and Tush just got this shit down because we been at it longer than y'all."

"Well, I ain't gone go through all that," Brianna said, standing up to stretch. "Next time I'm just gone bust a bitch head for real!"

"And now can we wrap up this little meeting so I can get paid and get the fuck outta here. I got shit to do."

Tuesday went into her Louis bag and pulled out a brick of cash. She carefully counted it out into five separate stacks then began to pass out the dividends. As the girls took their individual shares, Tuesday could see the disappointment on their faces. They were expecting more and she was too.

She passed two stacks to Doll, who took one then handed the other to Brianna. Bree made a quick count of the cash then dropped the sixty-five hundred onto the loveseat as if it were nothing. "What the fuck is this?"

Tuesday sighed because she knew this was coming and knew it would be from her. "Look, I know it's kinda short. Shit fucked up all the way around. I got twenty for the truck, seventeen for the work, and my mans said I was lucky to get that."

After doing two months of surveillance on Tank, Tuesday had put Baby Doll on him. It took another couple of weeks of Doll's sweet manipulation to get everything they needed for the lick: personal information, alarm codes, copies of his house keys, the location of his stash, and a head so far gone that he wouldn't risk Doll's life to protect it. The girls had hoped for a big score but found out that Tank was not the hustler they thought he was. The scouting report said that he was heavy in the brick game and the team targeted him expecting at least a six-figure payoff, but when they opened fat boy's safe all he had was forty-two thousand in cash and twenty-four packaged-up ounces of hard. Disappointed, the girls took his Denali even though it wasn't originally part of the plan. They split the cash that night but it was Tuesday's job to slang the truck and dope; now the girls didn't even get what they hoped for that. Minus what was due to their sixth silent partner, almost four months of work had only grossed them a little over thirteen racks apiece—if you factor in the expenses of renting a temporary place for Doll's alter ego, Simone and the Pontiac G6 she drove, they actually netted a lot less. The team typically went after bigger fish, and while they only did about five or six of these jobs a year (sometimes having a few going on at once), they were used to making twenty-five to thirty stacks each, so a lick that only pulled seventy-nine total was a bust.

Tuesday leaned back against her desk. "Look, ladies, I know shit ain't really come through how we wanted on this one. That's my bad but I promise we gone eat right on the next one." She took the blame because as leader of the group the responsibility always fell on her.

Code name: Tuesday aka Boss Lady. Tuesday was light-skinned, five foot nine, and thick. She didn't have junk like Tushie but her booty was bigger than average and had been turning heads since puberty. Aside from a pretty face and juicy lips, she had cat eyes that shifted from green to gray according to her mood. Tuesday had put this team together and was the brains behind it. She realized when she was just a dancer that clapping her ass all night for a few dollars in tips wouldn't cut it for a bitch who had bills and wanted nice shit. At nineteen she started hitting licks with A.D., and after he went away, she continued on her own. Over time she recruited Tushie then slowly pulled in the others. Each of these girls had come to The Bounce just as broke and desperate as she was and Tuesday saw something in each of them that made her think they would be a good fit for the team. Tuesday's best asset was her experience. She had years on every other girl in the group and none of them could crawl inside a mark's head better than she could. She gave them all their game and therefore had each of their skills. She knew how to make a read on a nigga and adapt to the type of girl it took to get him. She could play the innocent square better than Doll, the cool homegirl better than Jaye, and the high-maintenance trophy bitch better than Brianna. She could play one role to a T or blend a few of them together if it was necessary. Her strength was that she was not one-dimensional like the others. For Tuesday, her secret weapon was actually her secret weakness. None of the girls knew she suffered from obsessive-compulsive disorder. Her illness caused her to reorganize things over and over until they were perfect. Her nature to obsess over every little detail did make her a neat freak, but also the ultimate strategist. Tuesday had a way of seeing all the moves ahead of time and putting together airtight plans that accounted for every problem that might arise.

"He only gave you twenty for the truck, rims and all?" Bree asked with some skepticism in her voice that everybody heard.

Tuesday nodded. "He said he couldn't do no better than that."

"You know that was the new Denali, right? That's at least a fifty-thousand-dollar whip."

Tuesday frowned. "It's a fifty-thousand-dollar whip that's *stolen*! You think he gone give me sticker price for it?"

Brianna shrugged and studied her nails again. "I don't know. Just seem like you got worked to me. Either that or somethin' wrong with yo math!"

That made Tuesday stand up straight. Every other woman in that room felt the sudden shift in the vibe as her eyes quickly changed from lime green to icy gray. "Bitch, is you tryin' to say somethin'?"

Bree didn't retreat from her stare. "All I'm sayin' is that we done put in a lot of time for a punk-ass thirteen G's! If you figure it all out we basically got a little over three thousand a month. A bitch can get a job and do better than that!"

"The lick wasn't what I thought it was and I apologized for that." Tuesday inched closer to her. "But when you got to talkin' all this bullshit about my math, I thought you was tryin' to hint at somethin' else. So if you got anythang you wanna get off yo double D's about that, feel free to speak up!"

Jaye and Doll just sat there silent because they both knew what Brianna had tried to insinuate and knew that Tuesday had peeped it.

Tushie was quiet too but she was more alert. She knew Tuesday better than anybody, and she knew if Brianna said the wrong thing that Tuesday was going to beat her ass. The girl was just tits on a stick and Tushie figured Tuesday could handle that skinny hoe alone, but Doll and Bree were tight. Jaye fucked with Brianna too even though Tushie didn't know how cool they were. She was getting ready just in case she needed to have Tuesday's back.

The tension that swelled in the room seemed to have distorted time so after a second that felt much longer Brianna tucked her tail by looking away. She snatched up the money and threw the straps to her Fendi bag on her shoulder. "Well, if we ain't got no more business, then I'm out." She pushed off the loveseat and started for the door. "Doll, if you wanna ride, you betta come on!"

Just as Baby Doll got up to follow, Tuesday called out to Brianna. She paused to look back just as she grabbed the knob.

"You done got you a li'l Camaro, a couple purses, and some shoes and let that shit go to yo head. You the same broke bitch who pulled up in a busted ass V-Dub Beetle three years ago beggin' for a job; the same bony bitch who used to be out there on the floor looking all stiff and scared, barely making enough to tip out. I pulled you in, gave you the game, and got you together. Bree, don't forget that you came up fuckin' with me, you ain't make me better."

To that, all Brianna could do was roll her eyes.

"But if you ever decide that you don't like what we doin' in here, that door swing both ways." Tuesday looked around, making eye contact with each of them except Tushie, then added, "And that go for everybody!"

"Is you finished?" Brianna tried to redeem herself from getting hoed out earlier by trying her best to look hard again.

Tuesday just waved her off. "Bitch, beat it."

Bree left out the office with Doll right on her heels. Jaye got up too but threw Tuesday a *we're still cool* nod before she dipped.

When Tushie got up and went to the door it was only to close it behind them. She smiled. "I thought you wuz 'bout to whup dat bitch."

"I was. She did the right thang!" Tuesday went behind her desk and fell back into her chair. "I don't know where this bitch done got all this mouth from lately but she startin' to talk real reckless. If she keep it up, what almost happened today is definitely gone happen soon."

Tuesday dug into the inside pocket of her bag and pulled out a quarter ounce of kush that was tied in a sandwich bag. She passed the weed to Tushie along with a cigar because her girl rolled tighter than she did.

Of the team, Tushie had been down with her the longest and been through the most shit. Even though she was five years younger, they were tight and if Tuesday were ever asked to name her best friend, there was no one else more deserving of the title.

Back in the early part of '05 that ass had already made Tushie a legend in the New Orleans strip clubs. Magazines like *King* and *Black Men* were calling her the new "It Girl" and for a while rappers all over the south were clamoring to have her pop that fifty-six-inch donk in their videos. She had milked that little bit of fame into a brand-new house and a S550 Benz until Katrina came along and washed it all away.

Then she found herself living in Detroit and having to start from scratch. Tushie featured in a few clubs, and because she still had a strong buzz, she was the most sought-after free agent since LeBron James. All the big gentlemen's clubs were shooting for her and as bad as Tuesday wanted her, she didn't think she had a chance. She quickly learned that this country girl had a sharp business mind because Tushie agreed to come dance at the struggling little spot that Tuesday had just bought, but only if she made her a partner.

Tuesday was leery at first but it turned out to be the best decision she ever made. When Tuesday took over The Bounce House it was losing money faster than she could earn it, but when Tushie the Tease became a regular featured dancer, all that turned around. She was like a carnival attraction as niggas from as far as New

York came to see if she could really walk across the stage with two champagne bottles on her ass and not spill a drop, or clap it louder than a .22 pistol. The club was packed like sardines whenever she performed. Within months The Bounce House was turning a decent profit. Tushie kept the place jumping for five years, until she finally hung up her thong and retired from the stage.

Single-handedly saving the club made her a good business partner but years of loyalty and her down ass ways made Tushie a good friend. Tuesday trusted her so much that she put her up on how they could make some real money together: by robbing niggas who couldn't report the losses.

Tushie finished rolling the blunt, lit it and took her first three hits. She was passing it across the desk to Tuesday when she spoke in a voice strained from the smoke in her lungs: "I already know you gone talk to Dres 'bout dis shit."

Tuesday accepted the weed with a nod. "Hell, yeah," she said in between puffs. "I'm on my way to do that soon as I leave here. I'm damn sure 'bout to find out why he sent us on this dummy mission."

Chapter Three

After leaving Tushie at the club, Tuesday was headed to meet their silent partner, Dres, at a motel on Telegraph that rented rooms by the hour. She had pushed for a more public location but Dres had insisted on the motel and Tuesday already knew what that meant. As much as she hated this, she preferred to do business here rather than having him show up at The Bounce.

She parked her gleaming white Caddy into a slot next to his silver Charger. The motel had three separate buildings with sixteen units apiece and he was waiting in room 304. Tuesday didn't miss the joke.

When she got to the room the door was unlocked and Dres was inside sprawled across the bed watching a porno where a pair of white blondes with obviously fake tits were sharing a two-sided dildo. Tuesday sighed as she came in and closed the door.

"Now that's truly a thing of beauty," he said, nodding to the screen. "You should take a good look because these are what *real* women look like."

Tuesday rolled her eyes. "Can we get this over with? I gotta be somewhere in like twenty minutes."

"I don't give a shit where you have to be!" he snarled in that gravelly voice that always grated her nerves and had scared the shit out of Tank. His deep, raspy tone had a frightening quality, which was why Tuesday used him to make the recordings in the first place. She and the girls could disguise themselves as men but not fake a masculine voice.

"And you can bet your fat black ass you're gonna miss that appointment," said Dres. "Now gimme what you got for me."

Tuesday sat her purse atop a small bureau next to the door and dug inside it. She found the envelope with his cut of the score, but next to it she had a small Heckler & Koch P7M8 that was small enough to conceal in her bag without producing any bulges. Tuesday gave serious thought to pulling that out instead.

As if reading her mind, Dres whipped a huge .454 cannon from underneath a pillow. "Ms. Knight, I'll have you know that I never walk into a room that I don't know how to walk out of."

Tuesday slowly pulled out the thick envelope then held it up so that he could see it was harmless. "What, you scared of a paper cut?"

She tossed it onto his lap and he quickly thumbed through the bills inside. "There had damned well better be another envelope for me in that bag!"

"No, that's it!" She threw up her hands. "And you can thank yourself for that." Tuesday explained that she and the girls had pulled the job off without a problem but the fact that it had earned so little was due to his own bad information about Tank.

"That's bullshit!" Dres swung his legs off the bed. "I know for a fact that he was a major mover. Narcotics has been watching him for months, almost from the day he got out of prison."

"Dres," or Lieutenant Kyle Dresden, was a dirty cop that Tuesday had had the misfortune of crossing paths with two years back. The team had knocked a nigga for two bricks and eighty thousand in cash not knowing that he was a snitch under Dresden's protection. After months of investigation in which he watched them get two other D-boys, Dresden tracked Tuesday down and muscled her into a partnership. In exchange for an equal share, he would use his connections within the police force to point them toward the biggest dealers.

Dres peeked inside the envelope again as if the amount might change. He dropped it on the nightstand then glared at her. "How do I know you bitches aren't lying? How do I know there wasn't a lot more in that safe and you and your little team of sluts aren't trying to steal from me now?"

"You always get an equal cut," Tuesday lied. She shorted him every chance she got and had clipped him for fifteen hundred this time for what she knew was about to happen. "Believe whatever you want!"

Tuesday turned to leave but in a flash Dresden overtook her. He pinned her against the door, his beefy forearm on her throat, with the barrel of the gun pressed into her cheek.

"What makes you think I'd believe a black lying thief whore bitch like you?" he sneered in a low, guttural voice.

Kyle Dresden was a very muscular six foot six with blue eyes and sandy brown hair that he wore in a military-style buzz cut. He reminded Tuesday of the big Russian that Rocky fought in the fourth movie played by Dolph Lundgren. She might have actually found the white boy attractive under different circumstances but there was an ugliness about him that his looks couldn't mask. His blue eyes were cold and hard and he was never without a scowl. On top of being a crooked cop who was cruel and sadistic, adding to his charm was the fact that Dresden was an unabashed racist who always spouted his Aryan views.

"Where's the rest of my money at, bitch?" He kept the gun in her face but took his free hand and swept it up and down her thighs frisking her. Tuesday could tell by his heavy breaths and the bulge in his pants that this had nothing to do with the money.

She knew coming in that she was going to be raped today. This was another unfortunate condition of their partnership. From the beginning he had made it clear that everything was to be on his terms, so when they met for Dres to collect his cut, sometimes he only wanted the money but most of the time he wanted more. There were instances when Tuesday was able to sweet-talk her way out of it but some days Dresden refused to be denied.

"I told you I have to be somewhere in twenty minutes," she said with neither terror nor malice in her voice.

He moved his large hand up her skirt and groped roughly at her 36C's. "And I told you I don't give a fuck what you gotta do. You ugly-ass yellow bitch, you're gonna pay me one way or another!" Dresden reached around, grabbed her butt, and squeezed it hard. "You know I've been waiting for this. You knew I wanted it as soon as you walked in."

Tuesday couldn't push him off and didn't dare try. The Heckler was still in her bag but there was no way she could reach it and get off a kill shot before that .454 made her head pop like a balloon filled with Kool-Aid.

"You think you're pretty don't you bitch? With your high-yellow skin and green eyes." When Tuesday didn't answer, he pressed the gun harder into her cheek. "Don't you, bitch?!"

"Yeah."

"Say it," he demanded through clenched teeth.

"Yeah, I think I'm pretty." Tuesday sounded like a robot. The words were flat with no emotion.

"Bitch, you ain't shit!" he spat furiously. For Dresden it wasn't enough to violate Tuesday; as always, he needed to degrade and humiliate her before committing the ultimate act of female disrespect.

"Bitch, you're ugly!" he cooed, still running his hands over her body. "My wife puts your black ass to shame—long blond hair, eyes bluer than mine, perfect tits—she's not a whore like you. Say it, say you're a whore!"

"I'm a whore," she repeated in that same mechanical tone. There was no fear or shame in her eyes because Tuesday knew that this was a part of his twisted little game and during her life she'd been through far too much to ever let a piece of shit like Kyle Dresden break her. Plus, the sad truth was that he wasn't the first man to have sexually abused her.

"I see you ghetto rats with your painted-up monkey lips and big gorilla asses!" He spun Tuesday around and threw her face-first into the door. He groped at her butt hungrily and stared at it mesmerized. "Look at it, it's disgusting!" He put the gun aside so that he could enjoy her body with both hands.

Tuesday mocked him with a dry laugh. "It's so disgusting but you can't keep yo damn hands off it?"

"Shut up, whore!" He threw his forearm into the back of her neck again then pulled his wallet out and brought the badge up to where she could see it. "Do you know what that means?" he whispered while rubbing his hand between her legs. "That means within the city of Detroit I've got the God-given right to take whatever I want from you niggers! Your houses and cars, your money, your drugs, and even your pussy!"

He quickly undid Tuesday's pants and forced her tight jeans down to her ankles. He groaned with delight when he saw her thick, flawless legs and the pink bikini panties she wore underneath. He pulled her close and began to grind his crotch into her soft bottom. "It's your fault. You put African voodoo on my dick!" He grumbled in her ear, "I haven't fucked my wife in months!"

Dresden dropped his pants and boxers in one motion. He fished the condom from his wallet and slipped it on. He then snatched down Tuesday's panties and aggressively pushed inside her.

He pumped her from behind then yanked her head back with a fistful of hair. His voice was now whiny as he whispered to her: "You ugly ass black bitch, this pussy is sooo good! It's your fault I don't fuck my wife anymore. I jack off every day to you."

Tuesday might have been molested when she was younger but never allowed herself to play the victim's role. She learned that in situations like this it was better to take the initiative to get it over with as soon as possible. She threw her ass back into him and played on his secret desires. "You know I ain't ugly. I'm a sexy-ass bitch, ain't I?"

Pumping faster to keep up with her pace, he moaned: "Yes!"

She snapped at him. "Say it!"

He groaned in ecstasy. "Oh, Tuesday, you're so damned sexy!"

She began to throw it even faster, practically bouncing him off her ass. "The reason you so mad is because yo wife ain't black! You wish she looked like me, don't you?"

His whines were louder and more pathetic. "Yes! Yes!"

"You wish she had my pretty skin, my lips, my fat, juicy ass and my sweet black pussy. Don't you, you little-dick muthafucka?"

He cried, "Yes!! Yes!!"

Tuesday was bucking wildly, her ass slapping loudly against his pelvis. He reached beneath her shirt for her titties then let out a feminine cry: "Oh shit, Tuesday!" He grabbed her slender waist and his body went stiff as he began to fill the condom with a fat wad.

When he was done, Dresden collapsed on her back breathing hard. Tuesday had taken him from penetration to climax in only ninety seconds.

She checked her watch then looked over her shoulder at him. "I told you I had to be somewhere in twenty minutes, and if you get the fuck off me I can still get there early."

Tuesday didn't actually have to be anywhere in twenty minutes. She had just hoped that faking a previous appointment would help her to avoid Dresden's dick but since it didn't work there was no need to keep up the front.

She took a quick ten-minute shower in the motel bathroom then spent another ten in the mirror. She had a hair appointment tomorrow but used the tools in her purse to make herself look presentable until then.

When her hair was done she just took a moment to study her reflection. She noticed the formation of the laugh lines around her mouth that would only deepen with age.

However, what troubled her the most were her eyes. They were still that pretty shade of green but even to Tuesday they seemed to lack something. They looked tired and vacant. If they were truly the windows to the soul, she imagined only a black emptiness was inside her.

She was thirty-seven now. Still fine, but still thirty-seven. Still setting niggas up, still being abused and still getting fucked in cheap motel rooms. She thought she would've been past all of this by now. Pained, she slammed her palms down onto the counter that held the sink but did not cry. She had cried too much in this life already and that well had dried up long ago. She had no more tears to give anybody, not even herself. Besides, Tuesday learned that anger was much more productive than self-pity.

She was as angry at herself as she was at Dresden. She hoped he would have left during her shower but still heard him moving around in the anterior room. She took the Heckler from her purse and again thought about going in there to kill him. First she'd make him beg for his life then shoot him in his tiny dick. Then only after he'd whimpered and cried long enough to satisfy her vengeance would she almost mercifully put a bullet between his pale blue eyes.

The thing that stopped her was the same thing that had stopped her every time before: the gold shield he had taunted her with. If she killed a lieutenant in that fashion, not only would she incur the wrath of his precinct, but the entire Detroit police force and possibly the feds would be at her head. That was heat Tuesday didn't need.

Another reason she didn't kill Dres was because, as much as

she hated to admit it, the bastard was useful. Being a dirty cop meant that he had connections within the force and criminal world that made him a valuable asset. He had a line on the dope boys pushing the most weight, the gun dealers, the chop shops, and forgers. Thanks to Dresden their bulletproof vests were police-issue and when one of the girls had a mark they could produce phony ID's, Social Security numbers, and even birth certificates to get fake phones, rental spots, and cars. He had his ear to the streets and knew who was out there doing what in the game. Plus his sources were typically reliable; Tank had been his only fuck-up. Sometimes she convinced herself that having to give up a little pussy was just the cost of doing business.

Then there were times like this when she felt that it wasn't. Dresden was a sad contradiction in that he was a white suprema-cist with a yearning for black women. But sad or not, Tuesday knew that this little arrangement couldn't go on forever and that eventually he was going to have to be dealt with.

When she came out the bathroom he was sitting on the edge of the bed with the TV off. He still wore the perpetual frown that seemed to have been chiseled onto his face but the blue eyes were not so hard.

"Tell the girls I'm sorry about how things went with Humphries," Dresden said in a voice that was now thin. "I know you would never try 'n' pull one over on me. I know you're better than that." He glanced up into her now gray eyes then looked away meekly.

Tuesday wasn't surprised by this sudden change in Dresden's personality because she'd seen it before. The racism and the tough-guy act always melted away after he got his rocks off, to be replaced by this sad-puppy-who'd-just-got-caught-pissing-on-the-carpet routine. Each time after he'd strong-arm Tuesday out of some sex, he would instantly become this new person who was bashful and eager to give in to her, as if he were ashamed of what just happened. She figured a long time ago that this pathetic pic-ture was the real Kyle Dresden; the hard one was the facade.

Tuesday started for the door but he took her arm. "Wait a second." She spun around and shot the lieutenant a glare that made him quickly take back his hand.

"Tuesday, please, just hear what I got to say."

She stood staring at him icily with her arms folded, bag draped over her shoulder, and keys in hand.

He was still unable to meet her eyes. "I'm not a man who's used to saying he's sorry, no matter how terrible a thing was I did, but it's just that, uh . . ." Dresden looked into his hands as if he had crib notes to what he was trying to say written on his palms. "You're the first black woman I've ever, uh ur . . . It's just hard for me to control myself when I'm around you."

"So you basically sayin' I'm the first black woman you've found pretty enough to rape! You think I'm s'posed to be flattered by that shit?"

He looked from her Prada shoes up to her knees and couldn't seem to go any higher than that. "I'm sorry."

It never ceased to amaze or infuriate Tuesday how her entire life she'd been blamed for her own sexual abuse. It began with one of her mother's many live-in boyfriends when she started to develop at twelve. Inappropriate looks and comments escalated to fondling when they were alone. When she finally got up the nerve to tell her mother, she believed his denials over her accusations and blamed a young Tuesday for misinterpreting his fatherly affection. Then one night after her mother caught him trying to sneak into Tuesday's bed, they both blamed it on her for enticing him with her new body. It was the beginning of a recurring theme that happened again at fourteen with her aunt's husband, and again at fifteen with this older lesbian who had been a family friend. Each time she was to blame as if her beauty was some sort of curse. They all swore she possessed some magic ability to change them into pussy-hungry monsters and before Tuesday learned to master and profit from that power, she felt guilty and blamed herself too. Now Dresden's lame attempt to pin his perversion on her brought up all those old memories and the anger attached to them.

Despite his being six foot six with arms like boa constrictors, Tuesday thought Dresden looked as small and fragile as a child. She was almost certain that if she were to slap him he would curl up on the bed and cry like a bitch. She stared at him shaking her head with some odd combination of anger, pity and disgust.

"I'm through fuckin' with you. As of right now, me and my girls no longer work for you or with you. You can burn down my club, you can put cases on us, you can even put bullets in us, but we're done!" These were all threats he had made against her in the past.

She turned to walk away.

"Tuesday, don't be stupid. We've made a lot of money together."

She was still headed for the door.

"I didn't just call you here to collect. I had something else lined up. Something big!"

"Fuck you, Dresden!" She pulled it open and was crossing the threshold.

He called out: "I'm talking about a seven-digit lick, Tuesday! The kind that would set you up forever!"

That made her stop. She knew he was lying, knew that he was trying to reel her back in. She knew this but still could not walk out that room. "You fulla shit!" she said, looking back at him.

"No, I'm not," he said, standing up. He was able to meet her eyes again and that electric blue intensity had returned to his. "Something really juicy just got dropped in my lap and we have to move on it right away. This one lick can pay you more than the last ten put together."

"You fulla shit!" she repeated while turning away, but still was unable to find the will to walk.

He approached her. "I know you're tired, Ms. Knight. You've

been at this a long time and it's gotten old. From dancing to tricking to robbery, you're ready to be done with all this. The Bounce House might keep the bills paid but it'll never get you rich, and these scores for twenty and twenty-five grand are too few and far between. I'm talking about that big payoff you've been waiting for since you started this shit! A million, two, maybe more!"

His raspy voice was eerie and melodic. She hated the sound but was mesmerized by the content even though she was sure it only spoke lies. Tuesday felt like Eve when the serpent was trying to convince her to bite the apple.

He continued toward her dangling the bait. "You could get your boyfriend a really good lawyer or maybe even do the smart thing and say fuck him! No one would blame you. Change your name and buy you a condo down in Miami. Get floor seats to all the Heat games and sit right next to the bench—close enough to smell Dwyane Wade's sweat."

She turned to him. "Nobody ever told you that you s'posed to start a fairy tale with 'once upon a time.' Before you get to the happily ever after, gimme the name of this imaginary mark who's gonna move me to South Beach."

Dresden smiled when she allowed him to push the door closed because he knew he had her.

"Well, once upon a time, about twenty years ago, a small-time dealer that nobody ever heard of got tired of the crumbs and started murdering his way to the top of the food chain. In just five years he had the most feared name in the city without anyone really knowing who he was."

Tuesday's eyes went wide and flashed bright green. Dresden's smile grew wider when he saw the recognition in her face. "You already know who I'm talking about."

"Sebastian Caine!" she scoffed in disbelief. "Get the fuck outta here!"

"Oh, so you've heard of him?" he asked innocently, already knowing that she had.

"Everybody and they momma done heard of the nigga. He like a urban legend in the hood."

He asked, "And what would you say if I told you I could get you next to him."

"I'd say you was fulla shit!" she blurted without hesitation. "For twenty years niggas been throwing that name around to make it seem like they doin' big thangs but it's always just some frontin' muthafuckas blowing game. A nigga might say he fuckin' with some niggas who fuck with some niggas who fuck with Sebastian Caine. Or like this one time these guys hit The Bounce and made it rain with about sixty G's and had the girls all gassed up sayin' they worked for Sebastian Caine.

"But everything you ever hear about this nigga is always third- and fourth-party shit. As much as I've heard his name, I've never seen the nigga anywhere and I never met one person who actually seen him or met him in person. Truthfully I don't even think the nigga exists!" Tuesday shook her head. "So again, I say you fulla shit! Niggas who say they fuck with Caine is just like them hillbillies out in the boonies who swear they saw Bigfoot."

"Sebastian Caine is very real!" Dresden assured her. "Plus he's back around the city and has been for a while."

Tuesday was unconvinced. "So you sayin' that you done actually met somebody who's really met or seen him?"

He explained that he had a friend in the DEA and Tuesday knew that whenever Dresden said 'friend' he meant another cop who was just as crooked as him. "My friend tells me that the DEA, the FBI, and the Justice Department have been secretly working together for the past six years building an airtight indictment against one of the biggest but low-key dealers in the country. He swore to me that they have active surveillance and are very close to executing a warrant on the Invisible Man himself, one Sebastian Caine!

"He gave me the whole run-down but, like I said, we have to move quick. The alphabet boys are gonna be coming soon but just think of what type of score we'll be looking at if you and the girls can get to him first."

There was no longer doubt in Tuesday's eyes but some mixture of excitement and fear. "He's here and you know where?"

Dresden nodded with a smile that reminded Tuesday of a hungry alligator.

Chapter Four

Tuesday lived downtown in a twenty-two-hundred-square-foot condominium in a plush building called the Seymour. In addition to high ceilings, hardwood floors, two beds, two baths and walk-in closets, twenty-six hundred a month also got her underground parking, tight security, and access to the in-house gym/spa, swimming pool, and tennis court.

Tuesday didn't feel that the ten minute shower at the motel was enough to sufficiently wash the dirty cop off her so she spent another hour soaking in her Jacuzzi tub. The jets were running and the water was hot enough to scald but Tuesday sat in that bubbling caldron as content as a carrot in stew.

While she scrubbed Dresden's scent from her body, she couldn't exorcise his words from her mind so easily. She spent the last fifteen minutes of her bath just soaking and thinking over his proposal while having the occasional staring match with Nicholas.

Nicholas was an all-white long-haired Persian with eyes greener than hers. Tuesday had a suspicion that he'd been some freaky nigga in his past life because since he was a kitten he always made it his business to be present whenever she got undressed. The cat sat on the rim of the tub methodically grooming himself as if waiting for her naked body to emerge from the bath.

"Get yo pervy ass outta here!" she said, playfully splashing him with her bathwater.

He merely shook the excess water from his coat, gave her a *bitch, please* look and went back to brushing himself with his rough tongue.

Under Nicholas's watchful eyes she finally climbed out, dried off then wrapped herself in a terrycloth bathrobe. She padded out of the bathroom on bare feet and the cat followed closely behind.

In her bedroom Tuesday slipped into a lacy black bra and matching thong. She chose the sexy underwear because she was going to visit A.D. tonight and when he asked about her panties, as he always did, she wouldn't have to lie to him. She shimmied into another snug pair of jeans and a form-fitting V-neck top that showed enough cleavage to tantalize but not so much to get the visit denied—she learned early into his bit that she had to carefully select her outfits because Tuesday had once tried to surprise A.D. by wearing his favorite minidress but was turned away at the front desk. She then went into her closet and from her extensive shoe gallery selected a pair of Jimmy Choos that she felt complemented the look. While she applied her makeup, Nicholas scampered out of the room, deciding there was nothing more to see.

For the next three hours she gave her condo a thorough cleaning that it didn't really need. She went from room to room sweeping up imaginary granules, mopping spotless floors, and wiping surfaces that already looked to be sterile. Even casual acquaintances knew that Tuesday had a penchant for neatness but Tushie was the only one she'd told about actually being diagnosed with obsessive-compulsive disorder.

OCD had countless faces and degrees; it could be as little as a meticulous grooming ritual that almost escaped notice, or take shape as a crippling phobia and neurotic behavior that required a person to be institutionalized. Tuesday had a mild form that manifested as the uncontrollable desire to clean and organize her space. She was not a full-fledged germaphobe like Howard Hughes but could potentially become one. A one-time visit with a psychologist had taught her that the excessive cleaning was her attempt to organize a life that she felt was chaotic in what the doctor had termed "transference."

Tuesday would clean a window or mirror, imagine that she saw streaks then clean it again; and this might happen half a dozen times. She remade her bed five times before she was satisfied that the spread hung an equal distance from the floor on all sides. She spent an hour checking the canned and dry goods in her cupboard to make certain they were stored away according to her orderly system, then spent another one checking the dates on the perishables in her freezer. Sometimes Tuesday would open and close the refrigerator door nine or ten times in a row convinced that the items would shuffle themselves out of place the moment she looked away.

What gave Tuesday hope was that her OCD wasn't as pronounced at the club as it was at home. At work she had a high standard for cleanliness that some called excessive, but at home it was cranked up times one thousand. The psychosis was centered around her living space and, since it didn't intrude too heavily into the other areas of her life, she was hopeful that she might one day conquer it.

She was leaving for the prison at five o'clock. As the hour approached, she took a final tour of the condo, checking the lights in each room. She had to flick the light switch on and off three times while counting the number aloud. Regardless of the urgency, she could not leave until she completed this ritual, and when she thought she missed one, she had to start over.

Tuesday reached the Ryan Road Correctional Facility within fifteen minutes of starting her car. As much as she hated to see A.D. locked up, she loved the convenience of having him close by. Tuesday knew people who had loved ones imprisoned so far upstate that visits had to be planned like vacations. As long as it was his assigned day, she could drop in on A.D. whenever the thought crossed her mind. It was as simple as running an errand.

More than once he told her about the stresses of being incarcerated in a prison that was built in the middle of the hood. According to him, the worst part were the summers: children at play, cars riding by with speakers pounding, the barbecue on the grills, all these sounds and scents reached the gated inmates reminding them that they were home but still a world away. Tuesday had never done time so she didn't insult him by pretending that she could fully relate, but she could vaguely imagine how torturous that had to be for them.

Since she was a regular, the officer working the reception desk was familiar with her. She was a thin blonde with short, spiky hair who always kidded Tuesday about her name. She said, "Your parents must've really had a sense of humor to name you Tuesday Knight."

There was something in her eyes and smile that Tuesday recognized as subtle flirtation; since she'd already pegged the CO as a dyke, she accepted her visitor's pass with a comment that was friendly but not encouraging.

After changing twenty dollars for quarters to pump into the vending machines, she took a seat in the lobby and waited. A.D. was expecting her so it usually didn't take long for him to get ready. Waiting a few chairs down was a woman close to her age wearing open-toed heels that Tuesday admired, and seated next to her was a hyperactive little girl wildly swinging her legs, struggling to obey her mother's unrealistic command to sit still.

Tuesday was staring in their direction at nothing in particular when the little girl locked eyes with her and smiled.

The little girl favored Tuesday so much that she was momentarily stunned because it was like gazing into some magic mirror and seeing herself as a child. At first she was sure that the girl was a hallucination, some new symptom of her OCD starting to manifest.

The girl waved. "Hi."

"Hi!" Tuesday said, using that same friendly tone and phony enthusiasm that all adults use when speaking to a stranger's child.

"I'm here to see my daddy!" the girl volunteered happily.

"That's nice," Tuesday said, unable to think of anything better.

The girl was admonished by her mother. "Kyra, quit bothering that lady!" she said in a voice that was friendly but firm. To Tuesday she said, "I'm sorry, she's not exactly the shy type."

After a better look Tuesday realized that the child's resemblance to her was not as close as she thought. It was mostly superficial. They were the same complexion and did have the same gray-green eyes but the rest of their features, such as nose, lips, ears, and facial structure, were cast from totally different molds. She was a beautiful child but not Tuesday's clone.

"Oh she's not bothering me," Tuesday assured her mother. She asked the girl, "So your name is Kyra?"

She bobbed her head emphatically.

"How old are you, Kyra?"

The green-eyed darling held up three fingers and when her mother corrected her she added a fourth.

Tuesday said, "Well, Kyra, you are just about the cutest li'l girl I've ever seen."

Blushing, she covered her face, embarrassed, beaming a smile that just melted Tuesday.

"Kyra, what do you say back when somebody says something nice to you?" her mother urged.

She pulled her tiny hands away from her face and giggled a "thank you." It was then that Tuesday noticed the indescribable something in her green eyes, the same thing she noticed was missing from her own at the motel.

For another ten minutes Tuesday sat having a delightful discussion with Kyra about friends, video games, and a pet hamster named Fathead. Tuesday was telling her about Nicholas the cat when the mother was informed that it was time for their visit. While little Kyra was being led away by the arm, she spent the whole time smiling and waving back to Tuesday until she disappeared through the door.

Tuesday found herself still smiling a full minute after she was gone but it slowly faded away as she began to think.

Tuesday had decided a long time ago that motherhood was not for her. When she was younger, the reason was that her own mother had failed so miserably at the job. Tuesday feared she inherited her faults—her mother had jumped from man to man her entire life, always choosing the thrill of a new relationship over the needs of her child, and this made Tuesday feel more like a burden than a blessing. As she grew older it was her lifestyle that made her a poor candidate; she was playing a dangerous game with some really bad characters and knew that at any moment she might have to pay for all the dirt she'd done. Then as her OCD progressed, it was the illness that made her feel she was unfit to raise a child because a screaming, puking, pooping baby had no place in her meticulously clean and organized world. In the past, carelessness had led to two pregnancies—at eighteen and twenty-three—and Tuesday had terminated each one as soon as she learned of conception.

Up until now she had been comfortable with those choices, but seeing the little girl with the eyes like hers made her reconsider. She thought about the two lives she aborted. Her oldest would already be nineteen with a sibling five years younger. Tuesday didn't regret not bringing children into that life; she regretted living a life that was too unstable to bring children into.

She was thinking about that, Dresden, Sebastian Caine, and a thousand other things when she was called.

"Are you the visitor for Hollister?" asked a fat, bald corrections officer who came from behind a sliding glass security door. Tuesday thought it was a stupid question since no one else waited in the lobby.

She got up and approached him. "Yes."

He said, "I just need his inmate number for verification." Tuesday recounted those six digits as easily as her birthdate.

Beyond the sliding door one officer held her driver's license while a female frisked her in a way that always made Tuesday uncomfortable. After being wanded by one of the small handheld metal detectors, she was asked to walk through one of the large arch-type ones. As much as Tuesday hated this, it still wasn't as bad as going to the airport.

After checking her driver's license to make sure she had no outstanding warrants, she was permitted through a second security door and escorted through the facility's control center to the visiting room.

On a Monday the visiting room was not as lively as it was on the weekends. There were only three groups in huddled conversation in separate corners. Kyra was chatting animatedly to a brown-skinned nigga in prison blues who she favored more than her mother, another Muslim brother in a kufi was reading the Quran to a white girl who was almost fat enough to need two chairs, and then there was a frail white boy sitting with his elderly parents trying to comfort his mother as she quietly wept into her palms.

At the rear there was a large rounded podium where the officer sat to monitor the visits; A.D. was seated on a bench next to it in a no-name golf shirt and jeans that he wouldn't have been caught dead in on the street. He and Tuesday met with a hug and kiss.

She said, "Nice fit!"

A.D. didn't miss the sarcasm. "Fuck you."

He led her to a table that allowed him to be as far as he could from the officer while putting equal distance between them and the other visitors. They took seats next to each other.

Even though she came to visit at least once a week, Tuesday

still couldn't believe how much he'd changed. When she met him he had been six foot five, thin, dark-skinned with thick eyebrows that she found sexy, but twelve years of weightlifting had added a hundred pounds of muscle to his lean frame. He used to wear his hair in long French braids but now he kept it cut short with deep spiraling waves. His perpetually yellow eyes were now bright white without alcohol and weed, as were his teeth, and Tuesday figured he must've brushed them as diligently as his hair. He looked so damn good to her that she cursed Michigan for not having conjugal visits.

"Did you get that?" she asked in relation to a three hundred dollar money order she just sent him.

He nodded. "Yeah, good lookin'. That came last week."

"If you need it, I can shoot you somethin' else."

He waved her off. "Naw, baby, I'm straight. That plus what I already had gone keep me tight for a while."

"Ebony said, 'What up!'" Tuesday said, remembering their conversation. "Me and her was talkin' 'bout you earlier."

A.D. didn't respond. He made a face to suggest that he didn't care one way or another about the bartender's well wishes.

Tuesday could tell by the look in his eye and overall demeanor that something was bothering him, but she also knew A.D. well enough to be sure that if she were to ask he would just dismiss it. Since she didn't want to spoil their time by constantly pressing him to open up, Tuesday just smiled and hoped it was contagious.

"Damn, Debo! You shopping at Baby Gap now?" She felt one of his huge biceps. "You look like you 'bout to Incredible Hulk out that tight-ass shirt."

This earned a smirk but not the smile she wanted. "Just like all that ass look like it's 'bout to explode out them tight jeans."

"I wanted to give you somethin' to think about later while you raped some li'l white boy in the shower!"

"Oh, you got jokes today," he said, finally favoring her with a smile. "You got me fucked up, all I need is magazines and Vaseline. Plus the memories of all the times I pounded you to death!"

It worked because at least on the surface A.D. appeared to be in a better mood. They ate chicken wings, chips, and drank pop from the vending machines while talking about old times and actual acquaintances. Tuesday wasn't used to having to cheer him up; he was usually a rock for her. She figured it to be just a minor funk because over the next three hours he was back to his normal self.

She talked about her condo, her cat, the club, and how slow things had gotten. She told him how close she came to beating Brianna's ass but when she talked about the Tank lick, his mood seemed to darken again even though she didn't mention Dresden or what he'd done.

Recapping, she said, "So basically we walked away with about thirteen stacks apiece, which ain't shit when you consider how much work we put in."

A.D. leaned back in his chair and made a sound that was a combination of a sigh and snort. Tuesday didn't necessarily know what it was but knew that it meant he disapproved.

"What's wrong with you today?" she asked in a low voice filled with concern.

After a long pause he turned to her and said, "Baby, I'm sorry."

Tuesday was confused. " 'Bout what?"

" 'Bout everythang!" he said, shaking his head. "But mostly 'bout what I did to you. You on that shit you on right now because of me."

It was A.D. who had introduced Tuesday to that game. When they met she was dancing at nineteen and he was a twenty-four-year-old jack boy. After fucking for a couple months, A.D. had the idea to use his pretty little stripper to help him stick niggas.

Being that she was always an attention-getter, he started off just using her as a distraction. A.D. would convince a nigga to meet him at a motel to either buy or sell dope and while they did business Tuesday would be showering in the adjoining bathroom.

Then on cue she would innocently walk out toweling off her naked body, and by the time the mark finished scoping her ass, he would be staring down the barrel of A.D.'s 12-gauge pump.

Over time her role slowly expanded to where he started using her as bait. From the club Tuesday would lure off-brand niggas back to a room where A.D. would be waiting in a closet.

Getting a nigga for what he had in his pocket was cool but getting everything he had period was better. So it was Tuesday who ultimately had the idea to play the whole girlfriend role to peep a nigga's alarm code, stash spots, and safe combinations. Years later, after A.D. got sent up, she brought Tushie in the game the same way.

He said, "I feel fucked up because I took a young girl who was still at the age where she could've done anything with her life and basically corrupted her."

Tuesday shook her head to disagree. "I never saw it like you corrupted me, Adrian; if anythang, I felt like you gave me game. While every other nigga I met back then was just tryin' to use me, you was breaking bread wit me."

"Naw, Bright Eyes, I was using you too. I was just doin' it in a different way."

Tuesday always loved that pet name but couldn't remember the last time he called her Bright Eyes. This scared her as much as it touched her because something told her that this conversation was about to go somewhere unexpected and unpleasant.

He took her hand and began to play with her fingers. "As much as I love seein' you, it break my muthafuckin' heart to hear that at thirty-seven you still out there on the same bullshit I had you on at nineteen."

Tuesday felt that was an insult and tried to pull her hand away but he held it tighter.

"Naw, baby. I ain't tryin' to judge you on how you get yo money. I'm just sayin' you could've done a lot better without a nigga like me in yo life. You could've went back to school, even been a model—you fuckin' over half the bitches I see in these magazines. You could've blew up, pimped that shit into an acting career, and be on TV right now getting money."

She used her thumb to trace circles on the back of his palm. "Baby, we can't talk about wouldas and couldas. Life is what it is and we gotta deal with reality."

"You damn sure right about that," A.D. said, nodding. Then he was eerily quiet for a long time.

When he finally spoke again, there was a despondent tone in his voice that Tuesday didn't like. "I'm 'bout to ride up out this joint, have 'em transfer me to a different spot up north somewhere. I don't expect you to drive all that way to see me."

She said, "I'll come see you no matter where you at."

"Naw, baby, you don't get me. I don't want you to come see me. I'm not gone be calling or writing like that no more either."

Tuesday had no comeback. She just stared at him trying to make sense of what he was saying.

"Tims just came and hollered at me yesterday." Travis Timmons was his lawyer. Over the years Tuesday had paid that man close to eighteen thousand dollars to take A.D. through the various steps of his appeal.

"They shot down my sixty-five hundred!" He blew out a weary breath. "It's a wrap."

This wasn't the first time he'd heard bad news about his appeal and Tuesday didn't understand why he sounded so defeated. "Well, what do we gotta do next. You the one who told me that there's always another route, another card you can play."

While Tuesday had footed the bills, she never learned the ins and outs of the appellate process. She'd sat with Travis Timmons while he talked about briefs, affidavits, and writs of habeas corpus without really grasping what any of those things were. All Tuesday cared to know was how much would it help A.D.'s case and how much he charged to do it. So she just handed over the money in good faith that he would find a way to get her man home one day.

What she didn't understand was that for a Michigan inmate

the 6.500 Motion for Relief from Judgment was his absolute last chance at justice. It was only to be used after the appealing party had exhausted every other remedy from the lower courts to the higher to the federal level. The 6.500 motion was metaphorically a big gun with only one bullet: if it was granted the courts automatically vacated the prisoner's sentence, but if it was denied, like in A.D.'s case, the prisoner was left with no more options. To employ a better metaphor, it was a Hail Mary pass.

After taking a minute to explain this to Tuesday, he said, "Baby girl, I ain't never comin' home!"

A.D. had natural life and in Michigan it meant just that. Without a governor's pardon or a special commutation, he would spend the rest of his natural life in prison. After serving thirty years of his sentence, a special review board would examine his case every five years but they rarely, if ever, recommended a lifer for release.

Tuesday felt numb. It was like she was hearing what he was saying but the message hadn't sunk in yet.

A.D. looked at her with earnest eyes. "You a down-ass bitch! You done had my back for six years out there and held me down for twelve in here—and that's eleven more than the average bitch would have. But I'm not 'bout to have you waste yo life hoping for something that's not gone happen. You done already wasted enough money and time on me. I gotta cut you loose now!"

She frowned at him. "Nigga, you don't tell me what to do with my money or time! And I don't feel like I wasted any on you. Plus I still can't believe you just giving up on everythang like that—on yo freedom, especially on us!"

"Tuesday, you just sat here and talked about dealin' with the reality of shit. The reality is I got *life without parole*! It's a good chance I'm gone die in this bitch and I can deal with that. I ain't boohooing about the time. I can do my bit.

"But I can't do it here like this with you: in the middle of the D with you comin' up every week. I'm a nigga who been shot six times but don't shit hurt more than having to watch you walk out that door while I'm headed back to my cell. I was only able to deal with the shit this long cause I honestly believed I was gone make it out, but now—" He just shook his head. "This is the hardest thing I ever had to do, but I gotta do it for both of us or we'd never let each other go. I had to be the strong one. You gotta move on with yo life out there and I gotta move on with mine in here."

Although Tuesday had never admitted this to herself consciously, in the back of her mind she always knew this day would come; the day when her faith, optimism or delusion ran into a reality that was as hard and cold as the bars used to cage him in. While she didn't know much about the law, she knew that a guilty murderer going free on appeal had about the same odds of her hitting the lottery. She also knew that he was right about them needing to let go. This was why Tuesday couldn't put together a strong argument against what he was saying.

Even though the mood and the moment didn't seem proper, for some reason she began to laugh. Tuesday just got caught up in a sudden fit of uncontrollable laughter and soon he did too. The others in the room wouldn't have guessed they were ending an eighteen-year relationship but rather sharing some fond memory—which was in a sense what they were really doing.

Still smiling, she asked, "So you don't wanna see me no more ever?"

"I'm not gone say *ever* but at least not for a few years. I'm taking you off my visitor's list, and like I said, don't look for me to call or write either."

The smile waned. Tuesday was looking serious when she said: "Well, you can't control what I do on my end. I'm still gone keep in touch so you can expect to get mail from me."

"I'm ripping up all yo letters without reading 'em!" He was lying and Tuesday knew it.

"Now you gotta be the strong one," he said with a pain in his eyes that Tuesday had never seen. "You gotta get up, walk out that door and hurt me one last time."

"No. I don't. At least not yet anyway." She glanced up at the wall clock. "It's only eight fifteen, visiting hours ain't over."

"Tuesday, just go," he said mournfully. "I don't like this long sentimental good-bye shit!"

She sat there stubbornly. "Like you just said. I held yo black ass down for twelve years nigga, you can give me forty-five minutes!" She laced her fingers into his and locked eyes with him. "You still my man until nine o'clock."

Chapter Five

When Tuesday left the prison, she went straight back to The Bounce and almost wanted somebody to be parked in her spot. The Caddy braked with screeching tires and she slammed the door so hard when she got out that old Mr. Scott, who was standing next door, knew better than to speak to her.

DelRay was on the door but as she walked up he could tell by the color of her eyes and the look on her face that Tuesday was in no mood for games. Everybody who knew her understood that her eyes being gray was a clear sign that she was pissed and not to be fucked with. DelRay just held the door open for her and let Tuesday breeze past without speaking. He didn't care what she owed him or how smackable her ass looked, he made damn sure to keep his hands to himself.

Inside, Tuesday didn't throw a glance to the stage or the crowd; she went straight for the bar and took the empty stool. She told Ebony to line up five shots of 1800 tequila.

The bartender thought it was an odd request since Tuesday was only a social drinker, and then never at work, but certainly wasn't about to refuse her boss. Ebony lined up five shot glasses, filled them and then watched amazed as Tuesday slammed them back to back like a pro. Tuesday had hardly drained the last one when she asked for five more.

After pounding the second round she demanded the entire bottle and a sixteen-ounce glass to take back to her office. In it she sat behind her desk in the dark sucking down huge gulps of Cuervo for the effect rather than the taste.

Even with twelve years to process it, Tuesday still found it hard to believe that one of the coldest, most calculating stick-up men she'd ever known, who had gotten close to half the ballers in the city, would end up doing life over a poker game. At a weekly game in his cousin's basement, A.D.'s hot streak and trash talk had built animosity between him and a long-time acquaintance named Speedy. A.D. scudded them for sixteen hours in a game that was typically friendly, but on that night was filled with tension and mounting hostility. Things finally came to a head when A.D.'s boat cracked Speedy's flush, winning him another sizable pot while dealing equal blows to the man's money and pride. In a weak moment, Speedy called A.D. a "bitch-ass nigga" and doused him with a cup of Hennessy, sparking that well-known Hollister temper. Others around the table watched dumbstruck as A.D. responded by upping his .40-cal and blowing away a portion of Speedy's skull.

The whole thing was so petty and stupid to Tuesday that even after he was arrested, spent eighteen months fighting the case, and was ultimately found guilty, it still didn't seem real to her. A.D. had a knack for slipping out of some tight spots whether it was being shot, a car accident, or a run-in with the police; so Tuesday always imagined that he would slide out of this too, a few years lost but wiser for the experience. After dealing with court appearances, prison visits and attorney's fees for almost a decade and a half, the reality that her man and mentor had thrown his life away for nothing only sunk in that night.

She needed to get drunk. Fucked up.

Five minutes later Tushie came in and switched on the light. She found Tuesday pouring another glass from a bottle half empty.

"Gurl, whut tha fuck you doin'? It ain't like you ta get faded like dat, especially at work."

When Tuesday looked up at her, Tushie instantly knew that her girl needed a shoulder and not a sermon so she ran back to the bar to fetch a second glass. She pulled the door closed when she returned, then took the seat in front of her desk.

"So whut we toastin'?" she asked, pouring herself some.

Tuesday held up her glass. "The best day of my life!"

Tushie clinked her glass without bothering to ask what that meant. She wasn't going to press because she knew that Tuesday revealed things at her own pace and in her own way.

So without conversation that was phony or forced, they just sat and got wasted. After killing that first bottle of 1800, Tushie went and got another from the bar. They smoked some more of that kush Tuesday had and neither of them made a sound other than the occasional cough from the good weed. It was moments like this that truly defined a real friendship. While a weaker person might try to pump for answers or spit a bunch of clichéd quotes that have been used a million times and provided no comfort, a true friend knew when to just shut the fuck up and drink. Sometimes more love and support was communicated through a silence than ever could be with words.

They butted the tail of the blunt and were halfway through the second bottle of Cuervo when Tuesday finally opened up about the crazy day she had. She told it in reverse: starting with the split with A.D., then ending with what Dresden had done to her at the motel.

Tushie was the only other one in the group who knew that their silent sixth partner was a dirty lieutenant who treated her girl like his personal ATM and fuck doll. While she was saddened to hear about A.D., it only pissed her off to hear about Dresden. She said, "Gurl, it might be time to get dis nigga up out our mix!"

Tuesday shook her head. "You don't know how many times I done thought about killing that bitch but we just can't do it." The girls were thieves, not a hit squad, and definitely didn't want the drama that came with killing a cop, even a dirty one. For Tuesday there was only one solution for dealing with Dresden and that was hitting a lick that gave her enough money to get out the game for good.

Tuesday wanted to put Tushie up on the new lick but didn't want to do so until all the girls were together. She left the others texts about an emergency meeting. Jaye, who must've been close by, was there in ten minutes, but it was thirty-five more before Brianna and Baby Doll called back, and then they didn't show up until an hour after that. They came in together, both quiet and looking equally pissed off to be pulled away from whatever they were doing. With Doll's sleepy eyes and sweated-out perm, Tuesday figured that she was just somewhere getting fucked.

Once the door was closed and all the ladies had taken seats, Tuesday stood up at her desk. "Hey, I'm sorry for callin' y'all in like this but something done just got thrown in my lap today that we need to move on fast."

This was the first time they had ever been summoned to an emergency meeting and they didn't know what to expect. Plus they could tell by Tuesday's bloodshot eyes and slurred speech that she was peeled so Bree, Jaye, and Doll looked at Tushie for a clue to all the secretive shit. Since Tushie knew no more than the rest of them, she just shrugged then turned back to hear what the business was.

Trying her best to sound sober and failing, Tuesday said: "First off, I want to apologize again for how bad the Tank thing went. We good at what we do and we worked too hard and too long to only walk away with thirteen racks—it almost felt like we took a loss. We got fed some bad info on that but regardless, I'm willing to take the blame."

Tuesday went into her desk drawer and pulled out four envelopes. She passed them out to the girls and they found a little bit of money in each one: thirty-two hundred fifty dollars.

"That's my cut split between y'all," she said, leaning over her desk. "It's my way of taking responsibility for what happened."

Tushie said, "Gurl, you ain't gotta do dis."

"Yes the fuck she do!" Brianna snapped, tucking her envelope into a purse.

"Well, now, it's time to put that behind us and focus on this next thing!" Tuesday fell back into her seat. "We got another job, a big one. The biggest we ever had."

Jaye looked around to gauge the other's reactions before she spoke: "Already? It's kinda soon but long as it make up for the last shit I'm in."

Tushie and Baby Doll made agreeable comments too; of the girls, Brianna was the only one who seemed skeptical. She made a loud sputtering noise. "Is this comin' from the same source who put us on Fat Boy? 'Cause if it is, I'm straight! I ain't 'bout to be putting in four and five months to crack a nigga for less than what I spend in one trip to the Gucci store."

Tushie smacked her lips. "Bitch, please! Havin' five pairs of heels don't make you da shit."

Brianna fired back. "Bet yo big country ass can't see my shoe game. Real Prada don't come in a size thirteen, Boo-Boo."

Doll giggled and gave her girl some dap.

Tushie stood up. "I betcha my big country ass can see yo shoe game and *you,* bitch." She stuck out one of her black Louboutins. "It's only a size five but it's gone feel a lot bigger up in yo ass!"

"Y'all bitches, chill!" Tuesday said, restoring the order. Then, turning to Brianna: "And for yo information, I'm talkin' 'bout a seven-figure lick! Shit, we might fuck around and walk away wit a mil apiece!"

All the girls stared at Tuesday as if she were on some bullshit. There was even doubt on Tushie's face, who always rode with her girl.

"A mil apiece?" she asked. "Who you got lined up?"

"I said *might*!" Tuesday clarified, giving them a warning glare. "And this is who we goin' after." She reached into her purse and pulled out an eight-by-ten black-and-white surveillance photo that she got from Dresden. She handed it to the girls, who passed it around seeing nothing remarkable about the dark-skinned man in dark sunglasses and a dark-colored suit who was either climbing in or out of the backseat of a dark sedan. The shot was taken from about thirty feet away and in poor light so there wasn't much about him that could be identified from the photograph.

"So who the fuck is this nigga?" asked Doll, who had the picture in her lap. "And if he so helluva how come we ain't got at him before now?"

" 'Cause before now most of us didn't even think he was real, let alone knew where to find 'em."

Tuesday had been purposely drawing this out for dramatic effect. She wanted to get a good read on the girls faces to see who would be fascinated and who would be frightened when she finally dropped the bomb. "That's Sebastian Caine!"

For a full minute after that, the room was unnaturally quiet. The girls seemed to have had trouble processing what they were told. It was like Tuesday had set up some joke and not delivered the punchline. The four of them just sat there looking confused.

This was because each of them was familiar with the story of Sebastian Caine. Everybody knew that he had started off as a real person but for twenty years that infamous name had been entangled in so much gossip and rumors that no one could separate the man from the myth. Whenever a nigga in the game blew up and became major, it was whispered that Caine had made that happen, and whenever one of those same niggas came up dead, it was whispered again that Caine had made it happen. His name was attached to half the murders in the city and put a twinge of fear in the hardest nigga. The stories that were spread about him elevated his status to that of an urban legend. Some said he had moved to Mexico and took over one of the cartels, others believed he secretly owned the Motor City casino and was living in the hotel's penthouse. Some believed he was in prison, others believed he was dead, then there were those who swore he walked the streets of downtown Detroit at night disguised as a hobo. It was said that he kept the heads of his enemies as trophies and took baths in their blood. The conspiracy theorists believed he was a high-ranking Mason with ties to the Illuminati while those with a religious bent believed that he had sold his soul to the devil or was possessed by Satan himself. Sebastian Caine was a hood nigga's version of the Boogeyman; while your mind told you he couldn't be real, you still remembered those stories whenever you had to walk alone at night.

"Bullshit!" Brianna called out from her spot on the couch.

"This is *the* Sebastian Caine?" Doll asked, pointing down to the photo. "How old is this picture, 'cause I heard he doin' a million years in the fed? I heard they got his ass up under the jail over there in Guantanamo Bay with them terrorist niggas."

"I heard that nigga was dead!" Jaye broke in. "My cousin said the police killed him a few years back but kept it on the hush. They say they buried him under a different name so his family don't even know where he at."

Brianna snatched the picture off of Doll's lap and studied it with a frown. "This could be any muthafuckin' body! How do you know it's really him?"

Tuesday rolled her eyes. "I already knew you would be the one with something negative to say. Why you just can't take my word for it?"

Tushie wasn't trying to side with Brianna over her girl but had her doubts too. There was an apologetic tone in her voice when she said: "You gotta picture of a nigga we can barely see claiming it's a nigga dat ain't nobody *ever* seen. I know y'all done had ya little disagreements but damn, even I can see why a bitch would be skeptical."

Tuesday did understand. Neither Brianna, Jaye, nor Doll knew about Tuesday's connection to Dresden and she wasn't about to explain everything that he had told her when she voiced the same concerns to him. Along with the photo, Dresden produced enough evidence to convince her that the DEA thought he was the real Sebastian Caine and that had been enough.

Tuesday explained her position. "The nigga on that picture is either the real Sebastian Caine or some helluva-ass dope boy who just using that name. We not sure which but it really don't matter. You gotta be doing some real, real major shit to even pretend to be that nigga. If the feds think it's him, then he gotta be layin' like that. So whether this is the original or just some nigga frontin' with his name, we still gone get his ass."

Brianna stared down at the grainy black-and-white photo for a long time in deep thought. As much as she wanted to, even she couldn't argue with the logic in that, but as she continued to focus on the faceless dark stranger, doubt of one kind was replaced by doubt of another brand.

"Whether he's the real deal or not, this nigga gots to be a straight-up kingpin. How is one of us s'posed to get next to him?"

Tuesday smiled to let Brianna and the others know that she was peeping the weakness in her. "What, Bree, you don't think we can do it?"

Brianna's pride wouldn't allow her to say no but she wasn't confident enough for a yes. "I'm just sayin' we ain't 'bout to run into him at a car wash somewhere. We done knocked cats before but nobody this bossy."

This time it was Jaye who agreed with her. "She right. It's gone take a long-ass time to get next to him. I'm tellin' you, niggas with that much cake be naturally paranoid."

"That's another problem right there," Tuesday said, leaning back into her favorite chair. "I got it on good word that the feds 'bout to come at dude real soon. I know we like to scope out a mark for a few weeks before we make our move but we can't do that this time. We gotta reel him in and get him super-fast."

Jaye suddenly needed a drink. She took one of their glasses and poured herself some of the leftover Cuervo. "You want us to go on the most dangerous mission we've ever had without being one hundred percent sure of who our target is *and* without time to put together a proper plan? I just think we shooting dice like a muthafucka on this one! The reason we done always got down in the past is because we organized."

Tushie agreed. "She right about dat. I don't like dis goin' in headfirst shit either!"

Truthfully Tuesday didn't like it herself and she was usually the main one preaching the need for caution; however, it was the latest shit that happened with Dresden at the hotel that had her desperate for a way out the game and she, somewhat selfishly, was willing to put all of them at risk for that chance.

"Ladies, I feel everything y'all saying," she said with genuine empathy. "But in life you can't always play it safe, sometimes you gotta strap 'em on! Look, I know it's dangerous for all the reasons y'all said and a few dozen more, but if we pull this off, we'll be lookin at the biggest payday we done ever seen. The type of money that's gone get a bitch life right!

"I've been doin' this longer and I got all y'all by a couple years so take my word, this ain't shit you wanna make a long-term career out of. It's hard to bait niggas when yo titties and ass don't sit up like they used to—you see how older bitches get treated at the club. I'm thirty-seven and should've been done with this shit a long time ago, but now we all got a chance to leave this game with enough paper to do our own thang. Y'all can open y'all own clubs or even keep at it if you want, but as for me, I'm tryin' to get the fuck out the way. I think we need to do this!"

Tuesday tried her best to sell it, and for a while the girls just sat there searching themselves. It surprised her more than anybody else when Brianna was the first to jump on board. "If this nigga is

Sebastian Caine, he got cake out this world. We ain't gone get another chance at this type of money."

There was a little more discussion, but eventually the whole team agreed that this was an opportunity they just couldn't pass up.

"All right," said Tushie. "Everybody down. But how do we get close to da nigga?"

Tuesday explained to them what Dresden had told her. "This dude stay real low-key, don't handle no business in person, and don't do the club scene or no shit like that. The only time he show his face in public is to drop off and pick up his daughter from school. She six years old and go to one of them expensive private schools out in Romulus. He's there at seven forty-five and two thirty every day like clockwork."

Jaye smiled. "At least he's a devoted father. You gotta admire that."

"What about security?" asked Tushie. "Any goons rollin' wit 'em?"

Tuesday shook her head. "That's the strange part. It just be him and the girl."

Doll nodded. "Okay, the school is our best shot, but which one of us is it gone be? We usually scope a nigga long enough to see what type of chick he go for. How do we know who to sic on 'em?"

"I think it's gotta be me!" announced Tuesday. She'd spent the whole day giving this matter a careful amount of thought. "Caine gotta be in his early forties, and like Jaye said, niggas with paper like that be real cautious. I'm closer to his age and got the most experience. I think that make me the best choice."

"What if his type ain't hit up redbones with big foreheads?" Jaye asked, teasing her.

Tuesday laughed. "Bitch, I'm a dime! Plus I'm everybody's type."

Brianna couldn't help but take a shot at Tuesday. "You sure you can still do this? I'm just sayin', it's been a while since you personally went at a nigga. You might've lost it."

Tuesday stared at her with a *bitch, are you serious* look. "My whole life I been making niggas want me without even tryin'. Slut, I ain't worried 'bout losing it; my problem is that I can't turn the shit off!"

They all got a laugh out of that, except Brianna, who just rolled her eyes and folded her arms beneath her plump breasts.

While the rest were still smiling, it was the usually silly Jaye who suddenly became serious. "Something else we gotta keep in mind: any nigga wit pockets that deep gotta have a bunch of shooters on the payroll. We gone need plenty of heat and be ready to get some serious gone after we do the deed."

Tuesday agreed. It was a part of the plan that even she had overlooked. She gave her a slight nod just to show that she appreciated Jaye being on her shit.

Even though they were close to the same age, Tuesday had peeped a long time ago that Jaye was a lot sharper than Bree and Doll. She was funny, and used her humor to make people feel at ease—just like she did with her marks—but beyond those soft brown eyes Tuesday had gleaned a very analytical mind that was always calculating, just like hers.

"First thing tomorrow I'm gone see what's up wit some guns and everybody else might wanna put together a travel bag. Like she said, when it's over, we all gone have to bust up from the D, at least for a while."

Nobody was thrilled about having to leave Detroit but everybody agreed that it might be necessary to disappear until the heat died down.

For another half hour after that the team broke down the Caine game plan, but from there the conversation slowly shifted to what each of them would do with their cut of the money. They talked about Benzes, Bentley coupes, hundred-grand shopping sprees, vacations to Cabo, and even celebrities they planned to fuck. They got another bottle from the bar and smoked some more weed, and to Tuesday, there was a celebrating attitude that she thought was premature. She sat behind her desk watching the girls party up as if they just won the lottery.

Tuesday didn't want to disturb the mood but had to. She would prefer to have them overconfident and excited rather than doubtful and too afraid to go on the mission, but one last important detail had to be relayed to them.

She calmed them down. "There's somethin' y'all need to know before goin' in and it goes back to what Jaye said. Any nigga this helluva got mad goons and he gone know without a doubt that I set this shit up. He ain't the type of nigga who just gone take that kind of loss lying down. He gone come after all of us!"

Jaye looked at her, puzzled. "We already figured that we gone have to get out the city for a while."

"No, you don't get it," Tuesday said, turning to her. "What if this is the real Sebastian Caine? A nigga like that will find you no matter where you go. Ain't no running from him. It ain't a place on the map that he can't reach out and touch you in."

With that, the mood was officially changed. The girls now all had concern on their faces. In the past they had left all their marks as lovesick puppies who counted the loss of their money and dope as nothing when compared to losing them, but never had they considered the true repercussions that came with stealing from someone who was a true boss and certified gangster. Tuesday knew he wasn't just going to sit at home like Tank and boohoo about having his heart broken. This type of nigga was definitely going to get at somebody's ass about his.

"Which brings me back to my original point," she continued. "Once we get to his stash, ol' boy gots to go. We gone have to murder this nigga! If not, he'll be to see all of us: family, friends, the whole nine."

This was a nut-check moment for the team because up until now Tuesday always planned these missions so that a nigga's feelings were the only thing that got hurt. Brianna swore she had the heart but as far as Tuesday knew, none of them had actually killed anybody. Not even her. They had always been able to avoid the uglier side of the jack game, but this time, it would have to be done.

Boss Lady stared at the rest of her team from across the desk with eyes that were closer to gray than green. "If any of y'all wanna back out, you better speak up now. Shit 'bout to get thick on this one!"

Chapter Six

Tuesday was up early the next morning running errands—hangover and all. A whole lot went into creating a whole new person, which was exactly what each of the girls did whenever they went after a mark.

By 6:30 a.m. she had already traveled out to Grosse Point to meet with Percy, a forger she met through Dresden. She gave him thirty-five hundred and posed for a picture; in a few hours he would give her a Michigan driver's license with the name Tabitha Green, a Social Security card, a birth certificate, and a valid passport. For a few grand more she could've gotten a more elaborate package that included a phony credit history, medical records, and a degree from any college of her choosing. Percy's documents were identical to the real thing and for the right price he could basically make you anyone that you wanted to be.

By 7:30 a.m. she was out in Romulus parked across the street from the Bishop Burchram parochial school. From behind a dark pair of Yves St. Laurent sunglasses she watched as a convoy of parents dropped off their uniformed children.

It was 7:46 by her dashboard clock when a metallic gray Audi A8 pulled up and let out a little black girl, maybe six, in pigtails and barrettes. She was strapped in a colorful Dora the Explorer backpack and gave the driver an energetic wave before scampering into the building. As the Audi raced past, Tuesday saw that the man behind the wheel was alone and fit the description of her mark. She didn't bother to follow him because she knew exactly where he would be at 2:30.

From out in Romulus she had to drive back to the west side of Detroit, and after stopping to pay a few bills and hitting a beauty supply for a bag of Malaysian number fifty-four black weave, she made it to the salon in time for her 9:30 appointment. Tuesday pissed off all the women who were waiting when she stepped in and was immediately called to a chair. It took two and a half hours to get her hair styled into a Chinese bob with a low bang clipped right above her eyes.

While she was still under the dryer Percy texted that her package was ready, so from the hairdresser it was back out to Gross Pointe to pick it up and then a return trip to the west side to use the new ID. First she stopped at a cell shop to buy a phone, then drove out to Hertz, where she rented a green Honda Civic that she planned to pick up the following day.

Next she went out to the Town Square apartment complex on 8 Mile and Greenfield where she rented a one-bedroom unit for seven hundred dollars a month. The place was small and not even close to being as exclusive as the Seymour building, where she lived downtown, which was why she chose it. When the manager showed her the apartment, Tuesday paid no attention to the amenities because it was only going to be used as a front. Since there was no extensive background check, she cashed out first and last month's rent along with a security deposit, then was handed the key.

Her alter ego Tabitha Green now had a phone, a car, and a place to live.

After wrapping up her business at Town Square, she swung through a Checker's for a quick burger then reached Face's Auto Collision and Repair on Grand River at half past one. It was a small garage sitting on a two-acre salvage yard. She pulled up to the front gate and blew the horn three times. When the security camera craned in her direction, she gave it the finger and the electric gate rolled to the side, permitting her entry.

She weaved through the stockpile of junk cars where the sparkling CTS-V looked like a rich cousin visiting family in the slums. She parked at the garage, which was basically a poorly constructed shed of corrugated sheet metal wide enough to accommodate three auto bays and a customer service area. Tuesday got out to catcalls from two greasy crackheads under the hood of an old tow truck.

Tuesday hated coming here but it was necessary. The filth and disorganization of a junkyard was essentially the antithesis to everything she was. The cars were not lined up in an orderly way, just wedged in any way they would fit, with some stacked as many as three high. They were dirty, with crumpled bodies, shattered windshields, and scarred paint. They didn't even bother to group them according to make, model, year, or color, and this drove Tuesday even more crazy than all the dust. Her OCD was flaring like a rash that couldn't be scratched. She often thought that if only she had a forklift and four months to kill she'd have this place as tidy and organized as her kitchen cupboards.

In the first stall there was a busted burnt-orange '68 Chevelle with dented fenders, mismatched tires, and a raised hood. There was a mechanic lying beneath it on a creeper taking a ratchet to something under the engine. She stood next to the car and pounded on the roof with her fist.

Face slid out on the rolling sled in oil-soaked coveralls. "Girl, don't be banging on my shit. Respect my whip!"

Tuesday laughed. "That pearl thing you see out there is a whip. This is a piece of shit!"

"Yo problem is you seeing it as it is and not as it will be." Face rose to his full six foot three inches. "A little body work, custom paint, and new interior; plus I already got a motor from a Corvette ZR-l that I'm 'bout to drop in here. After I slap some twenty-sixes on it, in two months I'm gone have the coldest Old School in the city."

She waved him off. "Whatever, nigga, I ain't here to talk cars with you. We got business."

He led Tuesday through an adjoining room that had a cash register and a counter where Face did all his legitimate business, into a door behind the counter that led to a small office where he did all his real business.

Cars were Face's business and everybody knew this, but only a few knew that he dabbled in chopping up and retagging stolen ones as a lucrative side hustle; and of them, only an even smaller percentage knew that the garage and all the scrap cars were just a cover for how he made his real money: guns.

Everything in Face's office lent itself to function rather than fashion. All the furniture had either been found on the street or taken from junk cars that wound up in his scrap yard. Against the wall was a set of bench seats supported by milk crates that came from a church van. His desk was no desk at all but rather a dining table a neighbor had thrown out, and in front of it were two wicker chairs that came from someone's old patio set. Behind the table was an old patched-up leather recliner that served as his office chair.

He fell into it and wiped his hands on a greasy rag he pulled from his pocket. "Whatcha need, baby girl?"

Face had been a longtime friend that she met through A.D. back when they were doing sticks together. He earned his name due to the terrible acne scars that marred his face and made him resemble the similarly afflicted singer named Seal. He was cool, he was reliable, and could get a nigga nearly anything they wanted in the way of guns. He could also take hot cars off their hands, which was why Tuesday had brought him Tank's Denali. However, the gritty grease monkey persona was as much a front as the garage itself: Face owned a million-dollar house out in Allen Park, a fleet of cars, and was married to a fine-ass Colombian bitch who pushed a triple-white Range Rover and worshipped the ground this ugly mechanic walked on.

He offered her a seat but Tuesday looked at the set of raggedy wicker chairs and decided to stand. "We got another situation coming up and we need heat. A lot of it."

"Y'all must be expecting some trouble." He ran a hand over his bald head and beamed a smile that revealed a set of perfect white teeth. Despite his face, there was a rugged sexiness about him that Tuesday and many other women saw; just as his counterpart had snagged the supermodel Heidi Klum, Tuesday could see how he had knocked someone as beautiful as Maria, his wife.

Tuesday nodded in response to his statement. "We think things might get a little nasty on this one. We just wanna be ready."

Face rubbed his palms together in anticipation of a big sale. "Well, let's go shopping then."

He got up, went to the rear corner of his office then threw back the carpet that wasn't tacked down. Hidden under it was a trapdoor set within the wooden floorboards. He keyed a bolt lock and it swung outward to open on a set of stairs that led to a cellar. He descended first and Tuesday followed, taking the stair treads carefully in her high-heeled leather riding boots.

At the bottom he flicked a switch and the fluorescent lighting overhead was reflected in all the polished black steel. The twenty-by-thirty-five-foot room beneath Face's office was called The Gun Store. The walls had pegboard racks which displayed every type of rifle, shotgun, and handgun one could think of, and a few they never heard of. More of them were stored in crates and set out on the long metal tables. From tiny Derringers to hide up your sleeve to a big .50-caliber that could crack a tank, even to the extreme shit like grenades, RPG's and C-4 plastic explosives; anything a nigga needed to bring war and death on his enemy, Face either had or could get for a special fee.

The place smelled of gun oil and steel. There was enough heat down here to get Face all day in federal prison. Whenever Tuesday came through that little trapdoor in his office, she always felt like a secret agent on some James Bond shit.

He leaned against a counter that held a dozen AR-15's and SKS's with the ammunition boxes stacked neatly to the side. "So what was you lookin' for?"

Tuesday explained. "For looks the AK is cool because it's recognizable and it intimidates, but for actually shooting it's kinda heavy and it got too much kick for a woman. I need something that a girl can handle easy if it goes down and she find herself in the middle of it."

Face listened to her with a slow nod. He reached behind him, pulled a gun off the pegboard that looked like a small Uzi and showed it to her. "I think the M11 is exactly what you lookin' for. It's small and light enough for a woman to handle, and while it ain't got the power of a K, it damn sure gone get a nigga off you. Especially if it's converted to fully."

He passed it to Tuesday, who examined the weapon more closely. She maneuvered it as if she were fending off multiple attackers. She liked that it was short, lightweight and fit well in her small hands.

"You sure this ain't got too much recoil? I don't want this bitch jumping out my hands in the middle of a shootout."

"Hell, naw. I'm feeling this for a chick so much that I make the wifey carry a M11. I custom-built a stash spot in the Rover wit one of these in it, even took her to the range a couple times. Maria smaller than you and she handle that bitch wit no problem.

"But if you want, we can go out back and tag a couple cars. You know, just so you can get the feel of it."

Face took the M11, loaded it with ten rounds, then led her up through his office into the yard behind the garage. He gave the gun to Tuesday and watched her spray bullets into the side of an old Delta 88, shattering the passenger side windows, punching holes in the doors and rear quarter panel, and flattening a tire. Firing the gun charged her with a rush of adrenaline.

When the weapon was spent, she gave it back to him with a smile that said she approved. "That's all right! You say wifey got the same one?"

"Only I switched hers from semi to fully automatic and I put a laser sighting on it to help her aim."

"Good. I want you to hook me up five the same way."

"Damn, five!" He squinted. "Y'all must be goin' at somebody helluva! It ain't me, is it?"

He tried to mask it with humor but beneath the smile Tuesday could see that the question was earnest. This was a reminder that while they did go back twenty years, they weren't friends. Doing business had been mutually beneficial but with all the money that had changed hands, trust had never been purchased.

"Nigga, will you stop it, ain't nobody lookin' at you. Besides, you know how I feel about dark-skinned niggas!" She gave him an air kiss.

They returned to his office and he to his old recliner behind the table. "Five M11's switched over with the beam." He rubbed his chin thoughtfully. "Since it's you, just gimme fifty-eight hun and they be ready in two days!"

Tuesday added, "Plus I wanna good pair of binoculars, some night vision goggles, and a silencer that'll fit my Heckler."

He gave her a strange look. "Damn, girl, you 'bout to become a Navy Seal or somethin'?"

"Just tell me what the ticket is, and show me some love since you already stuck dick to me on the Denali."

"Again, since it's you," he said with the smile that always impressed Tuesday in how it could distract from his leathery skin, "I'll do the whole package for seven racks, and that *is* love!"

Tuesday tried to use her own smile. "Let me get it for forty-five?"

Face shook his head. "Damn, baby, and you just said you wasn't out to rob me."

She came around to his side of the table and sat on it. "So me and my girl Tush at the mall the other day and I'm lookin' at these fire red Prada joints wit a five-inch heel. I'm wondering, damn, do I already got somethin' in my closet like these."

Face looked away from her with his eyes closed. "See, you 'bout to get on that bullshit again. Let's just do this business and keep it clean."

"So after that we went for mani-pedis out at this new spot in Ypsilanti. They massage yo soles real good and soak yo feet in this oil that s'posed to make the skin extra soft. I got my nails did in this plum-red polish."

She could see that Face was starting to breathe harder. He dropped his hand into his lap and she watched with a smile as it found its way to his crotch.

Face was a smart businessman, a dedicated hustler, and had plenty of game; but Tuesday had learned his one weakness a long time ago and knew how to exploit it. Face had a serious foot fetish. A pair of pretty feet in open-toed shoes did more for him than lingerie did for most niggas. He was so into feet that even conversations about pedicures and toenail polish were enough to take him out of his zone.

He struggled for control of himself. "You a dirty muthafucka, TK! I'll do sixty-eight but anything less than that and you gettin' down on me."

Tuesday made a show of crossing her legs then seductively stroked the thigh-high Stuart Whiteman riding boots that she purposely wore for this meeting. "I already know you gettin' this shit from a wholesaler for next to nothin', Face. Tell me a better number and I'll unzip these boots and show you what we both know you wanna see."

Face was massaging his dick through the coveralls. He watched mesmerized as she teased him by toying with the zipper on her boot. "I'll do it for sixty-six."

She slowly tugged at the zipper but stopped about an inch below the knee.

He said, "I thought you was takin' 'em off!"

"No, no, no," she cooed softly. "You know how this game is played. The lower you go, the lower I go."

He let out a frustrated groan. "Sixty-three, but I'm tellin' you it's the best I can do!"

Face watched with wide and excited eyes as the zipper slowly traveled south again but grumbled curses when it stopped right at her ankle.

"C'mon, Tuesday, you killin' me!" he whined almost like a child. "Sixty-two fifty!"

She pulled the zipper halfway back up her calf.

"See, that's some bullshit!"

She wagged a finger at him. "Don't insult me then, nigga! Ain't nothin' fifty-dollar about me."

"Did you forget I'm tryin' to run a business here?"

She countered. "And did you forget how suckable my toes are?"

Tuesday inched over until she sat directly in front of him on the table. She dropped her left foot in his lap and, using the toe of her boot, she lightly stroked the length of his hard dick while he let out pleasure-filled groans.

"Sixty-one!" he said between heavy breaths.

"Make it an even six and I'll let you taste 'em."

Face agreed with a grunt and when she raised her right foot so that he could finally remove the boot, he stripped it off like a kid hastily unwrapping a Christmas gift.

At first he just stared at her flawless foot, appraising it the way a jeweler might do an exceptional diamond. Tuesday wore a four and a half in women's, which was a little small for her height. She didn't have bunions, corns, or calluses and the skin was a brighter shade since her feet didn't see the sun as often. The toes weren't bent, curled, longer, or shorter than they should be, perfect symmetry from the big toe down to the pinky, and she wore a gold toe ring on the second one. The nails were pedicured and painted in the plum-red polish that she had told him about. Tuesday had always taken care of her shit because her shoe game required that her feet be on point.

He took a long deep inhale as if ecstatic by the soapy scent then devoured her foot, kissing and sucking with a delight that only those with an identical fetish could appreciate.

Tuesday giggled as she felt his squirmy tongue wriggle between her toes. "Don't forget, I got another foot too."

When Tuesday pulled away from Face's it was already a few minutes after two and she was heavy on the pedal because she had to be back out in Romulus by two thirty.

She left the gun dealer in his office feeling like a sucker but a satisfied one. She'd gotten the entire package for fifty-six hundred; he'd even thrown in a few extra boxes of ammo. She left with the silencer, shells, goggles, and binoculars with Face promising that the modified M11's would be ready for pickup in two days.

To her, the funniest part was that she didn't even have to fuck since Face's bizarre fetish didn't involve him wanting the pussy. Tuesday did feel weird having to jack the nigga off with her feet but for the price of a Wetnap she'd saved fourteen hundred dollars.

Tuesday didn't take advantage of him every time they did business; she just really needed to save a few dollars. The club wasn't doing very well and everything she bought today—the ID package, the apartment, and the guns—had taken a huge bite out of her savings. Plus it didn't help that she gave up her share of the last lick.

She had to speed but was back out in Romulus and parked across the street from Bishop Burchram in time. The Audi swung through to collect the little girl and again the driver was alone.

Only when he pulled off this time, Tuesday followed. She performed an illegal U-turn down the block from the school and trailed them at a safe distance. She knew that the white Caddy wasn't very discreet so she purposely kept a car or two between them.

Tuesday had enough experience with tailing a mark to know better than to copy every stop and turn. On the surface streets she took corners a block or two after him and on the freeway she fell back as much as half a mile.

She tailed them on the highway at about five car-lengths until they got off and led her into a residential area that was about three miles from the school. The streets were clean and besides the occasional DUI, crime was probably an anomaly. Behind manicured lawns and neatly trimmed hedges sat large houses that would easily fetch eight or nine hundred thousand in a fair real estate market.

When they made an unexpected stop at a Dairy Queen, Tuesday had to take a quick right turn into the parking lot of a bank that was a block behind them. She whipped into it with a squeak of rubber, narrowly avoided the sign and parked in a slot that gave her a view of the Audi. She grabbed the binoculars off the passenger seat and used them to study the driver as he got out to approach the service window.

He was about six foot one, dark-skinned with his hair cut so low it was close to bald. He had thin sideburns that stretched into a short trimmed beard and goatee. While his eyes were concealed behind dark sunglasses, Tuesday figured that he was reasonably handsome, at least fuckable, since the mission would most likely require that she have sex with him.

Tuesday didn't know why she half expected him to have horns, huge bat wings, and a forked tail. Not only did this guy not look like Satan, he didn't even look like a run-of-the-mill dope boy.

This was meant only in a sense that he wasn't dressed flashily. He wore a plain white Lacoste golf shirt and dark jeans; the car blocked her view of his shoes. His sunglasses were stylish but probably less expensive than the YSL's she had perched on her head. He didn't wear any jewelry other than a watch and a platinum pinky ring on his right hand.

Tuesday was pleased to see that he didn't have on a wedding band; but while that meant he wasn't married, she knew that there was still a good chance he was involved with somebody.

Dresden had not given her a good picture but she had spent all the previous day and night studying it. Right then, watching him through a pair of high-powered military binoculars as the man paid for a small sundae and medium Blizzard then walked them back to the Audi, there was nothing about his look or swagger to suggest that this was the real Sebastian Caine or a phony. He looked as innocent as a bank manager or computer geek.

After the Dairy Queen, Tuesday followed them for six more blocks until he turned onto a short tree-lined street that ended in a cul-de-sac shaped like a horseshoe. The gray Audi pulled in at a large Bavarian-style house with stained-glass windows and a circular drive. The father got out holding his Blizzard and guided the buoyant youngster to the front door while she happily scooped heaping spoonfuls of ice cream into her mouth.

Parked at the corner of the block, Tuesday studied the house with her binoculars. It was impressive, sizable—she guessed four bedrooms and two and a half baths—and set in a decent neighborhood, but this was far below the level of someone like Sebastian Caine. The man who had quietly spent twenty years as the king of cocaine could afford something way more extravagant than this. For someone with his money and power Tuesday had expected a twenty-room mansion protected by privacy fences and cameras with armed goons in dark suits stationed at the front gate, not some nondescript house in middle-class suburbia surrounded by dentists, office managers, and anyone with a seventy grand a year income. Tuesday guessed with what she made off the club, minus doing sticks, she could afford the mortgage on a nicer place than he had.

"And what about security?" she wondered out loud. She didn't see any henchmen, goons, gunmen, or even friends, for that matter. Tuesday was confused because at the Dairy Queen he didn't even appear to have a pistol on him. Would the real Caine really be driving around with his daughter and no protection while living in a house without so much as a chain-link fence and two pit bulls in the yard? Would someone who was reportedly getting thousands upon thousands of bricks just walk around in the open like that and leave himself so naked?

There were a few children outside on the block and an elderly couple seated on their porch, and since Tuesday didn't want to appear too suspicious by just sitting on the corner, she slowly pulled away from the curb.

She cruised past the quiet little house, did a 180 in the rounded cul-de-sac and cruised by it again. There was a large picture window in front and through it she could glimpse cartoons on a wall-mounted TV.

She was looking for anything that might help her make sense of this mystery but nothing about the plain little house or factory-standard Audi said seven-figure lick.

Tuesday turned off his block and found her way back to the freeway thinking that Dresden must've fucked up again.

Chapter Seven

It was around five o'clock when Tuesday returned to The Bounce and since she was in a better mood than last night, she flirted with old Mr. Scott and made his day.

She went inside and was greeted by a typical Tuesday afternoon crowd: fourteen customers on the floor, two more at the bar, and three girls on stage.

She went over to the bar and called over Ebony, who was being chatted up by a drinker on the first stool. She cut their conversation and joined Tuesday at the other end of the bar. "What's up, Boss Lady?"

"Eb, I just wanna apologize for the way I came through here last night. I was goin' through something but I don't want you to think that I'm gone come in every night and try to drink up the bar."

Ebony leaned over the bar on her elbows so she could be closer to her. "First off, I knew you had something on yo mind but I felt it wasn't my place to try and pick yo brain for it. I'm a bitch who know her role: I pour liquor, it's not my job to be yo therapist.

"But second, and most importantly, you don't have to apologize for shit you do in this muthafucka! TK, this is yo shit and if you wanna drink up every bottle of tequila we got in stock, you can and not have to say sorry to me or any other bitch in here."

Tuesday nodded. "I know. It's just that I try to carry myself like a professional when I'm at work." It was more than just about carrying herself like a professional; Tuesday always tried to appear in control, especially at work. The break with A.D. had put her in a bad place and she had allowed Ebony to peep her in a moment of weakness.

Ebony said: "Can't nobody round here say you don't handle yo business. Every now and then a bitch might complain—you the boss, you gone get that—but all in all, you treat everybody in here right. From the dancers, to the waitresses, to the customers."

"Ahh, girl!" Tuesday reached across the bar and gave her a one-armed hug. "I know it sound corny but I needed to hear something positive like that."

Tuesday had a few more words with Ebony about the liquor supply then turned away from the bar, but just as she started for her office: *whack!* She flinched and spun around, only to see Del-Ray grinning at her.

"We at six!"

"Naw, nigga," she said, pointing a finger at him. "That was yo last one!"

He didn't understand. "By my math ten minus six equals four."

"And what math did you use to figure that Tushie's ass is worth more than mine? You ain't think I was gone find out about the bet you made with her?"

DelRay could only give her that guilty smile of a nigga who'd just got busted with another chick's phone number.

"You done already got down but now you go back to looking and admiring 'cause if you touch me again I'm gone shoot you in the dick."

DelRay shook his head. "That's some bullshit, Boss Lady. You reneging on our bet."

"Don't feel bad, Fatboy," she said, patting on his big belly. "Like everybody else, you still get to enjoy the view."

She turned around, made her ass bounce a couple times, then strutted off. DelRay called out over the music: "You wrong as hell for that, TK!"

When Tuesday reached her office, she was texting someone with her phone. She threw the door open but was so fucked up by what she saw that she froze and almost dropped it.

Baby Doll was sprawled out on her couch butt-ass naked and between her legs was this brown-skinned dancer that Tuesday had just hired. Crouched on all fours in nothing but boy shorts, the girl looked up at her boss, shocked, with wide eyes and lips greasy from eating Doll's pussy.

"What the fuck is y'all trifling bitches doin' in my office?" Tuesday barked angrily.

The dancer, who called herself Passionfruit, grabbed her top and bolted out of the room covering her bare breasts. She was too embarrassed to speak or even look at Tuesday.

Baby Doll was nonchalant. She just casually sat up and reached for the pack of Newports that she had left on Tuesday's desk. She tapped it against her palm, fished one out and lit it.

She leaned back on the sofa blowing out a trail of smoke. "Damn, TK, why you scare off my li'l thang-thang?"

Tuesday came inside and pulled the door shut. "Why is you and yo li'l thang-thang making it jump off in my office? Bitch, is you out yo rabbit-ass mind?"

She smiled as if she either didn't truly appreciate or care how pissed Tuesday really was. "I was feeling some kinda way. I was just tryin' to get me one real quick."

Tuesday dropped her purse in a chair and stood over her. "Well, you shoulda took that bitch to a room or something. And I done told yo ass before I'm tryin' to run a business here. This ain't yo personal candy shop!"

Tuesday didn't mind that most of the girls were bisexual because she sometimes went both ways; she also didn't mind that

some of them fucked with each other because even she occasionally picked out some new cutie that she wanted to taste; but the problem Tuesday had with Doll was that she was fucking everything at the club and all over the club. She'd been caught getting down in the dressing room, the stockroom, the restroom, and now in Tuesday's office—which, considering her OCD, was a major violation. Baby Doll was knocking so many of the dancers that it was causing unnecessary drama at The Bounce. Jealousy had made a few girls actually come to blows over the short, hazel-eyed vixen, and one time gunplay was even involved.

"I told you to slow yo roll on fuckin' with all my dancers up in here. It keep up too much shit!"

Baby Doll was still sitting on the couch naked with her legs open. "And what am I s'posed to do if a bitch choose me?"

"You gone pull a bitch up in my office and then top the shit off by playin' me like it's a joke!" Tuesday pointed a finger at her. "You betta be lucky I don't whip yo li'l midget ass!"

Doll's clothes were on the floor. Tuesday scooped them up into a ball and threw them at her. "Bitch, put on yo shit and get the fuck outta here!"

Doll untangled her outfit. "Bitch, stop actin like you ain't never dipped off with none of these hoes."

"That's right, *dipped off*!" Tuesday said, stressing the two words with her hands. "This is where I get my bread. Bitch either respect my club or don't bring yo ass up here!"

Tuesday watched with hands on her hips while Doll got dressed in a camisole top that she was wearing with some denim shorts. She slipped her feet into some ankle socks and a tiny pair of Air Force Ones most likely bought at a kids' shoe store.

As Doll was leaving out the office, she muttered, "I wonder if being fake just natural or if it's somethin' that happen to a bitch when they get old."

Tuesday spun around because even though she was talking to herself, the words were spoken loud enough for her to hear. "I got yo old right here, bitch! Whenever you think you ready to see this old fake bitch just run up. That go for you and yo girl Bree. All y'all gotta do is run up and I'll smash both y'all bitches! My bad, all one and a half of y'all bitches!"

Doll didn't respond. She just walked out her office never saying a word and never looking back.

Tuesday kept some air freshener in her desk drawer for when she smoked weed in the office. She walked throughout the room spraying until she no longer smelled their scent, doused the sofa, then flipped over the cushions.

Tuesday understood that the little pint-sized bitch had done this to make a statement because Baby Doll, as much as anyone, knew how she felt about her personal space. There once was a time when the girls followed her lead without question but lately Brianna was challenging her at every turn and Doll was starting to do the same. Yesterday Bree had all but accused her of stealing and now today this—there was an escalating level of disrespect that was going to culminate in somebody getting fucked up. This was just another reason why Tuesday knew this had to be their last lick since it was so obvious that it was time to break up the crew. When role players started demanding the ball from Kobe, there was definitely something wrong with the team chemistry.

Tuesday wasn't so stupid as to think that Bree and Doll didn't talk about her behind her back. One was too short and the other too bony to give her any trouble in a fight, but then again, who actually fought anymore in the Age of the Gun. If the two of them wanted to break camp and do their own thing, Tuesday would support that, even though she knew neither of them had the brains to do so. However, until this job was over, she intended to keep a close eye on both of them.

Tushie walked into her office just as Tuesday was putting the can away. She frowned because the flowery smell of potpourri was so strong that it was actually offensive.

"Gurl, what wuz you in hurr doin' dat you need to cover it up wit a whole thang of air freshener?"

"It ain't about what I was doin'!" She took two minutes to explain the confrontation she had just had with Baby Doll.

"Hell, naaaaw!" Tushie said with even more New Orleans in her voice than usual. "And you ain't whup dat li'l bitch from one end of the room to tha otha?"

Tuesday laughed at her girl's accent. "Haw, I gave her a pass this time."

"You been givin' out a lot of dem lately," Tushie said as a warning. "A bitch might think you goin' soft round hurr."

"If a bitch think that, it'll be a mistake!" Tuesday flashed her a serious glare even though she knew that Tushie was not referring to herself.

Tushie said, "I just came back from Aziz's. I got those cases of Grey Goose and got 'em to throw in a few otha thangs." Their liquor distributor was a young Arab who was raised in Hamtramck and had a thing for the sistas. Even though he was Muslim, he worshipped Tushie's legendary body almost as much as he did Allah, which was why when it was time to restock their booze, Tuesday always sent her to handle that business. While tight-fitting denim might look good on her, that ass didn't move quite like it did in lighter fabrics. So when Tuesday saw that Tushie was wearing stretch pants, she knew that a little flirting and some booty shaking had probably gotten her the order for next to nothing.

"And where wuz you at while I was over thurr getting felt up by bin Laden's cousin?"

"I just got done tailing ol' boy but something don't seem right about him." Tuesday took a minute to explain how she had followed Caine today and shared all the things that gave her doubts about him being heavy in the game.

"That don't necessarily mean nuthin'," said Tushie. "Maybe dat nigga just playin' low-key. It's a lot of niggas out thurr who got it but ain't tryin' to stunt. Tha smart ones know betta."

"I understand that but it's just hard for me to believe that a nigga who's basically a kingpin would just be walking around out in public by himself and parking at some shit no bigger than what we grew up in. This nigga s'posed to roll like the president whenever he out and about: one hundred killers, thirty cars deep with him ducked off in the backseat of something bulletproof. Not whipping around in some plain-ass Audi that ain't even got chrome rims."

Tushie countered by saying, "But ain't no nigga tryin' ta stay unda the radar gone be able to roll like dat."

She was right. Tuesday was surprised that her girl was actually peeping angles that she should've seen for herself. It all made sense when viewed in the light of Sebastian Caine's reputation for being incognito.

She tapped her chin thoughtfully while considering all the myths she'd heard about him over the years. The most important one was that he never did business in person, always through a front man. His anonymity was essentially the key to his power and was the primary reason he'd had such a long, lucrative run. It had earned him the moniker "The Invisible Man." He couldn't be snitched on, robbed, or assassinated if nobody knew who he really was.

Tuesday figured that a man so clever would also be smart enough not to draw attention to himself with some big luxurious mansion or even a flashy car, and he definitely wouldn't need security since nobody knew his face to begin with. Maybe someone slick enough to keep their identity a secret in the dope game for over twenty years would pick the simplest disguise: A plain '01 Audi-driving suburban father who watered his grass, paid his taxes, and took his daughter for ice cream after school. Tuesday began to smile to herself because the more she thought of it, the more she appreciated his genius.

But as she continued to think on Caine's genius, the smile began to fade because she realized that it would be all the more difficult to seduce him. A nigga like this would peep a game-running bitch coming from a mile away. In the past her fat ass, green eyes, and pretty smile had been enough to draw marks in, but this was no ordinary mark. It would take more than just sex appeal; Tuesday decided that she was somehow going to have to earn his trust.

She propped her elbow on the desk and perched her chin atop her fist struggling to decide exactly how she was going to do that.

While Tushie parked herself into the chair in front of her, Tuesday shared all the revelations that had just come to her and asked for some input on a scheme to get close to him. Tushie agreed with her assessment of their mark but in terms of advice on how to get to him, she was just as dry.

"Gurl, you just gone have ta watch 'em fo the next coupla days and wait fo yo openin'."

Tuesday made it back to her condo at about eight that evening, leaving Tushie, her co-owner, at The Bounce to oversee things. She was tired from the long day, but had a ritual for coming home that must be obeyed just like the one for leaving. She went room to room checking each light with three flicks and making certain that everything was still arranged according to her system.

Her stomach grumbled a reminder that she hadn't eaten since she grabbed that burger from Checker's earlier. She went into the kitchen, popped a ready-to-eat meal into the microwave, and sat quietly at the breakfast table picking over what Lean Cuisine had the audacity to call Chicken Alfredo.

Tuesday found it funny that so many girls at the club thought she lived some glamorous life filled with champagne parties when the truth was, most of her nights were spent exactly like this. While some people might find her existence lonely, or even a little pathetic, she was cool with it. Tuesday's motto was: *Being alone is only a problem when you don't enjoy the company*. She had been raised as a single child under a mother who was way more interested in each new boyfriend than in her. She only had a few cousins, and those who she hadn't fallen out with over money or jealousy were uptight Christian squares who looked down on her for being a stripper. Because her mother moved so often when she was little (sometimes as many as three times a year), she never forged those lasting friendships that could weather the years and span into adulthood. Other than Tushie, none of the people she dealt with could be classified as friends: most were casual acquaintances like Ebony, who she was cool with but not too personal, while others were just business associates like Face. Since A.D. had been away, she'd had several brief flings with men who she was using strictly for dick, but she always had to break it off because without fail the nigga ended up catching feelings and tried to get possessive. Despite it all, though, Tuesday didn't count the absence of any of these things as losses because she had herself and that had always been enough. She had no family, no friends, no man, but most important, she didn't feel she needed any of these things to complete her. Tuesday sat there in her quiet condo, alone at her kitchen table taking in forkfuls of gummy pasta and rubbery processed chicken, telling herself how complete her life was, and making herself swallow that as well.

After dinner she spent two hours cleaning a condo that already looked sterile enough to perform surgery in. During this period she only had one minor OCD hiccup in which she spent fifteen straight minutes wiping at an imaginary spot on the glass of a three-hundred-gallon saltwater aquarium that decorated her living room.

Then, after being inspired by the sight of the tropical fish, she jumped on her computer and spent forty-five minutes at a travel website considering vacation spots to hit up if the lick was a success—she was torn between St. Maarten and Costa Rica. Then she spent another half hour on Black Planet live chatting with a thirtysomething SBM out of Atlanta who claimed to be partner in a brokerage firm but was in all likelihood probably an unemployed white guy in Montana who was closer to fifty.

After logging off her computer, she took a quick shower in a large glass booth with mint-green marble walls. She paid special attention to her feet since she had used them to pleasure Face's pervy ass. She scrubbed so hard with the abrasive sponge that she was going to need another pedicure, because she was taking the plum toenail polish right off.

The gross part aside, she did enjoy having her toes sucked; plus, the sight of Doll getting served on the office sofa was a sad reminder that it had been a while since someone had fed on her. She had a couple of her own li'l thang-thangs on line who she could have had come lick the clit but right then there was no stud on deck, and what she really wanted was dick.

Tuesday was horny as hell. She felt hot and swollen between the legs. She looked down at her pretty Brazilian-waxed pussy and imagined A.D. on his knees tasting the juices. She would hold the back of his head while the water cascaded off her body and rained on the top of him, grinding into his face as his strong hands held the back of her thighs. He was the one man she knew whose tongue game was as sick as most bitches' and once he made a nice fat one bubble up inside her, she would explode right onto his sexy lips.

Then when her legs were done shaking, she would turn around and offer him a full serving of what Dresden's small unsatisfying dick had stolen just a sample of. He had groaned about how good her pussy was, but really, he had no idea; what he'd done was as impersonal as a gynecologist's exam. He had never experienced how wet and wonderful Tuesday could truly be when she was with a nigga that she cared for and desired—like A.D. Again she imagined him rough-fucking her from behind just the way she liked it: thug-style; spanking her ass and telling her that the pussy was his. She could almost feel his hands tracing the curvature of her body from her small waist to her plump titties, his long, stiff dick plowing deep into her receptive hole as he groaned with pleasure, the sound of his pelvis slapping into her so hard that he sent shockwaves rolling through her butter-soft ass, making it bounce to his rhythm. And just when his frantic pace coupled with his ecstatic groans told her that he was close to a nut, she would turn around and reciprocate with some marvelous head until he busted in her mouth.

That was the one thing that separated Tuesday from chicks who went all the way dyke: to her there was no substitute for a sexy nigga attached to a big, hard, throbbing dick that could actually come—a bitch in a strap-on just couldn't duplicate that for her. Girls were okay in that some of them were beautiful and most could really eat some pussy, but she just absolutely loved looking into her man's eyes and seeing the pleasure that she was giving him up until that moment when she sucked him off and swallowed all that he had to offer.

Tuesday was leaned back against the shower wall, eyes closed, with a hand between her legs. She was teasing herself with her middle finger and honestly didn't even know when she had started. She only knew when she would stop.

But she stopped sooner than she wanted to because the vibe was broken up by the sound of her doorbell. It startled her because it was such a hardly-heard sound; in fact she couldn't remember the last time she'd heard it. She would be paged from the front desk via intercom if she had an outside guest and she was not friendly with any of her neighbors. The only people who would pop up at her door unannounced were building management and even they wouldn't come at this hour. The clock on her waterproof radio that hung in her shower confirmed it was after eleven p.m.

She was ready to dismiss the phantom sound as a fluke, someone at the wrong door, but when the bell rang again, she killed the water and stepped out the stall. She wrapped her wet body in a dry towel, then quickly padded into the bedroom for some clothes.

She slipped on a black-and-red silk peignoir with a Chinese pattern that came mid-thigh. She stepped into some fluffy bunny slippers that she was way too grown for but liked anyway. She didn't bother to put on panties.

The bell rang again and this time it was accompanied by a knocking that sounded urgent. Forceful.

Tuesday grabbed the Heckler from her Louis bag and went to answer it. She approached slowly, warily, with the gun at her side. The safety was off.

Tuesday thought about screwing in the new silencer she just bought, then decided against it. If an intruder did try to barge inside her apartment, she would be justified in blowing his heart out of his back, but the police would be suspicious when none of her neighbors claimed to have heard the gunshots. While she wouldn't do a day for the actual murder, the illegal sound suppresser might still get her five to ten years in federal prison.

The bell rang again. More knocking.

From the living room she crept down the short hallway that led to the front door. Tuesday didn't know what type of wood it was, but it appeared to be of high quality. The door was thick, heavy, and wide as the ones in most medical centers that accommodate hospital beds.

Light from the hallway spilled in from the crack beneath it. There were only two shadows, representing one pair of feet.

She looked through the peephole and was presented a fisheye lens view of the gentleman from next door. He was an older nigga, Tuesday guessed early fifties, that she could tell had been really fine back in his day. His unit was to the left of hers, and although they'd passed each other a few times in the hall, they had exchanged no more than courteous smiles. She couldn't imagine what the fuck he would be doing at her door at eleven thirty at night when in two years of being neighbors he'd never so much as come by to borrow sugar.

Tuesday disarmed the alarm, disengaged the bolt lock, but left on the security chain. She cracked the door and peeked out between the one-inch gap that the short chain allowed.

"Can I help you?" she asked with enough attitude to let him know she considered this an intrusion. The muzzle of the gun was pressed against the door ready to fire straight through the wood if he presented a problem.

The handsome neighbor beamed a smile that instantly defused her. "My apologies for disturbing you at this late hour. I was just about to entertain company out on my terrace when I noticed this little fella stuck out on the ledge." He was gently stroking a bundle of white fur he had cradled in his arm.

"Oh, my God!" Tuesday quickly unchained the door and threw it open to receive her cat. It only dawned on her then that in the three hours she'd been home she hadn't seen Nicholas once—even when she got undressed for the shower, which should've instantly alerted her. She accepted him, then brought his face up to meet hers. "Fur face, what the hell are you doin' out the house?"

Still smiling but cautiously eyeing her pistol, the neighbor explained: "You know that one-foot ledge of decorative molding that goes around the building? Well, my guess is that the little guy climbed out onto it from your terrace to try and get after some pigeons and just went out too far. He was actually closer to my side than yours and it took me about twenty minutes to lure him onto my balcony with a can of sardines."

"Bad kitty! Bad, bad kitty!" She playfully admonished Nicholas with a finger trying to look cute for the nigga. She dropped the cat and he instantly scampered into the apartment for his water dish or perhaps his litter box.

"I am so embarrassed," she said with a flirty smile. "I promise to keep a better eye on him."

"It's no problem. I'm just sorry that I had to interrupt your shower."

Tuesday had forgotten to take off the shower cap that she wore to protect her new do from the water and humidity. She quickly snatched the plastic bag off her head, now genuinely embarrassed.

He was brown-skinned with naturally curly hair that suggested he might be some sort of mixed breed, with just a touch of gray at the temples that made him look dignified. He was wearing a blue pin-striped suit that Tuesday's expert eye told her was tailored for his build and not some ninety-nine-dollar off-the-rack shit from Men's Wearhouse. With a glance she also did a quick appraisal of his gold watch, diamond cufflinks, pinky ring, and the Italian loafers he wore with the suit. The nigga was bossed up with a white-collar swag.

He said, "As many times as we've passed each other in the hall, I just realized that this is our first conversation." He was checking out her exposed legs in a way that made Tuesday horny again.

"It's nothing personal, I'm just really private," she said. "But if there's anything I could ever do to thank you for this."

"Well, I was kinda hoping you could pay me back by allowing me to take you to dinner sometime!" He was wearing a boyish grin with eyes wide and hopeful for a yes.

Tuesday considered it, rejected it, wavered, reconsidered it, almost accepted, and reconsidered again before she finally said: "I'm sorry, but things are really crazy for me right now! I just broke up with somebody and—"

He held up his hand to indicate that she didn't need to explain. "It's okay, I know how it is. It's just that I've wanted to approach you for so long and I would've never forgiven myself if I didn't at least take my shot. Lord knows when I would've had another chance."

Tuesday smiled, truly flattered. That's what she loved about older men with game, because even in rejection they still came off smooth. It was almost enough to make her reconsider his invitation again.

"I can't do dinner, but can I at least repay you with a hug?" she asked with her arms extended.

"My father told me to never refuse a beautiful woman wearing a nightgown and holding a gun."

When they embraced, Tuesday pressed her entire body into his and held him tightly. His cologne had her going and a man felt so good in her arms right then that she had to resist the urge to pull him inside and jam her tongue down his throat. She held him so long that he actually started to rock up, and Tuesday squeezed him even tighter, loving how his piece felt pressed against her inner thigh.

"Derek!" A shrill female voice echoed from down the hall and startled them both into parting.

"Monica?" He looked at her confused as if his guest had already been forgotten. "I'll be with you in just a minute," he said with a guilty smile. "Why don't you go get yourself another glass of champagne?"

Monica gave him a *yeah, right* look then just stood there mugging Tuesday with her arms folded.

Sizing her up, Tuesday thought the girl was pretty but not quite on par with her: she had a nose that didn't fit her face and too much chin, like Jay Leno. She wore a red Dior dress that Tuesday knew would've looked better on her, with gold shoes that even she had to admit were pretty damn fly. Tuesday rated her a 7.9, points deducted for the nose and chin.

"Well, good night then," Derek said to Tuesday with an apologetic look on his face.

Tuesday stood there for an extended moment wanting him to notice the erect nipples poking out the silk fabric of her peignoir. "Good night then," she said, then finally closed the door.

Back inside, she closed the sliding glass door that she usually left cracked so that Nicholas could enjoy his favorite spot on the terrace. She then found him curled up on her bed.

She pulled the cat onto her lap and stroked him while she thought over the dinner invitation. Having dick right next door might be convenient, but she also knew that it was potentially disastrous. Niggas started off loving the idea of a purely physical relationship but they ultimately began wanting more time and attention. This was the one place she had to escape all the craziness and drama in her life, so the last thing she wanted was a disgruntled ex-lover living right next door. Tuesday knew she had made the right choice; it was just her hot ass making her think otherwise.

Chocolate had always been a good substitute for sex so Tuesday fetched two Snickers ice cream bars from the freezer, then watched TV from her bed. She took large bites, still wishing that she had someone to fill her other holes. To help keep her mind off dick she watched her favorite movie, *The Usual Suspects,* for the thirty-somethingth time.

She cut off the TV and tried to crash at about two a.m., but suddenly an idea hit her like a lightning strike. It made her eyes pop open as she sat up in bed. Beyond her window was a view of the Detroit River and Ambassador Bridge, so she stared at that dark landscape plotting the ins and outs of her plan.

It was brilliant, but would need perfect timing and precision to pull off. It would also require a little help from Tushie in a role that she would need some serious convincing to play.

As she sat there putting it all together in her head, Tuesday began to hear loud moans and the sound of a squeaking bed coming from the next condo. Obviously Monica had forgiven Derek and he was over there putting the smash on her to show Tuesday what she'd turned down.

She rolled her eyes jealously as she listened to the big-chin bitch get dick that was meant for her. After a while she went into the kitchen for a third ice cream bar.

Chapter Eight

The next day Tuesday made everything all about studying her mark. She parked the Caddy and jumped in the low-key green Honda that she rented so she could follow him more discreetly. She met him outside the school in the morning when he dropped off the girl and just tailed him the entire day. She wanted to know where he went, why he went there, who he went to see, and when he was going back.

The squad typically took months to study a mark before finally approaching him, but everything had to be rushed in this case. In an early phone conversation, Dresden confirmed that the feds were indeed about to move on him and Tuesday felt like she was actually in a race with them. She normally wouldn't even consider taking a look at someone who she knew was in the process of being indicted but, just as she explained to the girls, this was potentially a life-changing lick. She wanted to take a big wet bite out of his ass before the alphabet boys seized and froze everything he had.

After dropping the girl at school, he returned home and spent about three hours working around his yard: mowing the lawn, trimming hedges, etc.

Then at around eleven he emerged again in athletic gear and

jogged to a gym that was about three miles from the house. Since she couldn't creep behind him without drawing attention, Tuesday cruised past him several times yet he didn't seem to notice her.

Finally peeping his face without sunglasses, Tuesday saw that he was a straight-looking nigga. Dark-skinned and tall, just the way she liked them. She could also tell that he was a regular at the gym because the nigga was cut up—not overblown like some steroid-pumping juice-head—lean but ripped, like a middleweight boxer.

While he jogged, Tuesday found herself staring at his bulging calves and the way his muscles strained against his tight wifebeater when he moved. Much like her stomach had done yesterday, it was now her pussy sending constant reminders that she needed to be fed.

Tuesday didn't have a membership so she couldn't follow him inside the gym, but his workout lasted an hour and a half, after which he took his lunch at an eatery across the street with open-air dining. Using the binoculars, Tuesday watched from a block away as he washed down a club sandwich with Gatorade. He ate alone and spoke to nobody other than the smiling waitress who tried several times to converse with him, but he seemed far more interested in his newspaper than the obvious flirting that she was doing.

By the time he jogged back home, she imagined that he only had a minute for a quick shower before he left to pick up his daughter. She followed the Audi back up to Bishop Burchram and then they returned to the house after hitting Dairy Queen again—apparently an after-school ice cream was a daily ritual they shared. Daddy and daughter didn't leave the house again except for a quick trip to the supermarket around six that evening.

If he was a big-time dope boy, Tuesday couldn't tell, because he made no moves that suggested he was involved in anything illegal. He didn't meet with anybody, didn't go drop anything off or pick anything up. The nigga was so laid back that he obeyed all the traffic laws when he was driving.

She kept reminding herself that the feds weren't at him for no reason, so all she could do for the next couple of days was watch and wait for her opportunity to get close to him.

Over the next three days Tuesday, Tushie, and Jaye took turns watching him. Each morning someone would be waiting outside the school for him to drop the girl off, whether it was Tuesday in the Honda, Jaye in her Chrysler 200, or Tushie in her big (and not exactly low-key) Hummer H2.

During the morning while most of the neighbors worked, they could get away with being parked on the street watching the house for hours, but in the afternoon and evening they would look suspicious. In the spring when the weather was balmy and the children were playing outside, any strangers parked for a long time on a residential block with a pair of binoculars would probably have the police called on them.

For this reason they had to be creative in their surveillance. Because he lived within a cul-de-sac, there was only one way on and off their block, which meant they didn't have to watch the house directly. Whoseever day it was could simply park along the cross street and wait for the Audi to leave, and she would catch a glimpse of it from practically anywhere along that side street, since the military binoculars Tuesday had got from Face had a maximum range of twelve hundred yards.

Doll was the only one in the crew who didn't have a car, and since Tuesday didn't bother asking Brianna to help tail him, it was the fourth day and her turn again.

Learning his schedule had been relatively easy because, after comparing notes with Tushie and Jaye, Tuesday peeped that the man had a daily routine that he kept to without fail. Tuesday hadn't spent that morning parked outside the school because she didn't need to know where he was if she knew where he was going to be.

She had spent that entire day coordinating with Tushie so they could set up their plan. Because the daddy-daughter duo stopped for ice cream after school each day, Tuesday decided this small window was the best opportunity to lay down their play. But timing was everything: neither her or Tushie could be a minute late or the whole thing would be a bust and there wouldn't be a second chance.

That morning Tuesday put more thought into her outfit than the average seventeen-year-old headed for prom. She wanted to look hot but couldn't walk up wearing a backless gown from Oscar de la Renta either. Since he did the gym every day, Tuesday wanted to look like they had that in common. After rejecting four options, she finally chose a black sports bra with pink and black vertical striped tights—because the stripes would accentuate her curves more than a solid color. To round out the look, she chose a pair of black Nike cross-trainers with pink trim and wore her hair pulled back into a ponytail. She needed to look natural and not all glammed up so she went light on the makeup; just a little bit of eyeliner and some lip gloss.

By two thirty p.m. Tuesday was parked at the bank down the block from the Dairy Queen making herself ready for their first meeting. Her mark was probably picking up the girl right then and would most likely be there in five minutes. Tuesday had to time their arrival just right so it wouldn't look as if she was waiting on him. At 2:33 she sprinkled herself with some bottled water to look like she'd worked up a sweat, then checked herself in the mirror one last time before climbing out the car.

She jogged down the street to arrive at the Dairy Queen just as they were pulling up. He parked the Audi, leaving the girl inside, and stepped to the window just behind Tuesday, exactly the way she planned it.

Tuesday ordered a small caramel sundae and made a subtle show of leaning into the service window with her butt poked out while she waited. Using the reflection in the glass, she wanted to see if he was checking her out, but the mark just stood there waiting patiently for his turn. She didn't draw his attention the way she had hoped.

After receiving a dish of caramel-covered soft serve, Tuesday paid and turned away from the window, when she suddenly screamed: "Hey! Get away from her!"

Startled, he looked over to see a ratty-looking homeless woman standing next to his Audi. She was leaning into the back passenger window trying to offer the girl a handful of candy.

Before he could respond, Tuesday dropped her sundae, ran over and slammed her up against the car. Tuesday grabbed hold of her grimy coat and they got into a brief tussle.

The insane woman cried out: "I want to eat her eyes! I want to eat her eyes!"

Tuesday shook her up then slung her to the ground. The hag scrambled to her feet and Tuesday kicked her square in the ass before she took off around the corner.

"That's right! You betta run wit yo triflin' ass!"

Tuesday turned to the little girl, breathing heavily. "Sweetheart, are you okay?"

From inside the car the girl nodded that she was, even though the little darling looked more afraid of Tuesday than she did of the homeless stranger.

He ran over. "Dani, you didn't take anything from her, did you?"

The little girl shook her head for an emphatic "no."

After checking on her, the father turned to Tuesday. "Thank you. I'm glad you were here. We stop here every day and nothing like this has ever happened before."

Tuesday nodded. "You can't be too careful. It's a lot of sick people out there. I mean, anyone who would try to do something to a child is just the worst in my book."

He smiled. "Well, I'm glad you was here. You jumped in there and took care of business like some type of superhero—need to call you Wonder Woman."

Tuesday shrugged. "Two kickboxing classes and a self-defense course. Never thought I'd have to use it in an area like this."

"It's normally a nice neighborhood. I only live six blocks from here, which is why this whole thing is so weird. Do you live nearby?"

Tuesday shook her head. "Actually I'm from Detroit. I just left the gym and had a little business at the bank up the street. The lines were long so I thought I would zip down here for a quick treat while it thinned out. I didn't expect the trip to be so adventurous."

She looked down at the ice cream splattered on the cement. "Maybe this was God trying to tell me that I shouldn't be cheating on my diet."

He led Tuesday back to the window. "Well, I think the very least I could do is buy you another. Besides, I don't see any reason for you to be worried about a diet anyway," he added with a sly smile.

Tuesday smiled back, but it was only because he took the bait just like she thought he would. By now the homeless hag, who was actually Tushie in disguise, was back in her Hummer, which she left parked around the block, and headed back to the city.

Tuesday had gotten the idea from her neighbor when he rescued Nicholas. It had been a great way for him to break the ice and cut into her for a date. Even though it didn't work for him because of Tuesday's own personal reasons, she intended to make it work for her.

Caine replaced her sundae while buying treats for himself and the girl, and when he offered Tuesday a ride back to her car, she reluctantly accepted. As he drove her down the street, Tuesday quietly admired him and the luxurious interior of the A8. He pulled into the parking lot of the bank and she directed him to the green Honda. He slotted his car next to hers.

For about a minute there was a brief but awkward silence between them before she pushed the door open. "Well, thanks again for this," she said, holding up the ice cream. "And the ride." She turned in her seat and waved good-bye to the girl, who waved back in between scooping mouthfuls of her own sundae.

When she got out and closed the door, Tuesday was practically willing him to give chase. She was headed back for the bank entrance because she told him that she had business inside but was purposely taking slow steps to give him time to catch her.

She watched, disappointed, as the Audi whipped out of its parking space and headed for the exit. She thought she had him on the hook and gave him all the openings he needed, but for whatever reason he just didn't shoot his shot. Brianna's words echoed in her mind as she began to wonder if maybe she had lost it.

But while she slowly headed for the entrance, Tuesday noticed that the Audi wasn't leaving the lot. It just sat there idling at the outlet with the blinker going and wouldn't pull out into the street despite traffic being clear.

She was going through the door when he finally hit reverse and backed all the way up next to her. Tuesday came to meet him when he jumped out. She thought to herself, *'Bout time, mutha-fucka!* but concealed it with a smile.

"I'm sorry, but I never got your name," he said, rounding the car to approach her.

"Tabitha," she said with a tone that let him know it was an invitation and not just a response.

He looked around anxiously for a second and Tuesday could see that he was trying to work up the nerve to holla. She thought his shyness was kinda cute but a little out of character for someone who was supposed to be a kingpin.

"I normally don't do this, but are you seeing anybody right now?"

Her lips slowly stretched into a smile. "Why?"

"I was just thinking that the sundae wasn't enough to show my appreciation for what you did back there."

"And what did you have in mind?"

"I don't know," he said, nervously rubbing the back of his neck. "Maybe I could take you to lunch or somethin'?"

Tuesday nodded. "I would like that."

She took his phone and put her number on his call list—not her real number, but the one to the Tabitha Green phone. "Give me a call."

"I most certainly will," he said, accepting his phone back.

When they parted, Tuesday went into the bank just to play it off and waited for him to leave before she headed back to the Honda. When she got inside, Tuesday looked in the rearview and told herself, "Yeah, bitch, you still the shit!"

Part one of her plan had gone off without a flaw. Now all she had to do was wait for his call.

Straight back from Romulus, Tuesday went to the club feeling better than she had in a long time. To her there was nothing more satisfying than seeing a plan come together with perfect timing and execution. Plus the ease with which she put her mark on the hook was enough to shatter any insecurities she had about her looks or age.

Since she hadn't eaten yet, she stopped in at Bo's BBQ for half a slab of short ribs and intended to have the sundae for dessert.

She was in high spirits but sometimes Tuesday avoided coming in here because seeing Mr. Scott at work was always bittersweet. His shop was pretty much just a hangout for him and his old-school partners to sit around, play dominoes, and talk shit, but Tuesday was bothered that his money wasn't straight enough for him to retire. She respected the fact that Mr. Scott was still hustling at his age but thought it was sad that he still had to be. When she reached that age, she planned to be somewhere getting waited on and not still waiting on people. These thoughts did fuck with her sometimes, but on this day it wasn't enough to sour her mood.

Tuesday came in still wearing her gym clothes and to all the gray-haired players and ex-pimps she was both a fond memory of what they had in their prime and a painful reminder that their time had passed. Mr. Scott got offended when she tried to pay, reminding her of the lifetime pass she had at Bo's, and Tuesday showed her appreciation with some harmless flirting then gave them a show when she headed for the door by putting on such a scandalous strut in those pink-and-black tights that she could've given every old nigga in there a stroke.

She left out hearing more "Oh my Gods" and "Dear Lords"

than you would at a church revival, and even though they were all seniors, she still sucked it up. Today she was getting ego boosts from left and right and didn't care where they came from.

When Tuesday stepped into The Bounce, she was so up that she smacked DelRay on his ass. She beamed smiles at everybody then went to the bar to eat her ribs. She devoured bone after meaty bone, not thinking about the food but how well things had gone out in Romulus.

She couldn't believe that she'd ever doubted herself, because her entire life she'd had niggas wrapped around her finger. She was sexy-ass Tuesday Knight: the green-eyed cutie with all the booty. All she ever had to do was dangle bait and the marks came running with their lips drooling and wallets open. In Tuesday's mind she had always been like one of those chicks on *X-Men*, only her power was to control men's minds through manipulation and sex appeal. Her eyes, her smile, and the unspoken promise of pussy had always been enough to get what she wanted from niggas. If she even hinted that she might be hungry, they brought food. While shopping, anything her eyes gave a second look to would either be purchased on the spot or presented a few days later as a gift. If she wanted a nigga to come, he came, and if she wanted him to leave, he left. Tuesday had been mind-fucking guys so long that the only thing that excited her more than getting away with it was running across that rare one who was immune to her powers.

That was exactly what made her fall for A.D. When Tuesday met him she was nineteen years old and physically at her baddest, but while she could make other niggas jump through hoops like trained puppies, A.D. never went for her bullshit. A.D. was the first man to tell her "No!" The first man to be aggressive with her and put Tuesday in her place. The first man who didn't run behind her like a little boy: the first to actually be a *man*! Who could dominate her without being abusive. Who with a look could tell her to "sit down and shut the fuck up!" and she'd do it. He was the first nigga who wasn't so caught up on her looks that he forgot that she was just a girl; not some beautiful goddess who should be given everything on her terms. Niggas had her on such a high pedestal at the time, but A.D. kicked it right out from under her and brought her back down to reality. He didn't worship her or put Tuesday above him; she was his partner, his friend, and most important, his woman. She thanked God that he put the boundaries and restrictions on her that a man is supposed to put on his woman because if she would've never met him, she'd be one of those fucked-up snotty bitches who swore their shit didn't stink. For this reason A.D. was the first and only man to truly have her heart and was the prototype for any man who might have it in the future.

She hadn't seen A.D. in a week and thinking of him like this didn't darken her mood. She had her mark on the hook and a million-dollar lick in her grasp.

Methodically gnawing the meat off another rib bone, Tuesday was replaying their last conversation and scripting their next one when Ebony stole her attention.

"Hey, Boss Lady, we low on Schnapps and ice."

Tuesday blinked then nodded dumbly. Usually checking on the liquor levels was the first thing she did, but she had been so distracted that it slipped her mind. "Okay, I'ma get Tushie on it."

"Girl, you okay?" Ebony stared at her quizzically. "You looked like you was kinda zoned out there for a while."

Tuesday dropped the last bone and sucked the sauce from her fingers. "Naw, I'm just trippin' on somethin' that happened earlier today."

"Well, girl, from the way you're smiling, you must've found a bag full of money and dicks!"

Tuesday laughed. "Maybe the first part. I don't know about the second." Tuesday didn't go into details about the lick because while Ebony was cool, she was not part of the team. Tuesday would much rather have somebody like Ebony in the circle than

Brianna but she could read people well enough to know who was built for this game and who wasn't. She had peeped that Ebony wasn't a long time ago, which was why she never pulled her in.

Just then Tushie came in, no longer wearing her disguise and looking like her fly self again. Tuesday pulled her in the office so she could put her up on everything that happened after she left.

Tushie listened to the whole story while rolling a blunt. "Fo real? He almost let you jus' get away? What you think made him turn around at da last minute?"

"I don't know," Tuesday said, choking off the kush. "He just seemed real shy and kinda scared."

"I know you checked 'em out real good when y'all was in tha car together. What he look like up close?"

"Uh, he straight," Tuesday said, shrugging her shoulders to downplay it.

"Bitch, c'mon?" Tushie pressed as she took back the weed. "Iz he fuckable or whut?"

The voice in her head screamed *Hell, yeah*! but all that came out her mouth was: "I could if I had to. I done had to do way worse."

Tushie bobbed her head, blowing smoke out her nose, because that was part of the game. Just like she and Baby Doll stressed to Brianna, sometimes you had to let an ugly nigga or a weak one get down. If you were able to open a mark up with your looks, swag, and game, cool; but more often than not, it took some pussy to seal the deal.

Tushie passed the blunt back to her. "So how long you thank he gone wait to call?"

Tuesday thumped off the ash before she took another hit. "I know the nigga feelin' me but he ain't gone wanna come off too eager either, so he gone wait long enough to look like he ain't pressed, but not so long that I forget about his ass. He gone hit me up in about three days."

"I hope it's sooner den dat cuz from the way you said Dres was talkin', we might not even have three days."

Tuesday nodded to agree. "We damn sure pressed for time."

They sat there for a while smoking and talking about the lick a bit longer when Tushie suddenly broke out: "Oh yeah, bitch, you ain't say nuthin' 'bout kickin' me in my ass!"

Tuesday laughed. "I had to make it look real."

Tushie snatched her blunt back. "Put yo feet on me again, bitch, and next time it's gone be real!"

Chapter Nine

For a week Tuesday was in a holding pattern waiting for her mark to call.

While the plan couldn't go forward until he did, the girls were still keeping tabs on him around the clock to see if he made any moves out of the ordinary, or if the feds snatched him up. He never deviated from his schedule.

During that time Face came through with the modified M11's, a little late, but with all the extras he promised. She kept them in a drop-safe that was hidden in the bedroom closet of her condo. Tuesday had no intention of passing them out until it was time to go on the mission, but with the way Brianna and Doll were acting, she considered not giving either of them one at all.

Meanwhile business as usual went on at The Bounce where the girls danced a whole lot for a little bit in tips.

With every day that passed without the phone ringing, the girls lost more hope. It was beginning to look as if all that talk about a seven-figure lick was just a short-lived fantasy. Brianna and Doll were the most vocal, implying that Tuesday had lost whatever magic she'd once possessed. Tuesday assured them that he was going to call: explaining that he was just slow-playing it so he wouldn't look too desperate.

Secretly Tuesday was trying to sell this to herself as much as the skeptical members of her team. Her confidence wasn't exactly through the roof right now with just ending a relationship she'd been in for most of her life. At thirty-seven she still had niggas twenty years younger trying to holla, and while she was a lot more seasoned as far as her game, Tuesday knew she wasn't the same bitch she was at twenty. She wasn't feeling herself as much as she was the day she gave out her number. Times like this she really felt her age.

That was the main reason why this come-up was so important to her because she couldn't do this shit much longer and didn't want to. She had told Tushie more than once that if she still had to do this at forty, she'd rather let a .40-cal bust in her mouth before she sucked off another mark. Tushie would always laugh at this, but Tuesday was not joking.

Six days had passed since that little stunt at the Dairy Queen and the friends had spent that morning out at Somerset Mall. They had gone shopping then hit Hooter's for some wings, but despite doing two of Tuesday's favorite things, Tushie noticed that her girl had been usually quiet during most of it.

They were in Tushie's H2 and headed back to the city when she finally turned down the Lil Wayne they had pounding for a little heart to heart. "Gurl, iz you straight?"

Tuesday was staring out the passenger window looking dejected. "Yeah, I'm good. Why you ask that?"

"Cuz you ain't said three words to me all day and tha whole time we been out you been actin' like you got somethin' stuck up yo ass." She paused thoughtfully, then added, "Or maybe the real problem is that you *ain't* had nuthin' stuck up yo ass!"

Tuesday never looked at her. "Bitch, fuck you!"

She tried to play her off by cranking the music back up, but Tushie brought it right back down to a whisper. "I'm serious, TK.

I know you still down on this A.D. thang and shit moving slow wit ol' boy, but not gettin' no dick ain't helpin', either. You need a boy-toy! A young nigga 'bout twenty years old who don't know how ta do shit but fuck and play X-Box."

"I can get dick whenever I want!" Tuesday shot back. "I just got my mind on this mission right now."

"Look, I done been round you long enough to know you can get it from any nigga you want. The problem is you only want it from the one nigga who you can't get it from."

Tuesday didn't have a response for that because she was right. Since A.D. had been away, Tuesday had a few casual flings with niggas—and a few females—but it had been a long time since she'd even tried to meet a guy who wasn't a potential mark.

"Look, as soon as we take care of this piece of business I promise to turn into a real slut. I'm a let fifty niggas line up and just have a field day with me."

Tushie smiled because that was the closest Tuesday had come to making a joke all day. "I'm just tellin' you what I know, TK. When you meet somebody new dat you really feelin', tha shit improve yo attitude." She looked over at her girl beaming a really big fake smile.

It took a second for Tuesday to catch on. "Bitch, you didn't?"

Tushie bobbed her head. The smile was genuine now. "'Bout a week and a half ago. His name De'Lano. He 'bout six foot two, big-ass Jay Z lips. Da nigga is *FINE*!"

That made Tuesday finally shift away from the window until she was facing her. "How did y'all meet?"

Tushie checked the traffic in her mirrors before she merged into another lane. "Well, I'm comin' out tha market over thurr by my house and I run right into tha nigga, damn near runs his ass over wit my cart. Tha nigga holla'ed—you know, in a respectful way—and it was just somethin' 'bout him I was feelin' so I took his number."

Tuesday's expression became serious. "Is he doing something? You want us to take a look at 'em?"

Tushie frowned. "Naw, bitch! I told you I was feelin' 'em fa real."

"How many times you done seen him since y'all met?"

"Every day," Tushie said with a sly smirk as if she were embarrassed. "Last night we hit up Joe Muer down at the Renaissance. Dey lobster was tha shit!"

Tuesday gave her an accusing glare. "You fucked him, didn't you?"

She shook her head. "Oh, trust me, he definitely coulda got it already, but naw, we ain't did nuthin' yet. He ain't like dat. I mean I know he want it, but it ain't like he pressed, you know. Dis nigga like a real gentleman. He know I work at a club and dat I used ta dance and he ain't trippin' on none of it."

Tuesday could tell by the look in her eye that Tushie thought this nigga was special. She was happy for her because she knew how hard it was to find a quality man. They both had the Pretty Girl Curse: The right ones were too intimidated by their looks or assumed they already had a man, while the wrong ones either came at them disrespectfully or saw them as toys to be played with until they weren't fun anymore.

It was even harder for Tushie. Having a body like that made most niggas view her as purely a sexual object. Any man in a relationship with her would have to understand that, no matter how she presented herself, Tushie would always get whispers, stares, and "God Damns!" when she was out and about. It took a strong, secure nigga to deal with his woman getting that much attention, and unfortunately they were in short supply.

Tuesday thought it was out of character for her girl to keep this new nigga a secret when they usually talked about everything. "I mean I'm happy you met somebody that you really digging, but why wouldn't you tell me about him?"

Tushie sighed. This was the question she knew was coming but wasn't looking forward to.

She explained: "I jus met somebody at da same time you jus' lost somebody. I know you took dat shit wit A.D. real hard—harder den you lettin' on. I ain't want it to be like I'm throwin' my little situation up in yo face."

Tuesday understood but figured that her friend should've known that she would never be so petty as to be jealous of her happiness. If anything, being able to share in it would've been more helpful for Tuesday during this painful time.

"So when do I get to meet this De'Lano nigga?"

"Whoa, bitch, slow down, it's only been ten days. I gotta get 'em used to all my crazy before I introduce 'em to yours."

Tuesday laughed and she realized it was her first one all day.

Tushie continued. "Besides, I ain't gone stamp 'em certified until I take 'em fo a test drive. I gotta whole lot to deal wit back thurr and if he can't handle tha ride, we ain't gone make it."

Smiling, Tuesday said, "So what you sayin' is if he don't last long, y'all ain't gone last long."

Tushie laughed. "Thurr you go!"

After answering a few follow-up questions about De'Lano, Tushie turned the Lil Wayne back up and had it slapping hard enough to rattle the fillings in Tuesday's teeth. Tushie loved his music and swore that she had actually met and fucked the rapper back in the day when she first started dancing in New Orleans. Tuesday didn't doubt her because Tushie had never been on no fake shit; plus if Wayne had ever seen her clap that fifty-six-inch donk, he would've definitely wanted to hit it.

Tushie had four twelve-inch woofers in the back, each running off separate amps so Tuesday barely heard the phone ringing from inside her big Fendi bag. When she checked it, her breath caught in her throat because it was not her personal phone. It was Tabitha's, and only one person had that number.

She looked over at Tushie, her eyes wide from shock. "Ooh, girl, it's him!"

Tushie lowered the volume, wondering why she looked so confused. "Answer it, bitch! Whutchoo waitin' fo?"

Tuesday didn't understand herself why she was so shook. The fact that he called should've boosted her confidence, but instead she was more nervous. She was acting like she was new to this. Whether it was the amount of money at stake or just the small possibility of him actually being the real Caine, something had Tuesday rattled. Her breathing was short and fast. Her heart was thumping harder than Weezy's bass line. The delicious lemon pepper wings they smashed at Hooter's now felt sour in her stomach.

A fifth ring. She finally made herself answer it before there was a sixth. "Whaddup?"

His speech was very proper: "You probably don't remember me, but we met about a week ago at the Dairy Queen."

Tuesday regained a portion of her cool. "You have to be more specific. The Dairy Queen is one of my favorite pickup joints."

"Out in Romulus when the homeless person tried to attack—"

"I'm just playin'," she cut him off. Tuesday couldn't believe he missed the sarcasm. "I remember you. I'm just wondering why it took you so long to make a smart decision."

"Life is a series of serious choices," he extolled philosophically. "You have to weigh your options carefully before you make your move. Fools rush in."

"But he who hesitates is lost," Tuesday fired back.

He countered by saying, "Ah, but haven't you ever heard that patience is a virtue."

Tuesday looked at the phone and frowned. What kind of dope boy was he? The nigga actually sounded more like a preacher.

"Well, if patience is a virtue you sure gave me a lot of it because I've been waiting for you to call." Tuesday was purposely playing into the passive role because right then she wanted him to feel as if he were in control. She had to play the conversation just right because if he jumped off the hook he wouldn't call back and there would be no way she could set up another encounter without looking like a stalker.

Tushie also knew what was at stake. She was so into their exchange that she'd been neglecting to watch the road. Tuesday had to poke her with an elbow when she allowed the Hummer to drift out of their lane.

"I just wanted to say thank you again for what you did."

She said, "You already did, but you never had to."

"I know you enjoy ice cream, but how do you feel about steak? You're not a vegetarian, are you?"

Tuesday smiled because she knew where this was headed. "I didn't get this thick only eating salads."

He laughed. "Well, there's a place out in Northville Township called Gaucho's. Can you meet me there for lunch tomorrow?"

The world ending was the only thing that would make her miss this date, but Tuesday still paused for a moment, fronting like she had to think about it. "Tomorrow? I could move some stuff around to free up my afternoon."

"I appreciate you squeezing me into your busy schedule." From his tone of voice, Tuesday couldn't tell if he was being sarcastic or not. "How about I meet you at noon?"

"That works," she said, trying to sound nonchalant.

"Until then."

He seemed to be ready to end the call when Tuesday suddenly broke in: "So are you ever gonna tell me your name or do you want me to just make up one for you? Personally, I always liked Jayshawn."

"Jayshawn?" he said as if considering it. "I could get used to it. All my partners could call me J-Smoove or J-Dawg?"

"Or just Jay," she chimed in. "For real, though, what do all your partners call you now?"

"I don't have any. That's kinda sad, ain't it?"

"What's sad is how you tryin' so hard to dodge a simple-ass question. What's your name?"

He was quiet for so long that Tuesday actually started to think that he had hung up on her. Finally he said, "Marcus. My name is Marcus."

Tuesday gave no clue that she knew he was lying. "Well, Marcus, now I know who to tell the waiter to give the check to when lunch is over."

"I thought we were going Dutch!" he said, joking. "I'll call you around eleven thirty just to confirm."

They clicked off after parting words and she tucked the phone back into her bag and looked over to see Tushie waiting as eager as a dog at feeding time. "Wuz up wit' 'em?" she pressed. "Sound like y'all hooked up somethin' fo tomorrow."

"Lunch," she answered with a nod. "Oh yeah, and he's calling himself Marcus now."

Tushie laughed. "Da mark's name is Marcus. Marcus what?"

She shrugged. "He didn't say. Just Marcus."

"Well, tha hard part done now. You got his ass on da hook, ya jus gotta reel 'em in."

Tuesday heard her girl's words but as they rode, the feeling in her gut told her that Tushie was wrong. Things were moving forward, but outside of his boring lifestyle, there was something else about this guy that just didn't quite fit and Tuesday couldn't put her finger on it. Plus, the hardest part was still to come because this mission was going to be filled with challenges that she and the team had never faced before.

The same nagging feeling also told Tuesday that this was going to end up a lot more bloody than she planned. She had a dark premonition that not all the girls would be walking away from this one.

Tuesday didn't dare tell Tushie this out of fear she might somehow jinx her best friend.

This new development forced the girls to turn around and head right back to the mall, where they spent another two hours at Neiman's picking out the perfect outfit for tomorrow, then they headed back to The Bounce, where they got the rest of the crew together and told them the news. Jaye and Baby Doll were excited that he finally called, but Brianna sat there quietly, looking like a hater. Despite that this could possibly mean a six-figure cut for her, it seemed as if she would've preferred it all fail just so she could hold it over Tuesday's head.

They smoked, they talked a little bit more about the money and Tushie's new man, but mostly they discussed strategies on how to come at boy.

"I ain't really got a tight read on this nigga yet," Tuesday confessed from behind her desk. "He come off kinda square but I know it's more to him than he letting on. I'm gonna have to freestyle through lunch until I know more about his personality. Then I'll know what role to play with him."

Doll asked, "So what's wit all this Marcus shit he tryin' to pull?"

Tuesday shrugged. "Maybe he thinks he's hiding. When his name started getting too hot in the city, maybe he slid out to Romulus and changed his shit up. It ain't like it's hard to take on another identity—shit, we do it all the time."

Jaye was sitting in a chair right before her desk. "I'm still not a hundred percent sure that this is even him. In all the days I've been watching him this dude ain't so much as threw a piece of trash in the street. What if we going through all this just to find out he only some lame-ass nigga who work at Best Buy?"

"Dat would make mo sense if we eva seen tha nigga go to work," Tushie added from the chair next to Jaye's. "All da nigga do is take tha girl back and forth ta school and go to da gym. It's like he ain't got no life."

Tuesday leaned forward. "And that's the thing that fucks me up the most about him. If he don't have a job, then how does he get his money? And if he's so squeaky clean, why are the feds lookin at him in the first place?"

The girls all stared at one another as if waiting for somebody to come up with good answers to those questions.

"Well, did yo connect tell you when tha feds was movin' on 'em?" asked Tushie. She didn't throw out a name even though she knew Tuesday was talking about Dresden. "It'll be a lot betta if we knew how much time we had ta work wit."

The others made agreeable comments. It would be more convenient to plot their moves if they knew what type of window they were working with. Things could then be set according to a timetable.

Tuesday shook her head. "He just said they would be comin' soon. Fucking with the government, that could be days or it could be months. But I still think we should play it like we on short time."

Brianna made sure to interject some negativity. "Well, even shorter now since you took a week to get next to him and another one to get him to call."

Tuesday shot her a look but didn't feed into the bullshit.

Jaye said, "Well, you gone have to put that pussy down somethin' scandalous to make him fall this fast."

"I don't think he's gonna be lookin to jump in bed with me off rip. He's too disciplined for that. I know this guy's type, he moves slow—which makes time another problem. You see he set up a date for lunch and not dinner."

Jaye nodded thoughtfully.

She continued. "Plus in all the days we been on him, he ain't never went over a bitch's house or had one come through his. He ain't even sneak a peek at my ass when I flexed on him at the Dairy Queen."

Doll said: "Maybe that nigga gay?"

Tuesday shook her head. "No, I'm not pickin' up no gay vibe from him. That nigga like pussy, he just not reckless with his dick.

"I don't know what it's gone take to get him yet, but I know it's gotta be more than sex. If he is who they say he is, he got the type of money to trick with the baddest chicks in the world if it was just about busting a nut, but he needs more than that. Smart men respect intelligence and I'm going to have to be a challenge for him upstairs if I stand a chance."

Brianna sat on the couch next to Doll adjusting her tits in a tiny camisole top. "And while y'all waste time playing all these mind games with each other, the feds swoop in and take everything! Why not do this the quick way by just putting a gun in his face and making him to take us to the shit?"

Tuesday gave her a look that said *stupid bitch*. "Is this yo first day? We can't do it for the same reason we ain't never did it in the past. In all these years you ain't learned that our whole MO is knowing where the shit is before we come and get it?

"What if he say 'Suck my dick, bitches, I ain't tellin' y'all shit!' Now we got the heat on us for catching a body *and* without gettin' no money."

Tushie said, "I guess it's true: tha bigga da boobs, tha smalla tha brain."

Brianna frowned. "Well, what about the little girl? Put it to her head and I bet he tell us where it's at!"

"No!" Tuesday said forcefully. "We ain't goin' that route!"

"I'm not sayin' we hurt her," Brianna explained. "I'm just figuring if it come to it, we could use her to make him cooperate. If he *thinks* we might hurt her, then—"

Tuesday was adamant. "No!! We ain't never did things that way and we ain't gone start now."

Doll took up the argument for her girl. "She just sayin' it could be a plan B. It's too much money on the line not to do whatever we gotta do! You said yo'self that we killin' this nigga anyway, so what difference it make?"

Jaye agreed with her. "She make a good point and I think it's worth considering."

"Is y'all bitches deaf, I said *NO!!*" Tuesday roared in a furious tone the girls had never heard her use. They looked at each other surprised that she'd snapped so hard about that.

Tuesday looked over them. "Some of y'all might think I'm old, some of y'all might think you can do this shit better than me. Well, you gone get yo chance to prove it cause no matter how this end, I'm out!" She pointed to Brianna. "And y'all can let this little bitch run the show if y'all want. I wouldn't give a damn what y'all do then, but as for now, I'm still the HBIC in this muthafucka and we gone do shit my way!"

"Okay well, fuck it then," said Baby Doll. "What is your way? 'Cause so far all you told us is how hard this gone be but ain't said shit 'bout how we gone do it!"

Tuesday calmed herself a bit. "I'm gonna do it the same way I always do; I just gotta do it better and faster this time. Ain't enough time to make him fall in love, I just gotta get him to trust me. After that I'll be able to peep what he doing."

"And what if you can't ever get him to trust you?" Brianna shot at her.

"I can and I will!"

"And whut about when it's ova?" Tushie asked, staring at her best friend steely-eyed. "After being around them and spendin' time together, iz you gone be able to take dat little gurl daddy away from her if it mean gettin' away wit dis money?"

Tuesday matched the intensity of her stare with the green totally bleached from her eyes. They were hard and gray as dirty ice. "If it mean getting away with this money," she said in a voice that equaled their temperature, "I'll put two in the back of his head right in front of her."

That harsh statement dropped the room into an eerie silence that lasted for a while. It wasn't so much that Tuesday admitted she could execute a man with his child looking on; knowing that she meant it was what had them all so shook.

Chapter Ten

That night Tuesday had trouble getting to sleep. She flopped from her back to her side then over to her stomach and back to her side, but couldn't find a position that was comfortable. The problem had nothing to do with her bed, her mind was too active; it leaped to and from a thousand different random thoughts. Tiny little hobgoblins were tampering with the machinery of her brain forcing her to think over every single thing that was wrong with her life.

She was thirty-seven years old, unmarried, and the only man she'd ever loved was going to spend the rest of his life in prison. She had no family, no children, and only one real friend. She owned a struggling business that covered little more than her condo and car payments. She had a mental disorder that made her think the cans were moving themselves after the cupboards were closed. She had no education and no real talents other than manipulation and robbery. She had a psycho dirty cop on her case who used her like a fuck doll, and the really sad part was that she was so pressed for dick that she probably wouldn't mind it except that the racist bastard couldn't fuck. Not to mention her team was falling apart right when they were about to hit their biggest lick ever.

That twisted comment about killing Marcus right in front of his daughter had the desired effect. Men weren't the only people Tuesday could manipulate. Brianna's bullshit had already poisoned Doll and she couldn't let it spread to the others. Refusing to let them go after the girl could've been viewed by some as a sign of weakness. As their leader she must never permit them to challenge her authority or doubt the gangsta in her. They had to believe that she could be straight-up ruthless, even if she wasn't so sure of it herself.

Too many thoughts were swirling like snowflakes in a blizzard. Her bedroom was dark and still.

She looked in the corner and saw that Nicholas was sleeping peacefully on his tiny cat bed. Curled into a furry white ball with his tail cradling his body, he was dreaming of catching pigeons, fine tuna, or whatever the hell cats dreamed about. Tuesday was so jealous that she thought about waking him up and forcing him to keep her company.

She thought about Tushie having a new friend, and despite what she had said in the car, she was a tiny bit jealous of her too. She imagined herself going to the supermarket and literally running into her dream guy. Tushie the Tease was notorious for keeping a mark waiting forever, but Tuesday wondered how long she could hold out on a nigga she was really into. When the alarm clock next to her bed revealed that it was after two a.m., she thought that Tushie could be somewhere with De'Lano right then getting her action on.

Picturing her girl somewhere having her humongous ass pounded by a ripped-up stud was enough to get Tuesday going again. She slipped her hand inside her panties and fingered her clit for a while before she went into the drawer where she kept her toys—none of which were made by Hasbro. She chose a vibrating massager with three speed settings. She climbed back into bed then got herself together.

She finally got her rocks off at around three and apparently that did the trick, because she now felt relaxed enough to sleep. She was drowsy and ready to doze off even before she put her toy away. When she got back into bed she was out two minutes after her head hit the pillow.

Her plan was to wake up at around nine thirty, hopefully feeling rested and ready. The most important date of her life was in nine hours and she couldn't show up looking like shit.

The actual name of the restaurant was Gaucho's Brazilian Steakhouse and it was a freestanding building located on 7 Mile and Haggerty roads in Northville Township. With its architecture and cuisine the owners—who were actually Brazilian—had succeeded in bringing a little slice of Rio to this otherwise bland and milquetoast suburb.

Tuesday had made it a point not just to be punctual but fifteen minutes early. However, when she showed up at 11:45, she saw that his Audi was already parked there.

Inside, the rooms gleamed with Brazilian cherry wood and the white gaucho shirts worn by the staff. Beyond a long buffet offering cheeses, beans, and salads, he was seated at a rear table waiting patiently.

Tuesday had decided to downplay her sexy so she and Tushie had chosen a black knee-length skirt with a burgundy silk blouse that only showed a little bit of cleavage. The skirt hugged her but wasn't supertight. She rocked her black Prada heels with the ankle straps.

He remembered his manners because as she approached he stood to greet her. He was wearing a navy-blue Polo golf shirt, dark jeans, and crisp white Air Forces.

Tuesday hadn't noticed how tall he was before then. He towered over her by at least six inches. She liked tall men.

There was a brief hug in which she noticed his unique scent. His cologne, soap, and aftershave had mingled in an agreeable way.

He made certain to pull out the chair for her as she sat.

Tuesday said, "This is the part where you tell me how good I look."

He seated himself across from her. "You didn't come across as the insecure type who went fishing for compliments. You know you look good today, isn't that enough?"

"I'm gonna tell you a little secret about women." She leaned toward him then scanned around as if she feared someone might overhear. He leaned in and offered his ear.

She whispered: "All women are insecure—every single one of us! When you have a vagina you need three things to survive: food, water, and *compliments*."

He teased her by making a face like she had just told him the mystery of life.

"While you being funny, I could lose my womanhood card for telling you that! This is the top-secret shit that get discussed at our meetings."

Laughing, he asked, "So you mean a woman could actually die from not receiving enough compliments?"

"Compliment deficiency is no laughing matter," she said with a grim expression. "I lost my grandmother to CD when I was a little girl."

"You look beautiful today. Feel better now?"

Tuesday closed her eyes and sighed as if she'd just received a drug fix. "Oh, thank you. I didn't know how much longer I could've held on."

Someone came to drop off a pair of menus along with a basket of bread. Tuesday used that interruption as a chance to guide the conversation to a more serious place. "So, Mr. Marcus, what do you do?"

He took a piece of bread and broke it in half but didn't eat it. "I'm sort of in what they call a transitional phase."

"That's usually just a slick way that people have of saying they ain't got no job!"

"I'm not one of those people." He took a bite and chewed it slowly. Tuesday was waiting for him to explain but he never did.

She pressed the issue. "So you do work?"

"Not in a sense that I leave the house every morning wearing a suit with a briefcase, but yeah, I work."

"So we go back to my original question: What do you do?"

He tasted more of the bread. "It's complicated. Not so much what I do, just explaining it to people can be difficult."

On the inside Tuesday was frustrated that he was being so evasive but on the outside she maintained her cool. She should've expected this because just getting a name out of him had been like pulling teeth. Even though this was normal first-date conversation, he might get defensive if she kept pressing it, so Tuesday dropped the subject.

"This is a nice place," she said, looking around. "You ever ate here before?"

He nodded. "A few times."

"Is the food any good?"

"Actually it's really bad, but I just keep coming back anyway."

Oh, so now you understand sarcasm! Tuesday thought to herself.

"Okay," she said, forcing herself to smile. "So that was a stupid question."

"No I'm just messing with you. The only stupid questions are the ones we don't ask. For real, though, the food here is on point."

Tuesday glanced over her menu. "So do you mind if I ask another question that might or might not seem stupid?"

He gave her an agreeable nod.

"Are you single?"

"Yeah, I'm single."

Tuesday sighed in relief. Finally a straight answer from this nigga.

"Well?" she said, looking at him expectantly. "Aren't you gone ask me if I'm single?"

"I'm assuming you are. It would say a whole lot about your character if you weren't."

"You don't know that, though. For all you know I could be here creepin' on my man."

"You're not the type." He said this as casually as if he'd known her for years.

Tuesday squinted at him. "You think you already know what type of person I am?"

"Yep," he said, staring down into his own menu.

"So you done already figured me out?"

"Pretty much." He never looked up at her.

"Well, go ahead then, break me down. If I'm such an open book, then read me a page."

He sighed as if he were a magician being asked to do a card trick he was tired of performing. He set the menu aside and stared directly at her.

He took a breath then started: "People might think because of how you look that you're disloyal, money-hungry and will drop any guy quick the second you see something better, but that's just a misconception we make against pretty women. You're confident without being conceited, you can appreciate nice things without being materialistic, and I'm willing to bet that when a man has your heart you make him your entire world. You learned a long time ago that you have a look that men go for and while you have used the pretty face, green eyes, and banging body to your advantage, those aren't really the things you feel that define you. Men want to possess you and women mostly envy you, but you've never wanted to be a trophy or an object of jealousy. You'll play on a guy if he allows himself to be played but really, you're tired of those games. You're a natural-born leader—the type of woman that other women follow—and while you put up a front of being so strong and in control, deep down you're hurt and lonely. You've only allowed yourself to love once and that person broke your heart. Maybe he cheated, maybe he left, maybe he died, I don't know, but you've never opened up to anyone else like that again."

Tuesday was thrown into a stunned silence. All she could do was stare at him with her mouth hanging open.

She understood exactly what he was talking about because since she could remember, people had misjudged her based on her appearance. Tuesday had started as a quiet and humble girl, but so many guys before A.D. had treated her like a high-maintenance diva that she slowly adopted the attitude. Even other women assumed that she was a stuck-up bitch without knowing her. Men either wanted to possess her like a trophy or were so intimidated by her that they didn't want her at all—and both stemmed from their insecurity. Tuesday had always taken pride in her appearance but she never did think that she was absolutely defined by her looks. Good genes were a product of her parents and she couldn't take credit for that, but Tuesday had always taken the most pride in the things that she had developed in herself, such as her intelligence, style, personality, and game. Beauty is a blessing, but wisdom is earned.

She was even more surprised by the deductions he made about her being hurt and alone. Was it that obvious? Was it all written on her face so plainly for anybody to see or was this nigga something unique?

He had a way of reading her that was just uncanny; no one had been able to do that since A.D. She couldn't help but compare the two. Tuesday had noticed the physical resemblance immediately because their complexion and build were so similar, but she thought it ended there, because when they first met he came off as so shy. She now realized that they were so alike in personality that it was fucking with her head.

Before she got lost, she had to stay focused and remind herself what this was all about. He was good but apparently he wasn't that good, because if he could read her as well as he thought, he wouldn't be here. He would know what she and the girls had in store for him.

She asked, "What if I told you that I was a shallow, gold-diggin' bitch who only cared about the size of a man's wallet and dick?"

He slowly chewed more bread. "I'd say you were full of it!"

"How do you know I'm not lying?"

"Simple," he said in between bites. "I can tell by how you dressed today that you're not too materialistic. A true gold-digger would've wore something way more provocative to entice me and would've played a lot of jewelry to let me know what she was accustomed to.

"Plus you've already shown me through our conversations that you're intelligent and no woman who is truly shallow will do the necessary soul searching to ever discover that fact about herself. By nature, ignorant people are never aware of their ignorance."

Tuesday nodded to agree. "So you would have to be a deep person to even admit that you're shallow in the same way that the second a person realizes their ignorance, they have already taken the first step toward being wise."

He leaned back in his chair and Tuesday could tell by the expression on his face that she had just impressed him.

When their waiter arrived, Tuesday allowed him to order for them both since he'd been there before. The sides were self-serve from the buffet but Tuesday was surprised to see that the beef tenderloin he selected for them both was actually brought out whole on long skewers from which servers carved healthy slices right onto their plates.

While they ate, the conversation didn't extend much further than how delicious their meal was. He chose black beans and rice from the buffet; she, soup and salad. The tenderloin was succulent and juicy and the servers brought out a parade of it. The moment a slice was devoured, a server showed up to carve another onto their plates. There was a small wooden marker on their table shaped like a cylinder that was painted red and green on each side—flipping it red side up was the only way to stop the endless beef onslaught once they could stand no more.

As she sat there feeling full up to her throat, Tuesday didn't know if the place served dessert, but she hadn't left any room for it. She was a little self-conscious about eating so much, then told herself she was being silly. Her body type should've made it obvious to him that she had a healthy appetite.

Earlier Tuesday had allowed the focus to be shifted to her just when she was just beginning to dig into his personal life. Besides being single, he hadn't revealed anything about himself and she figured this was a good time to get back to that conversation.

"Have you ever been married?" she asked, suddenly breaking their post-lunch silence.

Tuesday had meant to ambush him and there was only the tiniest flicker of surprise in his eyes before he composed himself. "Never married. Came real close, though."

"What happened?"

"She died!" he said bluntly, then stared off into the distance.

Tuesday could tell from his tone and expression that this was not something he was willing to discuss. It was still a sensitive wound. She didn't press because a dead ex was a little too heavy for first-date chitchat.

Sensing a shift in his mood, Tuesday knew she had to bring the conversation back to a brighter subject. "So what do you do for fun?"

"I run, I work out. I do the gym thing."

"That's all? That's your idea of fun?"

He shrugged. "I wouldn't necessarily say it's fun, it's just what I'm into."

Tuesday leaned over the table some to expose a bit more of her cleavage. In a voice meant to be seductive, she said: "I've been lookin to get in better shape, improve my flexibility. Maybe you could teach me a li'l something? You know, work me out!"

The not-so-subtle innuendo either went totally over his head or he just didn't feed into it, because his expression was deadpan when he responded: "I'm not actually a personal trainer but there should be some on staff at whatever gym you go to. If not, you could find some local ones online."

When Tuesday rolled her eyes and grunted in frustration, he didn't seem to catch that either.

They sat there for a while longer and talked without really discussing anything. Tuesday fired off a series of questions, which he gave short answers to or skillfully deflected like a politician. He treated her most mundane questions as if she were a foreign spy trying to learn his country's military strengths. To Tuesday it seemed less like a conversation than a boxing match and after what felt like nine rounds of sparring with him, she was actually grateful when he looked to his wristwatch and called for the check.

They left Gaucho's and he escorted her to the green Honda. He opened the door for her, and after she got in, he poked his head inside. "I had a really nice time."

Tuesday faked a smile. "Me too."

"I hope we can do this again," he said. "Soon."

She nodded but rolled her eyes dramatically when he looked away. Truthfully, she'd rather lick a wall socket before she had to endure another date like this.

Tuesday had been worried that the feds might be tailing him so while they ate lunch she had one of the girls camp outside the restaurant. Since Tushie had plans with De'Lano and she didn't trust Brianna or Doll enough for the job, Tuesday had Jaye parked down the street from Gaucho's in her 200 with a Tigers hat pulled down low over her face, peeping the scene with Tuesday's binoculars.

After she left him at the restaurant, Tuesday had Jaye follow him and she confirmed that he shot back to the house for a minute then went to pick up the girl from Bishop Burchram. Jaye also reported that as far as she could tell no one else was following him.

She didn't tell Jaye how bad lunch went because Tuesday felt they were already losing faith in her skills. It wasn't just that he was so closed off about his life but what really bothered Tuesday was the fact that he never seemed to take a real interest in hers—especially after she went through so much trouble to create Tabitha Green. He said that he wanted to see her again soon but to Tuesday that just sounded like a polite kiss-off. With everything else that was going wrong with this case, she had just compounded another problem.

He had read her so easily but she was never quite able to figure him out. Tuesday's strength had always been that she knew niggas and knew what it took to get them on the hook, but for whatever reason this dude just wasn't taking the bait. Lunch was awkward for them both and if this nigga just decided to lose her number, there was no way she would be able to explain it to the team after Tuesday had been so adamant that she was the only one who could get him. Brianna was going to have a field day if she lost her mark.

While his being so secretive was enough to frustrate Tuesday, it was also confirmation that had something worth hiding. He quickly shot down any questions that pertained to his job and that had sounded alarm bells in Tuesday's mind. She couldn't know if he was actually Sebastian Caine, but he was way too game-conscious just to be the square nigga he was pretending to be.

A few hours passed and Jaye met her back at the club with nothing more to report. After scooping his daughter up from school, they stopped at Dairy Queen then went straight back to the house with no stops. She spent another hour and a half watching his block from the side street like Tuesday had told her but she swore that the Audi never left.

As Tuesday sat in her office with Jaye, she realized that it was one of the few times she had to talk to her one-on-one. Jaye was the newest member of the team, only having joined fourteen months ago, and while Tuesday had seen enough in her to extend an invitation, it sometimes occurred to her that she really didn't know much about the girl. Outside of Tushie, she didn't socialize with any of them personally because she'd tried to keep their relationship professional. But while Brianna and Doll were like open books that could be read at a glance, it wasn't so easy with Jaye. She was funny but not as reckless as those two; Tuesday also peeped that she was a lot sharper than either of them. Tuesday felt she could trust her enough to do what was necessary for the team but she didn't know whose side Jaye would be on when she and Brianna finally had the big blow-up that was coming. Tuesday used this rare alone time with her to pick her brain.

They had already smoked some of the premium kush that Tuesday kept stashed in her office. Jaye was on the couch stuffing her mouth with steak fries that she dunked in Mr. Scott's legendary barbeque sauce.

Tuesday called to her from the desk. "Jaye, if we hit this lick and get a nice piece of change, what are you talkin' 'bout doing?"

She chewed a wad the size of a golf ball then swallowed hard. "Gettin' the fuck outta dodge like we talked about."

"Naw, I mean after that. Have you ever thought about an exit strategy— a way to get out the game?"

"Look, I know what you getting at and I'm not planning on making a career outta this. No disrespect, but by the time I'm forty I plan on being well established."

Tuesday laughed. "First off, bitch, I'm not quite forty but I do see where you comin' from. So when you do hit the big four-oh, where are you trying to be?"

Jaye put aside the empty Styrofoam container. "I'm only twenty-three so I ain't gave forty a lot of thought, but by the time I'm thirty, I plan on being in Hollywood."

"So you wanna be famous?" asked Tuesday.

"I wanna be rich but I'll take the fame if it comes along with it." She explained: "My whole life I been silly as hell and I was actually thinkin' 'bout tryin' my hand at being a comedian. If you blow up from there you can pimp that shit to the movie business and that's when you start makin' the big money."

"Well, you do be havin' us rollin' up in here," said Tuesday.

"But can you really see yourself up on stage doin' it for real? Niggas gone be too busy staring at you to even pay attention to the jokes."

"Me and my brother talked about it and I think that's what's gone actually blow me up. If they see that I'm not just a pretty face, but can get on stage and kill it. Plus I got a look that's made for TV. My brother done already wrote up a comedy routine for me, and a treatment for my own sitcom."

Tuesday smiled. "Sound like y'all pretty close. I don't have any brothers or sisters."

Jaye nodded. "Yeah I got him by three years but I've been basically raising him since I could remember. My moms had always been sick and she finally died when I was fifteen. Now me and him ain't got nobody but each other."

Tuesday thought it was cool learning this little bit about Jaye. She had taken an immediate shine to the girl but liked her more now that she knew she had a dream beyond doing sticks. She could actually see Jaye up on stage doing comedy like Mo'nique and Sommore or one day having her own TV show.

"So do you think Doll and Bree got any plans for gettin' out the game?" Tuesday tried to make the question sound as innocent as possible but really wanted to check her temperature about what's been going on within the crew.

Jaye let out a dry laugh. "Look, everybody and they momma can see what's going on between you and Bree and I know you just tryin' to get my spin on the situation."

Tuesday nodded. Jaye had been smart enough to see through that so she respected it. "Okay, just being straight up, why don't you tell me what you think about the situation."

"Look, I ain't the type of bitch who talk about muthafuckas behind they back but I can tell you my honest opinion on shit without necessarily throwin' hate on anybody."

Tuesday said, "I appreciate that."

"Well, anybody with eyes can peep that Bree jealous of you. She see the club, the condo, and the new Caddy and to a bitch like her that mean you got it all."

Tuesday's eyes went wide at that comment. Jaye had just said something that didn't make sense to her at the time but she filed it away for later.

Responding to her, she said: "If I had it all, would I still be out here on this bullshit?"

"Me and you smart enough to see that, but then again we talkin' 'bout Bree."

She continued. "But more than what you got, it's how you so respected up in here. You Boss Lady, and I'm willing to bet that when she first started here she admired all this stuff about you but we both know how fast admiration can flip to envy."

Tuesday nodded.

"Challenging you at every turn is her little way of trying to convince us that you ain't really *dat Bitch*! She thinks she can run shit but you can tell she's not a leader. Bree can slide up under a mark and reel him in but she ain't got the game to know which ones to choose or the brains to put together the moves to go get it. She's not a planner and if you ain't a planner you damn sure can't be a leader."

Tuesday found herself smiling at Jaye, not in a way of trying to flirt but just because she was so impressed by her insights. She saw a lot of herself in Jaye but Tuesday was honest enough to admit that she wasn't even that polished at twenty-three.

Jaye's analysis of Brianna was so spot-on that Tuesday was eager to hear her take on Baby Doll.

"So what do you think about her sidekick?"

"Oh, you talkin' 'bout li'l Knee-High?" She shook her head. "In my opinion Doll is even more fucked up than Brianna. The reason why she play the little girl role so well is because she basically a kid in real life. She ain't got no self-control. All she wanna do is fuck and get high—you see how she is around here on the bitches! Out the crew, she the only one who ain't got her own car and crib. You ever notice that no matter how much we hit a lick for, Doll always broke again in a few weeks?"

Tuesday did notice this. It was something that she and Tushie had talked about but she didn't know if anyone else had peeped it.

"But to me the worst part about Doll," Jaye continued, "is that she's a straight-up follower! She just sniffing behind Bree because she's talking the most shit right now. If Tushie stepped up tomorrow and started speaking out more, Doll would be walking around with her nose between her ass cheeks. Just like a child, she gonna listen to whoever shows the most authority."

Tuesday had reached the same conclusions about Doll and for a while they sat there discussing the team, the lick, and a dozen other things until they were interrupted by her phone; actually it was Tabitha's.

Tuesday wasn't sure he would ever call again but definitely wasn't expecting him to call so soon. She answered it, trying to downplay how relieved she was to him and to Jaye, who was watching with interest.

"What?" Tuesday answered with a sharp tone.

"I'm sorry. Did I catch you at a bad time?"

"Actually you did, but what's up anyway?"

His tone was apologetic. "If this isn't a good time to talk, I can always call back later."

She snapped at him. "A good time to talk would've been when we were at lunch, but you didn't seem too interested then."

He was quiet for a while. "So that's what all this attitude is about. You didn't enjoy lunch?"

"Lunch was cool. It was the company I didn't particularly care for."

Jaye was giving Tuesday a look that said *Bitch, what the fuck are you doing?* This was a million-dollar mark that she was flipping on. In Jaye's mind Tuesday was supposed to kiss his ass until it was raw and tell him that his shit smelled like butterscotch.

Tuesday responded to her with a *Girl, I got this* look. She had a plan, and while it could potentially blow up in her face, she had to play it this way if she was going to have any chance of getting him to open up.

He asked, "Can you at least tell me what I did that's got you so upset?"

She fired back, "How about acting like a suspect who was being interrogated?"

"So you expect me to share my whole life story on the first date?"

"First off, don't call it a first date because that implies there will be a second. And no, I don't want to hear your life story but I don't wanna catch a headache just trying to learn simple shit like what's your name or what you do for a living?"

He laughed. "You know what I think? I think you're just so used to guys laying down for you and making things easy that the first one who gives you a little bit of a challenge you automatically feel like is on something different."

It was her turn to laugh now. "Listen at Dr. Phil! You really don't know me as well as you think! I don't have a problem with a man who challenges me, actually I prefer it. What I have a problem with is people treating me like I'm some type of agent when I'm just trying to meet them."

"Okay, okay," he said, trying to calm her. "Maybe I came off a little cautious."

"Cautious is a person who sits with their back to a wall. Cautious is a person who parks their car where they can see it. Nigga, you flat-out paranoid, and I think you need a therapist more than you need a friend right now so I'm good. You can lose my number!"

When Tuesday hung up on him, Jaye's eyes almost exploded out of her skull. Before she could ask her if she was crazy or leap over the desk at her, Tuesday paused Jaye with a raised hand. "Don't worry, he's gonna call right back. Trust me."

Jaye nodded, but Tuesday could tell by the way her chest rose and fell that her heart was going a mile a minute; and despite how confident she tried to look, Tuesday figured hers to be going about the same. She had played the whole "lose my number" routine before and usually a mark called back all humble and apologetic, but she couldn't be sure it would work this time. It was a hell of a risk considering what was at stake. If he took her advice, there was no way to call back, because she had never taken his number. The ball was totally in his court.

Jaye came and took the seat across from her desk and for a while they just stared at the phone waiting for it to ring. Time stretched out like rubber and with each languid second that passed a bit more doubt crept into them both.

"I know what I'm doin'," she said, reading the look of concern on Jaye's face. "He gone call back!"

Jaye smiled. "Look, I ain't trippin'. I just plan on being right there with my marshmallows when the others roast yo ass for fuckin' up the lick."

After thirty tension-filled seconds that felt like as many minutes, the phone finally rang and Jaye gasped in relief.

Tuesday winked at her as she picked it up. "Yeah!"

He said, "Damn, you don't think that was a little too much."

"Look, you seem cool but I've already been through so much shit in my life that I just don't have time for somebody else's drama."

He countered: "You don't think maybe I am the way I am is because I've been through so much drama myself? But anyway, I'm not trying to use that as an excuse. You felt like I treated you rudely and I apologize for that."

Jaye didn't know what was being said on the other end but could tell from the way that Tuesday was beaming that the conversation was going the way she wanted.

"Why don't you let me make it up to you. Tonight!"

"I don't know." Tuesday pretended to think it over. "What you talkin' 'bout?"

He said, "I'm talking about dinner at one of the finest restaurants in Michigan."

"Okay." She loudly smacked her lips hoodrat style, still fronting like she wasn't excited. "What time?"

"How 'bout we meet in the parking lot of that bank at seven and you can follow me from there."

Tuesday agreed, and after parting words she hung up the phone, then looked at Jaye. She screamed, "I does this shit, bitch!"

Chapter Eleven

Tuesday only had enough time to shoot home, take a quick bath, and change before meeting him.

She made up her face then squeezed into a tiny black minidress she had bought earlier in the week and had been waiting to use on him. She saw it more as a weapon than a piece of clothing. This was a dinner date, which meant she could break out the big guns. Now that she had him off balance and somewhat at a disadvantage for the first time, she was definitely going to play up the sexy.

Again, Tuesday tried to beat him to the meeting place, but even when she reached the bank ten minutes early, he was already there. He was leaned against the hood of the Audi playing a white button-up with dark slacks, and she was happy to see that he'd changed clothes too.

They were alone in the parking lot since the bank was closed. She pulled up nose to nose with him and made her car lunge forward pretending like she was going to run into him.

She let down the window when he came to her door. He looked in at her tight, hip-hugging mini and shook his head. "Either you got too much body or not enough dress on."

She frowned at him. "So whatcha sayin', you don't like it?"

"No, I'm not saying that at all." He smiled with his eyes glued on it. "And where we're going, you definitely will be turning heads tonight."

He got back in his car and she followed him out of the lot. She rode his bumper for a couple miles as she tried to imagine what type of place they would be dining at. Tuesday had her hopes set on seafood by candlelight, good wine, and maybe a little dancing afterward so she could see how he moved.

For forty-five minutes she tailed him along the highway in the wake of a westering sun. As the day eased into dusk more of the eastbound commuters were driving with their headlights aglow and just to fuck with him she switched on her brights.

Tuesday was a little confused when he finally pulled into a shopping complex because the upscale eateries she was used to weren't stationed between Rite-Aids and Blockbuster videos. She followed him through a maze of cars in the parking lot telling herself that he most likely had to stop and pick up a prescription before leading her to some white-linen establishment where a five-star chef with French training waited to delight their palates with exotic cuisine. His standoffish attitude made lunch tedious, but Gaucho's had been an excellent choice so at no time did she doubt his taste in restaurants.

However, when he parked his A8 in front of a Chuck E. Cheese, she actually thought that he had to be joking. She assumed this was a little bit of get-back for annoying him with the glare of her bright headlights, but when he cut off the engine and started to get out, she didn't think he would take it that far.

She was in a four-hundred-dollar dress and six-hundred-dollar heels. She had expected Alaskan king crab and a well-aged cabernet, not cheese pizza and sipping cherry cola from a crazy straw. There was a conversion van slotted between them. When Tuesday parked the Honda, she jumped out and stormed toward his Audi, ready to go off on this nigga for making her waste a bomb outfit—which was a clear violation of diva law.

Gray eyes pinched, lips snarled and nostrils flared, she circled the van with a thousand different curse words on her tongue and was about to let them fly when suddenly she saw him unloading the little girl from the backseat. Her and Tuesday caught sight of each other at the same time and they both seemed to be equally surprised and nervous.

"Dani, this is my friend who I said would be coming with us tonight. Her name is Tabitha. Do you remember when we met her at the Dairy Queen?"

She nodded but still clung to his pant leg, being shy the way children were around a stranger. "Hi, Tabitha," she said, waving a tiny hand.

"Hi, Dani!" Tuesday said with a big phony smile, still trying to downplay how shocked she was. The girl had been sitting so low in the back of the Audi that Tuesday hadn't noticed she was in the car. "What's Dani short for?"

Tuesday directed the question to him but he looked to the child as if she should answer for herself. She replied in a small mousy voice: "Danielle."

"Danielle, that's a really pretty name."

She giggled a "thank you" while covering her mouth with her hands.

Standing in the glow of a neon sign that featured a cartoon rodent on a skateboard, Tuesday turned on him. "So this is one of the finest restaurants in the state?"

"Yeah." He took Tuesday by one hand and Danielle by the other to lead them. "They've got great food, nice atmosphere, and reasonable prices."

For Tuesday, walking inside was like having an ambush sprung on her senses. The place was decorated in the bright reds and yellows designed to make a child feel hyperactive. There were enough swirling beacons and flashing lights to throw an epileptic into a seizure. Pizza, sweat, and disinfectant thinly masking the pungent stench of vomit assaulted her nose. The owners seemed to have cranked up the thermostat to ten degrees past hell just to make sure they sold plenty of pop. Adding to this was the raucous sound of a hundred screaming children at play, parents and staff in conversation, the noise coming from countless arcade games, and an animated puppet band playing "Wheels on the Bus" to the delight of their toddler audience.

He smiled at Tuesday. "See, and they got live entertainment," he said, having to yell over it all to be heard.

After checking in with the reception desk, they were directed to a booth in the rear, but as they made their way Tuesday noticed that she was drawing a lot of attention from the over-twelve crowd. Mothers gave disapproving frowns and a few of the fathers got checked for staring too long. She was wearing a cocktail dress in a place that specialized in root beer floats. The people were leering as if she were a prostitute who'd just stepped into church and it took everything Tuesday had in her not to show how embarrassed she was.

He leaned and whispered in her ear: "I told you that dress was going to turn heads."

He grabbed her hand and squeezed it in a way that said *Fuck these bitches, you with me!* and Tuesday felt good to have that little bit of support.

After reaching their booth, Tuesday studied the girl without openly staring. In the days of watching him pick her up and drop her off Tuesday had seen plenty of Danielle, but it was only in seeing them seated right next to each other that she noticed that they didn't share much of a resemblance. Dani was more of a peanut butter—in contrast to his chocolate—with a pug nose, slightly protruding ears, and brown eyes that were not the color or shape of his.

She had an elfish smile that had most likely come from her mother too. Her front two adult incisors had grown in among a row of baby teeth, giving her a cute beaverlike grin.

It wasn't long before a waitress showed up with a large pepperoni pizza, garlic sticks with cheese dipping sauce, and a pitcher of cola.

Tuesday had her hopes set on something a bit more sophisticated, but she soon found herself reaching for a second slice before either of them had finished their first.

Tuesday only handled children well in small doses. She could watch an infant for five minutes while a parent left the room or engage a child for a brief conversation, but having to deal with one for an extended period of time was a whole other matter. By nature, children were messy and irrational, and this ran contrary to the obsessions brought on by her OCD. Tuesday couldn't let them see how uncomfortable she was, which was why she was using the food as a crutch. She figured if she was too busy chewing, she wouldn't have to do much talking.

Not wanting to look like a pig either, she forced herself to chat up the girl. "So, Dani, are you in school?"

Danielle bobbed her head up and down, her cheeks swollen with pizza like a squirrel hoarding nuts. She started to speak, but Marcus stopped her. "Dani, swallow first. You know we don't talk with our mouths full."

She gulped hard. "Yeah, I go to Bishclop Burtstrumm."

"It's called Bishop Burchram," he said, pronouncing it correctly for Tuesday. "It's a private school not far from where we live. She's in kindergarten."

Danielle huffed and looked up at him, exasperated. Either she wanted to say these things for herself or felt that he was telling this stranger too much of her business.

We live! Tuesday keyed in on those two words and asked Marcus another question that she already knew the answer to. "She stays with you?"

He nodded. "Yeah. I'm actually her legal guardian."

"Uncle Marcus?" The girl looked up at him expectantly.

Without her having to ask, he went into his pocket and passed her a handful of the tokens he purchased at the reception desk. She immediately slid from the booth and raced toward an elaborate play maze with about thirty other children crawling through it. He cried out, "Stay where I can see you!" but no doubt his words were drowned out by the noise.

This confirmed the suspicion Tuesday had that Danielle was not his real daughter. She was curious to know who the girl was to him and how she wound up in his custody but wasn't going to press him about it. She wanted to know despite not seeing any strategic advantage in having that information.

"You're not too comfortable around kids, are you?"

"Huh?" Tuesday had heard him but she was so unprepared for the question that she could think of nothing better than playing deaf.

"Kids!" he said, leaning closer to her over the table. "They make you uncomfortable. I can tell!"

He was doing it again: reading her in a way that nobody besides A.D. had ever been able to do. It wasn't like she was straight-up fidgeting, trembling, or anything like that, and despite all she'd done to appear relaxed, he peeped it anyway.

"I used to be the same way," he said, taking a sip from his glass. "In fact, I'll go so far as to say I actually hated kids. But that was a long time ago."

"That was you," she said defensively. "I don't have any problem with children. I'm cool wit 'em."

You a goddamned liar! He said it with his smile without actually mouthing the words. "I've seen you flinch three times when kids have run past our table. And each time you scoot further into the booth, away from the aisle."

Tuesday decided to be real with him because he'd already seen enough to know that the atmosphere was bothering her, but she wasn't going into detail about her OCD. "It's just kinda crazy in here." Right when she spoke, three kids in party hats shot by their table screaming. "I guess I'm not used to this level of excitement."

"I understand," he said. "I should've told you what I had in store. It was wrong for me to just surprise you with all this. I'm sorry I tricked you and made you get all glammed up for nothing."

Two apologies in one day. Tuesday felt like things were finally starting to get on course with him.

"And for the record, you are killin' 'em in that dress!"

She smiled. "Finally, a compliment, and only seconds before I blacked out!"

He laughed. "And you didn't even have to fish for it that time. You see, I'm learning."

He took one of her hands and met her lime-green eyes with his own black coffee. "But seriously, though, I'm gonna make this up to you, Tabitha. I promise!"

There was something about his promise that made the fine hairs on her arms stand up and sent electricity through her body. Maybe it was the feel of his strong hand clasping hers or the direct way he was staring at her but she started to get that all too familiar warm and wet feeling between her legs. She was already forced to keep her thighs clamped shut due to the length of her minidress but now she had to break eye contact and snatch her hand away or risk ruining her finest pair of satin panties.

Apparently Danielle was not the shy type, because Tuesday noticed that she was now playing in the ball pit with two girls close to her age; she was pleased to see the girl had a talent for making friends. Tuesday had told herself she wasn't going to ask this, but she needed to talk about something that would take her mind off of jumping onto this nigga's lap and going buck right here in front of all these kids. "What happened to Dani's real parents? If you don't mind me asking."

Tuesday saw him hesitate and thought that he was about to get back on the same shit he was on at lunch but then he finally opened up. "Dani was my best friend's daughter. When he died, she didn't have anybody else so I took her."

"How did he die?" she blurted out curiously, then caught herself. "Again, if you don't mind me asking. If I'm being too nosy, just let me know."

"He got murdered over some dumb shit down in the city!" And again Tuesday could see the same pain in his eyes that he had earlier when talking about his fiancée. Pressing him about this would be like peeling the scab off a wound, so she didn't dig any deeper into the hows and whys.

"It wasn't all that long ago, was it?" She asked this in a tone meant to convey sympathy despite the fact she was basically forcing him to talk about a subject she knew he'd rather avoid.

He took a big swallow of his cola then said, "Five years ago in February on the fourteenth."

Tuesday was surprised that he remembered the exact date. This could only mean that for him the loss was particularly traumatic.

She asked, "So it's just you and Dani?"

He smiled because he knew that she wasn't referring to any relatives he may or may not have. "I already told you I'm single."

She fired back, "Yeah, but you haven't told me much of anything else."

He nodded thoughtfully as he took a bite of the pizza that had spent several minutes cooling on his plate, then wiped his hands on a napkin. He downed the last of the pop in his glass then looked back to her.

"Since you think I'm being so secretive, here's what we'll do: I'll answer any five questions you can think up, but—" He raised his hand to emphasize the stipulation. "But only those questions that require yes or no answers."

She laughed. "And I thought the kids were the only ones playing games tonight!"

"Let me explain the rules. You can ask me any five questions you want that have yes or no answers, but each question costs you something, and with each one the price goes up:

"The first question costs you the last piece of pizza," he said, pointing to the final slice on the tray between them. "The second question costs you a hug at the end of the night. The third costs you a kiss from those sexy-ass lips."

"Okay," Tuesday said, smiling. "I see where this is going."

"Wait, let me finish because the fourth question has a special price." He leaned forward over the table and again gave her that direct stare that turned her on. "During our kiss—"

"The kiss that the third question cost me?" she interrupted.

He nodded. "Let's just say that while I'm kissing those sexy lips, the fourth question allows my hands to roam around and appreciate certain aspects of your anatomy."

Tuesday smacked her lips because she already knew he was talking about her ass. It was just like the bet she'd made with Del-Ray. Since she could remember, niggas had always been obsessed with her butt and Tushie was the only other chick she ever met who had gotten more attention than her because of that one body part.

"What about the fifth question?" she asked in a seductive voice. Tuesday was reeled in now and wanted to hear what he had in store for her past the stages of kissing and ass grabbing. "What does the fifth question cost me?"

He was still looking her square in the eyes. "The fifth question costs you the most of all!"

"What?" she asked, curious, unable to look away or even blink.

"The fifth question requires that you do me a special favor. A big one that you can't say no to."

"What favor?"

"You'll find out when the time comes. But like I said, you have to do it regardless of what it is. Do you agree to the rules?"

Tuesday's mind was deep in the gutter as she tried to imagine what type of freaky sexual favor she might have to perform for Question Five. She hoped it was some real nasty shit. "I agree."

He sat back and folded his arms. "Go ahead, then, ask me anything."

Tuesday was flush with things she wanted to ask him but they were either too suspicious:

Are you really Sebastian Caine? Are all the stories people tell about you true?

Or they couldn't be answered with a simple yes or no:

I know you gotta be rich as fuck even though you ain't stunting, what the hell did you do with all the money? Where's the god-damned safe at, nigga?

Any of those questions would immediately kill the mission, so she started with something simple. "First question: Are you from Detroit?"

"Yes." He picked up the last slice of pizza and sat it next to the half-eaten one already in front of him.

She started to ask him the second question, then had a thought. "How do I know you ain't just gone lie to me?"

He placed his hand over his heart. "On my word I'm being straight up."

For some reason that was enough for Tuesday. Even though they were both pretending to be other people, something in his eyes said that he was going to play the game honestly.

However, just to be certain, Tuesday decided to test him with another question that she already knew the answer to. "Second: Do you and Danielle live somewhere in Romulus?"

"Yes. And I hope you understand that I mean an open-mouthed kiss. Ain't no pecking me on the cheek like you'd do your grandfather."

She said, "If my grandfather looked like you, he'd probably get a lot more than a peck on the cheek!"

He made a face at her. "Wow! That was kinda nasty, babe."

They shared a laugh and Tuesday noticed how he called her *babe*. She liked this because it meant that he was beginning to feel more at ease with her, which would lead to him eventually lowering his guard—and she tried to tell herself that was the only reason she liked it.

Two down. She only had three questions to go and wanted to get something useful that would prove without a doubt that he was really Caine or at least in the game. The only way she could see getting closer to what she wanted lay in finding out about the so-called job he touched on at lunch. He'd alluded to having some type of profession that didn't require him leaving the house each morning with a suit and briefcase, and as Tushie pointed out, in all their days of watching him they had never seen him go to a place of employment. Yet when she tried to probe deeper into that, he shut her down, claiming it was "complicated to explain." That had been her first clue, because only secret agents and drug dealers had complicated jobs that they weren't allowed to talk about. Most hustlers from Detroit used either real estate or being in the construction business as a cover for the lavish lifestyles funded by their illegal money and Tuesday knew he was too clever to use those lame excuses. Just finding out what Marcus pretended to do for a living would be the first step in locating the cash, but he was playing that close to the vest.

"Third question: Do you really have a job?"

He looked at her, disappointed in how she was playing the game. "I already told you earlier that I do. Now you've basically wasted your last two questions. First you ask me if I live in Romulus when I told you the day we met I only live six blocks away from the Dairy Queen. Now you blow your third question by asking me something I already told you at lunch. You only have two left, so I'd advise you not to waste them."

He was right and as Tuesday sat there racking her brain on how to approach her last two questions it occurred to her that she was still limited by the Catch-22. Just asking him straight out would gain her nothing because it was not a yes or no question and if she began to hint about drugs or anything illegal it would put him on to the fact that she knew who he really was. She couldn't get the information she wanted this way so she decided to switch it up.

"Fourth question: Did you give Dani all the tokens?"

Marcus was expecting another stab at his personal life or profession. He looked at her confused as he pulled a handful of them from his pocket. "No. I didn't give 'em all to her. I still got a lot."

Tuesday kept a straight face. "Last question: Are we just gonna sit here all night or are we gonna go have fun too?"

He smiled. "That's technically not a yes or no question, but I'll let it slide."

* * *

In time Tuesday stopped feeling so self-conscious about the minidress and was able to ignore all the adult eyes staring at her. They spent another hour and a half playing arcade games and were soon laughing louder and enjoying themselves more than the kids around them. He crushed Tuesday at Skeeball, but she got back when she ran him off the road on some Formula One racing game in which they had to climb inside huge car simulators with steering wheels and pedals.

Tuesday had a ball and the sad part was that she couldn't remember ever having done anything like this. Her mother had always been too focused on her boyfriends to bring her to a place like this when she was a child. She started dancing at sixteen and was jacking by nineteen, living a life that left no room for carnivals and amusement parks.

They didn't part at Chuck E. Cheese despite taking separate cars. She followed Marcus back to Romulus and they said their good-byes in the parking lot of the bank where they met up. By that time it was fifteen minutes to ten and an all played-out Danielle was asleep in the back of the Audi.

Standing face to face with him outside their idling sedans, she said, "I really had fun tonight." And meant it. In fact it wasn't just the most fun Tuesday had on a date, it was the most fun she'd ever had period and she couldn't help but realize how pathetic that was.

"Okay, so next time the tokens are on you!" he said, joking.

She laughed. "Don't forget that promise. You gotta make it up to me for having me waste this dress."

He slowly spun her around so he could take in how it clung to her body. "I'm sorry, but I don't see anything being wasted."

"So when should I expect to hear from you again?" Tuesday usually didn't press in situations like this, but time was too precious.

Giving her a look, he said, "Not before too long."

She responded with: "But not soon enough."

There was a lull between them as each one seemed to be waiting for the other to say something else. After a while, Tuesday reached for her door handle. "Well, good night then."

When she opened the driver's door, he instantly pushed it shut. "I know you haven't already forgot our little arrangement?"

Of course she didn't forget, but Tuesday didn't want to stand out there all night waiting for him to make his move, so she did a bit of a pump-fake. "I didn't think you were serious about that," she said, being coy.

"Very serious." He took her into his arms and she draped hers around his neck. "And I always collect what I'm owed."

Their lips met and after tasting them Tuesday parted hers to invite in his tongue. The kiss was deep, slow, sensual; soulful more than it was erotic. He probed her mouth in lazy circles, not being too forceful, with just enough moisture.

His big strong hands glided up and down her sides, caressing her hourglass curves the way a sculptor would mold potter's clay. He seemed to be appreciating her womanly form on an aesthetic level and not just groping at the softest parts like most niggas did.

Then the kiss grew in intensity; it became hungrier, more passionate.

He finally had to pull away from her just to catch his breath. "Whoa, hold up!" he said, looking at her surprised and a little concerned. "Let's take it down a couple notches before we get arrested out here."

Tuesday nodded, embarrassed that she'd momentarily lost control of herself. Her heart was pounding, her breathing short and fast, her nipples were poking out, and her panties were soaked.

"Yeah, you're right." She kept her eyes on her shoes, desperately trying not to look at him.

Marcus peeked through the rear window at Danielle, who was still sound asleep with her head resting against the safety belt. "I guess I better get her home. I probably shouldn't have done this on a school night, but report cards came out today and she handled her business. I wanted to do something special for her."

Tuesday smiled, finally able to look at him. "I can tell she's smart."

"Too damned smart. Five going on twenty-five. You know what this little girl had the nerve to tell me last week?"

"What?"

He couldn't even get it out without cracking up. "One morning I was making her breakfast and let some bread burn in the toaster. She actually told me that I need a woman!"

Tuesday's eyes got big. "You bullshittin'? No, she didn't."

He was still laughing. "Five years old! Can you believe that?"

"Maybe she's right," Tuesday said, trying to look seductive again.

He shrugged. "I don't know. Maybe she is."

There was another kiss, but just a peck on the lips with no tongue. They shared some parting words then left the bank parking lot headed in opposite directions. Tuesday watched his brake lights in her rearview mirror all the way until she lost sight of them around a corner.

Tuesday thought about hitting a U-turn, catching up to him and inviting herself back to his place. She thought about allowing him to put Danielle to bed then spending a few hours getting rammed by that big dick she felt throbbing against her inner thigh.

She didn't turn back.

Couldn't.

It was never like this with a mark before and Tuesday told herself that there was nothing special about him. She was just horny.

She thought about all the poor niggas who she'd sent home in the past all rocked up and pissed off because she'd spent the whole night dick-teasing only to shut them down at the last minute. She'd never been on the other end of it before, and even though he hadn't purposely teased her, she now felt their pain.

A few hours later on the west side of Detroit, Tushie was chilling at her crib with her new friend De'Lano. After spending the entire day together—which included a trip to the mall, running a few errands, and then going bowling—they kicked back for the rest of the evening on her couch watching movies on demand and washing down the Chinese food.

As the credits rolled on the last flick, De'Lano checked his watch, and seeing it was close to one, slipped into his leather coat. When she asked where he was going, De'Lano blamed the hour and claimed he'd already stayed later than he should've. So after collecting his phone and keys, he offered her a good-bye hug and started to leave.

Tushie was horny, working a strong buzz, and wasn't about to let his ass play Mr. Nice Guy. She blocked him at the door and before he knew what was happening, she began to undo his pants then fell to her knees.

He pushed her hands away from his zipper. "Naw, baby, chill. You ain't gotta do that!"

He helped her back up and she stood there with her arms folded defensively. "Whut's wrong wit choo? I know you ain't gay, so whut, you ain't feeling me or sumthin'?"

He touched her chin. "Naw, girl, you know better than that. I'm just not in a rush to go that way wit you."

"Why not?" she asked, sounding offended.

He laughed at her. He pulled her into his arms and Tushie's Hershey chocolate frame almost melted against him. The way his trimmed goatee framed those big sexy lips, his soft brown eyes with the long lashes, his deep, spiraling 360 waves all had her gone. It had only been two weeks but she was feeling this guy in a way she hadn't felt anybody in a long time. The only thing was that he was either missing her signals or just not interested in her sexually, which was a problem she never had with niggas in the past.

"Tanisha, you know I'm feelin' you!" Tushie liked that he called her by her real name, which was something few people did. Even to those in her family she had been "Tushie" since she was twelve years old, when puberty came and hit her harder than a Mack truck.

"Den why you actin' like you don't?" she asked, looking up at him solemnly. "I mean you don't neva try ta touch me or nuthin'. I undastand you tryin' ta be a gentleman but it's a such thang as being too much of a gentleman."

He lightly pecked her lips before he explained: "Comin' in I told myself I wanted to take my time with you. I know you used to dance and I know most niggas who come at you only wanting one thing."

Tushie blinked but didn't respond, because what he said was common knowledge.

"I didn't want you to look at me like the rest of them niggas!" he continued. "I didn't want it to be like I was just using you so I wanted us to connect on a deeper level first. Baby, I only care about what's on the inside and I'd be here right now if you was only ninety pounds and flat as an ironing board. You'd still be a dime to me."

She would too. Her body got so much attention that it was easy to overlook that Tushie had a really pretty face with sleepy cat's eyes and juicy pink lips. Plus not a lot of girls could pull off being that dark and still be fine like her.

Tushie was touched by the sentiment but explained to him that someone she truly cared for could never use her in that way. With some homespun southern wisdom she made him understand that she, like all women, wanted a man to respect her mentally but not to the extent that he ignored her physically. Even with all the negative attention she sometimes got, Tushie actually liked her body and wanted her man to appreciate it too.

"I'm glad you feelin' tha inside, baby, but tha outside need love too." She kissed him, then grabbed his hands and slid them down to her ass. "Ain't choo feelin' dat?"

As he rubbed the ridiculous round donk and squeezed its softness, she felt the proof that he was swelling between his legs. So when she led him away from the front door and back toward her bedroom, he followed like a dog on a leash.

After he got down to his boxers, Tushie made him watch as

she performed a little striptease. Tushie loved performing for her man because, as good as she looked clothed, she looked better undressed. She enjoyed seeing the look on a nigga's face as he marveled at her cartoonlike physique.

Her dark skin was flawless without a single blemish, scar, mole, or stretch mark, and the truly amazing part was that as thick as she was, her body still looked fit. As rare as it was to find a girl with her dimensions, it was rarer still to find one who was still toned. Chicks who were as thick as Tushie were usually on the downward slide toward being fat, but she broke the mold. The thirty-two-inch difference between her hips and her tiny waist complemented her shape. She had a flat stomach with visible ab muscles and her enormous thighs were not lumpy from cellulite but smooth and soft as baby fat. She took off her top then shimmied out of her Applebottoms while De'Lano wondered how she was ever able to get them on.

She stood before him modeling a red bra and thong set, then turned around so he could see that the ass was the same: no cottage cheese, no dents, not even a tattoo; just plump and round as two basketballs. It looked really firm but her slightest movements sent it quaking like a mountain of Jell-O. She hypnotized him by making it bounce to a silent rhythm.

When he couldn't take any more, he snatched her into bed and pulled off her Victoria's Secret. Tushie had perky up-thrust breasts with nipples that reminded him of Tootsie Roll candies and a waxed tight-looking pussy with lips that were thick like the ones on her face. De'Lano got the head he refused at the door and Tushie got her clit and ass licked from the back just the way she liked it.

A little later De'Lano was hammering her from behind and the clapping sound produced by her booty smacking up against him was almost loud enough to drown out her moans. Tushie was loving the dick and had practically painted his condom white because most niggas couldn't handle her backshot for longer than a few minutes. He had her hanging off the edge of the bed, facedown with her ass up, and had been killing her in that position for more than an hour.

The fact that he had stamina was like a pass of her final test. This nigga was official. She could now introduce him to Tuesday.

De'Lano gripped her slender waist and watched as he sent oceanic shock waves rippling through her stupendous ass with a satisfied but slightly sinister smirk on his face.

The big country bitch had gone for all that weak inner connection shit just like he was told she would. He had been plotting for this moment since he followed her into the supermarket that day and fronted like he bumped into her by accident.

This was deeper than just getting the pussy, though; she was falling for him, which meant that their plan was moving on schedule.

She came for the sixth time. "Oh, De'Lano!"

Tushie had her eyes closed, panting in ecstasy, with no idea that she was calling out a fake name.

Chapter Twelve

Tuesday made it home from her date around eleven and briefly indulged her compulsion to clean. By twelve she was indulging a different one in her bed, taking some personal time with another one of her toys, thinking of some imaginary lover who kept switching back and forth between A.D. and Marcus. By one she was snoring lightly, deep in a post-orgasmic sleep and probably would've stayed that way the entire night, but woke up at two thirty feeling like her bladder was about to burst from all the pop she drank at Chuck E. Cheese.

After going to pee, Tuesday was slipping back into bed when she was suddenly hit by the eerie feeling that something was wrong. It was a nameless fear without form or focus.

Her first thought was an intruder, so she immediately went for her gun. The Heckler she kept in her purse all day got transferred to the nightstand drawer right next to the bed every night. She withdrew it, switched off the safety, and tucked it at her side.

Although the night pressed at all her windows, there was enough artificial light coming in from the hallway to keep her bedroom from being pitch dark. Only the farthest corners lay in shadows.

She scanned around and noticed there was a six-foot silhouette standing in one of them and was just about to shoot when she realized that it was only the big stuffed giraffe Marcus had won for her playing Hot Shots. It was a new decoration and she hadn't got used to it being there yet.

She gasped in relief. Her heart was beating like a wild animal seeking to escape the prison of her rib cage.

Tuesday checked every room and closet in her condo for a burglar, letting the pistol lead the way. No one was hiding anywhere and the door had no signs of a breach.

She couldn't help but check the refrigerator and cupboards a few times. Everything was shelved just as it should be.

The condo was secure.

The eerie feeling remained.

It wasn't until she checked her cell that Tuesday realized the possible cause for her fear. Her eyes couldn't believe when the screen read: twenty-seven missed calls.

Somebody was dead. Tuesday could already guess that much because death was the only emergency that could trigger that many repeated calls at this time of night.

The rest was simply finding out who, how, and why.

Her caller ID showed the club's number listed in the majority, with Jaye's cell sprinkled in a few times.

The first one came from the club and went to voice mail at 1:38 a.m. When she checked the message, she heard Ebony the bartender speaking in an urgent whisper: "Boss Lady, you need to get down here right now. As soon as you hear this, just get out here. Don't even bother callin' back!"

At 1:41 there was a message from Jaye. "TK, some shit just went down. Some fucked-up shit! I don't care where you at or what you doing, hit me as soon as you can. Or better yet, just get to the club." This second one really disturbed her because Tuesday never heard the lighthearted joker sound so panicked.

Ebony was on her voice mail three more times and after that they just blew up her phone calling every minute or two. All of the messages were on the same tip: *Get to the club now!!*

The fact that they were too afraid to give any details over the phone only supported Tuesday's suspicion. She was about to find out that somebody she knew, and probably cared about, was dead.

But who?

Because there was no traffic at three in the morning and the CTS-V was built for speed, the twenty minutes it usually took her to get from home to work was shaved to ten.

When she pulled into the lot, she saw that every business in the strip mall was closed, as they should be, including The Bounce House. The sign was off and the only four cars in the lot were parked in front of the club.

Ebony owned a Honda Civic, but an earlier model than the one she was renting. Brianna's bumblebee Camaro was parked next to it. DelRay's raggedy-ass '87 Monte Carlo with the sagging bumper was in its usual spot. Tuesday slotted her Caddy between him and Jaye's charcoal Chrysler, rounding out the quintet.

Tushie's vehicle was noticeably absent. When Tuesday didn't see her big H2 or the '81 Cutlass on twenty-sixes she pulled out from time to time, nausea caused the fluids in her stomach to roll like a stormy sea. "Please don't let it be Tush," she mumbled to herself.

She stepped inside and something about the club made her uneasy. The stage lights were off and the house lights were dimmed. Drinks were still on the tables and the chairs were left in a way that suggested the customers had cleared out in a rush.

Yet the club being in disarray wasn't what bothered Tuesday. There was an ominous vibe that she couldn't identify or shake. She hadn't been afraid walking in The Bounce since that first night when she was sixteen, but what she felt at the moment was different in complexion because it was mortal fear, and not just a shy girl nervous about showing her body to strangers.

Ebony was seated at the bar with her face dropped into her hands and DelRay was standing over her. The bouncer was the first one to notice Tuesday.

As he approached, she could tell by the look in his eyes that it was bad. He had a fat, almost rubbery face capable of making some comical expressions he typically used to make her smile, but one would've never guessed it at the time. The woeful expression he wore seemed as permanent as if it had been chiseled onto a granite statue.

"What the fuck is up?" Tuesday asked, whispering with no idea why she was doing it.

DelRay didn't answer, he just turned and walked away while motioning with his head that she should follow.

He led her down the hall on the far side of the stage that served the dancers' changing room. It was a space twice the size of Tuesday's office that featured a makeup table, a couple of wardrobe racks strewn with skimpy stripper gear, and a large cardboard box full of wigs and accessories. Half a dozen wall lockers were there for the girls to keep their personal clothes in and there was an adjoining half bath with a shower in case they wanted to clean themselves up after their set. There was also an old sofa and a card table because on slow nights, more than a few of them used poker to pass the time and supplement their income.

When Tuesday came through the door, the stench sickened her even before the sight of the blood. The smell of shit fouled the air.

The body was lying to the right of the door. The bloody pattern that streaked the floor suggested that it had been dragged there from the hall. It was covered from head to toe with a bunch of crimson-stained towels and aprons from behind the bar.

"Who the fuck is it?" The only thing offering some relief was that Tuesday could tell from the size and shape of the body that it wasn't Tushie. It was obviously a man and a rather large one at that—small in comparison to the bouncer, but bigger than average.

DelRay reached down and pulled away the bloody towel that covered his face. Tuesday shuddered when she saw Tank staring up at her—their last mark who they took the loss on. His fat, greasy face was spattered with blood. His chapped lips were parted, although he could no longer draw breath.

By far the most gruesome part was that he was now a Cyclops. One huge eye was fixed on Tuesday while the other seemed to have been blown out of his head. The socket that had once contained his right eyeball was filled with milky pus and a bloody mass of scar tissue. Apparently the last thing he learned was that his Tiny Angel was really a Little Devil and unnamed fluids drained from the wound to make it look as if he were still weeping even in death.

"It's even worse on the other side," DelRay said in a hushed tone. "She pushed that nigga noodles right out tha back of his head!"

"What the fuck happened up in here?" Tuesday was speaking just as low as him and now understood why they were whispering. From the moment she walked in, she sensed a funereal atmosphere and as a species most of us had an abiding respect for the dead deeply rooted in our subconscious. We often chose to be discreet in their presence as if a loud, offensive sound would disturb their slumber and animate the corpses.

She repeated her question: "What happened?"

DelRay explained that because he was on the door he didn't see the actual shooting, but from what he saw for himself and the parts he got from talking to Ebony and a couple of the dancers who witnessed it, he was able to piece together the following story:

The fat, bug-eyed nigga came in the club about one looking for some chick named Simone. Apparently he saw Baby Doll and mistook her for this chick because he started following her around harassing her. She tried to get away from him but after he followed her into the restroom, Doll had tried to hide from him backstage in the changing room. She locked the door but Bug Eyes followed her back there and tried to force his way inside. That's when the shooting happened.

Tuesday was trying to figure out how this could've happened while at the same time deciding what to do next, but couldn't think clearly. She was disturbed by the body, and while towels had been put down to sop up most of the blood, there was still a lot, along with brain matter, sprayed on the walls and floor. This caused her OCD to flare up in a way that the kids at Chuck E. Cheese or the disarrayed furniture couldn't cause. Tuesday felt a tightness in her chest and it became difficult to breathe. Death had caused Tank to release his bowels; the stink of blood and shit suddenly seemed amplified, making Tuesday want to vomit.

She fled back into the hallway and leaned against the wall gasping for air like a swimmer only seconds away from drowning. She buckled down on all fours. Her body was wracked with a fit of dry heaves but she was able to keep her food down.

Big DelRay helped Tuesday to her feet. "You all right?"

She nodded. "So she just popped the nigga?" Tuesday asked, confused. "Did he have a heater?"

He threw up his hands. "Nobody saw one and I didn't find one either."

"We couldn't reach you or Tush so I just kinda quarterbacked the whole thing," he explained. "I shut down the club, sent the girls home, and pulled him in here. I didn't call the hook, TK, because I didn't know if that was the right thing to do."

DelRay had peeped enough to know that Tuesday and the girls were off into some criminal shit but he didn't exactly know what it was—he figured it was none of his business and was smart enough never to ask. Because he didn't know what she was into, he couldn't be sure if drugs, guns, or anything else illegal might be stored at The Bounce. Tuesday understood that he was only trying to protect her and her business.

DelRay looked at her with wide, solemn eyes that asked if he did the right thing by not reporting it. She gave a subtle nod and pat on the arm to indicate that he did.

This was fucked up but worse would be if they found themselves in the middle of a police investigation. They might start digging and learn what the girls had been doing and what they were planning next. Too much money was at stake; they couldn't afford to have the heat on them.

"Where the fuck is Doll at?" she asked with gray eyes. "I'm 'bout to choke tha life out that little bitch for doing this bullshit!"

"The girls in yo office but I think you should know it wasn't Doll who shot him." He closed the door to trap in the smell. He pulled a pack of Doublemint from his pocket and popped a stick in his mouth after Tuesday refused one.

"Bree the one who pulled the trigger."

When Tuesday burst through the door of her office, she didn't say a word to anybody. She looked over Jaye and Doll, immediately zeroed in on Brianna and attacked.

Before the girl knew what was happening, she was snatched off the couch by a handful of weave that Tuesday had twisted around one fist, and with the other she was smacked back and forth across the face. Each slap sounded like a firecracker and sent Brianna's head whipping from left to right like she was watching a long volley in a tennis match.

Baby Doll and Jaye could do nothing but look on stunned. They were either too shocked or too afraid to interfere. Tuesday continued to put down her Ike Turner while the two silently watched.

Tuesday slapped her ten times then let go of her weave. The girl fell to her knees and cupped her face with her hands.

"You stupid bitch!!" Tuesday roared at her as Brianna slowly crawled back into her seat. "Do you know what you just did? Do you know what type of heat you just put on us?"

Baby Doll tried to defend her girl. "She did what she had to do!" she said in a tone that Tuesday didn't appreciate. "That nigga came through here on some crazy stalker shit and tried to snatch me out tha club!"

Tuesday turned on her and pointed. "You shut tha fuck up, bitch, 'cause I'ma get to you in a minute!"

While Tuesday was focused on Baby Doll, Brianna went for the gun inside a Chanel bag she left on the sofa, but stopped short when she saw the mag from the corner of her eye. Jaye was on the other end of a .380 that was hovering only an inch away from her head.

"If you draw, better be Picasso!" Jaye said, quoting an old Jay Z lyric. "Naw, Bree, it ain't going down like that. You done did all the shooting you gone do tonight!"

"Bitch, I should slap you up again!" Tuesday said. She grabbed the strap out her bag and dropped it in with the Heckler she was carrying in her Louis.

As Jaye put away her gun, Tuesday shot her a glance that said, *Good lookin'*. She responded with a slight nod that said, *I got yo back*.

Tuesday was back on Brianna again. "What the fuck was you thinkin', bitch?! You do this shit in my place, and now? We got the most important mission we ever had on the floor right now! We don't need this shit!"

"What was I s'posed to do?" With no gun to reach for, Brianna was more willing to talk. "First the nigga followed her into the women's bathroom then burst inside the changing room. Since you so fucking smart and just got so much game, what would you had done?"

Tuesday looked at her with some combination of anger, pity, and disbelief. As pretty as Brianna was—and at times Tuesday somewhat envied her look—she honestly couldn't believe the girl was as dumb as she was.

Tuesday frowned at her. "Tank was by himself and the nigga didn't have a strap on him. Why wouldn't y'all just call DelRay to throw his ass up outta here? You know that big black muthafucka we got standing at the front door? That's what he gets paid to do!"

Brianna rolled her eyes, still giving attitude even though her cheeks were turning red from being slapped around. "Well, it's easy to say what you would've did after the fact. When all the shit was going down, I didn't think about that."

Tuesday wanted to go at her again but she didn't have the energy, plus it wouldn't do any good. The girl was so stupid that talking to her was tiring in a way that had nothing to do with the late hour or her lack of sleep. Tuesday went around the desk and flopped into her chair. She let out a deep sigh as if physically and mentally drained.

"Doll, how do you think he found you?" she asked, reclining her chair with her eyes closed.

She shrugged. "I don't know. He probably just saw me on the street and started following me."

Tuesday sat up, propped an elbow on the desk, and rested her head in her palm. "Simone's phone. You never got rid of it, did you?"

"So? Why throw away a perfectly good phone when all I gotta do is not answer it when he call?"

Frustrated, Tuesday closed her eyes again. She was then certain that she would never be a good parent. She felt like she was dealing with children and knew that she lacked the patience to do this full-time.

Tuesday spoke slowly and carefully as if she were actually talking to a five-year-old even though Doll seemed to have less sense than Danielle. "Baby Doll. I told you to lay low and to make sure you got rid of that phone. I stressed this to you because I knew what type of nigga he was. Insecure dudes like him will sneak and put GPS on your phone and car. That's why we only fuck with rentals and never use our own phones."

Brianna jumped in. "You don't know he found her by tracking her phone!"

"We don't know he *didn't*, either. And he damn sure ain't in no position to tell us!"

Doll had an icy stare. "He'd still be alive if he wouldn't have brought his ass through here like that! The ugly fat muthafucka should've got the hint when I stopped callin' his ass!"

Tuesday said, "The only thing Tank did wrong was fall in love with you and he didn't deserve to die because of it.

"Listen," she said, addressing them all. "Regardless of how some of y'all might feel about me personally, please believe that I know what I'm doing and everything I tell y'all is for a reason. I've been doing this shit for a minute and ain't never got caught up because I'm careful. I done ran into a few of my old marks on the street and got hugs; niggas never suspected I had anything to do with the loss they took. Some done even tried to hook up with me again!

"We watch a nigga and go through all this *Mission: Impossible* shit because it's about protecting us *and them*. We get the money and a dude might get his feelings hurt but that's it. Believe it or not, I actually like men and didn't come into this game to knock niggas' heads off. Nobody needs to die in order for us to get what we want. What happened here tonight was wrong and it should not have went down."

She looked at Baby Doll. "That nigga's death is on you as much as it is on Brianna. If you was more careful, he would've never followed you here."

"What about the one you on now?" Brianna asked with attitude. "You talkin' all this high and mighty shit when the whole plan is to knock his head off! What makes you so much better than us?"

Jaye and Doll looked at her as if to say it was a good question, and even Tuesday had to agree. She was coming off like a hypocrite considering that she was the main one stressing that Marcus would have to die after this.

"The difference is that my mark is in a whole other league than a nigga like Tank. When we hit him, he gone know I had something to do with it. Plus other niggas ain't connected to where they could have you whole family murdered, even from behind bars!"

Tuesday saw from the expressions on their faces that she had made her point.

"If we gone get through the rest of this shit, and stay the fuck outta jail, y'all need to start listening to me."

Just hearing the word "jail" deflated Brianna some. Apparently with all the things that could go wrong in committing a senseless unjustified murder, she never considered spending her life in prison to be one of them.

Tuesday said, "First things first, we gotta get this body taken care of."

"How we gone do that?" asked Doll. "Go buy some shovels, take his ass out to the country and just bury him somewhere?"

"Naw, I got a guy I know who handle this type of shit, but it's gone be expensive, though." She looked at Brianna. "It's about to take a whole lotta money to clean up yo bullshit and whatever it cost is comin' out your share!"

She made a face. "How much he gone want?"

Tuesday shook her head. "I don't know. I never used him for this before, but whatever he ask we gone have to pay. It ain't like we got a choice."

"We got another problem," said Jaye. "There was a couple girls working who saw the shit happen. What we gone do about them?"

Tuesday closed her eyes and massaged her temples as if developing a migraine. With everything else on her plate, she hadn't considered the possibility of any witnesses going to the police.

She breathed out a weary sigh. "Honestly, ain't nothing much we can do. We locked in now. We really need to hit this lick so we can get the fuck on!"

Tuesday let Ebony leave around three thirty but asked DelRay to stay through the night. When it was time to move Tank, she was going to need him to help with the heavy lifting and DelRay agreed with no complaints. Tuesday didn't have much money at the time but promised she was going to look out as soon as she could, for this and for keeping a cool head through the whole situation.

Tuesday set Brianna and Baby Doll to work on cleaning up the blood, since she placed the blame on them equally. Jaye offered to help them scrub the walls and floor but her assistance was voluntary.

DelRay helped Tuesday straighten up the front of the club, and as a joke, she told him that he'd earned a lifetime pass to smack her ass as much as he wanted.

She tried to get in touch with Face but wasn't surprised when he didn't answer his phone at four o'clock in the morning. She left an urgent message on his voice mail that he should call her as soon as he got it, regardless of the hour.

In all the confusion she almost missed that no one had heard from Tushie the entire night. Tuesday also left a message for her when the call was transferred automatically to voice mail.

The girls were tired but still awake as the predawn hours slid into morning. They sat around the club with red, puffy eyes, waiting for Tuesday to receive the call she was expecting from Face.

Big DelRay was the only one comfortable enough to sleep in the company of the dead. He was stretched awkwardly across the bench seat in one of the booths snoring loudly as if he were home in his own bed.

While Jaye sat at the bar with Tuesday, Baby Doll and Brianna were at a table across the room. They were huddled in a whispered conversation that Tuesday watched from the corner of her eye.

Even though Brianna was downplaying it, Tuesday knew she had to feel some type of way about getting slapped up and had kept on guard since it happened. The girl wasn't as hard as she thought but did have pride, and Tuesday didn't think for a minute that she was going to let that go. She wasn't going to let Brianna rock her to sleep. Especially now that she's proved that she could and would kill.

Jaye was a few stools down from her texting somebody, and Tuesday couldn't imagine who at five thirty in the morning. When she slid onto the stool next to hers, Jaye put the phone away and Tuesday leaned in to her ear.

"I need you to do me a favor," she whispered. "Keep an eye on them bitches for me until this shit is over with, because I think them hoes up to something. I'm gone be too busy with Marcus, and ever since Tush got this new nigga . . ." She didn't finish the sentence because just saying the words felt like she was betraying her girl.

Jaye smiled. "So you want me to go straight up Black Ops on these bitches? Hide some cameras in they crib, put a bug on her car and track 'em by satellite. If either of them hoes make any kinda move, I'm in they ass like a G-string."

Tuesday laughed. "Girl, just let me know if you see them doing anything shady."

Jaye gave a fake salute.

Just then Tuesday's phone rang. The number appeared as unavailable but when she answered Face was on the other end sounding as if he'd just rolled over from sleep.

"TK, what tha fuck? I just got yo message." His voice was low and raspy.

"I know it's kinda early, nigga, but I got a little problem. I got this junker I need you to come pick up!"

There was a long, thoughtful pause before he spoke again.

"Where at?" His voice was clear now as if he fully woke up in those ten seconds.

"A nigga broke down at my club last night. I need to get that towed away like now, ya hear me?"

"Yeah, I hear you, but you need to hear me. Towing ain't cheap and we don't just do that shit for any muthafuckin' body!"

"Nigga this me!" Tuesday snapped at him. "I ain't just any muthafuckin' body. And I'm damn sure not gone call at four in tha morning not wanting shit!"

He was quiet for a moment then said, "I'll be there in an hour."

When Tuesday put away her phone, even Brianna was smart enough to peep that she wasn't actually talking about a junked car.

Of the few people who knew that he dealt in stolen cars, and the fewer still who knew he was a major arms dealer, only a fraction knew that Face also operated a private cleaning business. He offered this special service only for his most trusted customers. If one found themselves jammed up with a body, Face could make their problem disappear. It wasn't much of a stretch since those who bought his illegal guns were bound to use them. The same resources that allowed him to strip a new Benz for parts, or just make the whole car vanish, were able to do the same for human bodies. However, Face assumed tremendous risk in doing this and he expected to be paid well for it.

The problem was that Tuesday couldn't afford it and seriously doubted they could even if she and Brianna pooled their money. She was really counting on the last lick, and because she gave the girls her share, her money was really funny right then. Her only hope was that Face would agree to do this on consignment for a piece of what they took from Marcus. If not, they were going to be hauling Tank's fat ass to the nearest Dumpster and praying for the best.

Because the decomposing corpse was locked away in the changing room and they had spent the last few hours away from the sight and scent, it was easier to convince themselves that they were waiting for someone as innocent as the cable guy or a plumber coming to fix a leaky pipe. It might have been a way to combat the nervousness or some defense mechanism employed by the psyche to deal with the guilt; either way, they were sharing the delusion that the morning's task was a mundane one, so when the subject of breakfast came up, everyone agreed that they could eat. Guilt didn't even quell Brianna's appetite: she claimed to be the hungriest of them all.

Just the mention of food made big DelRay sit up and Tuesday nominated him for the errand. She didn't trust Brianna not to disappear leaving them to clean up her mess, and Doll had no car. Plus she wanted Jaye to stay behind with her just to keep equal numbers with the two of them. Even though she had taken Brianna's gun, Tuesday was still playing it cautious.

She offered DelRay a fifty and the keys to her Cadillac then sent him to find the closest fast food restaurant open at a quarter to six. Mr. Scott didn't open Bo's until twelve so he would need to drive at least a mile to find something. She preferred that he take her car because it was more dependable. Tuesday was hungry and didn't want his shitty Monte Carlo to break down before he got back with the food.

Tuesday was behind the bar pouring herself a glass of cranberry juice that Ebony used to mix drinks when the knock at the door came. "That's my nigga Face right there. Bree, go let 'em in."

Brianna was closest to the door but she just sat there defiantly staring at her. Tuesday was about to lay into her about all this being her fucking fault from the jump when Baby Doll got up to answer it.

DelRay hadn't been gone two minutes and Tuesday hoped he didn't take forever, because she wanted him there for Face in case he needed help carrying Tank.

Tuesday took three big gulps of cranberry juice when Doll sprinted back from up front. Her chest was heaving, her face was pale, and her hazel eyes were so wide open that she might've seen the Grim Reaper at the door with cloak and scythe coming to collect Tank's soul before Face came for his body.

Baby Doll was wheezing so hard that Tuesday was barely able to make out the word "Po-po!" She took a deep breath then forced out in a single gasp, "Oh, shit, TK, it's the muthafuckin' hook at the door! What the fuck we gone do?"

Chapter Thirteen

Po-po. The Hook. One Time. Five-O. Them People. The Law. Heat. The Fuzz. Jake. Pigs. Blue Boys. Jump-out Boys. Heroes. Them Folks.

Each generation has called them something different and the names change with every city you visit, but no matter what they might be called in your hood, there are two things that niggas of all ages and in every part of the country can agree on:

1) It's never good when they show up at your door at six in the morning.
2) It's worse when somebody's stretched in one of your back rooms with their brains leaking.

Tuesday slowly approached the door with the girls on her heels: Jaye, Baby Doll, and Brianna, who wasn't looking as non-chalant as she had been a minute ago when Tuesday asked her to answer it. She was so nervous that she bit down on three of her fingers, probably to keep her teeth from chattering.

The world suddenly seemed eerily silent and Tuesday could

hear nothing over the sound of her wildly beating heart. It was like she was listening to herself through a stethoscope.

When they knocked again, it made all the girls jump. The second barrage was louder and more demanding.

The door to the club had a small window of tinted glass that allowed her to see out without being seen, but when Tuesday looked outside, the rhythm of her heart took on a much more frantic pace. There were two men standing on the other side in suits with badges that hung from chains around their necks.

One of them was Dresden.

She turned around and fell against the door. "Oh, shit!" It was inconceivable that he should be there. He and Tuesday had an unspoken agreement that he was never to come by the club and up until now he had honored that. She couldn't figure what his slimy ass was doing there and didn't know if she was better or worse off for having him versus some cop she didn't know.

Tuesday opened the door for him and his partner, who was a black guy who looked to be around thirty-two. He was brown-skinned, clean-cut, wearing cheap frames, and her first impression of him was that he was a square. She was actually surprised to see Dres paired up with a black guy after having listened to so many of his racist rants.

"Can I help you?" she asked, focusing on the brother and ignoring Dresden.

Dresden spoke for him, refusing to be ignored. "I'm *Lieutenant* Dresden and this is *Detective* Bates." He put emphasis on their titles as if to stress that he was the superior. "Someone reported there was a shooting that happened here late last night."

Apparently he wanted to play it like they didn't know each other and Tuesday was cool with that. "I'm sorry, officer, but you've been misinformed," she said. "There wasn't no shooting here."

Dresden smiled. "Misinformed, huh? Hey, sometimes those things happen, but would you mind if me and my partner took a look around anyway? I promise to be quick."

Little-dick muthafucka, you damn sure know how to be quick! Tuesday thought to herself. It was odd to her seeing him front like he was such a professional, even trying to be charming. It irritated her that this sadistic piece of shit could so easily hide behind this fake persona.

"Do you have a warrant?" she asked defensively.

"No, I do not," he confessed. "But I can make a phone call and park myself right here on your doorstep until one gets here, in, say, two hours. This is going to involve calling and waking up a lot of people who are going to be very upset. And then me and twenty or thirty of these upset people are going to spend the entire day going through your club, and because they're going to blame you for the inconvenience, I can promise they won't be gentle. They're gonna overturn every table, tear through every wall, and don't think for a second that the city is going to reimburse you!" Oddly enough, he was still speaking with a pleasant tone, saying this as if it were a fact and not a threat.

He continued: "Or you could save us both a lot of trouble by just giving me five minutes to look around. I see everything is cool and we're gone."

The black guy hadn't spoken, as if he'd been told not to or was just used to deferring to the ranking officer. Dresden added, "Ma'am, you really would be doing yourself a favor if you cooperated."

Although the girls were standing behind her, Tuesday could imagine the looks they must have worn on their faces. She could feel their nervousness and was worried that Dresden and his partner might pick up on it too.

A lot of the tension Tuesday felt was her own because she honestly didn't know what to do next. If she let him in and Dresden ran across Tank's body, she couldn't be sure how he would react. He had allowed them, even helped them to rob this nigga, but murder was a whole other issue. He might play it by the book and slap the cuffs on her right there. Or the dirty lieutenant might fear Tuesday snitching on his involvement and decide to silence her before that could happen.

But on the other hand, if she didn't let him in, the place was going to be swarming with cops in two hours. While she could certainly use that grace period, it wouldn't do any good with him right outside watching the place like a hawk. Plus, Face was due to show up at any minute and if he saw the police there when he arrived, that was going to create a whole other problem between him and Tuesday.

Unable to think of a better solution, she stepped aside and let them enter. As they walked past Tuesday, Brianna's wide eyes quietly asked her, *What the fuck are you doing?!*

She responded with a look that said, *Bitch, what else can I do?*

The two detectives stopped in the lounge area and surveyed the room. "Nice," Dresden said as if he was impressed. Because The Bounce was a small club located in a strip mall, many people were surprised by how elegantly it was decorated, so Tuesday wasn't sure if he was being sarcastic or not.

"Excuse me, miss, but I never caught your name." Like he didn't already know.

"Tuesday."

"Pardon me?"

"Tuesday! Tuesday Knight!" she spat with an attitude.

Dresden smiled. "That's a very interesting name."

"I guess my mother thought it would be funny!"

The black cop, Bates, asked, "Were you at least born on a Tuesday night?"

She put on a fake smile for him. "Actually, it was a Friday morning. Like I said, my mother was on some bullshit."

Dresden stood in front of her. "Ms. Knight, do you own this establishment?"

"Yeah, I do."

"You have a very nice place. It has a sophisticated feel."

"Thank you." Tuesday didn't bother to put on a phony smile for him. She was as much annoyed by this Officer Friendly act as she was with him being there.

While Bates looked around the stage, Tuesday noticed that he cut his eyes at Jaye more than a few times. At six in the morning on a night when she'd had no sleep, Jaye was still fine enough to turn heads. With a look Tuesday let her know that the square was feeling her and that they might have to use that to their advantage if the opportunity arose.

Just then Tuesday got a text message from DelRay. He was on his way back from Coney Island when he spotted the unmarked police car parked outside the club so he just cruised by. He had her Caddy parked down the street in the lot of a Home Depot that was still closed. He was wondering what she wanted him to do.

"Everything okay?" Dresden asked, eyeing her and her phone suspiciously. "People usually don't text you this early in the morning just to ask how you're doing."

Tuesday sneered at him. "Just a friend I was s'posed to meet for breakfast. He wanted to know if we were still on."

She put the phone away. Tuesday had an idea but couldn't text DelRay back with the details while Dresden watched her. She also needed to fill in Brianna, Jaye, and Baby Doll, but couldn't just call a huddle right in front of the detectives. It would look just as bad if all four of them tried to slip off to the ladies' room at the same time. She had to be subtle and hope that the girls caught on.

"You look familiar," Tuesday said to Dresden's partner. "I think you've been here before."

"Oh, no!" He shook his head with a nervous little smirk on his face. "I think you've mistaken me for somebody else. I don't go to gentlemen's clubs!"

"Why not?" Tuesday asked in a cute, pouty way.

"Two reasons. One: My wife would kill me!" he said, pointing to his wedding ring. "And two: My wife would kill me!"

Bates let out a goofy laugh as if he'd said something clever and Tuesday joined in. "Well, I still say you look familiar. Doesn't he look familiar, Jaye?"

"I was just thinking the same thing before you said it." Jaye stood in front of Bates, then looked him up and down. "You have been here before," she said, playing on what Tuesday had already set up. "In fact, I just danced for you the other night!" This was a lie because neither Jaye nor any of the other girls, except for Doll, had to stoop to dancing since becoming members of the team.

Dresden laughed. "So all that straitlaced family man stuff you're pulling at the station is just an act. I knew it!"

Bates was now blushing from embarrassment. "Lieutenant, I've never been here before in my life. I'm a Seventh Day Adventist and a happily married man."

Although Tuesday had set this in motion, she didn't quite know where it was headed. All she knew was that as long as they were standing there talking shit, they weren't searching the back rooms of her club. The problem was that she knew they couldn't keep this up for long.

As risky as Tuesday's plan was, she couldn't see any other way out of this situation for them. She needed to send a quick message to DelRay and Face—who probably would be showing up at any second—and get them working together. She figured if she and the girls kept the cops distracted, that would give the fellas a chance to get Tank out the back door. The upside was that DelRay already had keys to the club because she and Tushie often left him to lock up.

The downside was that Face might not be down with a move so dangerous. He was a man who had a lot to lose, and even though he and Tuesday went back, sneaking a dead body right under a cop's nose might be asking too much. It was bad enough that she didn't have the money to pay him in the first place. Tuesday didn't think Face would go for that even if she let him suck the toes of every single chick who took a shift at The Bounce.

Another problem was that in order for the boys to pull off their part, the girls would have to keep Bates and Dresden distracted for a long time. Tuesday had an idea on how to do this but couldn't be sure that Jaye, Brianna, and Doll would be up for it.

Tuesday asked, "Jaye, you sure this the same dude you danced for the other night?"

Jaye gave him a hungry stare that made the bashful cop look away. "I'm sure it's him. You think I'd forget a nigga this fly," she said, touching the lapels of his polyester suit. "And rockin' them fresh frames!"

Tuesday was almost unable to keep a straight face. "But this nigga say he don't remember you. Evidently you didn't do yo thang!"

Jaye now understood why Tuesday was geeking shit up but Brianna and Baby Doll were still just standing there looking lost and scared.

"I guess I didn't do my thang then if he just straight-up forgot me. I feel some type of way about that!"

"No, no, no!" he said, waving his hands. "Trust me, if I ever saw you dance I would remember it for the rest of my life. What I'm saying is that I've never been here before."

Tuesday came and draped an arm over his shoulder. "My girl takes a lot of pride in what she does—she's not just a dancer, she's more like an artist. So when you sit here and say you don't remember her performance, it's like an insult to her."

"No, I'm not trying to insult—"

Tuesday cut him off. "I think it's only one way to fix this. Doll, go hit the music. Jaye, make sure you give him something that he never forgets this time."

As Baby Doll headed for the deejay booth, Jaye gave Tuesday a look that said *Dirty bitch*. A few seconds later Trey Songz exploded out the system with deafening bass. While Jaye slowly began to move to the rhythm, Tuesday sat Bates in a chair so he could watch her more comfortably.

Bates's eyes got wide as Jaye began to strip out of her shirt and

Dresden was locked in too, just as Tuesday had hoped. He was so focused on Jaye's slow and seductive movements that Tuesday was able to slip out her phone and send a text to Face telling him to meet DelRay at the Home Depot down the block. Then she sent one to the bouncer telling him what the plan was.

Face must've been close by because he called back two minutes later, and luckily the music was so loud that only she heard the phone. By then Jaye had come out of her jeans and Dresden was so entranced with how she moved in the purple boy shorts that he didn't even notice Tuesday slip away to take the call. She went inside the deejay booth and ducked low behind the equipment.

"Bitch, is you crazy!!" were the first words Face said when she answered.

"Where you at?" she asked with her hand cupped over the phone to muffle her voice and drown out the music.

"I'm standing down the street with two of my people and yo mans right now, looking at the hook parked outside yo joint. You got the po-po on deck and yo boy talking 'bout you want us to sneak through the back door? Bitch, you out your mind!"

"Don't worry 'bout that. We gone keep these niggas busy and they ain't gone never see y'all. You and DelRay just gotta hurry up and make y'all move!"

Face explained something to her. "I don't know if you know the law but that's called 'Accessory to Murder After the Fact' and that shit carry as much time as killing a nigga. Tuesday, you my girl, and I hate to leave you hanging, but I'm not about to get a hundred years fucking with you!"

For fear that Dresden would notice she was gone, Tuesday quickly explained to him that they were close to taking down a major D-boy for nothing less than seven figures and offered him a hundred grand if he helped her out. Doubtful, Face fired a whole bunch of questions about the lick but Tuesday convinced him that she was on the level, and that they could pull this off without getting caught.

"Face, trust me, this is my bread and butter," she said, speaking urgently. "I know how to keep a man's attention focused on me. Pull up in the alley round back. We gone dance and put on for these niggas while y'all creep through the fire door and take the shit up outta here. But you gotta hurry up, though."

Face was quiet for a long moment and Tuesday peeked over the counter to make sure that Dresden was still watching Jaye and not looking for her.

Finally Face said, "I want three hundred G's and the CTS! And tell yo girl Brianna since this is all her fault, I'm gone need that Camaro too."

Tuesday exploded. "Three hundred racks and two cars! God-damn, nigga, you shittin' on me!"

"Look at what the fuck you asking me to do!" he fired back. "Three hundred ain't shit if y'all 'bout to hit for what y'all say. That's what it is or I can bust up right now and leave you to deal with the problem yo'self."

Tuesday didn't have the time nor was she in the position to ne-gotiate with him and Face knew it. Brianna's bullshit was gonna cost her three hundred stacks and her whip, and that's assuming they got away with it. If they got caught, it might cost all of them the rest of their lives in prison.

"All right, nigga!" she said, biting down hard on her lip. "Just hurry the fuck up!"

She got off the phone just as Gucci's song was going off. She put on a mix tape full of club shit that the girls could get loose to, then went back and joined the others.

Everybody was still standing around watching Jaye and it was obvious that Dresden hadn't even peeped she'd left until she switched songs. She pushed him into a chair and started dancing for him, then shot looks to Brianna and Baby Doll telling them to get in on the act. They paired off, with Brianna taking Bates with Jaye while hazel-eyed Doll partnered up with Tuesday to enter-tain Dresden. Within minutes all four girls were down to their bras and panties—Tuesday was just glad that she happened to have on a matching set.

Square-ass Bates had his eyes and mouth wide open looking like a kid who was sneaking to watch his first porno. As much as Brianna tried to push her big titties into his face, he was still more into Jaye than he was her.

Dresden's attention ping-ponged back and forth between Tuesday and Baby Doll's thick, pretty bodies. The same type of bodies that the racist bastard claimed disgusted him so much had him mesmerized like cartoons did children. As they danced on either side of him, he had a hand running up and down each one's inner thighs.

Tuesday had made sure that Bates was seated in a spot that didn't give him a direct line of sight down the hall with the rear exit or the changing room. Not that it mattered—he was too hypnotized by Jaye's gyrating body to notice even if the entire roof was peeled off the club.

Tuesday was most concerned about Dresden, but she knew how to deal with him. She waved off Baby Doll to go triple-team Bates while she took Dresden by the hand and led him to her office. Not only would this make sure that he didn't see Face and DelRay, but it would also let them talk in private.

Only Dresden caught her off guard, because the second she pulled the door closed, he slapped Tuesday hard across the face. Then before she could respond, he pinned her to the wall with a hand on her throat.

"I don't know what this little dog-and-pony show you're pulling on Bates is all about, but don't think that I'm stupid enough to buy into this bullshit. Just tell me what the hell happened here last night and thank your ugly black ass I was on duty when the call came in at the station."

Tuesday's gray eyes were beaming hatred. "It's nothing!" she spat through clenched teeth. "Two guys got into it, one of 'em pulled a gun. Nobody got hurt."

He looked skeptical. "Well, if nothing happened, then how come your little team of sluts is out there throwing their tits in my partner's face?"

Tuesday sighed and let some of the anger melt from her face. "We've got a couple guns here and a little bit of weed. I didn't know what the deal was with yo mans. He looks like the Super-cop type!"

"He is!" Dresden said, letting go of her neck. "But as you can see, he's also gullible as fuck! Just like every other nigger I've ever worked with, show him a little bit of skin and one of your fat jungle asses and their brains turn to mush. It's pathetic."

She didn't bother to remind him that he never took his eyes off Jaye either. Tuesday didn't let all this Klan bullshit faze her because she'd heard it so much that she was immune to it.

Tuesday stood there rubbing her cheek standing in almost the same spot where she'd smacked up Brianna several hours earlier. Karma *was* a bitch and it was the second time since last night that she had seen it come back on her.

"So if I turn this place upside down, all I'm gonna find is a few guns and some marijuana? Nothing else?"

She shook her head. "I never do dirt in the same place where I eat, sleep, or get my money!"

The dirty lieutenant seemed satisfied with her answer. He went behind Tuesday's desk and flopped down hard in her favorite chair. When he realized how comfortable it was and how perfectly it supported his back, he looked it over then gave her a thumbs-up. "Nice."

Tuesday smiled to hide how pissed she was that he was sitting there, but she needed to keep him in her office a while longer to give Face and DelRay enough time to take out the trash. Basically just trying to stall, she said, "I know it's early but if you want, I can run out to the bar and get you a drink or something."

"Never while I'm on duty." Dresden smirked at her and beneath the veneer of his Nordic good looks Tuesday saw something with reptilian ugliness. "But after watching your little performance out there, I'm actually more interested in giving you a drink!"

He unzipped his pants and summoned her with a finger. Tuesday rolled her eyes because once again she was going to have to take one for the team.

She came around to his side of the desk and got to her knees.

It sickened Tuesday to give him head but worse was the fact that she had to purposely go slow just to keep him in there longer.

But just like always, Dresden was too quick on the trigger. Even though the technique she used was designed to make a man last, he still busted way too soon. He then spent a little while leaned back in her chair with his eyes closed, either resting or just enjoying the moment.

Tuesday kept a toothbrush in her bag and immediately rinsed his taste out of her mouth with a mini tube of Colgate and bottled water.

She had hoped to keep him occupied for at least a half an hour but it wasn't fifteen minutes before they came from her office. Tuesday could only hope that they had already come and were gone but knew it didn't leave them with much of a window.

They surprised Detective Bates, who was out there bent over a table in plaid boxers with his pants dropped around his ankles while Jaye and Brianna took turns spanking him with a belt. When he saw his superior officer, he quickly yanked up his slacks and took his tie back from Baby Doll, who was wearing it around her scalp like a headband.

Dresden looked at him steely-eyed. "Detective, let's go. We're done here!"

Jaye had already confirmed with a subtle nod that the boys had come and were gone with the body. Tuesday should've been re-lieved to see the cops go, but after everything she'd gone through and what this little stunt was going to cost her, she actually wanted them to search the club. At least that way she would feel like Face truly earned his money.

"So that's it?" Tuesday asked with a note of resentment that the girls couldn't understand. "You don't need to see anything else?"

Bates looked to Dresden, who gave Tuesday a dry smile. "Naw. I think I'm pretty satisfied."

Tuesday followed the big white boy to the door shooting daggers at the back of his head all the way until he climbed into the unmarked squad car and pulled out of the lot.

DelRay showed up in her Caddy a minute later; then Face and two fiends were right behind him in a nondescript blue Ford panel van that had Tank in the back zipped up in a body bag. He left the strangers in the van when he got out to greet her at the door.

He smiled. "I ain't gone lie, I was kinda shook. I ain't never tried no shit like that, but you pulled it off. I promise to never doubt your skills again."

Face looked her up and down and the smile grew wider when he noticed she was only wearing a bra and thong set. "Damn, girl, I can only imagine what went down in your office to keep that nigga busy!"

Tuesday shot him an icy stare but didn't respond. She turned away from the door to go back inside and Face followed with his eyes bouncing from her ass to her feet the entire way.

Jaye, Brianna, and Baby Doll had already started to get dressed but Tuesday didn't bother. She went behind the bar for more cranberry juice but this time she spiked it with vodka.

Face said, "It's kinda early to be going in like that."

Tuesday gave him another *Fuck you* look then turned up her glass.

DelRay came in behind Face carrying the Coney Island that had now grown cold. Tuesday didn't care because when he set the bags on the bar, she immediately snatched out a burger and attacked it. The girls gathered around taking out burgers, onion rings, and fries soaked with cheesy chili, but the others opted to heat theirs up first using the tiny microwave behind the bar.

"This been a helluva muthafuckin' night," DelRay said, unwrapping a cheeseburger he was too impatient to warm up. "Y'all don't pay me enough to do this type of shit!"

"They sure in the hell paying me enough!" Face said, still beaming a smile.

The girls had never met him before, and of the trio, Brianna was the only one who seemed openly put off by his acne scars. She stared at him, repulsed, as she said, "I don't know what for. It ain't like you did nothing! DelRay and them fiends the ones who carried 'em out. Plus, they didn't even go back there to look around anyway!"

His smile never wavered. "And that don't mean shit to me, bitch!" He held out his hand. "And while we at it, I'll be taking those keys now."

Her eyes went wide. "What keys?" She looked to Tuesday. "What the fuck is he talking about?"

"The keys to that 'Maro!" Face said, making the gimme motion with his hand. "Come on in wit 'em."

"Nigga, you got me fucked up! You betta get your ugly ass out my face and go see a dermatologist!"

That remark finally killed his smile. "Ah, Tuesday. Tell yo girl I ain't the nigga to be playing with. The whip is mine—that's already a done deal."

Tuesday confirmed it with a nod. "I had to promise it to him, Bree. It was the only way he would help us."

She was still mugging him, hesitant to turn over her keys, but there was a hard look in his eye that made her believe he was not to be tested. Brianna knew that she really didn't want a problem with a nigga who was in the business of making people disappear. She smashed the keys into his hand. "I'm just gone report it stolen!"

"Don't matter," Face said, dropping them into his pocket. "In three days it's gone have brand-new paperwork, VIN numbers and everything. I'm giving it to my nephew as a graduation present in two weeks."

"And on that note. I hate to do it but—" He reached his hand out for Tuesday's keys. They all gazed at her in disbelief because everybody knew how she felt about the Caddy.

She nodded to DelRay and he dropped the keys into Face's palm.

Face noticed that she hadn't spoken to him the entire time and knew that the silent treatment was about more than him getting down on her. "TK, what's up with you?"

She chased a bite of her burger with another swallow of vodka and cranberry juice. "What's gonna happen to ol' boy?"

Face explained. "Well, in about an hour he's gonna be in the trunk of a '76 Buick LeSabre that's getting crushed to the size of a three-foot cube. Four hours later that cube along with sixty others are gonna be on a flatbed headed for a landfill in Arizona. Ain't no way this gone get traced back to you—or me, for that matter."

For Tuesday that was good to know, but she really wasn't concerned about a connection being made between her and Tank. "I don't want you to crush him or send him to Arizona. I want you to put him on ice for a couple days then put him where I tell you."

"Put him on ice?" Face looked at her like she was crazy. "Whoa, baby, I ain't running a funeral home or a mortuary service here! I get rid of niggas, not keep them in storage."

"Do this and you can add another hundred racks to my bill!"

This shocked everybody standing around including Face, who nervously rubbed his bald head. "All right. I don't know what you got up but I'm not sitting on him for longer than three days. Y'all just better make sure to pull off this lick and get all this money y'all owing me!"

After parting words, Face left them to their breakfast. One of his fiends drove the van, he took the CTS and Brianna watched with teary eyes as the second fiend pulled off in her Camaro.

Jaye went and fetched Tuesday's clothes even though she didn't ask for them. As she dressed, they all sat around the bar eating while secretly trying to figure out what was on her mind.

Tuesday was quiet because all she thought about was getting this money then getting the fuck away from Detroit and this life for good.

But before she left, she was going to stick some serious dick to Dresden for all the times he stuck it to her.

Chapter Fourteen

Once they did a little more cleaning and aired out the changing room to get rid of the smell, they locked up the club and everybody started to go their separate ways. Baby Doll caught a ride with DelRay, who joked that it would either cost her gas money or head; and while Doll swore to not having any cash on her, she still jumped into the passenger seat of his old Monte Carlo. Brianna called one of her male friends and within minutes some nigga in a new CLS showed up to get her. She wanted Tuesday to be jealous and made sure to throw her a look as she strutted out to his burgundy Benz. Tuesday was ready to take a cab home but when Jaye offered to drop her off, she thought long and hard before she accepted.

When they pulled up to the front of her building, Jaye seemed impressed by the gleaming waterfront tower. Just from seeing the outside she could tell that the condos were plush and you had to have your money right to live there.

She said, "I always thought you had some low-key apartment out in the suburbs."

Tuesday gave a suspicious look as she unclasped her seat belt.

"That's because I plays my shit like the Bat Cave. Only me, Robin, and Alfred know where this bitch at, and I like to keep it that way."

Jaye got the message and dapped her up when Tuesday offered her fist. "I got you, Boss Lady. I ain't the bitch to be putting yo business out there."

They had parting words and Tuesday got upstairs around eight a.m. with plans to sleep until eight p.m. After quickly going through the series of rituals required for just coming home, she fell across her bed fully dressed and was out before she kicked off her shoes.

The plan had been for twelve hours of sleep but she only managed closer to seven. She woke up around three p.m. with crusty eyes, a dry mouth, and in need of a shower. She spent fifteen minutes standing under scalding hot water and when she toweled off, as usual, Nicholas the cat was perched on a nearby windowsill to watch her lotion up.

She got dressed then checked her phone and was relieved to see two missed calls from Tushie. Not hearing from her girl in so long worried her, especially when she was spending so much time with this new nigga that Tuesday hadn't met.

She gave Tushie a call and spent half an hour putting her up on the craziness that happened at The Bounce. Of course, she didn't go into the details over the phone, but using a bunch of code words and slang, Tushie was able to get the gist of the story.

After the unpleasant news, the girls switched to brighter topics. Tushie gushed about De'Lano and, without even realizing she was doing it, Tuesday gushed a lot more about the time she had on her date last night. She told Tushie about the fun they had and the games they played and how he'd won her a big stuffed giraffe. She bragged about how well she handled herself around all those messy, screaming kids and how much Danielle liked her.

As Tuesday blabbed, her girl was quiet on the other end and there was a tension in the silence that she eventually picked up on. "Tush, what's up?"

"Nuthin', I'm jus listenin' ta you," she answered. "I ain't neva heard you talk like dat about a mark befo. In fact, I ain't neva heard you talk like dat 'bout no nigga! You still on game, right?"

Tuesday looked confused like some malfunction with her phone service was causing Tushie's words to come through in Chinese. "Bitch, I ain't never off game! What do you even mean by that?"

Tushie was quiet for a moment. She was never one to bite her tongue, but she wanted to choose her words carefully. "It's jus tha way you talkin' 'bout dat nigga, it sound like you really feelin' 'em. Then I know dat shit wit A.D. got you hurt and kinda vulnerable and I jus wanna make sho you ain't slippin'."

Tuesday got offended because her best friend was basically accusing her of breaking Rule One; the cardinal rule, the first and most important thing that was stressed to each new chick who joined the team, the same law that she herself had drilled into Tushie years back when she first got down: *You don't ever catch feelings!* It doesn't matter how fine a mark is, how good he can fuck, or how much he spoils her, the girl baiting him is never supposed to develop an emotional attachment. The lick is more important than the dick; her loyalty should always be to the team and the cream.

Tuesday said, "Bitch, are you forgetting that I'm the one who taught you the game?"

"I ain't neva forgot dat, my nigga! And you taught me well, dat's why I'm sayin' what I said. You can fool dem otha bitches, but I know you betta than dat—you lonely and you been lonely for a minute. Seeing dat nigga wit dat li'l girl make it easy to start dreamin' 'bout playin house."

Tuesday smacked her lips. "I know you ain't talkin'! You ain't known this De'Lano nigga two weeks and you ready to jump a damn broom."

"A bitch can't lie. I am fallin' pretty fast, but then again, I ain't the one on a mission either. It would be different if we was takin' a look at dis nigga, but dis my personal life. If I was workin' his ass, I would be on my shit sniffin' out dat bread!"

Tuesday snapped. "Oh, so now a bitch ain't on her shit! The same way you ain't been on yo shit lately. Wasn't you s'posed to be working last night when all this dumb shit happened? We needed you then, and I needed you to help wit the mission yesterday, but you wasn't around. It's like Jaye been coming through for me more than you. Got me wondering why I'm even fuckin' with you in the first place!"

Those were harsh words and Tuesday regretted them the instant they slipped out. People used to say "pause" after they said some fucked-up shit but right then Tuesday wished she had buttons to pause and rewind. If only she could suck the words back in the way you could blow a bubble then pull the gum back into your mouth. But she couldn't do that. All she could do was listen to the silence Tushie was giving her from the other end as both girls dealt with what was said and how each of them felt about it.

Tushie's voice was a lot softer and very sincere when she finally spoke: "Look, I know I been MIA for tha last couple of days, but don't let dat take away from all tha years I been holdin' shit down.

"Yeah, I been spendin' a lot of time wit dis nigga but dat's jus because it feels so good. I don't jus mean tha sex and goin' out ta eat; it feel good jus bein' able ta be real wit somebody. I'm tired of all dis manipulating and game-playin' wit niggas. I know dat's what we do but it feel good to be able ta be yo'self around a man, and to know dat tha person he feelin' is really *YOU* and not some fuckin' character you playin'! I been needin' this shit!"

Tuesday nodded solemnly as if Tushie could see her through the phone. She knew what her girl was talking about because A.D. was the only nigga she had that she could be real with. Even though it was only for a few hours at a time in a prison visiting room, Tuesday had appreciated having that and was really missing it.

Tushie continued, "TK, I got mo love and respect fo you than any bitch out here, and I ain't tryin' ta come at you sideways. I jus don't wanna see you get hurt cuz you ain't on yo shit. Don't forget fo one minute who we might be dealin' wit and what he can do!"

Tuesday was then able to appreciate that this was concern coming from a loving place.

"Tush, believe me, I'm still focused. And after this morning, I owe Face so much cake that I *gotta* make this happen. I'm locked in now, I don't got no other out. Plus, it's gone take a lot more than one night at Chuck E. Cheese and a big stuffed animal to take me off game."

Tushie enjoyed hearing that from Tuesday because as much as Sebastian Caine had a reputation for being smart and elusive, he also had one for being ruthless.

They talked a while longer and after a few minutes it was like that brief awkward moment never happened. They were setting up a date for her to be introduced to De'Lano when Tuesday's other phone rang. She told Tushie what the deal was and got off the phone with her so she could talk to Marcus.

"Get dat money to tha house, bitch!!" was the last thing Tushie said before she clicked off the line.

Tuesday dropped that phone and put the other one to her ear when he started in without small talk. "Look, I know this is incredibly short notice, but I've got a business dinner tonight and I need a date. I need to show up with somebody who's beautiful enough to turn heads, intelligent enough for great conversation, and classy enough not to embarrass me. But since I couldn't find anybody like that, I thought I'd ask you!"

Tuesday laughed so hard that her eyes began to tear up. She always liked men with a sense of humor who weren't afraid to bullshit around with her. Most niggas were too intimidated by Tuesday's looks to slip her like that because they assumed she was so stuck up and insecure that the jokes would offend her.

"And what makes you think I would go out with you again after the shitty time I had last night?"

He laughed now. "Because the band won't be playing 'Knick

Knack Paddy Whack' and all the guys trying to peek up your skirt will be grown this time."

"Wow, horny old guys instead of horny twelve-year-olds, how can I say no to that!"

"Well, if you gimme your address, I'll be to scoop you around six."

Tuesday gave him the address to the apartment on 8 Mile then checked her watch to see that she only had two hours to be there dressed and ready.

Dressed! She had no idea of what she was going to wear. While still on the phone, she sprinted into the walk-in closet to consider her options.

"And don't start trippin' about what you're gonna wear cause I got you," he said, reading her mind again. "I figured I owed you that much after I made you waste that sexy dress last night."

"You damn right you do! But what if you don't get my size right? And what if you pick out something I'm just not feeling?"

"Tabitha, trust me, you'll have a few choices. And as far as your size, you ain't the first girl I ever dated who had a little bit of ass."

"A little bit?" she snapped.

"All right, a lot of ass!"

"That's better."

"Still sniffing out those compliments any place you can get 'em, huh?"

"Always."

"Well, just make sure you're ready when I come at six because our flight's at seven."

"Flight?" Tuesday wasn't sure she heard him correctly.

"Yeah, flight!" he reiterated.

"You mind telling me where we're flying to?"

"Cali," he said nonchalantly. "Dinner's in L.A."

Tuesday wished she could've got something done to her hair, but just like the day before, he didn't give her much notice. All she had time to do was pack an overnight bag (since she assumed they wouldn't be back the same evening) and mash the Honda over to the Town Square apartment that she was using as a front.

She only had to hang out there for twenty minutes watching from her window before he showed. When his Audi pulled in front of her building, she hurried downstairs to meet him outside. She couldn't let him come to the door of her unit because there was no way to explain why her apartment was totally empty.

When she climbed into the passenger seat, she was a little surprised, but not disappointed, to see Danielle strapped in the back. She gave Tuesday an energetic wave, and she beamed a smile back at the girl. "Hi, Dani."

"Hi, Tabitha," she said, covering her mouth in that shy way that Tuesday thought was so cute.

She looked at Marcus, who was dressed in black jeans, a black T-shirt, and black fitted cap. "Oh, so you feelin' like a gangsta today, huh?"

"I never feel like a gangsta!" He checked his mirrors then pulled away from the complex. "If you think back on every movie you ever seen, gangstas always wind up dead or in jail." He smiled at Tuesday. "And I'm too young and handsome to wind up in either of those situations."

She said, "You ain't that young."

"Or that handsome!" Danielle chimed from the backseat and he reached an arm behind him to tickle her.

Tuesday wondered what type of business he could have in Los Angeles, but figured it couldn't be too dangerous if he was bringing Danielle along. She didn't see him as the type to be exchanging briefcases in an abandoned warehouse; Caine was too polished for that. So even if he was doing something illegal, she imagined that it would probably look legit on the surface.

The fact that he even brought her along on a business trip was progress for Tuesday. Getting closer to his business meant that she was getting closer to the money. She hoped that all his business wasn't out in California and that he had something put up in Michigan that she and the girls could get to.

When they arrived at Metro Airport, Tuesday wondered if they were flying first class or if he was going to keep trying to play the broke role. They left the Audi and the moment they hit the front door, they were immediately met by an attendant who'd been waiting to escort them. Tuesday couldn't believe it when she, he, and Danielle were ushered past the tedious gauntlet of airport security straight through a rear door that led to a hangar. Inside more attendants were waiting to take their bags and they placed them in the storage compartment of the private jet.

While Marcus shook hands with somebody who she guessed was the pilot, Tuesday looked over the gleaming white bird. This plane was like something she'd seen in a rap video and she couldn't help but wonder who he knew to get access to it. There was a logo on the side that read *Abel Inc.,* and Tuesday tried but couldn't guess how he might be affiliated with that corporation.

When Marcus was done chatting up the pilot, they were allowed to board. Tuesday couldn't believe how plush it was inside. The G-650 was the largest and most expensive model in the Gulfstream series. The cabin was large enough to allow a man of average height to walk fully erect and spacious enough to seat fourteen comfortably in fat leather recliners with eighteen-inch monitors that folded out of the armrests. The woodwork was done in dark maple with gold trim and some of the chairs were arranged around tables of the same grain. Beyond the passenger cabin was a small galley stocked with food and amenities. Beyond that was a modest suite with a full-sized bed and a bathroom with a shower. It was essentially a condo with wings.

As overwhelmed as Tuesday was, Danielle didn't seem too impressed. She climbed into one of the big cushy chairs and strapped herself in without having to be told or taught how. Evidently he traveled with her enough for this to be routine.

He strapped himself into a seat next to Tuesday and put a hand on top of hers. "You look nervous. You're not scared to fly, are you?"

"A little bit," she lied. The nervousness in her gut was more directed toward him than the flight because for the first time since meeting him, he actually *felt* like the real Sebastian Caine. This was how a real kingpin got around.

There were two pilots and a single flight attendant to attend to the passengers. She was a black woman in her mid-forties who made sure all of their belts were securely fastened before she took her own seat.

The jet taxied from the hangar to the tarmac, then after a brief announcement about the weather and flight time, they were off to sunnier shores.

Once they reached cruising altitude and were free to move around, Marcus immediately excused himself and disappeared in the back.

The flight attendant came around to see if she wanted anything and Tuesday asked only for water. Little Danielle wanted nothing; she was content with the headphones and *Dora the Explorer* on the screen in front of her.

Tuesday was half finished with her bottle of Evian when Marcus reappeared in different clothes. He was bossed up now in a navy-blue Ralph Lauren suit, a white shirt, and yellow paisley tie with the matching pocket square. He was playing it with some sweet-ass horn-rimmed frames by Tom Ford that looked to be prescription and not merely for show, and black ostrich-skin Mauris.

He brought out his ice game too because his cufflinks were diamond blocks the size of Now and Later candies. The six-karat studs in his ears were bigger than M&M's.

When he sat down, Tuesday couldn't take her eyes off him or close her gaping mouth. Soaking up this new swag convinced her that this was the real him and the Audi-driving babysitter was just a facade.

He looked over at Tuesday and pretended not to notice the "God damn!" look on her face. "You don't have to get changed right now if you don't want to. We've still got about two and a half hours before we get to L.A."

He confirmed the time by checking a platinum Greubel Forsey

Quadruple Tourbillion that Tuesday had seen in the *Robb Report Watch Buyer's Guide* costing over half a million. It was a big boy's watch, but he glanced at it then pulled his sleeve back over it as if he was just rocking a Timex. The fact that he wasn't trying to floss or stunt with it told her that he wasn't petty and was used to having nice shit.

"Huh? What?" Tuesday was so mesmerized that she hardly caught what he said.

"I was just letting you know that you can go get dressed now if you want. Everything's already set up back there."

Tuesday went to the rear of the plane, and inside the suite found three dresses hanging on a wardrobe rack with a different shoebox from Marc Jacob for each one. He had even thought to buy stockings.

She took all three, laid them across the bed, then zipped them out of their protective slips. Tuesday was beaming ear to ear because the nigga definitely knew his shit when it came to fashion.

The first was a floral-print dress by Oscar de la Renta made of Chinese silk, and while Tuesday thought it was fly, along with the shoes he had chosen with it, they didn't fit well together. The second one was a Vera Wang gown that was strapless with an intricate lace bodice. Tuesday thought that was pretty too, but it had a deeply plunging neckline and she didn't want to spend the entire night trying to make sure her titties didn't fall out. She passed on that one as well.

Tuesday literally struck gold with the third one. It was a gold chiffon backless gown by Rachel Zoe that was ankle-length with a slit running up the side to show off her legs. Tuesday liked that the fabric was light and clung to her body. Plus it was clasped at the neck and showed just enough cleavage. Although it came with an Hermès clutch that she was feeling, she wasn't too crazy about the shoes. She swapped them out with the Jacobs from the first dress and knew she had her look.

When she came from the back, the flight attendant in the galley was the first to see her. She gave her smile of approval but stopped

Tuesday before she could present herself to Marcus. "You look beautiful, girl, but there's only one problem. With a dress like that, the hair is supposed to be worn up."

Tuesday agreed. "I know, but this all happened so fast that I didn't have time to get it done."

"Don't worry," she said, pulling Tuesday back toward the bathroom. "I worked in a salon for five years before I started doing this. Now I ain't got no irons or weave on board, but with a comb and a couple of hairpins I can get you right."

And a few minutes later Tuesday was right. Her hair was pinned up in back; she combed aside the bangs covering her forehead and had two longer strands spiraling on either side of her face. The flight attendant even had a small makeup kit and gave Tuesday some eye shadow that matched the dress. She did so well on her face and hair that Tuesday jokingly asked if she knew anything about doing nails.

As they both stood admiring her reflection in the mirror, the flight attendant said: "Girl, I don't know how you pulled it off, but Mr. King must really like you. I've been working for his family for years and you're the first woman I've seen him with in a long time."

Tuesday was confused. "King?"

"Yeah, Marcus King!" she said, looking at Tuesday as if she were slow. "The man you're with. Whose private jet you're standing on. The one who bought that six-thousand-dollar dress you're wearing."

Tuesday tried to play if off like she always knew his name. "Naw, I just thought you said Bing. Like Dave Bing, the mayor of Detroit."

She said, "Well, between me and you, I'd take fine-ass King over Bing any day!"

Tuesday smiled to agree.

She leaned closer and whispered into Tuesday's ear, "And it don't hurt that his family's worth like six hundred million dollars either."

Tuesday's eyes almost exploded from her skull. *"Six hundred million!"*

She figured the woman had to be lying or overexaggerating. She knew Marcus had to have some money stashed from all his years in the dope game but that was a ridiculous number. Plus, how could this flight attendant possibly know what he was working with when he made it his business to keep so much on the low?

"What makes you think he has money like that?" Tuesday asked nonchalantly, trying not to sound like a gold-digger.

The woman looked at Tuesday as if what she said were common knowledge. "You don't know who he is, do you?"

No, you don't know who he really is, Tuesday thought to herself.

"He's Marcus King!" she said as if the name alone should explain it all. "Son of Brandon King."

The woman was speaking as if these names should be familiar to her. Tuesday knew it would look bad if she didn't know the first thing about the man who had brought her here and done all this for her so she just played it off. "Oh yeah, I just didn't know he was *that* Marcus King."

This nigga wasn't just secretive, he was a full-blown mystery. The more Tuesday learned about him, the less she understood.

When Tuesday finally made her appearance, Danielle was taking a break from her cartoons. "Wow, Tabitha, you look like a princess. Just like Ariel in *The Little Mermaid*."

"Thank you, Dani."

When she sat down next to Marcus, he offered his approval with a smile. "I was kinda hoping you picked that one."

"Why, because it shows the most skin?"

"That and because it goes best with these." He pulled out a jewelry box and passed it to her.

Tuesday opened it to reveal a set of diamond earrings. Each had a trio of six-karat stones with icicles hanging from them like chandeliers. She'd never seen anything so exquisite nor diamonds so flawless. The dress, the shoes, and now this. Tuesday was starting to feel like Julia Roberts in *Pretty Woman*.

As bad as she wanted the earrings, she knew it would score major points with him if she refused them.

"I can't accept these," she said, pushing the box back into his hand. "Those look really expensive. It's too much too soon."

His eyebrows shot up. "First off, they *are* really expensive. Second, I never said anything about you being able to have them!"

Tuesday looked confused.

"They're on loan from Cartier and have to go back in a few days. I just thought you would look fabulous in them tonight."

She practically had to pick her face up off the floor.

"Tabitha, I like you but I'm not the type of dude who'll pop for three-hundred-thousand-dollar earrings on a woman I just met." He smiled at her to cushion the blow. "Even one as fine as you."

Tuesday accepted the jewelry box when he forced it back into her hand. She couldn't hide how embarrassed she felt just assuming he was giving them to her. She stared down at the set, and while they were mesmerizing, it was mostly to avoid his face.

He turned her head to meet his eyes. "Hey, don't get like that. Tonight is supposed to be about us doing it all grown up, and after how I played you last night, I just wanted you to look as fly as can be.

"And Tabitha, the fact that you turned them down says a lot more about your character than assuming they were yours to have. It takes a special type of woman to refuse a gift like that on principle. I admire you for that."

Wow, that was a first for Tuesday: having a man say that he admired her. All niggas complimented her on her looks and a few on her brains, but she couldn't remember one ever complimenting her character. Refusing the diamonds was a calculated move, one that she hoped would earn his respect, but she still felt moved by how he articulated that respect. She was touched but stayed on game and hid it well.

She hooked the icy earrings into her lobes, then turned to him. "How do they look?"

"Amazing!" Although he never looked away from her eyes to examine the jewelry.

Tuesday stared into his eyes and again felt herself becoming lost in them. The moment seemed perfect for a kiss, but after last night she didn't trust herself to stop, plus Danielle was sitting just across the aisle from them.

Luckily, the flight attendant interrupted them. "Champagne?" She had flutes of Dom Perignon for the two of them and some apple juice for Danielle, so she wouldn't feel left out.

The rest of the flight was so smooth that some minor turbulence was the only thing to remind Tuesday they were thirty thousand feet in the air. She would've loved to join the Mile High Club, but having Danielle with them, it didn't seem right to try to sneak off and get it in.

On their approach, Tuesday got to look out over the coastal skyline of Los Angeles, and when they landed at LAX, there was a car and driver already waiting for them just off the runway. Their things were transferred directly from the storage compartment of the G-650 to the trunk of a big black Rolls Royce.

Tuesday was not a bitch who was easily impressed or some broke-ass hoodrat who'd never been off the block and wasn't used to being around money. She knew heavyweights in the game and a few of them had taken her on trips before—once to Vegas and twice to Miami.

But Tuesday had never fucked with a nigga on his level. She had never in her life done it this big and couldn't keep it from getting to her head. As they drove through downtown L.A. in the backseat of the Phantom with Danielle sandwiched between them, Tuesday had her face pressed to the window wide-eyed as a schoolgirl on her first field trip. On Hollywood Boulevard Tuesday saw many of the famous landmarks she'd seen only in movies. On Rodeo they cruised past all the high-end stores like Gucci,

Bvlgari and Chanel, with her secretly hoping they would get a chance to hit a few of them.

From there they crept up into those famous hills that held some of the most expensive real estate in the world. Beyond high fences, statement homes made bold claims about their owners' wealth, and the longer they drove, the claims got more outrageous. Tuesday made a game of trying to guess which of her favorite celebrities might live in those lavish cribs.

Then the Rolls pulled through the gates of someone's estate, where beyond a quarter mile of manicured lawn and trimmed topiary, the driveway opened onto a Grecian mansion that was so expansive it seemed more like a hotel than a private residence. With fifteen-foot beveled windows and huge Greek columns supporting the portico, Tuesday thought it looked like the White House but on steroids.

For the most part Tuesday was just going along for the ride and not bothering Marcus with a lot of questions, but when gazing upon this beautiful white palace with the decorative nude statues, she couldn't resist the temptation to inquire about the people who were lucky enough to call such a place home.

"This is my father's house," he said after a hesitant pause. "We're just dropping Dani off here for the weekend."

She flashed back to their conversation last night. "I thought you said you grew up in Detroit?"

He nodded. "I did until I was about ten. Then I lived out here."

There was something in his voice that sounded as if he were embarrassed to admit that and for the life of her, Tuesday couldn't understand why. Her childhood had been spent with her mother, bouncing from one roach-infested flat to another, but here he was acting all ashamed to have been raised in a mansion that looked as big as the malls she couldn't afford to shop in until she was eighteen years old.

As the driver opened the door for them, they were greeted by a man who came from the house. He was an elderly brother, maybe in his mid-sixties, with a head full of salt-and-pepper curls. From the way he bounced down the front steps, Tuesday could tell that he still had some life left in him. Also from the way he caught Danielle when she sprinted to him and leapt into his arms.

"Grampy," she screamed as he picked her up and spun her around.

"Hey, Funny Face!" He covered her cheeks with kisses and Danielle giggled with delight.

Just then a trio of golden retrievers clamored through the doorway and surrounded her, sniffing, licking at her fingers with enthusiastic tails wagging. They were leaping playfully to compete for the girl's attention.

To Danielle he said, "Berta made cookies." And this was enough to send her scrambling into the house with the dogs on her heels.

As Marcus approached his father, Tuesday looked for a resemblance, but just like with him and Danielle, she didn't see one. He was a smaller man with brighter skin and a better grade of hair. Nothing besides the age difference could've marked them as father and son.

They had a brief hug that to Tuesday seemed very formal. It was a split-second embrace with a pat on the back. Everything about their body language told her that they weren't very close.

"You look good," father said to son. "So how are you?"

"I am good."

"Dani's just growing like a weed, huh?"

"Yeah, I gotta go clothes shopping for her every few days."

There was an awkward silence between them and Tuesday could tell that he introduced her merely to distract from it. "This is Tabitha Green. The friend I told you about."

"Brandon King." He surprised Tuesday when he took her hand and kissed it. That was some old-school player shit that niggas nowadays never did. It made her smile because he was the first guy that Tuesday ever met who was pushing seventy and could still get it.

"It's a pleasure to meet you, sir. You have a lovely home."

"Thank you. I'd be happy to give you a tour if you guys have time for it."

"We don't!" Marcus interrupted coldly. "We have eight o'-clock reservations for Mastro's and we're already cutting it close."

Tuesday wasn't used to being in another time zone. They had left Detroit at seven and after a three-hour flight had landed in Los Angeles at seven. She couldn't wrap her mind around the fact that it wasn't as late as it felt to her.

"Well, that's too bad," the father said with a disappointment that seemed to be more than just about the tour. "But I still need to talk to you." And after Marcus shot him a look, he added, "Just for a moment."

Marcus apologized to Tuesday and excused himself with a peck on the cheek. His father led him to the entrance of the house but they didn't step inside. He took him just far enough for Tuesday to be out of earshot.

Tuesday stood with the driver next to the Rolls. She gave him a nervous smile, trying not to feel too awkward. He opened the car door to suggest that she might be more comfortable waiting inside and Tuesday agreed.

While the Kings spoke, she didn't openly stare but did glance repeatedly at them. Even though it was his father who had asked for a minute, Marcus did most of the talking. There was an aggressive flair to his gestures that made Tuesday think he was either going off or barking instructions to him. The old man just nodded compliantly as the son used his fingers to enumerate a list of things that he either hated about him, or needed him to do.

When the discussion wrapped up, Brandon trailed Marcus back to the car where he received an overnight bag for Danielle. When Marcus climbed inside, his father stuck his head inside the window for parting words.

"It's all gonna happen pretty fast," he said. "So you need to be ready."

Tuesday didn't understand what that meant but did understand the impatient glare his son shot back before he signaled the chauffeur to pull off. As the car lunged forward, his father practically had to jump back not to have his feet run over.

Tuesday was shocked by how rudely he'd treated his old man but knew it wasn't her place to say anything. There was obviously some history at work that she didn't know about or understand.

There was actually a laundry list of things about all of this she didn't understand. Tuesday assumed that this whole "Marcus King" thing was just a front he was putting on, but if it was, he sure put a lot more into it than she had for Tabitha Green. All she had was a phone, some bogus ID, and an empty apartment; he had a daughter and a paid-ass father with whom he had issues. His character was so convincing that Tuesday was beginning to wonder if it really was a character at all. Even if Caine had legally changed his name, and raised the little girl to believe that he was really Marcus King, she couldn't see his father changing his name just to go along with the plot. Plus from the way the flight attendant talked about the Kings, their name was known, just not in the circles Tuesday moved in.

Another thing that bothered her was their wealth. Nobody outside of Colombian and Mexican cartels made six hundred million dollars from selling drugs. Even if he had a strong run and hustled hard for years without ever spending a dime, Tuesday couldn't see that. Marcus said he grew up in this house, which meant he was born into money, and the way the flight attendant said "son of Brandon King" seemed to confirm that the father was already caked up. Of course Daddy might be fucking with the game too, but you don't drop a fat-ass mansion in Beverly Hills and a private jet without having some way of cleaning up your money.

As the Phantom cruised down the driveway, Tuesday took a final look back at the plush white palace. She couldn't see how someone who grew up there could end up hustling in the D. It was obvious that his family had plenty of money and Marcus seemed too smart to do something that dangerous just to make a name for himself.

No matter how she looked at it, Marcus King and Sebastian Caine just didn't match up as one person. The more thought she gave it, the more she began to suspect that she and Dresden had both got it wrong. This wasn't her mark. This was just the rich son of a multimillionaire who, for some reason, was living low-key out in Romulus. She'd spent all this time barking up the wrong tree.

Chapter Fifteen

Mastro's was a high-end restaurant that was obviously a favorite of the Los Angeles affluent and Hollywood celebrities. Tuesday played it cool, carried herself like she'd been somewhere before. She didn't stare at the famous faces or pester anybody for an autograph. She didn't want to embarrass Marcus by acting like some starry-eyed groupie, but she told herself that if Dwyane Wade walked in, then all bets were off.

They had dinner with Marcus's accountant and his wife. The couple was about ten years older than them. Even though they were black, Tuesday could tell they were the type with absolutely no hood in them at all. Marcus spent most of dinner in whispered conversation with the man about business while huddled over a stack of paperwork he needed to sign. They were at the same table but in their own world. Through it all Tuesday tried to kick it with the wife, but she was so uptight and bougie that their conversation quickly dried up.

Tuesday didn't make it obvious but did her share of ear-hustling while the boys were talking. They were speaking low and the noise from the other diners prevented her from hearing everything, but she heard enough being mentioned about offshore accounts and shell corporations to peep that Marcus was moving around a lot of money. Millions on top of millions. He was preparing to make some big move that neither of them would speak about in detail.

Tuesday didn't know how to play it from here because she was more convinced than ever that not only was he not Sebastian Caine, he wasn't even a dope boy. He spoke about investments, assets, and liquidation like a Wall Street yuppie, and every document he signed was as Marcus King. Sure, he had money, but the girls usually only hit up niggas in the game. Plus, his money was tied up in securities, stocks, and municipal bonds, not safes, duffel bags, and burial stashes they could easily get at. The fact that they dealt in cash was another reason she preferred to rob drug dealers.

Tuesday considered shifting her role to play him as the high-maintenance girlfriend, but dude was so sharp that he would peep if she switched up on him after seeing his father's mansion and jet. Even if she could reel him in as a boyfriend, that didn't change the fact that she owed Face four hundred G's and couldn't see Marcus writing a check, no questions asked. Then, to top things off, she still had to remember that the feds were about to kick in his door any day, whether he was Caine or not. That didn't leave time to build the type of trusting relationship that gave her access to his bank accounts or safe deposit boxes.

Things must've gone well for Marcus because he was in a celebratory mood and took her to a swanky downtown nightclub called Red. The place was jumping and Tuesday saw as many celebrities there as she did at the restaurant. They partied up in their own VIP lounge with bottles of champagne. Tuesday couldn't remember the last time she'd been in a club that didn't have a girl dancing on a pole.

It took some time and a whole lot of drinks to get Marcus loose enough to dance. When he got up, she pulled him close and spent the next five songs grinding her ass into his crotch until he was bone-stiff.

After a few hours, they left Red with such a buzz that Tuesday was glad neither of them had to drive. There was more kissing, more touching in the car, and Tuesday thought it would have been so perfect for them to fuck right there in the backseat.

The only problem was that his square ass wasn't down. He was cool with kissing and playing with her body, but every time Tuesday tried for his zipper, he pushed her hand away.

He whispered in her ear, "Not here, but soon. Wait till we get there."

This made a drunk and horny Tuesday curse at the driver to hurry the fuck up.

She expected a hotel, so she couldn't believe it when they pulled back up to the airport. She figured he was about to fly her home just like that. They weren't going to spend one night in L.A.

When they got back on the jet, as much as she tried, Tuesday couldn't hide how disappointed she was. He only needed her to be arm candy for some dinner, and now that she'd done her part, he was dropping her back off? She felt used. She knew how crazy this was considering that she'd spent the last two weeks planning to rob and kill him, but couldn't help how she felt. She was gracious to the friendly flight attendant who had hooked up her hair and makeup but was cold toward Marcus.

"You all right?" he asked from the seat next to hers, noticing that she'd been somewhat withdrawn since they boarded and took off.

"I'm fine." It was said in a tone that every man who ever had a woman knew meant that she really wasn't.

She pulled off the diamond earrings, put them back into the jewelry box she kept in the Hermès clutch and passed it back to him. "Thank you for letting me wear 'em," she said without ever looking at him.

"You didn't have to take 'em off so soon. I kinda liked the way they looked on you."

"I forgot; this is yours too." She dropped the purse in his lap, then turned to face her window. "You can get back the dress and shoes when they say it's okay to get up and move around."

He looked at her, confused. "Tabitha, did I do something wrong?"

She shook her head. "You did exactly what you said you was gone do. You needed somebody to go to a business dinner with you and that's just what I did. Now it's over."

Marcus now understood why she was giving him attitude. He smiled as he reclined his chair. "Well, since you aren't gonna be pressed for conversation, do you mind if I take a little nap?"

Tuesday smacked her lips. "It's yo muthafuckin' plane! You can do whatever you want."

"Actually it's my father's, but I get your point."

He closed his eyes, and not too long after that, the champagne, the stretched day with the extra three hours, along with the cushy leather chairs, all began to take their toll on Tuesday as well.

She dozed off trying to understand why exactly she was so mad at him.

Tuesday didn't feel as if she'd slept long but constantly switching time zones had her internal clock all screwed up. The windows on the G-650 were all lit up from the day outside and sunbeams filtered into the cabin through the ones on the port side. Along with light, the cabin was also filled with the smell of breakfast.

Tuesday had that brief moment of confusion that we all get when waking up in an unfamiliar place. It panicked her a little bit too when she looked over and saw that Marcus was gone.

Just then the flight attendant wheeled in a cart, which was the source of that delicious aroma. Scrambled eggs and a few strips of bacon accompanied a fat Belgian waffle with strawberries. There was a large glass of orange juice to wash it down along with a mug filled with black coffee.

The flight attendant said, "I don't mean to rush you but you may want to hurry. You only have a few minutes before we land and the tray has to be put away before we start our descent."

"And where exactly are we about to land?" asked Tuesday. "The trip coming from Detroit didn't take this long."

The woman just gave her a mischievous smile before heading back to the galley.

Tuesday was half finished with breakfast when Marcus finally appeared from the back. He had changed into a white Polo shirt with long shorts that were blue, and crisp white Gucci sneakers.

He said, "Hey, stranger, still not talking to me?"

"Where are you taking me?" Tuesday tried her best to make it sound like she still had an attitude even though she wasn't mad anymore.

He slid into the seat next to hers. "Well, for now just consider yourself kidnapped."

"My people will never meet your demands. They have been instructed never to negotiate with terrorists."

"I guess that means I get to keep you and do whatever I want." He reached over and stole a strawberry from her plate and she made a motion as if to stab him with her fork.

"Why don't you get your own?"

"I already ate while you were still sleeping." He pecked her on the cheek. "You're beautiful, but you snore."

Tuesday playfully punched his arm. "Is this the type of mental abuse you put all of your hostages through?"

He laughed. "I haven't even started abusing you yet."

Tuesday finished her breakfast just as the flight attendant came to collect her serving cart. She returned it to the galley and the captain announced for them to fasten their seat belts because they were starting their descent.

Tuesday kept pestering him about their destination until he finally told her to look out her window. Peering down through the clouds, she saw a group of four large islands surrounded by a bunch of smaller ones that looked like gumdrops from that height.

She turned to him. "Wow, Detroit sure looks different when you see it from up here," she said, joking.

"Baby, that's the Caribbean Sea you lookin' at down there, not Lake Ontario. That ain't Belle Isle either. Welcome to the BVIs— the British Virgin Islands. I thought you might be down for a quick tropical getaway."

"Virgin Islands, huh?" She smiled. "Sounds like the perfect place for a girl like me."

He gave her a *yeah, right* look. "Well, if you're a virgin when we get there, I promise you won't be one by the time we leave."

Tuesday gave him a sly smile. "Don't make promises you ain't gone keep!"

They landed in Road Town on the main island, Tortola, and did a little shopping for clothes better suited for the tropical weather. He laced her up with some sundresses, sandals, and a few swimsuits for the beach, then hit a couple more stores in the district picking up miscellaneous supplies they might need. Tuesday soaked up the sights and culture, still amazed by the fact that just hours ago they were half a world away.

From Road Town they took a chartered helicopter to Peter Island, which was the largest of the private islands. The Peter Island Resort was world-renowned for its luxurious accommodations and indulgent staff, but mostly for its seclusion. Being a privately owned island meant there were no people other than those staying at the resort and the staff operating it. As a rule they never booked more than one hundred guests at a time so couples would have no trouble finding privacy within its twenty-five hundred acres. In addition to hotel rooms, the Peter Island Resort also offered beachfront villas, of which the Crow's and Falcon's Nest were the two most elegant—and expensive.

The Falcon's Nest had been reserved by Marcus. As the attendant showed them around, Tuesday tried not to look so gassed up but couldn't help it. The villa was plush, the decor impeccable, and it was all surrounded by floor to ceiling windows with killer views of White Bay Beach and the Caribbean Sea. Boasting twenty thousand square feet of living space, an infinity pool with Jacuzzi, and its own personal stretch of beach, it was like having their own private mansion set on their own private island.

After they got settled in, Tuesday changed out of her evening dress into a blue-and-yellow two-piece that definitely wasn't designed for her body type. The top fit fine, but she was practically bursting out of the bottoms. When she came out and modeled it for Marcus, the *goddamn!* look on his face was enough to make her laugh out loud.

The first thing they did was hit the beach. The resort was designed to make guests feel as if they had the island all to themselves, which was exactly how Tuesday felt as they strolled barefoot through the warm, powdery sand. They didn't see another soul the entire time, and as usual, Tuesday thought they could've got it in right on the beach without being seen—which had always been a fantasy of hers.

The resort offered numerous activities for their guests such as nature walks, hikes, and bicycle trails, but neither of them were down to do anything like that. They rented jet-skis and clowned out on the water, took a boat ride where they were taught how to dive and catch their own lobster that was served to them later at lunch. They got their drink on at the island bar where they saw a few other guests, and then after massages, they spent some time just chilling on a big hammock that was strung up between two palm trees.

Tuesday had a lot of questions but knew she couldn't ask any of them. She still wanted to know exactly what he did for a living and what was this big move he had planned. If he wasn't selling dope, which she seriously doubted now that he was, what was he involved in that would make the feds mistake him for Caine? She was even curious to know what the deal was between him and his father. Most important, she wanted to know why, when the Kings had money up the ass the way they did, was he living so below his means out in Romulus.

The problem was that asking those questions would require a lot of answers from her. Even if she tried to warn him about the feds, she would have to explain how she actually knew they were about to come at him. How could she know that he was living beneath his means if she had never been invited to his house? Plus at this stage, asking about his relationship with his father and the money moves discussed with his accountant might only get her "None of ya damn business!"

So she just lay there quietly with her head resting on his chest in a lover's embrace, full off lobster, buzzed off mojitos, and relaxed from a deep tissue massage, slowly rocking in their hammock, being lulled by the swaying palm trees, the caressing breeze, and the rhythmic lapping of the waves against the surf, until they dozed off again.

The resort had its own nightclub, and going there was the only time the couple got a feel for how many other guests were actually staying on Peter Island. Tuesday had brought the two other dresses from the plane, and even though she still wished she had better shoes for it, she wore the blue Oscar de la Renta with the floral pattern—and without panties because that was just how she felt that night. The club played techno, pop, reggae, Latin reggaeton, but very little rap. Tuesday and Marcus still got their dance on and it only took a little bit of contact before he realized she was absolutely naked underneath that thin layer of Chinese silk.

Tuesday was typically a cognac drinker, but down there it was all about rum and tequila. She wanted to be loose enough to put it on him later, but not sloppy drunk; yet, sometime during the night she crossed that line. Some of those tropical creeper drinks were made so fruity and delicious that it hid how much alcohol was in them. The bartender introduced her to something called a "zombie" and Tuesday liked it so much that she got three refills.

All she remembered was waking up the next morning in the master bedroom back at their villa. Everything that happened past the club last night was a blank. She rolled out of bed, head pounding, stomach boiling, and still in last night's dress. She shuffled off to the bathroom looking just like the name of the drink that caused her condition.

While washing her hands, she caught a glimpse of herself in the mirror and tried to figure how in the hell did she get big red stickers on her face. It wasn't until she pulled them off and studied them did she realize they were actually rose petals. She looked at them confused, wondering why they were stuck to her face and arms. Had she stumbled around drunk and fallen into some rosebushes?

It took a little time for her rum-soaked mind to connect the dots and realize that she'd spoiled what was supposed to be a special night. She came out the bathroom to see that the bed had been covered with petals and a couple dozen partially used candles had been set up around the room. He'd most likely had the staff set this up while they were still at the club but she got so fucked up that the surprise was ruined.

So on top of all the regular hangover symptoms, she tacked on embarrassment and guilt.

She searched for Marcus and found him out back swimming laps in the pool. On the deck next to it, a table held two breakfasts: one devoured with a second under a tin. She peeked at it but quickly covered it back because the mere sight of the omelet made her nauseous.

She sat on the edge of the pool and dipped her legs into the water. When he caught sight of her, he swam over.

"The dead has arisen," he said, treading water in front of her shirtless.

She covered her face with her hands for a second. "I'm so sorry about last night. I swear to God I can usually handle my liquor but I don't know what the fuck they putting in this island shit. I woke up and saw the candles with the rose petals and just felt so bad."

He rubbed the back of his neck. "Aww, the more I think about it, that was kind of a corny look anyway. Some ol' high school prom night shit."

"Naw, that was a good look," she assured him. "You went through all that trouble and my drunk ass fucked it up!"

He calmed her with his smile. "Don't even trip, it happens to the best of us. You gotta be careful, though, because they make that shit that sneak up on you."

"You ain't never lied about that—I don't remember shit past the first few drinks. Please tell me I ain't do nothing to embarrass you last night."

He hopped out of the water and sat next to her on the pool's edge. "Well, all it took was a couple dollars to make things right with that old white lady you swung on. We were just lucky nobody got hurt in that fire you started."

Tuesday bumped him with her elbow because she knew he was just playing.

"Naw, you just kinda ran outta gas at the club, found a seat and passed out. And I only hurt my back a little bit when I carried you back to the villa."

She smacked her lips. "Oh, so now you tryin' to say I'm fat?"

"We call it *thick* when it's in all the right places."

She looked serious. "I'm sorry for real, though. It was supposed to go down last night and I left you hangin'."

"If it makes you feel better, I did sneak and cop a few cheap feels while you were passed out."

She laughed. "The sad part is that you probably did!"

He laughed. "The really sad part is that I'm not joking!"

Tuesday moved in for a kiss but he backed away from it. "No offense, babe, but did you brush your teeth? You did spend a little time in the bathroom last night throwing your life away."

"Did I really throw up?" she asked, looking surprised and embarrassed again.

Marcus confirmed it with a nod. "You made it to the toilet so you get points for that."

He kissed his two fingers and used them to touch her lips. "But you really should go hit yo grill, though!"

There wasn't much on the agenda for them that day other than a little tour that Marcus had set up. The docks were on the opposite side of the island, and when they got there, Tuesday saw the forty-two-foot powerboat that he arranged for them to have all that day. Marcus boasted that it was a single hull V-bottom XXX-47 GTX. Tuesday didn't know what any of that meant but was impressed because it was long, sleek, and painted canary yellow with orange flames, making it look to her less like a boat than a Ferrari that had been adapted for the sea.

It moved like one too. The craft was incredibly fast. Rather than cut through the water, it seemed to skip across the surface. As it zipped along spraying huge water wings and leaving a long trail of foamy wake, the engine even growled like an Italian supercar. Tuesday sat shotgun admiring how easily Marcus handled the beast.

They raced over the Caribbean at full throttle while touring some of the lesser islands in the BVI. Some of them were a few hundred acres while others were as small as the housing plots on a residential street. Marcus explained to her that many of those small island properties were privately owned—like Peter Island—and a few were capped with stately mansions looking like beautiful floating estates.

Dead Chest Island was the one closest to the resort, and that which Marcus gave the most attention. It was about seven hundred acres and they cruised around it three times in slow circles while he studied the coast with a pair of binoculars. When Tuesday asked him about his interest in the island, he tried to downplay it as just curiosity. Tuesday didn't press him but to her he seemed to be doing more than just sightseeing.

After spending a few hours zipping around on their tour of the islands, he took the boat a few miles off the coast and just killed the motor in the middle of the water. It was a calm day in the Caribbean with a cloudless sky and placid sea. They spread a quilt out over the long bow and lay out on the front of the craft feeling like the last two people left on Earth.

Tuesday was reclining on her elbows, sunning herself in a purple two-piece while Marcus was next to her shirtless in long board shorts that were turquoise. Salsa music came from the radio in the cockpit. Conversation was minimal.

"Can I ask you something?" he said, breaking a long reflective silence. When some of her hair got caught in the warm breeze and concealed her face, he tucked it behind her left ear. "And if I'm being too personal just let me know."

"Well, I'm actually kinda curious since you haven't asked me a personal question since we met."

It was true that he hadn't asked her a single personal question about Tabitha Green. It hadn't been necessary for her to invent a fake family, friends, or backstory about her character because as secretive as he'd been concerning his own life, he'd been equally silent on the subject of hers.

"You don't even know what I do." Her prepared line had been that Tabitha was a registered nurse on paid leave from Henry Ford Hospital after hurting her foot at work, but the topic had never come up.

"You're right, I haven't asked you a lot of questions about yourself. Do you think that makes me self-centered?"

"Self-centered would be if you weren't interested in my life and just spent the whole time talking about yours. But we both know that's not the case, don't we."

He smiled at her. "Maybe I just like for things to be a little mysterious."

"So for fun you'd fly off to the Caribbean with a woman you hardly know?"

"I might not know all the details about your life but I do know pretty much everything I need to about you, Tabitha." His smile remained but there was a sincerity in his eyes that made Tuesday ashamed he wasn't even calling her by the right name.

"Well, if you already know everything you need to, what was this personal thing you wanted to ask?"

Marcus took on a serious expression. "What was his name?"

"Whose name?" she asked, puzzled.

"That one man you let into your heart. The one who hurt you and caused you to lock that door forever."

"You think you just got me so figured out. You don't know me as well as you think you do."

"I know enough to see that I'm right and you're still going through it. That's why you're trying to duck the question."

It was obvious that he'd picked up on her pain and she saw no reason to deny it. "His name was Adrian. I met him when I was nineteen and we were together for a long time."

"What happened?"

Tuesday took a moment to decide how to answer that.

"He left me," she said after a long pause without bothering to elaborate.

Marcus pressed the issue. "So what, he just busted up one day?"

"Somethin' like that."

He leaned in closer to her. "Do you ever see yourself loving somebody like that again?"

Tuesday thought it might be better to lie but found herself answering truthfully. "No. Not like that, anyway. What I had with Adrian wasn't perfect but it was real. I would love to have something like that again but not in the same way."

He nodded because he felt where she was coming from.

"So what about you?" she asked, switching the focus to him. "What happened to that fiancée you didn't want to talk about at Gaucho's?"

"Long story short: she cheated."

"Do you ever see yourself loving somebody like that again?"

Marcus smiled because he then realized how stupid the question was when directed back to him. "No, not like that. But I could definitely see myself falling in love again." He paused for a second then added, "With the right person."

"And can the right person be light-skinned and have gray-green eyes with a bangin' body?"

He laughed. "Yeah, but she would have to have a few other things going for her too. She would have to be smart. She would have to be a bossy-type bitch because I don't respect weak women. She would have to be ambitious too; want something outta life for herself other than what I could give her. And no doubt she would have to be someone I could see being a good mother to Dani."

Tuesday felt he was describing her to a T until he made that last statement. As much as she liked Danielle, Tuesday couldn't see herself doing parent-teacher conferences, bake sales, or whipping up to soccer practice in a minivan. She didn't think it was a bad life, just not the life for her. She didn't think she had it in her to be "Momma" and Lord knows her own mother didn't provide a good example.

Her mind drifted back to a childhood of being left home alone while her mother went out with one of the many men who were always introduced as "Uncle So-and-so"—when Tuesday was little she had more uncles than she could count and they never stayed around for long. Tuesday was so lost in this past that she momentarily forgot he was still talking and had to tune back in to him.

"But most important, she would have to be straight-up with me." He pierced her again with that direct stare that quickened her heart rate. "I hate a fake-ass bitch more than anything! Shit need to be *one hundred* with me all the time." He used his hands to stress those two words. "Hurt me with the truth before you flatter me with a lie."

Again Tuesday felt so guilty that it made her shiver despite the temperature being above ninety degrees. It was one thing when she thought they were both pretending to be other people, but now that she was the only one being fake, it bothered her a little.

Then she thought back to her conversation with Tushie and reminded herself to stay on game. She didn't exactly see Marcus as a mark anymore, but she was in too deep now and had to play this thing out as Tabitha Green. Tuesday didn't know how this was going to end, but just because he was good people she couldn't start slipping and break Rule One.

She met his gaze and trumped it with the intensity of her own stare. Tuesday needed her green eyes to sell the performance she was about to give.

"The man who was the love of my life: a nigga I lied for, stole for, and probably would've killed for, just up and left me one day. But he didn't move away or run off with another bitch, he left me in handcuffs."

"What kind of bit he doing?" Marcus asked with a tone that was not meant to be intrusive.

"The worst kind. Life without parole."

He draped a consoling arm around her. "I'm sorry."

"Don't be. It's not yo fault, it's his!" she spat with repressed anger that arose from nowhere. "The stupid muthafucka threw his life away over nothin' and threw me away right along with it! I would honestly feel better if he had left me for another woman—at least that would make more sense."

Tuesday didn't even realize she was crying until she felt him smooth the tears away with his thumbs. She had started out acting but had mistakenly tapped into a real emotion. Each time she was certain that she'd come to terms with A.D. being gone, she always found hurt resting on some deeper level.

"It's not your fault either," he said in a warm, almost fatherly voice. "Sounds like you're carrying a lot of guilt about what he did."

"I know it's not my damn fault!" she snapped at him. "I did everything I was supposed to do. I got him a lawyer, I was at every court date, and after he got his time, I was there to see him every week and made sure he wanted for shit! I stood by that nigga's side for twelve muthafuckin' years when most bitches would've been outta there! Why in the fuck should I feel guilty about that?"

Marcus rubbed her back in slow circles to calm her. He knew that she was just venting and that none of this hostility was directed toward him.

Tuesday was looking off to the horizon, that place in the distance where the sky and sea were only separated by some invisible line. He turned her face so that she met his eyes again.

"Guilt and anger go hand in hand," he explained. "Life is a series of serious choices! It's hard enough living with all the mistakes we make for ourselves, we can't go carrying around other people's fuck-ups too. We're not built for all that. I know you pride yourself on being tough; but nobody's *that* goddamned strong, nor should they have to be." He pecked her on the forehead. "Baby girl, let that shit go before it kill you."

Tuesday tried to fight the rising tide of emotion swelling within her but broke down before she could get a handle on herself. She put her head upon his shoulder and began to sob hard. Yet this was no ordinary cry; the emotional dam she'd been constructing her entire life just crumbled under a torrent of tears. She wept about all the things that had been haunting her since childhood, plus a few ghosts she didn't even know were there: A.D., her mother, the two pregnancies she aborted, a youth wasted in the club rather than in school, even Dresden's abuse.

Marcus didn't know what it all meant and was wise enough not to ask. He just stroked her silky hair as she sobbed and shook. The only support he offered was his presence, allowing her tears to pour onto his shoulder and roll down his bare chest.

Again, this was no ordinary cry. A lifetime of accumulated regret seeped from her eyes in the form of tears, and with each one shed, Tuesday felt the breaking of an invisible shackle that had kept her tied down. The truly amazing thing was that this cry was so liberating that Tuesday instinctively knew that she would never weep about any of those things again. She felt like she was being cleansed of everything in her psyche that was noxious. For that reason she felt no shame about bawling like a baby in front of Marcus.

After a couple minutes she was done, and Tuesday felt buoyant, somehow lighter. She understood the metaphor of a weight being lifted, but she honestly felt that if Marcus took his arm from around her, she would float up into the sky and be forever lost like a balloon.

"Feel better?" he asked after she was finally able to look up at him.

She was beaming a smile even though her face was still streaked with tears. "I feel like I just had an emotional enema!"

He wiped her cheeks dry. "I could've done without the visual, but I'm glad you got it out of your system."

"And for yo information, you got it wrong about me, Mr. Know-it-all!" She rolled her eyes and pretended to be sassy. "Yeah, I have been hurt before but I didn't lock that door forever. I've just been waiting for somebody who had the right key to open it."

His smile returned. "And is that somebody tall, dark-skinned, with a killer smile and six-pack abs?"

She started to respond but he covered her mouth with his and silenced her with a kiss. It caught Tuesday by surprise but she quickly relented and invited in his tongue.

The kiss escalated in passion until it was something hungry and animalistic. They didn't break it even when he laid Tuesday on her back and crawled on top of her. His hands massaged her titties then rubbed her thick thighs. The feel of him growing hard beneath his shorts excited her so much that she began to push them down, not bothering to wait for Marcus to undress himself.

He hastily untied her bikini top, and after kissing on her neck, he took a moment to admire her breasts. Resting atop perfect C-cup mounds were perky nipples with silver dollar–sized areolas the color of caramel. He devoured one, then the other. Marcus took his time with them and Tuesday moaned with delight but it made her laugh out loud when he tickled them with his tongue.

When he began to kiss a pathway down her stomach Tuesday was pulling off her bottoms before he even reached her navel. She understood that he was trying to be sensual but she was way too hot for the slow romantic shit. She wanted to get ate out then fucked hard. Marcus was headed in the right direction, he just took his time getting there. He licked and nibbled on her inner thighs for a while, and by the time he made his way to her pretty shaved pussy, Tuesday's lips were swollen from anticipation.

The second his tongue made contact with her clit, Tuesday shuddered like she'd been zapped with a Taser. He teased it then sucked on it, causing her to moan his name. Marcus definitely knew what he was doing, but it was her celibacy more than his skill that made her cum so fast. Just three minutes in she was gripping the back of his bald head and squirting like a drinking fountain.

Tuesday knew she owed him some head and intended to repay him one day, but was so horny right then it made her selfish. She was starving for his dick. So after he hurried to put on the rubber he pulled from the pocket of his discarded shorts, she pulled Marcus back on top of her and grabbed his piece to help guide him inside her.

Tuesday had been playing with her sex toys but hadn't been really fucked in close to a year—she didn't count run-ins with Dresden because his shit was so little and they never lasted more than a few minutes. Being out of action had made her tighter than she realized. It took some time for Marcus to work the head in, but once he did, her incredible wetness practically sucked him in the rest of the way. She gasped. It had been so long since Tuesday had a big dick that she dug her nails into his shoulder and bit down on her bottom lip.

The ocean made the boat rock with a relaxing motion and he soon found the stroke to match that rhythm. She wrapped her legs around his waist and ground her hips in sync with his thrusts. She rubbed his back and the powerful arms he used to suspend himself over her; to feel the contraction of his muscles excited her.

What Tuesday didn't realize was that it had been a while for Marcus too and he was feeling the effects. Her pussy was so tight and wet that it made a slurping sound each time he stroked it; that along with the pleasure and pain-filled whines she let out was driving him crazy. He reached beneath her to grab that ass while whispering in her ear how soft it was. This made Tuesday cum again, and it took every bit of his concentration to fight back his own nut. Marcus didn't want to spoil the mood by busting too soon.

Tuesday didn't think that he had a bad stroke but the missionary position had played out for her back in middle school. She climbed on top and rode him like a porn star. Years of being an exotic dancer gave her a rhythm and coordination that many girls lacked. She rolled her hips in slow circles and used her muscle control for maximum effect. Soon she had him breathing heavy and moaning "Tabitha" in ecstasy.

Since they met, Tuesday had been ready for him so many times and thought that getting it on in the back of the Phantom would have been perfect, then thought the same thing about the beach yesterday, and the villa last night surrounded by candles, but none of those places compared to this. It was the setting as much as the sex that drove her: naked on the front of a long powerboat with nothing but the azure sky above and surrounded by crystal clear turquoise water. She was now glad they waited.

There was also something raw and primal about fucking outdoors. It was a throwback to some pre-evolutionary part of our savage ancestry. It was wild and uncivilized. It was also taboo, which heightened the appeal. As Tuesday went buck on top of him, she felt like a high priestess engaged in some sex ritual designed to appease the pagan gods.

Tuesday rode him forever; but what seemed like eternity was much closer to two and a half hours. She had switched positions from forward to reverse cowgirl and was popping her pussy like she was eighteen years old again back on stage at The Bounce. The time had been filled with bunches of orgasms for her, and Marcus's body held the proof as he was soaked from his navel to his knees along with the quilt under him.

Finally Tuesday climbed off of him then got on her elbows and knees with her butt in the air. With the day starting to wane, she could think of no better way to cap if off than him pounding her from the back as they looked out on the sunset.

"I hope you know how to ride a donkey." She smiled then playfully smacked herself on the ass.

"Like a muthafuckin' champ!" he said, eagerly positioning himself behind her.

The solar orb started its descent, changing from yellow to various shades of red. The reflection it cast off the water made it look as if the sea was covered with sparkling rubies and painted the sky in iridescent colors.

Tuesday had never seen anything so breathtaking but her limited vocabulary lacked the words to articulate the beauty or how humbled she was by it. These were thoughts best expressed by accomplished poets.

Marcus was more mesmerized by the view of Tuesday from behind than the one nature provided. His eyes never strayed from watching those rounded cheeks bounce against his pelvis with a loud clap. He held on to her tiny waist, pumping furiously, and the faster he went, the wetter she got, which in turn only made him want to go faster. He grabbed a fistful of her weave and began spanking her so hard that it made Tuesday's high-yellow ass turn bright pink.

He tried to hold back until the sun went completely down but couldn't last; Tuesday was too tight, too hot and wet, and the way she was throwing that pussy back at him was more than he could take. He exploded while a quarter of the sun was still peeking above the horizon. Marcus came so hard that his entire body shook from the force of it and Tuesday worked her muscles to make sure she milked him for every drop.

Tuesday slid down onto her stomach and he covered her like a blanket. He was too exhausted to pull out and she didn't want him to. So for a while they just lay there silent and satiated.

They drifted off to sleep. Afloat on the Caribbean. An entwined mass of flesh. Watched only by God.

Chapter Sixteen

Late that night the two of them left the resort and flew out of the Virgin Islands aboard the G-650. They had to pick up Danielle from his father's house before heading home. Tuesday was finally able to join the Mile High Club because en route to LAX, she pulled him to the back room and got it in once more before they landed.

After retrieving Danielle, the two hours they spent in Los Angeles was uneventful other than a quick lunch at the Beverly Palms. From there it was right back to the airport to leave the land of sunshine and movie stars.

For Tuesday, seeing the city again was like coming down from an incredible high. Flying into Metro Airport made Detroit a real place again, and all her problems returned with the sight of the Renaissance building and other Motown landmarks. The fantasy was over and reality was harsh as the chilly wind she'd become unaccustomed to in just those two days spent in the warm Caribbean.

Conversation was light on the drive back to her fake apartment at Town Square. A jet-lagged Danielle slept and they didn't talk about much beyond the weather. It bordered on awkward how they both tried to avoid the unspoken question on both of their minds: *Where does this relationship go from here?*

He walked Tuesday to the door of her building and there was a moment when they both seemed to want to say something more but neither of them did. There was just a quick kiss from Marcus and a promise that he would call soon before he smashed off in the Audi. Tuesday only waited five minutes then left behind him in the Honda.

Tuesday got Tushie on the phone and was telling her about the incredible weekend even before she reached her condo. All her girl could repeat was "Bitch, iz you serious!" as Tuesday described the plushed-out jet, his father's Beverly Hills mansion, the private villa they shared on Peter Island, and the beautiful blue of the Caribbean Sea as she got fucked on the front of a speedboat.

Upon agreeing that he was not Sebastian Caine, Tushie asked the same question as to why was he living so low-key when his family obviously had crazy money, and Tuesday still had no plausible answer.

There was no easy answer for what the crew's next move should be either. On top of owing Face a shitload of paper, Tuesday had lost her car and hyped the girls up with promises of a million-dollar lick that wasn't going to happen. Making matters worse was the fact that her personal bank was just about gone and it didn't help that she chose to keep The Bounce closed over the last few days to let the shooting incident die down.

Tuesday got home and did some deep thinking while she cleaned her condo.

For all she knew, the mission was over and the only thing left to do was break the disappointing news to everybody who had been expecting a payday. The team would be pissed and would take no consolation in that she had a fabulous weekend with Marcus in the Virgin Islands; but beyond bitter feelings from Brianna and Baby Doll, life would go on, and after hitting a few more licks, they would put it all behind them.

As usual, Dresden would be suspicious, assuming that the lick had went down and Tuesday was just trying to fuck him out his share. At worse she'll get slapped up again but nothing too rough, then he'd come back trying to kiss her ass when he learned from his fed friends that they had made a mistake. Then their relationship would go right back to the status quo: an endless cycle of rape and regret.

Face, on the other hand, would not be so easy to deal with. While she did go back a few years with the gun dealer, Tuesday couldn't be sure that he would not kill her about his money. The best she could do is offer to pay him off in installments until they were even—which meant she would most likely be seventy years old still trying to reel in marks. As a last resort she could give him her share of the club, which was the only thing left that she still owned.

Once she was satisfied that her place was spotless, Tuesday spent some quality time with Nicholas, who she had basically left to fend for himself while she was gone. Even though the feline still had food in his dish, Tuesday fed him a can of tuna then allowed him to curl up on her lap while she stroked his thick, white fur.

With all the other problems she faced, Tuesday couldn't stop thinking about Marcus. She had been fucked plenty of times in the twelve years since A.D. left, but this was the first time that it felt like more than just sex. During that period she'd been with a few niggas who could really put it down, but with them it still just felt like exercise—a purely physical act. Maybe it was the conversation before when she shed her pain or just the way he touched her; however, it was the first time since A.D. that sex had been intensified by a level of intimacy. They had connected emotionally. At least that's how it seemed to her, but of course, she couldn't speak for him.

Tuesday thought back to what Tushie had explained about needing something real. Marcus was handsome, rich, and could fuck pretty good too, but outside of all that, Tuesday thought he was good people and could see having something real with him. If the mission was over and she wasn't looking at him as a mark anymore, did that mean it was okay to pursue him?

The problem was that Tuesday knew she would never be able to establish something real that was founded on a lie. This meant that she would have to tell Marcus who she really was, and this meant having to explain why she lied in the first place.

As bad as she wanted to warn him about the indictment, that would also mean having to explain how she came by that information. She would have to break down who Dresden was and why she got on to him from the jump. Explaining that she'd manipulated her way into his life with plans to rob and kill him would be an awkward conversation. On the chance that he was big enough to respect her honesty, she didn't see any way that he could trust her after that.

Even when you sleep along the way, traveling has a way of exhausting a person. This was why after taking a quick shower, Tuesday climbed into bed and prepared to end her day even though it was hardly six thirty in the evening. With the curtains drawn to keep out the sun and Nicholas purring at her side, she was asleep within minutes.

But sometime between toweling off and dozing off, Tuesday had decided that she was going to tell Marcus everything. She had to give him a heads-up about this fed situation, even if it meant that he wouldn't want anything to do with her after that.

The next morning Tuesday placed calls to all the girls to have them meet her at The Bounce. None outside of Tushie knew about her weekend getaway or what the meeting was about. Tuesday arrived around nine a.m. and the others trickled in over the next half hour. The club was still closed in the wake of Tank's death so they didn't need to crowd into Tuesday's office for privacy.

The ladies seated themselves at the tables fronting the stage while Tuesday perched on the edge of it. She looked over the faces of her team, already knowing what needed to be said and how they would respond to it, just unsure of how she would say it to them.

After taking a breath, she started. "I don't know if Tush told y'all or not, but I just spent the weekend with dude and I learned some shit that seriously fucks up our whole play."

"What happened?" Jaye was the only one who answered vocally. Brianna and Baby Doll just smacked their lips and made faces to show how they felt.

"I got fed some more bad info from my inside guy. The mark's name really is Marcus King and he got a rich daddy out in Beverly Hills. He ain't Sebastian Caine. He ain't even fuckin' with the game!"

Brianna couldn't wait to get on her. "I knew it! I knew this was gone be some bullshit! I said from the start that I didn't want nothin' to do with this if it came from the same nigga who put us up on Fatboy."

She looked around to the others. "Y'all stupid bitches let her gas y'all up talkin' 'bout a seven-figure lick! I ain't believe that shit for one second."

Tuesday just sat back and took the heat. She could've pointed out that Brianna was right with the others bragging about Ferraris and Bentleys she was going to drop after they hit the lick but Tuesday didn't put her on blast by reminding them that she had drank the Kool-Aid too.

"Look, I know I got everybody hyped up," she apologized. "I was hyped up too! I would've bet the house on this being the lick that put us on, but I was wrong."

Brianna snapped, "Bitch, you bet my car on it!"

"I bet mine too, Bree, and a whole lot of money," she said, maintaining a calm voice. "I fucked up. I met this nigga's father, I saw where he grew up. He don't sell dope, he on some corporate white-collar shit."

"So whut we gone do now?" Tushie asked, hoping her girl had put together a backup plan since talking to her yesterday.

"I don't know." Tuesday threw up her hands in defeat and the girls looked confused because for them it was the first time that the boss bitch had no answer.

Baby Doll said, "I just can't believe we wasted all this time and energy for nothin'!"

Brianna stood up to let everyone know that she wanted the floor. "If this nigga got all this money, then why we not gone still try to get at it? You said the nigga paid!"

"But he not a dope boy," said Tuesday. "It ain't no safe loaded down with bundles of cash and bricks. His money in the bank. This nigga own stock and shit!"

"If his money in the bank, then we make that nigga go get it!"

Tuesday shook her head. "Bree, you know the rules. We only hit those who can't report the losses. Dirty money is good money."

Brianna erupted in frustration. "You and all these damn rules is what's holding us up! We stick niggas, stop frontin' like we doing something positive! Fuck if a nigga sell dope or real estate, if he got money I say we get his ass!"

Because Tuesday felt guilty about the lick going sour, she'd given Brianna a little bit of rope, but the girl had quickly used that to fasten a noose. She had lost all patience.

"Dumb bitch, niggas who earn they money legally can call the police and the police will start to investigate. How long do you think it would take them to connect the dots back to us?

"You see, if it wasn't for all these rules you keep complaining about, you'd already be dead or spending the next twenty years upstate gettin' ate by a muscled-up butch bitch wit a mohawk."

Brianna stood in front of Tuesday addressing Baby Doll, Jaye, and Tushie. "Now goin' in we were s'posed to murk this nigga and walk away with enough money for all of us to be straight. That was what she said," jerking a thumb back at Tuesday. "She done found out the nigga got millions on top of millions but now she don't wanna do nothin' because he didn't get it from the game. That don't make sense to me when we can still come out this shit right. I thank it's something else going on here!"

Tuesday snatched her around so they were facing each other. "First off, don't talk about me like I ain't standing here. But if you're gonna do it, be woman enough to speak yo mind and stop dropping hints!"

"All right, I'll say it!" Brianna yanked away from her grasp. "I don't know what happened on y'all li'l weekend, but I think you done caught feelings for this nigga."

Tuesday frowned at her. "Bitch, please!"

Brianna wouldn't back off. "Either you done caught feelings or you still on game and just trying to cut us out."

Tuesday pretended to be confused even though she had a good idea of what she meant. "Bitch, what the fuck you talking about?"

Tushie didn't understand. She rang in, "Yeah, cuz you ain't makin' no sense to me eitha!"

"Think about it," Brianna explained back to Tushie. "She find out his people got money up the ass, why hit him for a piece of change she gotta split with us when she can Boo up with the nigga and have a crack at everything? If she get a baby out the nigga, she set for life. Better yet, if she trick him down the aisle with no prenup, she all the way on! This bitch parlaying out in Beverly Hills, flying around the world on private jets while we stuck in the hood still living hand to mouth."

Tuesday had to keep her game face on because truthfully, all those same thoughts crossed her mind the moment that flight attendant said six hundred million.

"Look, y'all know I'm about the team first," she said, trying to take some of the steam from Brianna's argument. "Either we all eat or we all starve. That's the way it's been from the door."

"We all starving right now!" Doll said bitterly. "All of us ain't got condos on the Riverfront. You promised us a seven-figure lick and the shit still out there, but you want us to back off. I need this shit! I ain't 'bout to go back to giving lap dances and trickin' with niggas just to get tipped out."

"And you need it too!" Brianna said to Tuesday. "Last time I checked, Face had you in the hole for four hundred racks. Did you forget that?"

Tuesday spat, "And bitch, did you forget you're the reason I owe that nigga in the first place?"

Jaye, who had been quiet up until now, finally came in with her opinion. "Look, I'm not trying to take sides here, but Bree does make some good points. Coming in, the plan was to handle this business and then get out of Dodge until the heat died down. I know he's not who we thought he was, but I don't necessarily see why we have to fall back."

Baby Doll added: "You done already spent all this time getting in with the nigga and you know he got money. I say we finish what we started."

Brianna raised her hand to signify that she was calling for a vote. Doll's tiny arm shot up immediately followed shortly after by Jaye's. Tuesday could tell by the look on Tushie's face that she agreed with them but it was loyalty and nothing else that kept her hand down.

"It's still three to two," Brianna said triumphantly.

Tuesday had a good idea of what they wanted to do because it had been alluded to before, but she couldn't think of any way to deter them without looking like she was either out for herself or had broken the first rule.

"If we murder this nigga, it's gone be crazy crazy heat on us!" she said, hoping to scare them. "With the type of money his pops got, you know he can hire people to track a bitch down."

"A week and a half ago you said the same thing about Caine," Doll reminded her. "But you were still down with murking him. You even said you'd do it right in front of the little girl if it meant getting that money. So why is you trippin' now?"

Tuesday was pressed to give an answer but there wasn't one that would satisfy them. No matter how she tried to spin it, the truth was that she had caught feelings. She liked Marcus and she liked Danielle. And as badly as she needed the money to settle things up with Face, not to mention pull herself out the game once and for all, she didn't want it at the expense of hurting either of them. Even if she and Marcus never ended up together, she still felt that he deserved better than to die for the sake of their greed.

All Tuesday could do was just boss up. "We stick dope boys, that's our MO. We ain't lookin at this nigga no more and we ain't talkin' about this no more. The last time I checked this wasn't no democracy, so y'all can kiss my ass with all this voting shit! I make law in this bitch!"

The girls were upset and expressed it through body language and grumbled insults. Tuesday was surprised to see that even Tushie was giving her a disapproving look.

"Now gimme some time to put something together and eventually we'll get our money back right," she said, offering a little consolation. "But I meant what I said here and I don't give a fuck how any of y'all hoes feel about it!"

Grim-faced with hard gray eyes, Tuesday made certain to stare each of them directly in theirs after she made that last statement. Even Tushie.

The team didn't like the way she ended the meeting but coming in Tuesday had established to all of them that this was a dictatorship and she was the only one wearing a crown.

So an hour after spazzing out on them, she was at the scrapyard in Face's office delivering the same bad news to him. Tuesday explained that she'd been wrong about the lick and there would be no money coming.

Face responded just as she expected. He placed his head upon his makeshift desk and pounded the wood with his fist while shouting curses.

"Damn, Tuesday!" he cried, finally raising his head to look at her again. "What are we s'posed to do about this situation? We ain't talkin' 'bout a couple dollars here."

Just like when she was standing in front of the girls, Tuesday could do nothing but throw up her empty hands. "Face, I came into this thinkin' that I was 'bout to hit a million-dollar lick. Now I fucked up with you and a few other people because I was banking on that. I been at this a long time and all my instincts told me this nigga was laying like that but I was wrong. I could sit here and try to put the blame everywhere else but at the end of the day it falls on me. It was my bad."

Face methodically rubbed his bald head like it was a crystal ball and the answer to their problem might be provided through sorcery.

"Look, I appreciate you comin' here and telling me to my face. You get points for being real." He shook his head and let out a weary sigh. "But we talkin' 'bout four hundred racks here so a puppy-dog look and a 'my bad' ain't gone cut it. That was some real *Mission: Impossible* shit I pulled off for you—getting a body outta there with the po-po in the building. I needs my paper!"

There was an intensity in his glare that Tuesday had never seen before, and as much as it frightened her, she didn't look away. "The truth is, between the losses I took on this and the last lick, I'm wiped out. I'm broke, nigga. I got seventy percent ownership of The Bounce and that's it."

He laughed but there was no humor in it. "One hundred percent ownership of The Bounce ain't worth four hundred thousand, you know that."

Tuesday shrugged. "It's what I got."

He covered his face with his hands for a minute. "Damn, girl, you leaving me in a fucked-up spot. What am I s'posed to do, just take that as a loss? Charge it to the game?"

Her voice was calm, moreso than his. "I wish I had an answer for you."

Face looked at her with that intense stare again. "Me and A.D. go back to cartoon draws and you his woman. And it's only because you is who you is that I'm giving you a week to come up with somethin'."

Tuesday shook her head. "I ain't got four hundred racks now

and I doubt if I have it in a week. I owe you and I'm standing here telling you that I can't pay." She threw her hands out to her sides. "So whatever you got planned for me in seven days, you might as well do it right now!"

She glared right back at him, not backing down or retreating from his eyes. Face had never seen hers that shade of gray before and it chilled him even though he was on the giving end of the threat. He knew what Tuesday did to eat and knew she was a hard-core bitch but never expected this. For a moment he just sat there in his patched-up old recliner silent and dumbstruck.

"Tuesday, I don't wanna have to kill you about this!"

"Good," she said, never breaking eye contact with him. "Because I don't wanna have to die about it either."

There was a long pause in which the two became locked in a staring match that neither one of them wanted to lose. Tuesday's fierce gray eyes pierced his and his dark brown pierced hers. There seemed to be a battle of wills where each person tried to search the other for any signs of weakness, fear, hesitation, or doubt.

Tuesday was unreadable. She wasn't trying to look hard, but wasn't looking scared either. Her face was a blank slate; if this were poker, Face would have no idea if she had top pair or was just bluffing at the pot. She was giving him nothing.

He finally folded. "All right. If push come to shove, I'll take your share of The Bounce for a hundred and fifty, and that's love like a *muthafucka*!" he said, pointing a finger and giving her a stern look. "But I still need you to go make somethin' happen for the other two-fifty. And that's the best I can do for you!"

Tuesday did appreciate that he was trying to work with her although she didn't see the point. She couldn't see coming up with two hundred fifty thousand in a week any more than putting her hand to the whole four hundred.

"And if I can't do it, then what?"

Face gave her another look, this worse than any he'd given her before. At that moment Tuesday saw nothing handsome in the man. With his leathery skin and bald head, he looked like a burn victim; only one who'd escaped from the sulfur pits of hell rather than an ordinary fire.

In an eerie tone she'd never heard him take, he said: "Let's not even think about that, because I know you're gonna make somethin' happen."

There was something in his eyes so chilling that this time Tuesday had to look away first.

Chapter Seventeen

Tuesday needed a stress reliever after the day she had, so when Marcus called her around four with a dinner invite, she was with it. The last time they ate together it was at Mastro's in L.A. surrounded by celebrities and she was eager to see how he would top that.

She was surprised—but not at all disappointed—to learn that all he had in mind was a quiet dinner at his house with him and Danielle. Since Tuesday wasn't supposed to know where he lived, she asked for the directions and made plans for seven.

She arrived on time and he met her at the door after she parked in the crescent driveway behind his Audi. The only thing on deck was chilling at his crib for the evening so neither of them swagged it up too much. He looked crisp, though, in a white T, jeans, and a pair of throwback Penny Hardaway's. Tuesday chose a blue blouse with matching heels and played them with white stretch pants. They shared a quick kiss on the porch while checking each other out. Then he invited her inside.

Just like everything else with Marcus, his home had a plain exterior that hid something lavish. White suede sofas sat upon elaborate hand-woven rugs and those sat upon polished walnut floors. The pieces were situated around a slate-top cocktail table, creating a conversation area. Above it all, wrought-iron chandeliers hung from decorative coffered ceilings with walnut braces. It was definitely a man's house; the heavy use of dark woods gave it a strong masculine feel, but overall, Tuesday was very impressed.

She admired his style but Tuesday's OCD made her notice that the place was also immaculately kept. She figured that only a child as mature as Danielle could be trusted around white suede furniture because there wasn't a single smudge or juice stain on any of the pieces—which was one of the first things Tuesday's meticulous eye scanned for.

Just as she had that thought, Danielle came sprinting toward her from the dining room. She was smiling big, all teeth and gums, when Tuesday scooped her up into her arms. The little girl was so excited to see her that she was talking a mile a minute, hardly giving Tuesday a chance to answer one question before she fired off three more. Danielle was acting like she hadn't seen her in weeks when they were just together yesterday.

Danielle was eager for Tuesday to see her room and dragged her away by the arm before she could get off her jacket. As Tuesday was being led away, she looked back to Marcus, who smiled because he knew Dani was going to be on her heels all night.

After a tour of the house with Danielle playing guide and introducing her to all her favorite dolls, Tuesday was able to join Marcus in the kitchen where he was starting dinner. It was a huge English kitchen with a deep pantry and breakfast nook. Granite countertops with a Carrera marble backsplash complemented the cabinetry and stainless steel appliances, which included a massive refrigerator with deep freezer paired with a high-quality gas range with eight burners, dual ovens, and a broiler.

Tuesday was blown back because it was not the type of kitchen that came with the house but rather one that was custom-built.

Only a professional chef or someone who took seriously to the trade would invest in such a showplace.

Marcus stood over the center island dicing cauliflower into florets with an experienced hand. There was something about watching a man cook that all women found sexy, and Tuesday was no exception.

They all sat down to a dinner of grilled raspberry chicken served with a creamy Italian spiral salad. At first chicken marinated in raspberry jam and vinaigrette didn't sound too appealing to Tuesday, but tasting it was something totally different. She devoured every scrap on her plate and wasn't shy about taking seconds.

Rich, handsome, a good father who could fuck, *and cook*! Tuesday was ready to marry this nigga.

There was a comical moment during dinner when, out of the blue, a way too grown Danielle flat-out asked Tuesday if she was spending the night. Tuesday just looked at the girl with an embarrassed smile, unable to respond. Then when Marcus stepped in and politely told her that it was none of her business, Danielle began to clap excitedly because she was smart enough to know that meant Tuesday was staying.

As much as she enjoyed being with them, it made what she had to do even more difficult, because sometime during the night, she was going to have to sour their evening by telling him her secrets. Tuesday felt that Marcus needed to know what was coming his way and he deserved to know she wasn't who she pretended to be. Each time he or Danielle called her "Tabitha," she felt a guilty pain prick her in the side.

After dinner, when Danielle changed into Hello Kitty pajamas, they retired to the family room and the huge eighty-six-inch plasma TV that hung there. Danielle was always allowed to watch a movie from her collection before bedtime and she chose Disney's *Aladdin* for what Marcus said was the millionth time. He joked that he had heard the theme song "Whole New World" so many times that it would be stuck in his head forever.

Danielle was sandwiched between them on the couch, and halfway through the movie Tuesday looked down to see that she was leaning against her sound asleep. This stirred up something inside of Tuesday forcing her to be overcome with some strange mixture of joy, shame, pride, and guilt. Her eyes began to water but she blinked back the tears.

Even though she wasn't crying, Marcus still peeped the look on her face. "What's wrong?"

"Nothing," she said, trying to downplay it. "Just had a rough day, that's all."

He smiled. "Well, I'm gonna do my part to make sure it ends on a *high note*."

Tuesday laughed because she didn't miss the play on words.

Marcus carried a slumbering Danielle to her room and tucked her into bed while Tuesday watched from the doorway. The scene made Tuesday think back on what Tushie said about wanting to play house. She never thought she wanted this life before, but now she did. She could see being a woman to him, but more important, she could actually see being a mother to Dani, which was something she never considered before.

However, none of that really mattered, because Tuesday knew that after the truth came out, she would never see him or Danielle again.

Even worse was that in a week she expected to be crushed in the trunk of a junked car and headed to Arizona.

When Marcus led her to his bedroom, Tuesday only wanted to talk, and she planned to tell him everything, but then he took off his shirt. The sight of those ripped arms, chiseled abs derailed her train of thought and before she knew it they were kissing; then he was stripping off her clothes and she was helping him. Tuesday dropped to her knees and tugged down his jeans, eager to repay him for the head she got on the boat.

When it came to sucking dick, women generally fall into two distinct categories: those who do it out of obligation to their men and those who do it because they themselves love it. The latter pride themselves on being experts and derive as much pleasure from the act as they provide. The power and control they exert over a man as he twists and moans in ecstasy is almost as thrilling to them as having their own pussies ate. It becomes a mandatory part of foreplay. Some of these women have oral fixations that cause them to suck their thumbs well into adulthood; and the compulsion can be so deep in some that not allowing them to give you head is a form of punishment. These selfless lovers are not just a joy to be with, but they make the world a better place for men everywhere.

Tuesday belonged to that group. An older cousin had her practice on a banana when she was sixteen, but it was the years spent with A.D. that perfected her talents. In the crew, the wanna-be comedian Jaye had the reputation for being a head-smith, but Tuesday knew the girl was too young and inexperienced to fuck with her neck game. She knew how to make her mouth extra wet and relax her throat muscles to swallow every inch of the bigger ones. So when Tuesday took his dick with two hands and worked her head in a corkscrew motion with deep, slow strokes, Marcus fell back against the dresser with his eyes closed and groaned curses.

She let her mouth make love to him for twenty minutes or so, and was ready to go for an hour more, but he pushed her away then guided her to the bed. He kicked his pants the rest of the way off, snatched down her thong and seconds later he was inside her.

Tuesday didn't know if it was because she was feeling him so much or if it was the fact that this might be the last dick she ever got; either way, something in her mind took the sex to another level. Each thrust was magnified times ten and the freaky shit he whispered in her ear had her head gone. It felt so good that Tuesday came three times in the first few minutes.

When they fucked on the speedboat and on the jet, it was Tuesday who took the lead, but this time she played the submissive role. She just allowed herself to be bent and twisted into any position Marcus wanted. He flipped her from her back to her side then had her ride him again for a little while.

It blew Tuesday's mind when he picked her up and carried her across the room without missing a stroke. She was a thick girl with hips and thighs that put her close to a hundred fifty pounds, but Marcus handled her as if she weighed nothing. He pinned her against the wall and she wrapped her legs around his waist while he cupped her ass. Marcus drilled her, making her cum back to back. Tuesday let out those high falsetto notes that he joked about earlier but had to check her screams when she remembered that Danielle was sleeping just down the hall.

He carried her back to the bed and wanted to finish with Tuesday lying on her stomach. She had no problem with this because it was her favorite position. So when he climbed on top of her, she lifted her ass to give him access to the pussy.

It must've been his favorite too because he kept Tuesday like that for a long time just stroking her with slow but powerful thrusts. His deep groans and the sound of his headboard thumping against the wall kept Tuesday wet, but he rode her ass for so long that by the end she was in his ear begging for him to come. When he finally did, the feel of him erupting inside her was enough to trigger another orgasm for her.

When they were done, and as he lay on top of her dozing off, Tuesday didn't want to ruin the moment by telling him then, but it was on her mind. They were definitely going to have that talk in the morning and she was not looking forward to it. She just lay there awake, enjoying the warmth of his body covering hers, figuring it would probably be the last time.

Tuesday woke up the next morning to an empty bed. Marcus was gone; searching the house revealed that he'd taken Danielle with him. She looked out front and saw that only her Honda sat in the circular driveway.

Tuesday wondered why he didn't bother to wake her up if they were leaving and had no idea of where he was going or when he would be back. She thought that was awfully rude.

Then she considered the time and the fact that it was a school day and guessed he just went to drop Dani off at Bishop Burchram. It was a quick errand so he probably decided not to bother waking her. If so, he would be back in a few minutes.

Tuesday didn't know if he'd already eaten but thought it wouldn't be a bad idea to have breakfast waiting for him when he returned. It wasn't like it was going to cushion the blow, but she figured that hearing what she had to say on a full stomach couldn't hurt.

His being gone also gave her a chance to do a little snooping. She opened up a few drawers and peeked into a few closets just to see what she would find. Tuesday wasn't expecting to run across any bundles of cash or kilos of cocaine, but she was looking for anything suspicious. After all, Marcus wasn't a drug dealer but the feds had mistaken him for one for some reason.

Her trained eyes saw no telltale signs that he was involved in anything illegal. She found a bunch of paperwork from Abel Inc., which she'd already figured was his father's company, but she didn't find anything that made him look dirty.

The only thing that stood out to her was what she didn't find. There weren't any pictures of his family. The few she did see were just of Danielle, and Marcus wasn't in any of them. Tuesday didn't think too much of that because she wasn't cool with any of her family either and didn't have many pictures of herself lying around. She decided to stop being nosy and start breakfast.

Opening his cupboards did stir her OCD when she saw how disorganized his shelves were, but Tuesday resisted the urge to re-stock everything. She didn't want him to come home to the sight of all his food stacked on the kitchen floor while she had a mini freak-out because he had three different brands of canned peas.

Marcus did come home to the sight of her standing over the stove scrambling eggs in nothing but one of his long T-shirts.

"That's a good look," he said, standing in the kitchen doorway with a smile. "It don't take me long to get 'em trained."

"Boy, shut up! Did you eat something?"

He came and wrapped her up from behind. "I sure didn't, but I want to soon as I'm done with breakfast."

She bumped him with her elbow. "Stop being nasty!"

He kissed her on the neck. "I'm sorry, babe. I don't know how to be no other way."

There was a recess in the kitchen that served as the breakfast nook and that was where they sat down to eggs, sausage links, hash browns, and croissants from a can. The windows looked out onto a spacious backyard with a manicured lawn and privacy hedges. Tuesday noticed a chunk of it was roped off by the stakes that construction workers use to map out the area where something is being built soon.

"What you got planned back there?" she asked. "Adding on to the house?"

"Naw," he said, scooping a forkful of eggs. "Had thought about dropping a pool for Dani, but something came up that made me think twice about it."

"What? Is everything okay?"

"Nothing life or death," he said, responding to the concern in her voice. "It's just that I might not keep the house as long as I thought."

She flashed back to his dinner in L.A. and remembered the big move he and his accountant hinted at. Tuesday knew that it was all connected but he wasn't jumping to fill in the blanks for her.

They finished breakfast in silence because as Tuesday thought about her secrets, she realized that Marcus still had a few he was keeping from her. If he and Danielle were about to leave, then where were they going, and why was he keeping it so hush-hush? She also asked herself did she really need to come clean about everything when it was obvious that he was about to bail anyway.

Because of that, Tuesday decided to play at being "Tabitha" a while longer and didn't feel guilty about doing it.

So after breakfast she screwed him again right there in the kitchen. Tuesday was just going to use his big dick for all it was worth. If she wasn't going to get money, then she was damn sure going to get sex to make up for all those nights she went to bed horny. If nothing else, when Face came to collect, she was going to die a well-fucked bitch.

He hit her on the prep island with her legs wrapped around his waist, but when Tuesday complained about the granite countertop, he tossed her over his shoulder and fireman-carried her to the bedroom where they finished the deed.

They lay across his bed naked as newborns while Marcus used his finger to trace circles on the small of her back. He marveled at the curvature of her body, her pouty lips, and pretty green eyes. He snickered to himself then shook his head as if remembering some inside joke.

"What?" she asked, noticing his smile.

"Nothing."

"Why you lookin at me like that?"

"Nothing. I'm just thinking to myself."

She pressed him. "Then tell me what you thinkin' 'bout."

"Ain't no way to say it without sounding corny as hell!"

"Try."

Marcus propped himself up on his elbows and took her face in his hands. "How can I say you are the most beautiful woman I've ever seen without it sounding like some fake-ass line? How could I tell you how absolutely perfect I think you are without coming off like I'm running game?"

There was a sincerity in his voice and eyes that knocked Tuesday breathless. Over the years she had been told that she was fine a million times by a million different niggas but never with such eloquence or conviction. She actually blushed.

She looked away embarrassed. "Boy, shut up!"

"I'm serious," he said, turning her face back to his. "But the best part is that it doesn't begin and end with that, because your looks are just an outward reflection of your inner beauty. You're kind, you're smart and funny, and got a good heart. Plus, I just know that when the time comes, you're gonna be a great mother too."

Tuesday expressed a "thank you" with her eyes that she couldn't articulate with her lips, and he repaid them with a kiss. It sparked another make-out session with a lot of tongue-play and roaming hands but they didn't fuck again because they were still satisfied.

Although it did spill over into the shower, where they took turns lathering each other up under steaming hot water. As insane as his ripped body looked, Tuesday thought it was even sicker when it was wet and glistening.

They enjoyed watching each other get dressed too. She pulled fresh underwear from her bag and he admired the view as she squeezed her ass back into the stretch pants. From his boxers, he dove into another Polo shirt with a fresh pair of jeans.

It was time for Tuesday to go. As much as she hated to, she had to check on a few things at home, including Nicholas.

They stood at the door holding each other in silence. It was another one of those moments when they both seemed to be waiting for the other to say something.

"You know you still owe me," he said, gripping her hips.

She laughed. "Between last night and this morning, I paid you back and then some."

"I'm not talking about that. I mean from the game we played at Chuck E. Cheese: Question five. You owe me a big favor that you can't say no to."

She had already forgotten about that. "What is it?"

He whispered in her ear: "You gone find out in a little bit. I just thought I would remind you."

Tuesday still assumed that he was talking about something sexual. "Well, I don't take it in the ass without a commitment. I can't just hand out backstage passes to anybody."

He laughed. "You're such a classy lady. I'll make sure to keep that in mind."

On the drive home Tuesday thought that maybe it was time for her to get out of Dodge. Rather than just sitting around and waiting for Face to come kill her, she considered some places she might slip off to. There was no family she had a connection with here, A.D. was gone, the team was broken up, and even Marcus was about to leave with Danielle. From where she stood, there was nothing keeping her in Detroit.

Her money situation was the only thing holding her up. Things were so tight right then that Tuesday figured she probably couldn't scrape together ten thousand in cash to run with. Tushie had always been good with her money and Tuesday hoped she could tap her girl for some bands. That small piece of change wouldn't last very long, but it might be enough to put some distance between her and a bullet.

The longer she considered it, the more this seemed to be her best and only option. She was just going to leave. Get together what she could, borrow a few more, then jump in a car and put Face, Dresden, The Bounce, and all the other bullshit in her rearview.

She would go someplace where she didn't know anybody and that would allow her to start fresh. She would stop doing sticks and get a legit job. Over the years Tuesday had compiled enough fake identities that she could use any one of them to start a new life and have the paperwork to back it up. In fact, she had enough to start over as Tabitha Green providing nobody did an extensive background search on her. Plus with a little more money, she could get an identity package from Percy that only the feds would be able to see through.

Speaking of the feds, Tuesday still felt she owed Marcus a heads-up about that, even if she didn't owe him the truth about herself. She hoped to see him and Danielle one more time before leaving, but if not, she'd just give him a call while she was already on the road. She knew that was cowardly and preferred to tell him face to face.

But before she got ahead of herself, she needed money.

She needed her girl Tushie, who she secretly hoped would decide to come with her. Like Tuesday, Tushie had no children and no real ties to the city, being that she moved there from New Orleans after Katrina. Tuesday would even be cool with moving down that way if Tushie wanted to go back home.

She tried Tushie's phone, and when she didn't get an answer, she headed straight for her house.

When Tuesday parked in front of her house, she saw that both of Tushie's cars were slotted behind each other in the driveway. Her old school Cutlass was toward the rear, blocked in by the Hummer H2, which had become her everyday whip. This gave Tuesday hope that she was home but just too busy to answer her cell.

For Tuesday, hope was quickly changed to concern when she reached the side entrance to find the security door unlocked and hanging half open. She announced herself by calling Tushie's name but when she got no response, Tuesday cautiously went inside.

Concern became full-blown panic when Tuesday entered and found the crib ransacked. The kitchen right off the side door wasn't too bad, but the living and dining rooms were trashed. Furniture was flipped, the floor was littered with the contents swept from the shelves and countertops, along with the drawers, which had been yanked out and dumped. As a reflex she immediately pulled the Heckler from her purse.

When Tuesday saw that her girl's flat-screen and PlayStation were gone, she figured it was just a B & E by some young niggas from the hood. She prayed that Tushie was somewhere out with De'Lano. These type of niggas were typically cowards and only kicked in doors when they were sure nobody was home.

Tuesday went searching through the house but it was in the bedroom that she found what she most feared. It was wrecked in there too: emptied drawers, a broken lamp, a mound of clothes on the floor that had been snatched from the hangers in the closet. Tushie was on the bed.

Her best friend was naked, only partially covered by a sheet. Her eyes were still open; she'd been shot right between them. Blood spread out from her head and was soaked into the bedding.

Tuesday doubled over feeling like she'd been punched in the stomach. A scream exploded from her that sounded more like the cry of a wounded animal.

Chapter Eighteen

Pain, anger, pity, regret, but no tears. There wasn't any time and this wasn't the place to mourn. Tuesday had just stumbled onto a crime scene and there was still much that had to be done.

She was definitely going to call the cops on this one, but was going to make sure that she was long gone first. Tuesday had enough experience with the Detroit Police to know that they would treat her more like a suspect than the Samaritan who phoned it in. They would ask her who she was, what was her connection to the deceased, and Tuesday having her own unregistered gun would be the thing that got her driven away in cuffs. The last thing she needed was to spend the next seventy-two hours at the First Precinct being hammered by questions she couldn't provide the answers to.

Plus she had her own theories about what happened here. But they were only theories.

The primary one being that this was an execution disguised as a robbery gone wrong. Tuesday noticed that, while the place was trashed, it wasn't trashed in a way to suggest that the murderers were searching for anything of value. Just poking around, Tuesday came across some of Tushie's jewelry—which would get far more than the TV and game console taken from the living room. It was what made Tuesday suspect that they were taken just as a front. This had nothing to do with burglary: it was a hit.

It was only by chance that Tuesday stepped on Tushie's phone among all the debris and clutter on the floor. She picked it up and dropped it into her purse for the time being. She was going to check it later to see if there was anything in it that might help to explain why her best friend was dead.

If this wasn't about money, then what was it about? Sure, they had all made enemies, but of the crew, Tushie was just as cautious as she. Tuesday couldn't imagine that this was revenge taken by one of their marks. She sensed a much bigger and more complicated scheme at work here; Tuesday also sensed that she was very much a part of it.

Tuesday knew that Tushie kept her money in a lockbox on a high shelf in the closet, and checking, she saw that it was still there. This was another reason for her to have doubts about the burglary angle. Niggas who really did that B & E thang were trained to scout such places and would've thought to look there.

The girls didn't keep many secrets from each other, which was why Tuesday knew exactly where to find the lockbox and how to open it: 38-24-56. Tushie thought it was fitting that the combination be the measurements to the insane body that had earned her the money inside, as well as everything else she owned.

Along with some important documents relating to her house and ownership of the club, Tushie had stashed away twenty-seven thousand in cash. Tuesday did hope it would be more, but couldn't complain, because it was more than she presently had. She dropped the stacks of fifties and hundreds into her bag.

Before leaving, Tuesday wiped down the box, the door handles, and anything else she might have accidentally touched. She'd watched enough cop shows to know that all forensic technicians needed was a partial fingerprint or the tiniest piece of DNA to place you at the scene of a crime.

On the way out of the bedroom Tuesday gave her girl one last look. The dark and beautiful Louisiana stallion who had mesmerized men in life looked peaceful and serene in death. Wrapped in white linen with a crimson halo surrounding her head, she was like some macabre artist's interpretation of an angel.

Tuesday felt like a piece of shit for stealing her money, but figured better her than the dirty cops who were going to search the house. Tuesday justified it by telling herself that Tushie would rather she had it than them. That and her desperate situation was enough to convince her.

However, she still felt so trifling that Tuesday avoided her reflection in all the mirrors she passed on the way out.

Strange shit was going on, and while Tuesday didn't know what the fuck was up, she was almost sure that whoever killed her girl would be coming for her next.

While her first instinct had been to run, to protect herself by getting as far away from the city as possible, the sight of her girl dead had replaced the instinct to survive with the need to unravel this mystery—and the darker taste for revenge. She still planned to leave but was going to put a bullet in the muthafucka who did that to her partner and friend.

Tuesday did over a hundred on the Jeffries, stabbing downtown to her condo. Had she not been in such a rush or preoccupied with the image of Tushie's pretty face with a nasty bullethole right between the eyes, Tuesday might have noticed that the security booth outside the underground parking garage was empty. The guard, whose job it was to check the parking passes of all the incoming vehicles to her building, was not at his usual post. The booth was never left unattended. If one guard went on break, there was always another there to relieve him. Tuesday would've noticed this on any other day under any other circumstances and immediately known that something was wrong.

She parked the Honda in the spot that had once been reserved for her Caddy. With bag in hand, she got out and closed the door; seconds later, the sound of two more car doors slamming echoed through the cavernous structure.

Tuesday looked back and saw two niggas step away from a burnt-orange Cutlass that she'd never seen parked in there before. One was tall slim, and she even thought was kind of handsome, while the other was a short, round nigga who looked gay because he had no hair on his face. They both had on black skull caps but the tall one had on a leather jacket while Fatboy played a dark hoodie.

Tuesday knew they didn't live in the building but couldn't be sure they weren't there visiting somebody. As far as she knew, visitors were allowed to park inside the building as long as they didn't take any of the spots reserved for the residents.

Tuesday glanced back at the duo and something in her gut warned her of danger. She didn't see them pull in right before or after her, yet they didn't get out of their car until she got out of hers: like they were waiting for her. Neither man spoke as they walked side by side thirty feet behind her. Tuesday might have been a little less suspicious if they were laughing or making casual conversation, but they weren't. Both men were quiet, faces grim, and walking with purpose.

Tuesday had just found her friend murdered and knew something like that could fuck with her head. She figured she just might be tripping on some paranoid shit but still put some pep in her step. She also unzipped her big Louis bag and put her hand on the Heckler.

While she didn't look back to confirm it, Tuesday sensed that they picked up speed too. She couldn't hear their footsteps over the sound of her Louboutins snapping loudly against the concrete, but just felt they were getting closer to her.

At the rear of the garage there was a short hall that terminated in the doors to the elevator and an access to the lesser-used stairs. She knew the elevator would never get there before they did. She had the gun, but was certain they had guns too and didn't like her chances against them in a confined hallway. So as soon as she bent the corner and was out of their sight, she took that last dozen yards in an all-out run and exploded through the door that led to the stairs.

Tuesday was closing in on the second floor when she heard them burst into the stairwell beneath her. No longer could it be chalked up to paranoia or some mind game she was playing with herself; these niggas had come here for her. The sound of them scampering up the stairs in pursuit made her move that much faster.

The heels were slowing her down and the sound of them was allowing the duo to keep track of her progress. When she reached the third floor landing, she kicked off her red bottoms and didn't waste time bothering to scoop them up. The iron stair treads were going to be hell on her bare feet but she had better balance and was able to move faster. Plus without her shoes making so much noise, she was then able to keep track of them from the squeaking of their rubber soles.

Tuesday heard one of them grumble, "Hurry the fuck up" to the other and figured it was Slim talking to the fat one. From the sound of his voice she guessed she only had him by three flights, which was a floor and a half. She knew that lanky-ass nigga with those long legs was probably taking the stairs three at a time, in which case he would catch her quickly.

Tuesday bailed out of the stairwell on the fifth floor, hoping she could meet the elevator there. She lived up on twenty and had no plans on running the entire way. She was not that same girl who ran track her freshman year in high school. Going up twenty floors would be an effort if she was allowed to set her own pace, and she doubted if even a gold-medal sprinter could manage that distance at full speed.

Tuesday reached the elevator hoping that it would be at or at least close to the fifth floor. No luck. The overhead display indicated that it was up on eighteen and climbing. It would probably take three to four minutes to make its way back to the fifth floor, and Tuesday had less than a ten-second lead on her would-be killers.

The Seymour was a tall building with a long, rectangular base; and luckily, to accommodate its many residents, the fire code had insisted that it be constructed with a second elevator along with another set of service stairs. These were situated at the east end of the building in reverse position to the one where she stood.

Tuesday raced down the hall; bag leaping around her shoulders, feet bare and dirty, eyes wide from fright with the gun clenched in her hand. If she happened to bump into somebody stepping out of their apartment, they would most likely think that she was crazy and slam the door on her rather than help.

When Tuesday reached the elevator at the opposite end, the board indicated that it was on the second floor and headed her way. She looked back to make sure the lanky nigga had not appeared in the hall behind her. If she could just get inside before he came, then she could lock the doors with the emergency stop and call building security.

First the damn thing had to get to the fifth floor.

The display spent an inordinately long time at two before climbing to three, then spent a long time there. Fear had a way of warping time and made what was probably a normal wait seem much longer. Seconds were precious for Tuesday as she kept throwing glances back over her shoulder for Slim. She looked up to the board doing an anxious little dance like a child waiting to get into the bathroom.

Who sent these niggas? Why kill Tushie? Why in the hell were they trying to kill her? Tuesday's mind swirled with a dozen questions but her adrenaline was pumping too hard to deduce plausible answers.

She cursed out loud because the elevator was taking so long. Any other day there were hardly two or three people on at one time, but on this day it was moving like a hundred were getting on and off at every floor. From four it was slowly making its way to five. Behind the closed doors Tuesday could hear the elevator car moving up the empty shaft; the sound made hope and anxiety grow in equal degree.

Tuesday glanced back for Slim one last time just as the doors began to open and was thankful he still wasn't there. However, it was what she saw when she turned back that reduced her knees to jelly and sent icy spiders crawling down the length of her spine.

On the elevator was that sexy older Rick Fox–looking nigga who saved Nicholas and stayed next door to her up on twenty. Riding with him was Fatboy.

Tuesday then understood what it meant when his partner had told him to "hurry the fuck up." They knew she would try to go for this elevator because the other was too far away and she could never outpace Slim on the stairs. So this chubby nigga had left the stairwell at the first or second floor and circled around to this one, knowing she would run right into him. That also explained why the elevator was taking so long, because he was stopping it at each floor looking for her.

Again, fear has a way of distorting one's conception of time. What happened next took place in an instant, but for Tuesday it was played out in the slow motion of a Hollywood action sequence.

When the handsome neighbor saw Tuesday, he smiled and started to speak, but his expression quickly changed when he noticed the Heckler. This was the second time a door had opened and she had been waiting behind it with a pistol; he was probably starting to think she was some trigger-happy gun freak.

At the same time Fatboy's eyes lit up with recognition and it was at that moment Tuesday realized that Fatboy was actually *Fatgirl*. She was a butch lesbian with short hair and dressed in men's clothes—which explained the lack of facial hair and feminine features Tuesday noticed in the garage.

Fatgirl went for a gun that was tucked into the waistband of her loose-fitting jeans. Luckily, Tuesday had the jump on her, because her weapon was already in hand. There was no hesitation on Tuesday's part, no time to consider the legal or moral ramifications. While Fatgirl's gun hand was coming up, Tuesday's was extending forward. She squeezed the trigger, didn't yank it back or jerk it—just the way A.D. had shown her all those years ago when he first taught her to shoot.

There wasn't a bang but more like a hollow pop that was loud enough to make Tuesday's ears ring. Fatgirl's head jerked from the impact as the exit wound caused her skull to explode out the back of her wool cap. Blood and brain matter splashed against the rear wall and sprayed the neighbor, whose eyes went wide as golf balls. The round little dyke flopped onto her side with the Glock still curled in her fingers. She didn't even get off a shot.

Her neighbor's lips were moving but Tuesday couldn't make out what he was saying. She was wondering if the gunshot had temporarily made her deaf when suddenly a slug pierced his chest and knocked him backwards off his feet.

Tuesday turned and saw Slim running toward her from the far end of the hall with a pistol thrust out in front of him. He was about forty yards away and Tuesday didn't know if he was a skilled marksman or if her neighbor had been hit by a bullet meant for her.

She damn sure wasn't about to hang around to ask.

She hurried into the elevator and began frantically tapping the button to close the doors. Slim was still coming with his barking .40-cal leading the way. This forced Tuesday to flatten herself in the corner against the console as bullets poured in through the open doorway.

The elevator refused to close despite the fact she was laying on the button. In her panicked state it took her a second to realize that her neighbor had fallen into a position that left his foot obstructing the doors.

Tuesday had no choice but to put herself in the line of fire to pull him out of the way. She stooped down and tugged at his pant leg with Slim busting all the while. One bullet came so close that Tuesday heard it whistle past her ear before it tore into the rear of the elevator. He was twenty feet and closing fast with a gun that seemed to have an endless clip. When she cleared her neighbor's foot, the doors finally sealed themselves a second before he reached the elevator.

Tuesday let out an explosive gasp but took no solace in her temporary safety. She instantly pressed for twenty.

At one time her plan had been to lock herself inside and wait for building security. Things had changed because she'd killed somebody. Now the plan was to get to her condo and grab what she could, then get the fuck out of there.

The sound of gunshots had probably made more than a few tenants call the police along with building security. Tuesday was now thinking in terms of eluding them and Slim. She had no intention of leaving the Seymour in either handcuffs or a body bag.

Tuesday rode the elevator up in the company of the dead and dying. Fatgirl was done but her neighbor was lying on his back with a bloody hand clutching his chest. His tearing eyes were swirling around as if he was frightfully watching invisible phantoms surround him. All Tuesday could offer was the words "I'm sorry!" before he was claimed by the unearthly forces that stalked him. His head rolled to the side, his eyes fluttered, then closed, and Tuesday looked away, sickened.

Fatgirl was the only one Tuesday busted out, but she felt like she'd murdered him too. He was just in the wrong place at the wrong time. Tuesday knew this was true; yet, guilt still accompanied her for the ride, along with the stench of death.

As terrible as she felt about her neighbor, she was that determined not to join him.

Tuesday got off at nineteen instead of twenty then pressed for all the other floors leading up to the penthouse. Just in case Slim was checking the display board, she was hoping this would throw him off her trail a little.

From nineteen she took the stairs up to the twentieth floor, then sprinted down the hall to the door of her condo.

Tuesday was fumbling with the keys, ready to let herself inside, when she noticed that the door was already partially open. The wood in the jamb was cracked and splintered. There was a big grimy bootprint next to the knob.

Tuesday froze. The sight of that breached door revealed a violation that she wasn't ready to fully comprehend. Tuesday brought the gun up but it suddenly felt heavy in her hands. The pistol shook.

She nudged the door open with her foot. Even from the hallway Tuesday could see that her condo was a mess. Furniture was tipped, cushions ripped open, her pristine beige carpet covered with debris.

It was much like what she discovered at Tushie's house—but this was not Tushie's house. This was her home. Her sanctuary. This was the one place where she had order amidst the chaos. This had been the eye within the perpetual storm that was her life.

Tuesday experienced a panic attack brought on by her OCD. Her heart began knocking against her ribs. Her breathing was short and quick. The lack of oxygen made her feel dizzy.

Tuesday didn't want to go inside, but not seeing the extent of the damage would be more distressing than seeing it. Her imagination would torture her with pictures far worse than the reality could ever be.

She stepped inside tentatively; her legs so weak and rubbery that she leaned against the wall for support. Struggling with her purse and gun, which suddenly seemed to weigh a hundred pounds each, she collapsed when she reached the end of the short hall that served as her entrance. The carnage was so bad that she couldn't force herself beyond the living room.

Everything was destroyed. All the items had been pulled from the shelves and her glass tables were smashed into shards. The floor was littered with the soil from her potted plants. The vandals even broke her aquarium, leaving her angelfish to flop around on the soggy carpet until they suffocated.

Tuesday couldn't reach the kitchen but could glimpse enough from her position to see that it was the same. The refrigerator had been ransacked. The contents of her meticulously stocked cupboards were swept to the floor.

For a while Tuesday just sat there on her hands and knees trying desperately to draw breath. Her hands trembled so violently that she no longer could grasp the Heckler. The heart palpitations grew worse; there was a heavy weight crushing her chest. The room began to spin, then go dark. Tuesday wasn't sure which awaited her—unconsciousness or death.

Tuesday was ready to surrender to that darkness until she heard her girl's voice calling to her. *Bitch, get cho weak ass up!* she said in that Louisiana accent that got stronger when she was mad. *Dis shit ain't shit. Ev'rythang in here can be replaced. Dey just broke yo shit, dey didn't break you!*

Tuesday forced her eyes open then slowly got a handle on her breathing. As her breathing slowed, her heart began to decelerate. Her vision began to swim back into focus.

It was only after she composed herself that her oxygen-starved mind began to process the danger: If Fatgirl and Slim had already been there, then Slim knew exactly where she lived in the building and was most likely on his way.

That thought propelled Tuesday to her feet. She scooped up her bag and gun.

She was worried about her cat. Tuesday feared that Nicholas might be somewhere inside injured or dead, but couldn't bring herself to search for him. She fought off the panic attack but her sickness still wouldn't allow her to go deeper into the apartment.

She called out to him a few times but when Nicholas didn't come, Tuesday stumbled back out the door.

She felt better the moment she stepped into the hallway. It was as if the atmosphere in her condo was noxious; the doorway, a portal into a poisonous, inhospitable world that couldn't spill out past the threshold.

The condo was lost along with everything in it. Not only was residing there permanently out of the question, Tuesday knew that she would never be able to step foot in there again. This was no longer, nor could ever again be considered, home.

She bailed to the elevator opposing the one she rode up and took the stairs. After three floors she got off at seventeen and pressed for it there. Slim and building security weren't the only ones she was looking to avoid: she didn't want to ride again with Fatgirl's and her neighbor's bodies.

The elevator arrived after a minute's wait and Tuesday was grateful that it was safe to board. She caught a ride with an elderly white lady, maybe sixty, who was headed down to the garage. Tuesday tucked the Heckler in her bag before she gave the old bitch a heart attack.

Tuesday thought about taking it all the way down, then decided against the direct route. She pressed for four with plans of exiting there then switching back to the stairs on the west side of the building and taking them to the sub-basement.

Tuesday got off at the fourth floor and was halfway down the hall when Slim inexplicably appeared at the far end. He was coming out of the very same door she was headed to.

Luckily, she saw him first. Tuesday was already backpedaling before he spotted her and gave chase.

The white lady was already gone with the elevator so Tuesday had to take the eastside stairwell. She was down two flights when she heard him burst through the door above her.

Tuesday was taking the stairs as quickly as her tender feet would allow but Slim was taking only two or three then leaping down the rest to the landing. At that rate he was going to overtake her before she got to the second floor. She knew she had to find some way to make him back off.

Tuesday got to the landing between the third and second floor then just waited for him. She drew her gun.

The moment he jumped into view on the landing one flight up, Slim froze because he didn't expect her to be right below him. Tuesday busted at him three times and he stumbled, jab-stepped, then scrambled back upstairs out of the line of fire.

Tuesday's aim wasn't good enough to hit him but it didn't need to be. Killing him would have been great; however, her intention was only to slow him down. She took off again, knowing that he would have to proceed around those corners more cautiously after that. Slim couldn't be sure which landing she might be waiting on to ambush him again. This was one of those rare occasions in strategic warfare when having the low ground offered the advantage.

Having slowed him up, she reached the sub-basement two floors ahead of Slim. She ran back into the garage rummaging through her purse for the keys. She hit the button and quietly thanked whoever invented the remote starter.

The burnt-orange Cutlass was parked across from her Honda and Tuesday fired several rounds at it until she flattened the rear tire. The booming echo triggered the alarms to blare on a few of the cars around her, and if all the shooting didn't draw some attention, this surely would.

Tuesday really had to go because her gun was now empty.

Just as Tuesday was pulling out of her parking slot, Slim appeared behind her car with his gun raised. She threw it in reverse then launched toward him. He was able to crack off two shots. The first shattered the rear window but the second went wide because he dove out of the way as he fired.

She swung into the aisle then braked with screeching tires before she threw it into drive and hauled toward the exit.

Again Slim appeared behind her, shooting as he ran. She was putting more distance between them but she heard a few of the bullets puncture the car and ricochet off the metal. One of his shots was close enough to bypass the driver's seat and crack the navigation screen in the dashboard.

Tuesday raced up the service ramp and went over the speed bumps hard enough to damage the Honda's suspension. While pulling into the street, her last sight of Slim was him standing outside the building. He was breathing heavy, hunched over, with his hands on his knees.

Chapter Nineteen

Tuesday sped away from the Seymour not really sure where she was headed. It took her a moment to remember the Town Square apartment and she punched it there, doubting that whoever was behind the play knew she was keeping it. She used a lot of side streets and wasn't followed, as far as she could tell. She was also lucky that the missing back window didn't get her pulled over by police, since she had an illegal gun and a purse full of cash.

She parked the Honda behind her building, where it couldn't be seen from the street, then spent the first half hour pacing the empty rooms. The place came with two sets of vertical blinds, and Tuesday pulled them closed but was nervously peeking from the window every few minutes.

She wanted to call somebody. Tuesday felt like she needed to tell somebody about the crazy shit that just popped off but couldn't think of who. It was only then that she realized how incredibly small her circle was without Tushie. Tuesday literally didn't have a friend in the world.

After a while she walked to the closest store for soap, toiletries, and something to eat. This apartment was just supposed to be a place for Tabitha to get dropped off or picked up from, so it didn't have the basics for living, since Tuesday never intended to spend any time there. Now she imagined she would have to stay at least one night while she figured out her next move.

Upon returning, she sat on the floor cross-legged to a lunch of gas station hot wings, Doritos, and Fruitopia. After everything she'd been through, Tuesday was surprised not only to have an appetite, but that she ate voraciously. The energy she burned getting away from Slim seemed to have emptied her tank, so she refueled by devouring her meal and a couple of candy bars she grabbed as an afterthought.

After lunch there was nothing to do but sit and think.

She couldn't believe how quickly her life had gone from sugar to shit over the past few days. She lost her car, her home, her club, her best friend, and very soon she might be losing her life. The situation at her condo prevented her from getting to the few racks she had stashed there, so she was basically stuck with the clothes on her back and the bag on her shoulder containing the twenty-seven G's she took from her girl.

There had been no time to mourn for Tushie back at the house, but now the image of her pretty chocolate face and soulless eyes haunted Tuesday. It was just beginning to sink in that she would never see her again, never smoke with her again while hearing some of that deep southern game in that beautiful New Orleans accent. Tushie was dead and Tuesday knew it was somehow her fault. This, combined with the fact that she lightweight snapped on her the last time they saw each other, was enough to bring her to tears.

She got a hold of herself rather quickly because no amount of grieving has ever brought the dead back to life. Plus it was during her panic attack that she heard Tushie's voice just as clearly as if she were standing next to Tuesday. This gave her consolation that there was a small piece of her girl that she would always be carrying with her.

Instead Tuesday focused on the invisible enemies who did this and tried to see the motivation behind it.

Tuesday knew there was a short list of people who wanted her dead and Face was at the top. The only problem with considering Face was that her deadline to pay him wasn't up yet. The man had already admitted that he was more interested in seeing his money than seeing her dead. Plus she could think of no reason for him to kill Tushie.

Dresden was another possibility. He was ruthless enough and could easily find out where any of them lived. He had even made threats against her and the team in the past. He could've somehow heard that the Caine lick went wrong and was now looking to wipe them out as punishment. Dresden's crooked ass had enough contacts that it wouldn't be shit for him to hire a couple of goons.

It was plausible but Tuesday wasn't ready to accept that because something in her gut still told her that this was part of a much more complicated plan.

Tuesday felt that she owed it to the rest of the girls to put them up on what happened to Tushie. For all she knew, they might be in danger too and she wanted to give them a heads-up.

Considering their relationship, it didn't really surprise her when Baby Doll and Brianna didn't answer her calls, but she did talk to Jaye. She told her about the crazy day she had: starting with finding Tushie then having some niggas waiting at her building for her. Jaye listened, stunned, as Tuesday explained how she killed one and got away from the other after shooting it out with him. Jaye also seemed to take it to heart when Tuesday warned Jaye to be careful because niggas might be coming after her too.

Her conversation with Jaye lasted about an hour, and after that there was nothing to do but think some more. It was then that her mind went back to what happened in the elevator.

Tuesday had never actually killed anybody before and the point of planning her licks so carefully was so that she wouldn't have to. Sure, she talked a good gangsta in her office in front of the girls about killing Caine, but she always wondered if she could really do it when the time came. Talking about killing someone and actually shooting a person in the face at point-blank range were totally different things. She felt justified because she was certain that the bitch would have killed her had she not acted first.

Justified or not, Tuesday had crossed a line today that would leave her forever changed. The last shred of innocence that she could claim for herself was lost.

However, Tuesday doubted that she would lose any sleep about it because she also knew that in a case of life and death, it was a sin not to act. Every person on this planet has the God-given right to protect his or her life with deadly force. Survival is the first instinct of all living things and thankfully the human animal has not evolved beyond this. Even if the strictest proponent of nonviolence were to passively sit back during an attack on him and his family—when it be in his power to defend them—the world would not remember this man as a martyr. History would inevitably judge him as a fool, if not a coward. Life is too precious not to be defended by any means necessary.

With nothing to do and no one to call, boredom led to sleep. Tuesday was out for about forty-five minutes when she was awakened by her phone ringing from inside her bag.

Actually, Tuesday's phone was lying next to her; it was the Tabitha phone still inside her bag. She went for it, eager to speak to Marcus even though she couldn't tell him about what happened today.

She clicked on to hear him speaking quickly and panicky before she could even mutter a hello: "She's gone. She's gone. They got her. She's gone!"

Tuesday never heard Marcus sound so distressed. He wasn't making any sense to her so she tried to calm him down. "Whoa, baby, slow down! Who's gone? What are you talking about?"

He took a breath. "Dani's gone. Somebody snatched Danielle!"

Chapter Twenty

It all made sense now. As soon as Marcus told her that Danielle had been taken, Tuesday was then able to connect the dots to see the bigger picture. It became clear why Tushie was dead, why they had tried to kill her, and who was responsible.

Tuesday knew that Brianna wanted to run shit and there was plenty of animosity built up between them. Brianna had been openly pushing for the team to kidnap Danielle but Tuesday wasn't having it, so they took the next logical step. She came after her, and went after Tushie, who was the one person who had Tuesday's back. With her and Tushie out of the way, the team would be hers and Brianna could run it just the way she wanted—without all the damn rules.

Tuesday cursed herself for not seeing this coming. She didn't think Brianna had the brains or the heart to shoot a move like this, and Tuesday still wasn't convinced that it was all her. She had underestimated her rival and that mistake had cost her friend's life.

The first thing Tuesday did was call Jaye back and demand to know if she had anything to do with taking Danielle. Jaye swore on the lives of everyone she knew and loved that she knew nothing about it, but did admit that she wasn't surprised. According to her, Brianna and Doll were obsessed with the idea, but Jaye claimed to have no clue as to what they had planned. Jaye also swore that she would have warned Tuesday and Tushie if she'd known about the hit put on them.

Jaye was humble and apologetic and Tuesday didn't fault her for not seeing it coming—after all, Tuesday didn't. Jaye said that she was down for whatever and if Tuesday needed her help she shouldn't hesitate to call. Tuesday explained how she appreciated that, because without Tushie it felt good to know that there was still somebody on her team.

Minutes later she stood out in front of her building waiting for Marcus with no idea of how she was going to explain this to him. It would be hard enough just to tell him that she had been lying about who she was and her motivation for approaching him; how could she possibly tell him that his little girl was gone because of what she had set in motion? She had been taken by the very people that Tuesday had put together and trained. Worst of all, how could she possibly convince Marcus that she started this just trying to smoke him out but real feelings had developed?

When his Audi pulled up, Tuesday jumped inside not knowing what to say to him. Marcus was quiet, staring ahead as if he saw the kidnappers right in front of his car. He was gripping the wheel with both hands and the muscles in his arms made Tuesday think that he was about to rip it from the dash.

"I'm sorry!" was all she could manage. Tuesday wanted to say more but knew this wasn't the time. She could easily imagine those powerful hands reaching for her throat—and deep down she felt that he would have every right to choke the shit out of her for what she'd done. She tried but couldn't think of any words to comfort him.

"Tell me what happened?" she asked innocently.

Marcus sat there, car idling, still unable to look away from whatever he saw in front of him. "I get a call from an unavailable number around twelve forty-five saying that they got Dani and if

I go to the police she's dead. Of course I think it's some kinda joke, but just as I'm about to run to Bishop Burchram, the school calls me before I can even get out the door."

He paused, and because Tuesday could hear the pain in his voice, she didn't press him. She allowed him to tell it at his own pace.

"When I get to the school I see they're closing down early; parents are already picking up their kids. They take me into the principal's office and tell me that Dani got snatched right off the playground by two men dressed in black. They were wearing ski masks so nobody could see their faces."

"Brianna and Baby Doll," Tuesday said to herself. What she said aloud was, "What did you do?"

"I didn't want to, but I had to tell them about the call I got or else the school would've called the police. I don't know who these people are, but for right now, I have to take them seriously. I'll most likely be getting a call soon. They'll be wanting money."

"What are you going to do?"

"Whatever I have to do to get her back!"

They went back to his house, where they spent the next hour anxiously waiting for the call. Tuesday knew there was nothing she could say to ease the tension so she didn't bother to try. She just sat with him on the couch quietly squeezing his hand for support.

She heard his stomach growl and offered to make him something to eat, but Marcus refused. He did kiss her hand to show that he appreciated the effort, and it made Tuesday feel even worse.

Just then his phone shattered the silence and made Tuesday jump. It was from an unavailable number and he gave Tuesday a look to let her know it was them. While he spoke to them, she sat next to him nervously, wishing that she could hear who was talking and what was being said on the other end.

Marcus said, "What makes you think I got that type of money?"

Tuesday couldn't hear the response but could guess that it had something to do with what she told them about his father. "Well, you know it's gonna take me some time to put that together. It's not like I can just pull it out my ass!"

"Plus, I want proof of life!" he demanded. "For all I know, she could already be dead. Let me talk to her right now or you can kiss my ass from here to Kalamazoo!

"Or else that same money you asking for will pay for the contract I put on your life. I'll put a loaf on your head so goddamned thick that your own mother will knock your noodles out to collect it."

Tuesday was surprised to see him boss up on the kidnappers with Danielle's life on the line. She knew that he was concerned about getting Danielle back safely but liked that Marcus wasn't just going to let them call all the shots. It scared Tuesday but turned her on a little bit too.

Going gangsta seemed to work, because they put Danielle on the phone. His voice cracked with emotion as he spoke to her: "Yeah, baby, I know you're scared and I know you wanna come home. I'm coming to get you real soon okay, I promise. Just be good and do what they say and you'll be home with me real fast, baby. I love you. I love you so much!"

Tuesday saw that his eyes were glazed with tears; a few of them escaped from her own before she was able to blink back the rest. She felt his anger, felt Dani's fear. Tuesday told herself that no matter what happened, she was going to kill the bitches responsible. It was bigger than what they did to Tushie and tried to do to her. Just getting the girl back wasn't enough to satisfy Tuesday. She wanted blood behind this.

Marcus started to say something more but she could tell by the way he was cut off that they yanked the phone away from Danielle. After that he was quiet for a moment and sprinkled in a couple of *uh-huhs* that let Tuesday know he was receiving instructions for the exchange.

"I heard all of your demands and promise to do exactly what you say, but I need you to listen to me for a second." There was a scowl on his face that was so intense and seething with rage that Tuesday thought he could have been turning into a monster. It was the first time she'd ever seen him look ugly.

He said: "I just want you to know that if anything happens to that little girl, I'm going to find out who you are and kill your entire family. And no, I don't just mean your immediate family, I'm talkin' 'bout aunts, uncles, first and second cousins, grandparents. I'm even gone kill the people who ain't blood but been around you so long that they call themselves fam."

The way he went in sent chills through Tuesday because, despite the look on his face, Marcus didn't sound angry. His calm tone suggested that he was stating plain facts. He could've been listing the ingredients to a recipe rather than making vicious threats.

"And after I've killed everybody who's ever known and loved you, I'm gonna save you for last, but I'm not going to kill you. No, this is where it gets fun. I'm going to take a sledgehammer to your spine, crushing every vertebra, until you're paralyzed from the neck down. Then I'm going to snatch out your eyes, cut out your tongue, and pour acid into your ears. I'm going to leave you blind, unable to move, talk, or hear: basically a prisoner in your own body. And as you spend the rest of your life as a living corpse—in eternal darkness and silence, pissing and shitting on yourself with no way to communicate with the outside world or even kill yourself to end the misery—you're not going to have anything left but the memories of everybody and everything you lost. All this because you fucked around and put hands on the wrong child.

"I swear to whatever God you believe in, I will dedicate the rest of my life to this purpose. I will not rest, work, party, fuck, or make a new friend until this is done."

Marcus painted a pretty graphic picture, and while Tuesday didn't know if it fazed whomever was on the phone, it sure scared the shit out of her. He was describing a fate ten times worse than death: a lifetime of shame, helplessness, and pain, with an inability to put an end to any of it. She understood that he was upset about Dani, but the fact that he could even conceive of such a torture made Tuesday look at him in a somewhat different light. It was obvious that he had a dark side that she didn't know about.

When he got off the phone, she had a million questions. *What did they say? How much did they ask for? Did they threaten to kill Dani?*

She also wanted to know if he spoke to a man or a woman. Would Brianna be stupid enough to make the call herself or have someone do it for her?

But before Tuesday could ask anything, he turned to her, his eyes ablaze with some combination of anger and confusion.

He snarled at her. "Tabitha, tell me right now who these people are and what the fuck you gotta do with this."

Chapter Twenty-one

The price: three million in cash.

The conditions, the first of which had already been mentioned: no police. Second, they had until eight o'clock that night to get the money. Third, it was to be placed in a duffel bag and delivered to a place that would not be disclosed until minutes before the drop time. Lastly, and the part most baffling to Marcus, the ransom was to be brought by his new girlfriend; and if she didn't come alone and with the money, Danielle was going to be sent back to him in pieces.

"Why? Why would they ask for you?" He stared at Tuesday again, probing her with those dark brown eyes. "Tabitha, tell me you don't have nothing to do with this. Baby, please tell me what's good!"

For most of her life Tuesday had been manipulating and running game on niggas. They'd been nothing more than pawns to be used as ATM's, boy-toys, or goons when she needed. Lying to them came as easy as breathing. Tuesday couldn't remember how many times she'd lied about her name, address, her plans, or how she felt. Over the years she had used that smile and those beautiful gray-green eyes to sell more bullshit than all the fertilizer plants in the world combined.

However, at that moment she wanted nothing more than to tell this man the truth. She wanted to get it out, to be unburdened by it, because this lie felt like a heavy weight that she was carrying and she wanted nothing more than to just put it down. She wanted to tell him everything from start to finish. How growing up without a father and having no positive male influences left her with no empathy for men. How her mother didn't help because she changed boyfriends as often as she changed panties. How from the time she developed she was told that her sexuality was the best way to get what she wanted out of life. How spending years in the strip club caused her to see men at their worst on a nightly basis: tricking, cheating, and so disrespectful to women that it was easy to view them as targets. How coming in he'd been nothing but a mark she was looking to come up off of, but things had changed. How being with him and Danielle had opened her mind to the possibilities of being a wife and mother—things she'd never considered before. How in such a short time she'd come to care so deeply for them both. How guilty she felt because this was all happening because of her. How she was willing to give, not just everything she owned, but her very life to make sure that Danielle got back to him unharmed.

"Tabitha, how could they even know about you?" Marcus pressed. "Why are they so dead-set on you bringing the ransom?"

Again Tuesday wanted to say all those things that flashed into her mind during those two seconds since he asked the first time. She looked at him with a straight face, blinked those gray-green eyes and said: "I don't know. If they knew about Dani's school and how to get in touch with you, then they've probably been following you. In which case, they've seen us together.

"As far as why they want me to bring it instead of you, they probably figure that I'm less of a threat because I'm a woman."

She stared at him, hoping that he swallowed that, and after a while he nodded thoughtfully. If Marcus had any doubts or suspicion that she was lying, it couldn't be read on his face.

Tuesday really did want to tell him the truth but just couldn't bring herself to do so. This was different from the past when she lied to niggas because she didn't care. Now she was lying because she did.

Regardless of the reason, she still felt bad about it, though.

"Is getting the money together going to be a problem?" she asked, eager to change the subject. "You only got about six hours."

Marcus fell back against the couch and sighed. "Getting the money here on time is nothing; having to ask for it is the problem."

Tuesday's facial expression was one of confusion.

He sighed again and Tuesday could tell by his demeanor that Marcus didn't want to talk about this. "I work as a financial consultant in my father's company—I'm not some spoiled trust-fund brat! I put myself through school, I earn my own money, and the only reason I have access to his corporate jet is because my position in the company allows it.

"Tabitha, I do all right—I mean my money straight—but I don't have nowhere near three million dollars."

Tuesday then understood what the thing was with him and his father. Why he lived here and like this while Daddy had long paper and a fat-ass mansion out in Beverly Hills. Marcus was determined to be his own man. He was not content to slide through life on his father's money and name, but to earn everything he had for himself. He probably didn't even like the fact that he worked at his father's company, which could explain why he was so secretive about what he did.

Tuesday shook her head. "So now you've got no choice but to go to him with your hand out to save Dani?"

"Look, the old man loves Dani, and for her he'd give up three hundred million without blinking an eye. It's just that I haven't asked my father for money since I was thirteen and swore I never would. I know it's just foolish pride, but this is hard for me."

She grabbed his hand again. "I can understand you not wanting to be in your father's shadow, but this isn't about you and him. It's about Dani."

He nodded to agree. "You're right. It's about Dani."

Marcus stood up with his phone in hand. "And just so you know, I don't have any problem with being in the shadows: in fact, I try like hell to make sure I stay in them. It's being in the limelight that bothers me." He stepped into the kitchen to call his father, and Tuesday didn't fault him for not wanting to do it in front of her.

While he was away, she thought about everything that happened today and what was probably going to happen tonight.

Despite what she told him, Tuesday knew exactly why they wanted her to bring the ransom and actually thought it was clever for the girls to set it up that way. After missing her at the Seymour, Tuesday had no doubt that she was about to walk straight into a bullet. In a few hours, she would have to deliver the money and herself right into the hands of her murderers. The trick was for her to figure out how to get Danielle back, kill those bitches, and still walk out of there with her own life.

Tushie was the only one she socialized with outside the club and because of this she knew very little about Brianna or Baby Doll on a personal level. She didn't know who they fucked with, the places they hung, or even where they lived. The idea had been to keep things between them strictly business so Tuesday didn't know too much about them and didn't want them knowing too much about her.

Plus The Bounce was a cash business where the girls danced for tips rather than earned a wage. This meant that Tuesday never needed to keep the type of employee records that listed full names, addresses, or Social Security numbers for tax and insurance purposes. The girls didn't fill out applications; she and Tushie hired them simply on how they looked and danced, so all she had for many of them was a stage name and phone number. It was the same for Brianna and Baby Doll.

That thought gave Tuesday an idea, but in order to make it

work, she was going to have to practice what she just preached to Marcus. It meant having to swallow her pride and asking someone that she didn't like for help.

She needed Dresden. Tuesday would rather have a lit cigarette put out in her eye before asking the dirty lieutenant for a favor, but for Danielle she would do whatever.

Tuesday was almost certain that Tank had tracked Doll to the club by slipping a GPS chip into her phone. While she didn't have GPS, she figured that Dresden could somehow put a trace on Bree and Doll's phones to find out where they were hiding out. She didn't understand the science involved but had seen enough cop shows on TV to know that this was something the police did all the time.

She took her phone into the bathroom to make the call. Tuesday didn't want Marcus to overhear and didn't want to have to explain who she was talking to. She closed the door, locked it, then put the lid down on the toilet seat and sat there.

She had not talked to Dresden in a while, and as far as he knew, everything with the lick was still going according to plan. She knew he was going to grill her about the who, why, and what for needing these phones traced but Tuesday thought up a believable lie the moment the idea came to her.

When she called, he answered on the second ring. There was enough noise and people talking in the background for Tuesday to guess that he was at the precinct.

"What?" he barked sharply in that raspy voice that irritated her.

"I need you." She purposely said it with a strong sexual undertone hoping to soften him up.

It didn't work. "What you need is to explain to me why you been ducking me for over a week! You need to tell me how it's going with Caine and how soon I can have my money."

"I was just calling you about that. You not gone believe what happened."

"I don't wanna hear any bullshit!" he said impatiently. "I just wanna hear how much and where are we meeting to collect."

"The whole play goes down with no problem," she lied. "We get this nigga and make 'em take us to the safe. One point three million in cash and at least a million more in jewelry."

"Two point three million!" he gasped with excitement. Tuesday could hear the gears turning in his head as he tried to calculate his share after a six-way split.

"I knew you could do it!" he said, laughing. "You ruthless, cold-hearted bitch! You cast your spell and the poor bastard never had a chance against those wicked green eyes and that tight pussy!"

Tuesday pretended like his comment didn't bother her. She hated Dresden, and his opinion of her should've meant less than shit, but the fact he viewed her as some evil witch who only lived to torture men was actually a little hurtful. She also knew that it stung only because it was so close to the truth.

"So when do I get my money?" he asked eagerly.

"Now that's where the problem comes up."

"Problem? What problem?" Tuesday could hear the excitement in his voice get replaced by panic. "Don't think for one second you bitches are gonna fuck me outta my share!"

"You already got fucked! Both of us did."

Tuesday laid out a detailed story in which the girls were back at the club counting up the score when two of them double-crossed the team. According to her, Brianna and Baby Doll decided they wanted it all, pulled straps and took everything. No cut for her, no cut for him. He was ass-out just like the rest of the crew.

Dresden was furious. "Tell me where those bitches are right now. I'm gonna kill them both!"

Tuesday smiled because he was sucking it up just like she knew he would. "Calm down, babe, you're a highly decorated officer and you don't need to get your hands dirty on this. I can handle it, but I need a small assist from you."

The lieutenant was quiet for a moment and was probably deciding whether he could trust her or not. He finally said, "What do you need from me?"

Tuesday gave him the phone numbers and said she wanted him to run a trace. It took everything she had to convince him that she was on the level and that the next time he saw her she would be holding a bag filled with enough money for him to retire on.

Dresden was skeptical, but his greed won out over his suspicion and he agreed to run the trace. He tried to explain the procedure for having something like this done (the department heads to be notified, the trouble it entailed, the paperwork involved) and Tuesday only half listened as he spouted a bunch of codes and cop lingo. He promised that he was going to call as soon as he found out where the girls were at, and that was all she cared to hear.

When she got off the phone, she flushed the toilet and washed her hands just to keep up the front. She came out the bathroom to find Marcus standing right outside the door. Tuesday didn't know how long he'd been waiting or exactly what he'd heard.

"The money's coming," he said flatly. "It's being flown in and should be here with at least two hours to spare."

Tuesday nodded, trying to pretend that he hadn't startled her. "So fast. That was pretty easy."

He gave her a look. "No. It was harder than you could possibly know."

Tuesday understood. At the end of the day, a man's pride was all he had.

"The money's not going to be here till six," he said, walking back toward the kitchen. "Nothing to do till then but wait."

Marcus went into the refrigerator for the ingredients to make a sandwich: whole wheat bread, lettuce, tomato, condiments, and thin deli-sliced turkey. He sat everything on the prep island and began pulling lettuce leaves off the head.

Despite the fact that he hadn't eaten, Tuesday could tell that he was just doing this to fill the boredom. She saw in his overall demeanor that he was very worried about Danielle and was just trying to play strength.

He was spreading on the mayonnaise when she came and embraced him from behind, just sensing that he needed to be held. He dropped the knife and bread then laced his fingers into hers. For a long time they just stood there like that with neither of them speaking. She placed her ear to his back and listened to the rhythm of his heavy heart.

After about two minutes he finally said, "If anything happens to her—"

Tuesday cut him off before he could finish the thought. "Nothing will! We're gonna get her back and she's gonna be okay." It was a bold promise, being that she was basically powerless on this end.

As much as he tried, Marcus was unable to hold up under the emotional strain. He didn't cry out loud but Tuesday could tell from the way his body convulsed that he was letting out quiet sobs. She just squeezed him tighter and murmured some consoling words. Tuesday didn't turn him around because he probably didn't want her to see this weak moment.

"I've taken so much from her. She deserves better than me!"

Tuesday didn't understand what he meant by that and couldn't even be sure she heard him correctly because he was so choked up. She figured that he was feeling guilty about Danielle and just chalked it up to that.

When Tuesday took Marcus to his room and laid him on the bed, it had nothing to do with sex this time. They cuddled together and seemed to be drawing strength from each other's touch. This had been a crazy day for her too with finding Tushie and the shit that jumped at her building, so she needed his support as much as he needed hers.

Tuesday didn't know exactly when he dozed off, but after a while she looked and saw that he was sleeping. She was still rested from the nap she took at the apartment so she slid out of bed, careful not to wake him.

In the kitchen she finished making the sandwich he started and sat it in the microwave. She thought he might be hungry when he finally got up.

Next she cut on the TV in the den, eager to see if any of today's drama had made the news. Channel 4 broke a story about a carjacking on West Warren but nothing was said about Tushie or the bodies at her building.

Sitting there reminded her of how Danielle had fallen asleep in her arms during *Aladdin*. It was just last night that she'd sat safely between the two of them, but so much had happened since then that it seemed like a long time ago.

Tuesday brought her purse and thumbed through the money again hoping that she missed some in the rush count she made in Tushie's bedroom. Counting money fast and accurately had always been a talent, so it didn't surprise her to learn that she got it right the first time: $27,450 was all Tuesday had to work with. She had a couple thousand more stashed at her condo, but for obvious reasons she couldn't get to that.

Rifling through her bag, she came across Tushie's phone, which she had almost forgot she had. Tuesday still didn't really know why she took it. She snatched it up just on a whim, not knowing what she thought it might be useful for.

She went through it feeling bad about invading her girl's privacy—first stealing her money and now this. She saw her calls, some from her new friend De'Lano and a few with a New Orleans area code that must've come from family. Tuesday checked her voice mail and only found the message that she herself had left just before getting to Tushie's house.

Tuesday got a weird feeling when she saw De'Lano's name. This was the person that Tushie had been spending all her time with lately and Tuesday thought that she might only be suspicious of him out of jealousy or simply because she didn't know him.

Whatever it was, something about the nigga stirred a bad feeling in her.

Tuesday used Tushie's phone to call him but it went straight to voice mail. She didn't leave a message. Truthfully, she didn't know what she was going to say if he answered.

From the jump something had been nagging that this whole play was deeper than she thought, and it was then that she stumbled across the evidence to prove it. As Tuesday kept looking through Tushie's phone, she eventually made a discovery that blew her mind.

She was in the photo gallery scrolling through a couple pictures Tushie had snapped with her phone when she saw him. It was a shot of De'Lano taken while he was sleeping on her couch with no shirt on. Tushie must've thought that he looked so sexy that she'd taken it just as a keepsake.

Tuesday became so enraged that she momentarily forgot that Marcus was sleeping upstairs. She cursed out loud and began smashing the phone against the walnut table until the screen cracked.

Even in low light and taken from a bad angle, Tuesday instantly recognized him.

Tuesday then knew exactly who killed her girl. It was the same nigga who just tried to kill her at the Seymour.

De'Lano was Slim.

Chapter Twenty-two

Tuesday was still trying to wrap her mind around the implications of her girl being set up. This meant that the kidnapping and the hit on them had been planned for at least a month. They had known enough to put a nigga on Tushie and taught him exactly what to do to reel her in. Tuesday then realized that her enemies were far more clever than she had given them credit for.

The same thing had been done to her girl that they usually did to niggas, and Tuesday didn't miss the irony. She had taught Tushie how to get close to a mark, but not how to avoid being one. It was something that she never could've planned for.

She was thinking about all the other things that she might've slipped when Dresden's call came. The trace went through and he knew where Bree and Baby Doll both were. He tried to tell Tuesday about all the shit he had to go through to get it done, wanting her to kiss his ass, and she played along just to get the information.

He explained that using the different cell phone towers around the city, he could pinpoint their location within twenty feet. In front of him was a large map of Detroit with Brianna and Baby

Doll appearing as two colorful dots blinking on a screen. It wasn't a live camera feed but just as accurate.

Tuesday couldn't believe it when he said they were on Schaefer and 7 Mile because that meant they were at The Bounce. She couldn't be sure if Danielle was there with them or if that's just where they intended for the deal to go down. All Tuesday knew was that the system the police were using to live-track their phones put both of them there at that moment.

The audacity of those bitches to use her own club as their little hideout. With it being closed over the past couple days, they probably figured she would've never thought to look there—and truthfully, she wouldn't have. That De'Lano nigga must've taken the spare set of keys off Tushie, which was how they got inside.

Dresden got off the phone promising to let her know if either of them moved. She knew that he was only being so helpful in the hopes of her getting back his share of the money. He wouldn't have given a fuck if he knew this was really about trying to save a little girl's life, especially a black one.

Tuesday had to move quickly but didn't know what her next move should be. She had the element of surprise but not much else. If she went in there guns blazing, she risked getting herself and Danielle killed. If she went in there guns blazing and Danielle wasn't with them, she risked never finding out where she was.

She needed to come up with one of her brilliant, airtight plans that accounted for every possibility. The problem was that she didn't have enough information and was too emotionally involved to analyze this properly.

When Marcus woke up, he told her that his father was flying the money in on his jet and that it was almost time to go pick it up. Fifteen minutes later they were out the door and headed to the airport to meet him. Tuesday couldn't imagine anybody else putting together that kind of paper that fast, but she figured that his old dude probably tripped over three million dollars when he rolled out of bed in the morning.

They met him inside the hangar where the Abel Inc. G-650 was being refueled. Tuesday stayed close to the hangar doors; besides being nauseated by the fumes, she didn't want to be in the mix when he talked to his father.

She watched as Brandon King stepped off the plane carrying a black leather case about the size of a travel pen for a small dog. He passed it to Marcus and gave him a quick pat on the shoulder. Marcus accepted it with a nod, they exchanged a few words, and then he turned and was headed back toward her while the old man got back on his plane. It didn't take five seconds and Tuesday was fucked up because she used to have to go through way more than that just to get ten dollars from her mother.

Going back through the airport, Tuesday was a lot more nervous and walked at a much faster pace than he did. After 9/11 it just seemed like it should be a lot harder transporting a case full of cash; apparently it was just another one of the perks of owning a private jet. Marcus was calm, but Tuesday was sweating like he was carrying ten kilos of dope. When they made it out the front exit without being stopped or searched by anyone, she breathed a sigh of relief.

When they got back to his car, Marcus sat the case on the backseat and opened it. Tuesday couldn't believe her eyes. Ben Franklin never looked so handsome or had so many twins. Tuesday knew the difference between dope money that had changed hands a few times and that crispy shit straight from the treasury. Fresh new one-hundred-dollar bills were bound together in thick fifty-thousand-dollar stacks. She watched, mesmerized, as he pulled out each one and hefted it in his palm. Every brick contained five hundred C-notes, and he seemed to be checking it by weight rather than thumbing through all the bills.

Tuesday had never seen that much money in her life and the sight of it had her in a trance. She thought about all the nights she danced on stage for crumbs, all the trifling-ass niggas she had to fuck, and all the risks she took just to see a small piece of that. She would spend weeks, and sometimes months, putting together the perfect lick for a few thousand; meanwhile, this nigga made one phone call and had millions delivered to him on a silver platter.

Must be nice to have a rich daddy! she thought to herself. As much as she liked Marcus, and respected that he was trying to be his own man, there was a part of her that was really hating right then.

It took some time but he finally counted sixty of those 50K bundles. When he was done, Marcus stacked them neatly back into the case and zipped it closed.

"It's all there?" Tuesday asked innocently. She tried to pretend that her eyes weren't glued to the money the whole time he was counting it.

He nodded to confirm it was, then put the car in gear and pulled away from the airport. Tuesday heard it calling to her from the back-seat but resisted the urge to turn around and just stare at the bag.

They were on the Lodge Freeway and headed back out to Romulus when Tuesday began to feel sick. She was holding her stomach and rocking in her seat. She was moaning and her face was contorted with pain.

"You all right?" he asked, glancing over to her with a concerned look. "You say I make you, but I didn't think you meant sick for real!"

"It was the smell of that jet fuel at the airport," she groaned. "That shit got my head bangin' and my stomach fucked up."

"Don't worry, babe, I'm gone hit a Rite-Aid before we get to the house. Chase down a couple aspirin with some Pepto and you should be straight."

Tuesday shook her head. "I don't think I'm gone make it!" she cried. "Pull over. I think I'm 'bout to throw up!"

Marcus quickly made his way to the side of the freeway and Tuesday cracked the door then stuck her head out. He listened as she spent a minute making some disgusting sounds, but from his angle he couldn't tell if anything came up.

When Tuesday pulled her head back inside, Marcus asked if she felt better but she didn't answer. When she went into her bag Marcus thought it was for a breath mint or some gum. He didn't know what to think when she pulled out the Heckler.

Tuesday shook her head. "I'm so sorry about this. I like you, Marcus, I really do, but I need that money!"

He thought that Tuesday was joking but there was nothing in her face to suggest that she was. Her eyes were the color of dirty ice and she had the pistol aimed at his ribs. For a minute the only sounds to be heard were the vehicles racing past them on the freeway at eighty miles per hour.

Marcus was confused. "Tabitha, what the hell are you doing?"

Tuesday sighed. "Look, I'm not who you think I am, Marcus. There's a lot going on here and I don't have time to explain it. I need you to slowly undo your seat belt and get out the car. Leave the money!"

Marcus just stared at her with his mouth hanging open. He couldn't believe what he was hearing. "You would do this to me when you know I need that to get Dani back? If you steal this money, it's just like you're killing her yourself."

"I'm not gonna leave Dani hangin'. I promise you that I'm gone get her back, but I need to do it my way. The whole ransom drop tonight is just a set-up. They're gonna kill Dani and me then just take the money. I know how these bitches operate!"

"You know how they operate?" He paused for a second and Tuesday could see the exact moment when the truth hit him by the expression on his face. Marcus put his hands over his eyes and slowly shook his head.

"Sonofabitch! How could I be so damn stupid! That's why they wanted you to bring it in the first place." He looked at her with a little smirk. "You set all this up. You been playing me from the start."

The way he was staring at her made Tuesday's chest feel tight and she could hardly breathe. She wanted to tell him everything, but the explanation was too long and complicated to get into right then. She had a plan on how to get Danielle back but time was a factor.

Tuesday explained: "I'll admit that I came into this for the wrong reasons but I didn't have anything to do with Dani being taken; I done my share of dirt but I don't kidnap kids.

"Now I know who's got her and I'm gonna get her back, but I need you to trust me!"

"That's pretty hard to do while you're pointing a gun at me!"

"Look, Marcus, I don't have time for this. If you wanna see Dani alive again, you need to do what I say."

"That's funny, because you sounded exactly like a kidnapper just then."

"Get out!" she said, thrusting the pistol deeper into his ribs. Tuesday was wearing a vicious scowl. "Don't make me peel yo shit!"

It was a bluff because the Heckler was empty. Tuesday had spent her last few bullets flattening the tires on Slim's Cutlass.

Marcus seemed to be calling her bluff, because he just sat there staring at her defiantly. "You're not gonna shoot me, Tabitha. I know you won't."

Tuesday brought the pistol up to his head and cocked it. "Do you see my hand shaking? Do I look nervous to you right now?

"Quit acting like you know me because you don't. We didn't meet by accident—you was a mark. These feelings we got for each other ain't real. This what the fuck I do. Don't get it twisted just because I gave you some pussy and a little bit of head.

"Now you can give up the money or I can pop yo ass and take it! It don't make me none either way."

That seemed to be enough to convince Marcus. She ordered him out of the car and he slowly undid his seat belt just the way she instructed. He had to make sure traffic was clear before he opened the door and slid out on his side.

Tuesday scooted into the driver's seat. She pulled the door closed and spoke to him through the open window. "This might not mean much, but I'm sorry about this, and I'm really gonna get Dani back for you."

Marcus mugged her with some combination of anger and disgust. "Why should you feel sorry? You're just doing what you do, right?"

It wasn't exactly an insult but to Tuesday it felt like one. She would've felt better if he called her a "trifling bitch" or "scandalous slut" but even in a situation like this, Marcus was the personification of class.

She whispered the words "I'm sorry" one last time before she meekly looked away from his eyes and rolled up the window.

When Tuesday pulled off in his Audi, she looked back and saw that Marcus was just standing there as if he really did think it was a joke and expected her to come back. Once she merged into freeway traffic, Tuesday checked again in the rearview after she'd driven about a quarter mile and saw that he finally started walking along the shoulder.

Her emotions welled up and her throat got tight but Tuesday fought back the urge to cry. She reminded herself that this was the game she played. Marcus was cool and she really liked him, but three million dollars was enough to get her shit all the way together. Then she had already peeped enough to know that he was planning to leave anyway so it wasn't like there was any future for them. His father had enough money to where three tickets wouldn't be missed. Plus, she was about to risk her life to get his little girl back, so that ought to count for something.

Tuesday told herself all these things so she wouldn't feel so guilty.

It didn't help.

Chapter Twenty-three

Tuesday was on the freeway with a bag containing three million in cash on the backseat. It would've been easy just to bust up right then with the money but she was going to stay true to her word and get Danielle back first.

However, no part of her plan involved paying one penny in ransom. As far as Tuesday was concerned, that shit was already hers; and for what they did to Tushie, all she had for those bitches were bullets.

Speaking of which, the first thing she had to do was get to some heat. The Heckler was empty and was too little to get the job done anyway. The five full-automatic M11's that she bought from Face for her and the girls at the start of this mission were all stashed at her condo. Even if she could go back there, the problem was that the cops were probably sitting on the Seymour waiting for her to come home.

She called Dresden to see if she was hot and after he checked around with some friends within the PD, he called her back to confirm that she was. Dresden told Tuesday that the security cameras on the fifth floor had caught her shooting the lesbian at the elevator. Warrants had been issued for her and the unnamed suspect who shot the innocent bystander who lived next door to her.

Dresden also informed Tuesday that the police had already raided her apartment and seized the guns along with the last of her money. Although that case was being handled by a different department from his, Dresden said that the five converted assault rifles and the silencer offered a good chance that the case might get picked up by the feds. So to answer her question, she wasn't just hot, she was scorching.

In light of what already happened, the image of twenty officers going through her personal things didn't mean much to Tuesday. She had already chalked up the condo and everything in it as a loss. Her clothes could be replaced and the money they confiscated was just change compared to the three tickets in the backseat. Tuesday was only concerned about her cat.

Dresden grilled her about the shooting and Tuesday told him everything. She let him know about Tushie and how the situation popped at her building, but left out the real reason why it happened. Instead she tied it all into the lie she told earlier: Brianna and Baby Doll were behind the set-up, only Dresden thought it was all about them stealing their money and not taking a little girl.

Dresden was worried about Tuesday, but it was only because she might get arrested before he got paid. He warned that by tomorrow her face would be all over the news. His final piece of advice was to handle her business quickly and get that money back, then to just lay low somewhere until they could meet. Tuesday pretended to agree just to get him off the phone, but she planned to be long gone by tomorrow.

With the heat on her head, this made time even more critical. It was six thirty and the deal was in an hour and a half. The police might be swooping down on her before she could even get Danielle back.

Then Tuesday had another thought that disturbed her. What if the police were using her phone to track her the same way that Dresden was doing Brianna's and Baby Doll's?

She pulled the phone from her bag and tossed it out the window right there on the Lodge Freeway. It got crushed by a large auto-hauler that was behind her carrying a shipment of Hyundais to a dealership.

She still had Tushie's and the Tabitha Green phone; she pulled out the latter to call Face. She still had to deal with Dani's kidnappers, which meant she needed to buy more guns. Luckily, Tuesday now had more than enough money to clear up her debt with him.

It was just before seven when she got to Face's junkyard and the exchange was only an hour away. Tuesday parked the Audi outside his garage and left the car with her big Louis bag practically bursting with cash. It was loaded up with five of those fifty-thousand-dollar bundles and she figured Tushie's twenty-seven stacks was more than enough to cop something for the work she had to put in tonight.

Before she got there, Tuesday was smart enough to stop and move the big black case with the rest of the money to the trunk. It was so heavy that the effort exhausted her, but it had to be done. Face was notorious for hiring crackheads to work as mechanics and the last thing she wanted was for one of them to peek inside the car and get curious.

When Tuesday walked up, Face greeted her at the door. "Damn, girl, that's the new A8. Is that you?"

She ignored him. Tuesday made a beeline straight for his office without bothering to speak, went into her bag and just started slamming the cash bricks on his desk one after the other while Face watched with wide eyes.

When she was done, Tuesday stood there with her arms folded. "Two fifty nigga, just like I promised!"

Face picked up two of the stacks and began clapping with them. "I never doubted you for a second. Mind if I ask how you came upon it?"

Tuesday was in no mood to explain. "Don't worry 'bout it. I owed you and now you paid."

"You owed me four hundred!" he reminded her. "I took The Bounce for one fifty out of love."

"I don't give a fuck about that club, nigga, I'm on to bigger and better shit! I'll bring the paperwork over for you to sign tomorrow." That was only half true. While Tuesday didn't care about owning The Bounce House anymore, she figured that by tomorrow she would either be dead, locked up, or a thousand miles away.

Face thumbed through the crispy new bills and noticed that each bundle was wrapped in the official Federal Reserve band. He looked at her skeptically. "This shit look more like bank money than dope money. Don't tell me you and yo girls done went Queen and Jada and set it off?"

"I ain't got time for this," Tuesday said impatiently. "You got what I owed you, that's a done deal. Can we get on to new business?"

"Sho nuff!" Face found a plastic bag and swept the money into it. "What can I do for you?"

"Shit might get hectic tonight. I need something I can keep close to me. Heat ain't shit if you can't get to it, nigga! I need another one." Tuesday pulled out some more money to indicate that she was ready to go shopping.

Face nodded then reached for his phone. "Hold up, just let me text the wifey right quick. I was s'posed to be on my way to the cut an hour ago."

Face lifted the trapdoor and took her down into The Gun Store. While in the cellar Tuesday was adamant that all she wanted was another M11—a gun she'd already fired and was familiar with—

298 • Zaire Crown

but Face kept trying to show her a bunch of different models. This made her suspicious, because Face had never been one for the hard sell. Seeing that two-fifty must've given him the idea that she had plenty more to spend and Tuesday guessed that he was just trying to get a little deeper into her pocket.

It took her fifteen minutes to convince him that all she wanted was another M11, shells, and extra ammo for her Heckler. They came upstairs and concluded their business in his office where she cashed him out to the tune of two grand.

Face offered to knock off a few hundred to play with her feet but Tuesday passed. Her money was straighter than straight now so she didn't need to do any tricking for a discount.

Tuesday left after parting words but when she stepped outside, she thought her eyes were playing tricks on her and had to do a double take. She had parked the Audi only a few feet away from his garage but now it was gone. For a moment Tuesday was dumbstruck; she just stood there rubbing the keys in her hand as if that would make the metallic gray sedan magically reappear.

It didn't take her long to connect the dots: That text he was supposed to have sent his wife was really him telling one of his workers to bring a tow truck. All that bullshit in the cellar was just about stalling her so they could get the Audi hooked up and hauled away before she got back upstairs.

Tuesday snatched the M11 out her bag and charged back into his office but Face was already expecting this. He was standing behind his desk waiting with a bigger and much more destructive-looking assault rifle.

Tuesday didn't know what the fuck he was holding but it looked like the type of shit they used over in Iraq to shoot down helicopters. The sight of it stopped her in her tracks and made her forget everything she was about to say.

His voice was calm. "Don't be stupid, TK, just sit the keys on the desk and leave. Besides, you know I wasn't stupid enough to hand you a loaded gun."

Pulling out the clip revealed that it was empty. Tuesday had bought ammo but it did no good still being in the box. She had also bought shells for her pistol, and that was loaded; however, that was in her bag and the beast Face was holding would put a hole in her the size of a dinner plate before she ever got to it.

"So this for us?" she asked with a humorless smile. "After all we done been through—all the years we go back and all the money I done sent yo way—you just gone carjack me, nigga?"

Face wasn't affected by her bringing up the past. "You still owe me one fifty. I don't want the club but I'm taking the car to put us back right."

"Nigga, you already got me for my Caddy, now you want this too! Face, it ain't even my whip!"

"Then you shouldn't care," he said coldly.

Truthfully, she didn't. Other than having a ride to go deal with Bree and Doll, the car meant nothing to her. It was the $2.75 million in the trunk that she cared about.

Using force had failed in the face of his big-ass gun, and with sympathy not playing either, Tuesday tried to appeal to his reason.

"Look, this don't make no sense. You gone take the car for a hundred fifty racks when you can get two of them for that price?"

Face skillfully countered her argument by saying: "But you're not giving me a choice between a hundred fifty racks and the car. I made a choice between the car and The Bounce. And I would rather have that A8 than yo little hole-in-da-wall-ass strip club.

"I don't need another business to run—shit, I'm busy enough as it is. Plus, the club can't be doing all that great if you still out here stickin' niggas."

Tuesday was caught in a jam because she could easily pay him if she could get to the car, but if Face saw what was in the bag, then he was going to take it all. Her only hope lied in convincing him to let her take the Audi and bring back the money.

"Look, nigga, I got the other hundred fifty, I just need to go get it. Gimme the whip and I can have it back here in ten minutes."

Face rubbed the leathery skin on his cheek thoughtfully while still keeping her under the muzzle of the .50-caliber cannon. "How 'bout this? Have the money here in ten minutes, then I'll give you back the whip."

Chapter Twenty-four

Easy come, easy go. Tuesday had been a millionaire for less than an hour. No celebrity sniffing up mountains of cocaine could run through three million so quickly. She had betrayed Marcus and karma came right back around to bite her in the ass.

Tuesday could get the car back if she had the money but in order to get the money, she had to get the car back. It was another one of those ironic Catch-22's that plagued her life, like being so beautiful but lonely, a thief but with a conscience, so well known but without any real friends.

She had a little over twenty-five grand, but to Tuesday it was nothing more than pocket change. It would get her out of town, but being that she was hot, it wasn't much to run with. Getting away from niggas was one thing but getting away from the authorities took another comma and a few more zeroes.

She figured at any moment Face or one of his people would search the car and find the case. Then it would officially be over. Any chance she had of coming out this situation on top would be dead, right along with Danielle.

Tuesday walked away from Face's Auto Collision knowing that Jaye was the only person in the world she could call. Earlier Jaye had told Tuesday to call if she needed anything and right then she needed everything. She was headed north on Grand River, with no destination, when she got in touch with Jaye.

Tuesday didn't say too much on the phone but told Jaye that she needed her to pick her up and to bring all the cash she could put her hands on. She also told her to hurry the fuck up because it was already close to seven thirty.

Jaye was there in a few minutes to find Tuesday waiting at a bus stop. She was in her Chrysler 200, and the second Tuesday got in the car she began to grill her about the situation.

At first Tuesday deflected most of her questions because she really didn't want to tell Jaye about the money. Then she realized that Jaye was going to find out eventually, so Tuesday told her everything that happened from the airport until then. How she'd jacked Marcus for the ransom only to have Face jack it from her.

Jaye stared at her wide-eyed, not sure what part of the story to comment on first. Finally she asked, "His father just came up with the money just like that?"

Tuesday snapped her fingers. "Just like that."

"And you had it? All of it, and let it get away?"

Tuesday gave her a look that said *Bitch, I already know I fucked up!*

"How much was you able to scrape together?" Tuesday asked, doubtful it would be anything close to the one twenty-five she needed.

Jaye went into a large Birkin bag that was resting on the console between their seats. "The last lick got my money funny too, but I don't trick off like the rest of y'all bitches, so I keep a li'l something put up." She pulled out a thick stack of cash held together with rubber bands. "This about sixty."

"Cool," Tuesday said, taking it from her. "I got about twenty-five." She was hopeful that Face would trade the Audi back for eighty-five thousand.

Tuesday called Face a minute later, and when he agreed to the trade, the girls assumed that he hadn't searched the car. They couldn't imagine him being interested in eighty-five thousand if he just came up on three million.

When they pulled up, Tuesday saw the Audi was now in the garage next to the Chevelle he'd been rebuilding. She tried to take that as a positive sign but wasn't going to let herself get caught slipping again.

Outside the building that was his garage/office, one of Face's dope-fiend mechanics was now playing the role of a goon. He stood post in dirty coveralls looking so frail and thin that the recoil from the AK-47 he held would probably break his ribs. However, skinny or not, the weapon still made him a threat.

They approached the door with Tuesday carrying nothing but her bag containing her and Jaye's money. The fiend stopped them and demanded to inspect it. Tuesday opened it up and he seemed satisfied when he saw that it contained cash and no weapons.

Jaye got a quick pat-down but he took a longer time frisking Tuesday. It soon became obvious that the fiend was more interested in what God had given her over what she might be carrying.

After he spent over a minute running his grimy hands up and down her body, Tuesday finally snapped at him. "Damn, nigga, the shit turned into foreplay twenty seconds ago!"

When the fiend was done, he smiled at Tuesday—missing his two front teeth—then smacked her on the ass just because he could. She shot him a grim look, but he had the gun so there wasn't really shit she could do about it.

Jaye whispered, "He barely touched me. I don't know if I should feel happy or dissed by that."

He led them into the office where Face was waiting with another fiend carrying another AK. Tuesday knew that Face had always been cautious but not even she expected so much protection. He sat behind his makeshift desk looking like a junkyard mobster. His henchmen stood on either side of the room like bookends.

"Damn, nigga! What's with all this?" Tuesday asked, motioning to the fiends.

"I just believe in being cautious," said Face. "We didn't leave on the best of terms last time."

Tuesday shot back, "That's because somebody who I thought was my nigga jacked me for my shit!"

Face looked at her unfazed. "Now you said you put together eighty-five on the phone. Let me see it."

Tuesday stepped forward and emptied the bag onto his desk. Face fingered the cash for a moment, and when he was satisfied it was all there, he gave Tuesday a nod. "I said you could have the car back for eighty-five and I'm a man of my word." He pulled the keys from his oil-stained Dickie's and tossed them to Tuesday. "You can have the car but it's gone ride a little light."

He reached under the old dining table he used as a desk and slid the big black case into view. The sight of it made Tuesday feel as if she'd been punched in the stomach. Everything that could go wrong was going wrong for her today.

"Yeah. I found that little situation you had stashed in the trunk," he said in a comical voice that made his goons laugh. "I see why you was trying like hell to get that Audi back. You must've been praying yo ass off that I didn't search the car."

They all laughed again and Tuesday just stood there with a stare that could turn water into ice.

Face swept the other money to the side and sat the case on his desk. "This is why you don't give a fuck about The Bounce no more. All that shit you was talkin' about moving on to bigger and better thangs."

Tuesday looked at him coldly, her eyes bright gray. "Face, real talk—no bullshit. If I don't get that money back, a little five-year-old girl is gonna die."

Face mocked her tone. "Tuesday, real talk—no bullshit." He didn't blink, look away or retreat from her gaze. "I wouldn't care if a whole school bus full of little girls was gonna die. You got about as much chance as getting that bag back as you do of walking outta here alive!"

* * *

A minute later Tuesday and Jaye were being marched through Face's four-acre salvage yard at gunpoint. It was dusk, and as they weaved their way through a maze of junk cars, Tuesday noticed how the setting sun cast reflections off the dusty chrome, broken glass, and rusted metal. She thought it was ironic that not only cars were being brought here to die.

"What the fuck we doing out here?" Tuesday asked, pretending she didn't already know.

From behind her Face said, "I just wanted to put you up on some of the tools of my trade." This got another laugh out of his pair of crackhead cronies.

Jaye knew that she and Tuesday weren't being brought out there just to talk. At this point she began looking to save herself. "Look, I don't know what problem you got with this bitch, but it ain't got nothing to do with me. You could just go on and cut me loose, and I ain't seen shit or know shit!"

"I wish I could, sweetheart, but shit just don't work that way. When it's this type of paper involved, mouths don't stay closed on their own."

Tuesday rolled her eyes at Jaye. "Damn, bitch, way to stay down."

"Fuck you! I ain't trying to die behind your bullshit."

At the southernmost part of his property sat two large machines that were indispensable to his business. The first was a crane connected to a huge disk-shaped magnet used to lift and transport heavy metal objects. The second, and the one that frightened Tuesday, was the hydraulic-powered compactor that could reduce a car into a flattened slab of sheet metal or press it down into a three-foot cube. There were dozens of them back there stacked four and five high, making Tuesday wonder how many were cramped coffins with crushed bodies inside.

Face brought them to a stop in the shadow of that great machine where a '78 Bonneville was waiting. Tuesday told herself that dead was the only way he would get her inside that car.

Face took the AK from the second fiend and motioned for him

to operate the crane. With the agility of a spider monkey, he leapt on top of the tank tread and climbed inside the cab. He brought the crane around until the giant magnet was hovering ten feet over the car.

"By now you done probably guessed all that shit about trading you the Audi was just the underlay. I just needed you back here to find out where the money came from. Now why don't you tell me whose it is so I'll know who to kill when they come looking for it."

Tuesday crossed her arms. "Why should I tell you anything? You just gone kill us anyway."

"You're right," Face said with a smile that she no longer found appealing. "But you still have a choice in how you go out. A well-placed bullet can be quick and painless; over before you even know what happened. But being slowly crushed to death trapped in two tons of steel, crying in agony while you listen to the sound of your own bones breaking is a lot worse."

"Just tell 'em what he wanna know," Jaye said, frustrated.

Tuesday just stood there defiantly, not responding to either of them.

Face leaned against the hood of the Bonneville. "Look, adding in the two fifty you already gave me, I counted three mil even back there. Legit or illegit, ain't nobody gone be cool with taking a loss like that. I need to know if I'm gone have street niggas or the feds kicking in my door about that shit—"

"Whoa, whoa, hold the fuck up!" Jaye chimed in before he could finish. "*Three* million?" She looked at Tuesday. "Bitch, you said the ransom was only two. All that shit you was talking 'bout splitting it fifty-fifty, the whole time you was gone try to work me outta five hundred racks."

Face laughed. "Uh oh! I guess I wasn't the only one she was trying to hold out on."

Tuesday turned to Jaye. "Two million, three million; don't none of it matter now anyway. We ain't got shit!"

"It do matter!" Jaye spat back at her. "It shows that Brianna was right about you the whole time. You ain't nothing but a slimy-ass bitch. You probably been getting down on us from the start!"

"Slimy?!" Tuesday glared at her, furious. "I was the reason all y'all bitches was eating good, riding good, and could shop how y'all wanted. All y'all hoes would still be on the pole if it wasn't for me!"

"Yeah and if it wasn't for me, yo ass would be dead! I should've just gone and let Bree bust yo ass out that night you slapped her up. The bitch caught you slipping but you was lucky I had yo back. Being on that Chris Brown shit almost got yo ass murdered."

"Bitch, keep running off and see if I don't Chris Brown you!"

"Put hands on me, bitch, and I'm gone save these niggas the trouble of dealing with yo ass!"

Jaye turned back to Face. "Look, fuck this bitch, I'll tell you what's good. The money belong to this nigga named Marcus King and the only reason she trippin' is because she done caught feelings for his square ass."

Without warning Tuesday hauled off and slapped Jaye hard enough to whip her head around. Before Face could even get out an "Oooh, damn!" Jaye came back with a right, the two of them started to tussle, and then they were rolling around the ground in a full-on scrap. They kicked up dust as they struggled with and clawed at each other like wildcats.

If Face and his men had thought about breaking up the fight, they held up when Jaye's shirt got ripped and her titties bounced free. After that they just sat back and enjoyed the show.

The girls were biting, punching, pulling hair, and each one would spend a little time on top dominating the other; and to anybody else it would look as if they were really trying to kill one another. That was exactly how they wanted it to look because what the three men watching didn't know was that this whole scene had been planned before the ladies even pulled up to the garage.

Face and his henchmen were totally caught up in the action, laughing so hard that their eyes teared up, but after about three minutes it stopped being funny when the girls tired themselves out. He gave his man the order to break it up and the bony fiend who felt Tuesday up came over ready to pull them apart.

Coming in, Jaye assumed that they might be searched. She also guessed correctly that because Tuesday was thicker with a better body, the men would focus on her, allowing Jaye to slip past them with Tuesday's small Heckler tucked down the front of her panties.

The fiend reached for Jaye, who was on top, but didn't know that Tuesday had stealthily slipped the pistol out during their fake tussle. Jaye suddenly rolled out of the way to give her girl a clear shot. The fiend's eyes went wide when he saw Tuesday bring up the gun. It was like she'd just performed some type of magic trick and made it appear from nowhere.

Tuesday tried for his head, but being that she was aiming from an awkward position lying on her back, the shot was low. The bullet caught him in the throat, tossing him back onto the ground. He coughed and held his neck as blood squirted between his fingers.

The whole thing caught Face by surprise but he responded quickly. He started spraying the AK in their direction. Tuesday was able to scramble to her feet and dive behind an old Ford panel van.

Before running for cover, Jaye tried to grab the AK dropped by the dying fiend. But Face wouldn't allow her to reach it and the price of the effort was costly. As she turned for the van, she felt a bullet pierce her flesh. She stumbled forward with a scream and fell out of view just as another round went whizzing above her head.

Tuesday peeked out from her hiding spot and saw that Jaye was only a few feet from her. She'd been shot, but luckily it was only in the hand. The wound was bleeding pretty bad, but it wouldn't kill her.

However, the next shot just might because Jaye was still lying out in the open. In order for Tuesday to get to her, she would have to put herself in the line of fire.

Tuesday imagined that any man who sold guns for a living had to be pretty good with using them. She reached out for Jaye while trying not to expose too much of herself. Tuesday hooked her beneath the arms and dragged Jaye back behind the van. The *rat-a-tat* of Face's machine gun was accompanied by the sound of metal striking metal. A window exploded right above Tuesday's head raining glass down into her weave.

Tuesday stuck her arm out from around the van, squeezing off a couple of shots from the Heckler. She was firing blindly, just hoping it would make Face think twice about rushing in.

She looked over to Jaye. "Girl, you all right?"

Jaye nodded, clutching her right hand. When she showed it to her, Tuesday saw that the middle finger was bent and only hanging on by the meat. Tuesday made a face to try to pretend that it wasn't as bad as it looked.

Jaye smiled through the pain. "That bitch shot my favorite finger. I use this one to play with my pussy!"

Tuesday said, "Would've been nice if you could've got to that other AK."

Jaye looked at her. "Let me shoot you in the hand and see if it don't make you think twice about playing hero."

All jokes aside, their situation was still pretty bad. Face still had the advantage of an extra guy and extra gun. By now the one on the crane had probably jumped down and grabbed the other rifle. Two men with machine guns would win against two women sharing a handgun any day. If they split up and came around either side of the van, there was no way she would be able to defend herself and Jaye against both of them. Even if she killed one, the other one would gun them down.

Then the junkyard fell eerily silent; this made Tuesday nervous. Peppering the side of the van with bullets not only wasted his ammunition, but allowed her to keep tabs on him. Now Face was quiet and most likely thinking up a plan to sneak up on them.

Tuesday then came up with her own plan. It was crazy and had a pretty good chance of getting them both killed.

She looked at Jaye, who was still cradling her injured hand. "I know this might seem like a fucked-up time to ask, but when was the last time you had a pedicure?"

Jaye looked at her like she'd lost her mind.

It wasn't long before Face came creeping around the van just like Tuesday figured he would. He was crouching low with his weapon raised like a soldier doing recon in enemy territory.

He saw Jaye sitting there in the gravel, slumped against the rear wheel. Her hand with the broken finger was wrapped into her shirt to absorb the bleeding. Tuesday had lent Jaye her jacket to cover up with but was nowhere to be seen.

"Can't believe yo girl just busted up on you like that!" Face said, aiming the business end of the AK at her. "I learned that when shit get thick, people stay true to their nature."

Face looked down and noticed that Jaye had kicked off her shoes. She made a show of wiggling her painted toes.

Face didn't become mesmerized and start drooling. Her pretty brown feet only stole his attention for a second.

But a second was all Tuesday needed. She'd been watching from her hiding place within the passenger compartment of the van. The moment Face averted his eyes, she thrust her gun hand out the window and brought the Heckler to his head.

"You're right!" she said, slowly inching out of the passenger door. "People do stay true to their nature. If a nigga got a crazy foot fetish, he'll stop and check a bitch's feet even at a time like this."

Face smiled. "This don't change nothing."

"It change everything. Now drop that shit!"

Face still had his rifle on Jaye. "Even if you shoot me, you can't stop me from killing this bitch! Then my mans gone kill you."

"Yo mans might kill me, like you might kill her. But you the only muthafucka who gone die for sure." Tuesday pressed the muzzle hard into his forehead. "Are you ready to die today?"

Face hesitated a second longer, then decided not to call her bluff. He sat the AK where Jaye could grab hold of it with her good hand.

When they ushered Face back into the open, Tuesday made him call out to the second fiend, ordering him to drop his gun. At his boss's command he came out from his position behind the rusty Bonneville. He sat his weapon on the ground then kicked it away.

Tuesday took the first AK from Jaye while she went to retrieve the other. Jaye winced as she walked over the stony ground in her bare feet.

Disarmed and helpless, Face was now willing to bargain. "Look, Tuesday, you been in the game long enough to know this was just business. You got the car and the bag. Just take it and leave and let everythang be everythang."

Tuesday glanced at her watch to see that it was now ten minutes past eight. She had missed the exchange and for all she knew little Danielle was already dead.

She glared at him with cold gray eyes. "Naw, nigga, it would've been just business at 7:59. Now it's personal!"

When Jaye popped the trunk on the Bonneville and ordered them inside, the fiend climbed in but Face tried to play hard. Tuesday took the Heckler and shot him in the ass. Whimpering and bleeding, he was more cooperative. Jaye slammed the lid closed as he tried to bribe Tuesday with cars, guns, and all kinds of money she doubted Face even had.

Tuesday had never operated heavy machinery but knew she was smart enough to figure out the crane. It took a while, but with Jaye coaching from the ground, she was eventually able to hoist the big Bonneville and drop it into the car crusher.

Jaye hit the start button as Tuesday climbed down from the crane. Over the sound of buckling metal, Face's and the fiend's desperate cries could be heard from inside the machine. Jaye stared at her and she stared off into space as Face went from begging Tuesday to begging God for help.

She never heard the sound of their bones breaking but Tuesday wasn't listening for it either. She and Jaye just waited for their screams to fall silent.

Chapter Twenty-five

The very first thing Tuesday did was try to call Brianna and Baby Doll. She was about twenty minutes late but hopeful they hadn't done anything to Danielle as punishment. When she got no answer from either of them, she left desperate messages on their voice mail explaining that she had the money and would be delivering it soon.

She also tried Marcus, thinking that they may have contacted him again about the ransom. She couldn't reach him either. She left a long and apologetic message for him, promising revenge for Danielle if those bitches had hurt her.

Next, Tuesday went back to Face's office to get the black case. She also took back the two hundred fifty thousand she paid him from it to bring the total back to three million, plus the eighty-five racks they brought for the Audi. Tuesday gave Jaye back her sixty G's.

During their fake fight they had pretended to argue over their split of the money. Tuesday really did promise her an equal share this time, but once she finished her business with Brianna and Baby Doll.

She raised the trapdoor in the floor to go downstairs to raid

Face's arsenal. Tuesday loaded her arms with all the guns and ammo she could carry and made three trips. There was no reason for thinking she would need so much heat against two people, but then Tuesday wasn't thinking. She was preparing for a war. She even thought about grabbing some C-4 and grenades but Tuesday didn't know shit about explosives.

Jaye had never been in The Gun Store and when she saw all the merchandise, she wanted to come back with a U-Haul to clean him out. Tuesday explained that they didn't have time for that and reminded Jaye that she was about to get a million and a half in cash already.

Tuesday put the case back in the trunk of the Audi then began loading the guns onto the sedan's backseat. Jaye stood next to her in the garage and watched as Tuesday loaded the car like a survivalist preparing for Doomsday.

"Damn, Rambo! You got a plan or you just gone run up in there like SWAT?"

Tuesday appreciated her attempt at humor but wasn't really feeling it right then. Her mind was only on her mission.

"No more plans!" she grumbled, throwing another M-16 and AR on the backseat. "I ain't got it in me to mastermind some more long drawn-out *Ocean's Eleven*–type shit. I'm just going to wherever these bitches at, killing them both, and getting the girl back. Flat out!"

"But she might already—" Jaye didn't finish the sentence and didn't have to. Tuesday was haunted by the same fear each time she checked her watch.

"I don't care! Then it'll feel just that much better when I pull the trigger."

"Don't you see what I'm saying?" Jaye said, grabbing Tuesday with her good hand. "Fuck them bitches! You got the money, you got your way out now. It's like Face said, you done already won!"

Tuesday snatched away from her. "Fuck dat! This shit ain't about winning and losing. If that was the case, I could've busted up soon as I got the money.

"They set up Tushie. They sicced some nigga on her who played my girl and left her butt-ass naked with a bullet in her head. Tush wasn't no saint, but she was a good-hearted bitch who deserved better than that and I ain't letting the shit ride!" Tuesday hadn't even realized that she had started to tear up until she felt one race down her cheek.

Jaye nodded because she understood. Tuesday reminded her of O-Dogg in *Menace II Society*: not only had he uttered those same words when talking about the carjackers who killed Caine's cousin Harold, but he had the very same look in his eye. Jaye was smart enough to know that sometimes when a person had an appetite for blood, the only thing you could do was stand back and let them eat.

She said, "You know I'm down to roll with you."

Tuesday shook her head. "Yo hand all fucked up! Gone and get yo ass to the hospital before you lose that muthafucka."

"Shit, bitch, I'm even-handed. I can shoot lefty if I have to."

Tuesday didn't pull into the lot of The Bounce for fear that Brianna and Baby Doll might have somebody playing lookout. They parked in an alley one block over from the strip mall and planned to go the rest of the way on foot.

The girls weren't answering her calls but Dresden's trace had already confirmed they were still there. She wouldn't know about Danielle until she got inside.

Tuesday cut the ignition and turned to Jaye. "It'll be easier if you took some shit you could handle with one hand." Tuesday took the clip from her pocket, slid it into the Heckler, then passed it to Jaye. "I'm gone have this bitch right here," Tuesday said, patting the street-sweeper that was lying across her lap. "Just make sure you stay behind me."

When they got out the car it was a quarter to nine; forty-five minutes late for the exchange. Tuesday didn't know what it was but something in her heart said Danielle was still alive. She hoped it was more than just wishful thinking.

Tuesday crept low down the dark alley carrying the rifle with Jaye a few feet behind her. Thinking back, it had been stupid to bring so many guns when there was no way she could use them all. Plus, Tuesday seriously doubted that she would be able to run back to the Audi and swap out in the middle of a shootout.

From the alley behind the club, Tuesday peeked through the window that looked in on her office. She figured this would have to be the entry point. She wasn't sure if the alarm on the fire door was still disconnected from when Face and DelRay moved Tank. They couldn't maintain the element of surprise coming straight through the front door.

Tuesday was relieved to see that no one was inside and the door was shut. She used the butt of the rifle to break the glass and cleared it out of the frame. She let Jaye climb through first then followed her in.

It had only been about a day since she'd been in the club but the place already felt foreign to her. Maybe it was because so much had happened and she'd already checked out of there mentally and saw The Bounce as something from her past. Her office didn't feel like hers anymore; she literally felt like an intruder breaking into a stranger's place.

Tuesday and Jaye waited for a moment with their weapons ready but when the sound of the breaking window didn't bring anybody, they slipped out the door of her office as stealthily as ninjas.

The house lights were off, leaving the club almost pitch-black and silent as a tomb. Shadows laid claim to everything, offering a million hiding places for someone with a gun.

Tuesday and the street-sweeper had the lead. Jaye was so close behind that Tuesday could actually feel her breath on the back of her neck.

In the hall that served Tuesday's office, they searched both restrooms and found no one hiding in the stalls. There was also a small broom closet that hid nothing more sinister than a mop leaning against the wall, which at first glance looked like a skinny bitch with a bad weave. Tuesday caught herself before she opened up on it.

It was a little easier to see at the front of the club due to the strings of LED lights that decorated the stage and bar; however, it was still pretty dark without the house lights. The tables and chairs that surrounded the stage were revealed as dark silhouettes. Nothing could be seen of the restaurant-style booths that lined the walls and Tuesday felt an eerie presence in that blackness.

She held Jaye back while quickly scanning behind the bar for anyone who might be crouching there. A moment later she came back to report that area was all clear.

Then the house and stage lights suddenly winked on, startling them both and shocking their dark-adapted eyes. When Tuesday got done blinking hers back into focus, she saw him standing by the wall next to the front entrance. The .40-caliber was raised and aimed right at her.

Slim still had on the same black skullcap and leather jacket he wore from when he chased her through the Seymour. It looked like the same gun too.

He said, "Bitch, drop that shit!"

"Make me!" she spat back almost instantly. Tuesday wasn't about to surrender a street-sweeper to a nigga holding a Glock 40. Slim had the drop but there was about ten feet between them. If he shot first and happened to miss, she was going to mow his ass down before he got off a second one.

Slim said, "Drop it or the girl is dead!"

"Naw, bitch, you dead!" Tuesday raised the rifle and was ready to shoot but, with the same speed he showed on the stairs, he snatched something from inside the deejay booth.

It was little Danielle still in her Catholic school uniform and pigtails. A zip-tie bound her hands in the front and a swatch of gray duct tape covered her mouth. Physically she seemed unharmed, but she looked exhausted from the ordeal. Her eyes were puffy and red. Her face was streaked from the tears that had dried on her cheeks.

Seeing Tuesday made Danielle's eyes spring wide with some combination of excitement and fear. Even though the tape muffled her screams, Tuesday could make out the words: "Tabitha! Tabitha!"

The sight of the girl also made emotions well up in Tuesday. So young, innocent, and in the middle of all this bullshit because of her. Danielle should have been at home right then in her pajamas watching Princess Jasmine and Aladdin fly around the world on a magic carpet, worried about nothing more than the imaginary monsters under her bed and tomorrow's homework assignment. Everything about her being in The Bounce was just wrong to Tuesday on so many levels, even without the kidnapping and guns. By comparison, her purity made the place seem that much more foul. Even though there wasn't a dancer on stage clapping her ass for dollar bills, Tuesday hated Slim for exposing Danielle to this place. She also hated herself for owning it.

"Baby, don't worry. I'm here to take you home." Tuesday kept her voice as cheerful as she could, as if the girl wouldn't notice she was carrying a machine gun that was nearly the size of the five-year-old. "Everything's gonna be okay!"

Slim stole her attention back from Dani. "Don't make promises you can't keep."

Tuesday slowly inched toward him. "So where them two fake-ass bitches at who hired you? I already know they here."

"Hired me?" he said with a nasty grin. "Bitch, you ain't got a clue to what's happening here! But if you wanna know, yo home-girls right over there."

Tuesday really didn't want to turn away from him so she searched the room using her peripheral vision until she spotted Brianna and Doll. They were both in the far corner booth slumped over like they were sleeping. The white Styrofoam containers revealed that their last meal had come from Bo's BBQ, and Tuesday knew that the huge burgundy stain covering the table was not the old man's delicious sauce.

"That's some fucked-up shit!" she said, hoping he hadn't noticed she'd stepped about three feet closer to him. Slim was still using the girl as a human shield but Tuesday figured at or around five feet would be close enough for her to squeeze off a shot that would kill him without hitting Danielle. "What type of man could just kill women so easily and not feel shit?"

"Aye, don't look at me. I ain't even put in that work, but it's not like I wasn't going to. It wasn't like they had any of that money coming. Somebody just saved me the trouble. Shit, I thought it was you."

Tuesday stole another step closer to him. She wanted to keep Slim distracted by talking until she could get into range. "Bullshit! But I couldn't care less about them hoes anyway. I'm at that ass for what you did to my girl Tush."

"Now that was me!" he said with a proud smile that infuriated Tuesday. "For three million dollars, I'll kill in my sleep." He pressed the gun into Danielle's side. "And I'll prove it again if you keep trying to creep up on me. Now where's the money?"

Tuesday stopped her approach. "Don't worry about that 'cause you ain't gone live to see a penny of it anyway."

From behind Tuesday, Jaye called out, "You might as well put the gun down. We got you beat two to one."

Tuesday shook her head. "He not gone listen. He wanna do this the hard way, and for what he did to Tushie, that's exactly how he gone get it."

"I wasn't talking to him!"

When Jaye came into view, Tuesday realized that she had the Heckler aimed at her and not Slim.

Jaye smiled when she read the confused look on Tuesday's face. "You ain't never met my baby brother Jason. I guess that whole strictly business and keeping your personal life personal was a good rule after all."

Jaye went and stood next to her brother. "I ain't gone lie. I was pissed when he told me he missed you at your apartment. But always having a backup plan is something I learned from you."

Tuesday said, "I guess you wasn't listening all those times I spoke about loyalty to the team, though."

Jaye snapped back at her. "Bitch, how you gone talk about loyalty? You said fuck the team soon as you started catching feeling for that nigga. And you only called me when you needed my help getting the money back from Face."

Tuesday nodded. "And the reason you didn't just kill me after we got rid of Face was because you wanted to do it here like this—the big reveal to show me that you was really the mastermind behind it all. Ain't that why you wanted me to bring the ransom in the first place? Not just to kill me, but so I could see it was you first."

Jaye frowned at her and it revealed for the first time the level of animosity she'd secretly been harboring against Tuesday. "They all thought you was so damn smart but from the start I knew I was more advanced than you, TK.

"It wasn't shit to turn Brianna and Baby Doll against you. About a year ago I just started planting the seed that you was skimming us on the bread. Since Doll was always broke, it was easy to convince her, but Bree's stupid ass actually looked up to you before I started fuckin' with her head."

Tuesday said, "And all that you said about her being jealous of me was really you talking about yourself."

"Jealous of you?" Jaye laughed. "Bitch, please! What the fuck I got to be jealous of a old has-been hoe who pushing forty and still living hand to mouth? All you got is your looks, TK, and you only had about three more years of being cute before you lost that!"

Tuesday shook her head. "You been sitting here hating on me all this muthafuckin' time for what?"

"Because I knew eventually you was gone lead me to some real bread. As much as I hated it, I stuck in there going on these little dilly missions for twenty and thirty G's, but I knew sooner or later something big was gone come through. I was just setting up the pieces but the game didn't start until we got the Caine lick."

"Too bad Bree and Doll didn't realize they were just pawns about to be sacrificed."

Jaye laughed again. "You must be getting slow in your old age. All y'all were pawns! I was playing you and everybody else. You so busy putting together your brilliant plans to get these niggas, never knowing the whole time that y'all bitches were the real marks!"

"Why is you sitting here explaining all this shit to her?" Slim said impatiently. "Let's just kill this bitch, go get the money, and bounce!"

"Nigga, shut up!" Jaye flipped on him and the way he folded proved to Tuesday that not only was Jaye the older sibling, but she had the dominant role in their relationship.

Tuesday explained it to him. "Young dog, what you don't understand is that she been waiting to rub my face in this for a long time and ain't 'bout to let you spoil it. This is her moment to shine."

"That's right," Jaye agreed. "Because you s'posed to be the one with all the game, who can peep all the angles. But I was right up under your nose and you never saw me coming."

"Just like your girl Tushie ain't see him coming!" she teased.

It was at that moment that Tuesday had an epiphany. "You knew you couldn't poison Tush against me like you did them other bitches, so you kept her distracted instead. That's why you put this ole funny-looking-ass nigga on her."

"I couldn't believe how easy he pulled her. You see, I was able to read her just like Bree and Doll. She was smarter and more loyal than them but being lonely was her weakness."

Slim jumped in. "Yeah, and Sis right here told me just how to reel her in. She was used to niggas sweating her for it, so all I had to do was pretend like I wasn't pressed for the ass! And the more I downplayed it, the more she wanted to give it to me.

"But on some real shit, I hated having to murk that pretty

chocolate thick muthafucka, but Sis said it had to be done." He laughed. "I'm gone miss riding that big ole ass. Her pussy was so wet and her neck game was the truth."

Jaye checked him. "Nigga, quit suckerstrokin' over that big funny-talking-ass bammer bitch. When we get this money, you gone be able to buy ten hoes just like her."

Tuesday had to hide how much it bothered her to hear them mocking her girl like that. She kept her game face on and quietly promised her best friend that they were going to pay for it.

Jaye continued to break it down for Tuesday. "Tushie's body was her gift and her curse. I knew that any nigga who came along and treated her with a little bit of respect would have her sprung.

"Years of playing on niggas had taken its toll. In the end the bitch was so desperate for some genuine companionship that she practically fell in love with my baby brother before knowing him a week." Jaye shook her head. "Now that's sad!"

Tuesday agreed that it was, because she had peeped many of the same things about Tushie. Tuesday remembered one of their final conversations on the phone when Tushie talked about needing something real. The game had taken its toll on them both, which was why she fell for Marcus. Tuesday knew that if her girl had been in a better place emotionally, she would've smoked out this young punk-ass nigga before he even got her number.

"You was able to peep my weakness too," Tuesday said with a nod. "My OCD. That's why you had them niggas tear up my condo. How long did you know about my illness?"

"That was just a guess," Jaye said with pride. "I knew you was a neat-freak from the way you acted around the club. I thought that would fuck with your head a little more than what it did."

"That was your smartest move," said Tuesday. "That shit almost broke me down for real. Seeing my spot disrespected like that damn near gave me a nervous breakdown.

"Well, I got to give you props," Tuesday said, faking a smile. "One gamer to another, Jaye, you laid down a masterpiece. So what do you think is gonna happen now?"

Jaye brought the Heckler closer to her head and made Tuesday drop the street-sweeper. "Well, now you and this little girl are going to die. The sad part is that if you didn't catch feelings, you could've just took the money and busted up. In the end you brought this shit on yourself by breaking your own Rule One."

She cocked the pistol. "I just wanted the last thing to go through your mind—before this bullet—to be the fact that a young bitch like me outsmarted you.

"You see, with this money now I got a way out. I'm not about to end up some old, sad, dried-up bitch still sucking dicks and doing sticks when I turn thirty-seven. When we talked in your office that day, I told you I was gone be straight by the time I reached your age."

Tuesday looked at her calmly with absolutely no fear in her eyes. "Bitch, you ain't gone live to see my age."

"We'll see." Jaye put the muzzle of the Heckler to Tuesday's forehead.

"One gamer to another, you laid down a classic by murking Bree and Doll. I don't know how you got to 'em but I guess that's a secret you can take to your grave."

Jaye pulled the trigger. *Click.*

She tried it again and again but the gun was empty.

Tuesday took advantage in that moment of confusion. She smacked her hand away, cocked back and blew Jaye shit out. She stumbled back a few steps holding her mouth then looked up at Tuesday, stunned. When Jaye dropped her hand, her lips were bloody.

Tuesday snatched up the street-sweeper. "You so damned smart, telling me about the rules I broke, but look at you. What's the first rule when somebody hands you a gun to go on a mission? Stupid bitch, you check to see if it's loaded!"

"That don't change shit!" Slim said, motioning with his Glock. "We still got the girl and we leaving with that money."

"Nigga, it change everythang!" Tuesday called out, "Ay yo, bring it out!"

Neither Jaye nor her brother could believe it when they saw big DelRay jump out from his hiding spot behind the bar. He was carrying a .12-gauge pistol-grip pump. He stood behind his boss and took aim at Slim.

Jaye then realized why Tuesday waved her back and checked that area herself. When it dawned on her that Tuesday had seen through her so-called masterpiece the entire time, Jaye's face almost dropped to the floor.

"How did you know?" Jaye asked, still leaking blood from her mouth.

"Bitch, I always knew it was you!" Tuesday said with fierce gray eyes. "Remember that same conversation we had in my office when you said Brianna's not a planner and Doll will follow anybody. I knew they couldn't pull something like this off without somebody pulling their strings, and I knew that somebody was *you*.

"You fucked up when you said that Bree was jealous of my condo downtown because at that time Tush was the only person at the club who knew where I lived. That shit right there let me know that you done had me followed home at least once before.

"Then you tried to clean it up that day you dropped me off by pretending like you didn't know where my spot was, but it was too late—I had already peeped that you slipped. When you had them try to get me at my building, that was my first clue."

Jaye looked dumbstruck. She replayed the conversation in her mind and realized that she had actually told on herself.

Tuesday looked at Slim. "Your baby brother never knew that Tushie snapped a picture of him with her phone one day while he was taking a nap. When I found the picture I recognized him from the building; but when I looked closer, I saw the family resemblance. Y'all both got them same big dick-sucking lips!"

Slim was still holding Danielle against his chest with the gun thrust out in front of him. He couldn't cover DelRay and Tuesday both so he was swinging the Glock back and forth between them.

The bouncer had the gauge trained on him but couldn't pull

the trigger while he held the girl. DelRay could easily blow off Slim's head but the buckshot would take off a piece of Danielle's face with it.

Tuesday continued explaining it to Jaye. "Now I didn't plan on getting stuck by Face but I been had yo ass peeped by then. I knew you would be down for getting that money back and I did need your help.

"I called DelRay before I called you and put him up on my plan. He already had keys to the club and been here for hours laying low, just waiting for this surprise party."

DelRay added, "I was here watching before dog even showed up with the little girl. So the whole time you thought you was setting her up, it was really the other way around."

Tuesday nodded. "Sometimes good game can come from an unexpected place. A dirty cop I know once told me that he never walks into a room that he can't walk out of, and I took that to heart."

"Well, me and my brother walking out of this room," Jaye said, still holding the useless gun in her good hand. "You gone gimme the keys to the Audi and we gone call you and tell you where to pick the girl up."

Tuesday shook her head. "Jaye, that ain't even 'bout to happen. The only way y'all leaving this muthafucka is *shot!*"

"Whatever!" Jaye snapped as they slowly backed their way to the door. "She still my ticket up out this, bitch. You talk a good gangsta but as long as I got the girl, yo soft ass ain't gone do shit. Now gimme the keys!"

She was right. Tuesday wasn't willing to risk Danielle's life, not even for the money. It was the second time today she had to run those keys. She dug them out her pocket and passed them to Jaye.

Tuesday glared at her steely-eyed. "I promise you ain't gone get far."

Jaye jingled the keys and smiled with a big, busted lip. "Bitch, I'm gone get as far as three million dollars take me."

Slim was the first to back his way out of the door. Still holding Danielle with the .40-cal extended over Jaye's shoulder at Tuesday and DelRay, he took a step back into the awaiting night.

From Tuesday's view inside the club she could see nothing of the killer. All she saw was a hand wearing designer leather gloves bring a pistol with a silencer level to Slim's head.

There weren't any muzzle flashes, just two shots as quiet as whispers. *Psst. Psst.* The blood sprayed all over Danielle and the door to the club.

Jaye had no idea of what happened. It was only the *oh shit!* expression on Tuesday's and DelRay's faces that made her turn around. She saw her brother, already dead, as his lanky frame started to topple like a falling tree. Jaye screamed like she had been shot too.

Tuesday didn't know what just happened either, but she sure didn't hesitate to capitalize. She threw down the street-sweeper again and rushed Jaye before she could react. Tuesday pinned her against the wall and squeezed her injured hand until she dropped the gun and keys. The pain made Jaye howl as she went down to her knees.

DelRay tossed away the gauge and went for Danielle. She was lying on the walk outside with the tape still muffling her screams. Her face was sprayed with Slim's blood but she was not hurt. Luckily, when they fell, she landed on top of him.

DelRay scooped her and peeled off her tape. He turned her away from the dead body and tried to calm her down.

Then they heard a car door slam and tires peel out. Tuesday and DelRay both tried to get a glimpse of the shooter but they were too late. All they saw was a big sedan smash out the opposite end of the parking lot with the streetlights gleaming off its black paint. It bent a quick right off 7 Mile then disappeared down a side street before they could even recognize the model.

Tuesday went back inside, grabbed DelRay's gauge, and snatched Jaye up by a fistful of hair weave. She told her bouncer to take Danielle next door to Bo's because the girl had already seen too much and didn't need to witness what was about to happen. They figured she might be hungry too.

When they were alone, Tuesday led Jaye over to the bar and made her sit. Tuesday grabbed a bottle of Remy Martin XO and two double-shot glasses.

"What's this s'posed to be?" Jaye said, frowning at the drink Tuesday offered her.

She explained. "You usually give a dying man a last meal, but we ain't got shit in here to eat."

Jaye nodded thoughtfully. "I guess this your moment to shine now? The part where you rub it in my face how you outsmarted me. Boss Lady pulls off another brilliant plan."

Tuesday downed her shot then poured herself another. "Naw, it ain't about all that. I just thought I'd put you up on one last piece of game before we parted ways."

Tuesday sat the .12-gauge at her side and leaned across the bar, forcing Jaye to meet her eyes.

"You lost because you think getting older only means getting slower and losing your looks. I used to think the same thing. I'm starting to get those lines in the corner of my eyes and they don't sparkle like they used to. My titties don't sit up like yours no more. And I can admit that I don't turn as many heads as I did at eighteen.

"I'm cool with all that, because being fine was only part of what made me a bad bitch. I was never a dummy! You see, Jaye, getting older means getting wiser. Being a boss not only means being able to put the people around you in the right positions, it also means knowing what they are thinking and having your next move figured out before your enemies make theirs."

Jaye finally swallowed her shot. "TK, you don't have to do this. I know I fucked up, but you won. You got the girl back, you got the money, and you leaving anyway." Tears fell from her eyes. "I'm sorry 'bout Tushie but I lost my brother too and that should make us even. You could just gimme a pass."

"Give you a pass?" Tuesday downed another shot of Remy then grabbed the pistol-grip pump. She cocked it, then put the barrel right under Jaye's chin.

"Girl, you really should've been a comedian 'cause that's the funniest shit I ever heard."

Chapter Twenty-six

After the eventful day Danielle didn't have an appetite. At Bo's, DelRay bought her a wing dinner with fries that she hardly touched. He and Mr. Scott tried to get her to eat but she did no more than nibble on a few fries. One of DelRay's funny faces did get a thin smile out of her but the chicken wings still went wasted. The kindly old man didn't take that as a knock on his cooking.

While she wasn't able to eat, sleep came easy. By the time Tuesday came for her and DelRay, Danielle was already beginning to nod, and by the time they made it around the corner to the Audi, she had already fallen asleep in the big man's arms. Tuesday had him strap her into the passenger seat because the guns were in the back. After everything that happened today, Tuesday didn't want the girl to see anything else she could associate with death.

During the walk DelRay explained that Brianna and Baby Doll were already dead when he got there but Slim didn't show up with Danielle until later. Because Jaye and her brother genuinely seemed ignorant about who killed them, Tuesday chalked that up to the mystery gunman who popped Slim. DelRay thought that the killer waiting outside was part of Tuesday's plan and she let him believe that.

Being that DelRay had no particular beef with either Brianna or Baby Doll, he felt saddened by their deaths. Tuesday did too because in the end they were just innocent victims of Jaye's manipulation and not her true enemies.

Tuesday figured that they must have been killed while Slim was gone with Danielle; in which case, she wasn't there to see it. Tuesday knew something like that could scar her for life. Danielle had survived the ordeal, but Tuesday was worried that the experience had killed that something precious inside her. Tuesday hoped that she still had the same spirit; that same sparkle in her eye. She hoped that nothing had been done to change her personality from that bright, bubbly little girl she met at Chuck E. Cheese who made friends so easily. Tuesday felt like killing that part of her would be no different from killing her period.

Refusing to eat in itself was not proof that she was traumatized. Right then, she appeared to be sleeping peacefully, and if she was emotionally wounded, only time would tell to what degree.

When he closed the door on Danielle, Tuesday took DelRay to the trunk to settle up with him. She felt like she owed him big-time for coming through on this and the Tank incident, but he had no idea how much gratitude she was about to show him.

Tuesday watched DelRay make his funniest face ever when she unzipped the black case and started smashing 50K bundles on him: one after the other until she reached ten. Even with his beefy arms and huge hands, he fumbled to hold them all.

"Girl, is you serious?" He stared at the cash with wide eyes and his mouth hanging open like a dead fish. "What the fuck is this?"

Tuesday ignored his question. "Do you know where Face's Auto Collision is on Grand River?"

He nodded that he did.

She explained, "Grab all yo niggas, a moving van and get over there ASAP. There's an office connected to the garage, with a room hidden underneath that. It's enough guns in that bitch to make you millionaire."

DelRay looked confused. "Why is you doing all this?"

Tuesday said, "Because real niggas do real shit and loyalty should always be rewarded."

Then as an afterthought she added, "Oh yeah, The Bounce is yours too if you want it." She zipped the bag closed. "The paperwork gone still be in my name but open that bitch as soon as you ready and start getting your money. It's not a gold mine but it will turn a decent profit. I was just a greedy bitch feeling like I needed more."

DelRay either didn't or couldn't comprehend what she was doing for him. "I'll run it for you and handle the day to day if you need me to."

"I ain't promoting you to manager, I'm saying it's you now, nigga! You own it flat-out." She closed the trunk. "All I ask is that you look out for Ebony and throw Mr. Scott a couple racks from me for twenty years of free rib dinners."

DelRay agreed that he would. He also knew that without saying it, Tuesday was telling him that he would probably never see her again. It was unspoken but clearly understood.

He smiled. "This a lot of money but I'm still gone miss smacking that fat ass!"

Tuesday laughed and threw her arms around the big man. He leaned into it but couldn't hug her back without dropping his severance pay.

Tuesday was headed for the driver's side of the Audi when he called to her, "Boss Lady, do you know where you goin'?"

Tuesday shook her head. "Nope, but I know I'm gone be straight when I get there."

She climbed inside and couldn't resist taking one last shot at him before leaving. "Ay, nigga, you rich now. Buy you a new car and junk that raggedy-ass Monte!"

DelRay looked down at the pile of cash with a smile. "I guess I can finally get the bumper fixed, huh?"

She left DelRay with nothing else to do but drop Danielle off to Marcus then hit the highway. Little Dani slept the entire ride out to Romulus. Tuesday rubbed her head as she drove. As much as this had been about the money, in some strange way, Tuesday was actually more satisfied to have her back. She would have never thought she could care so deeply about someone in such a short time. Danielle had ignited maternal feelings in her that she never thought she could have and exorcised some of the demons Tuesday had about her own absentee mother. Tuesday kept glancing over at her as she drove. Not only was she thinking about how much she would miss little Dani, she was secretly wondering if there was even the slightest chance that Marcus could forgive her so the three of them might be together.

Remembering that she was wanted instantly killed any pie-in-the-sky hopes she had of them being a family. Marcus and Danielle had their own lives and Tuesday couldn't expect them to give up everything to go on the run with her. Even if he didn't hate her as much as she was sure he did, Tuesday could never ask someone she loved to make that kind of sacrifice.

They finally made it to his house and as she pulled into the drive Tuesday was trying to think of the quickest, most painless way to say good-bye. She would've loved to fuck one last time, because she was going to miss riding that big dick as much as anything else about him.

She tried Marcus's phone but again her call went directly to voice mail. She cut the ignition and was about to step out the car when all hell broke loose.

Out of nowhere a set of black GMC Yukons pulled in front and back of the Audi, boxing her in the circular driveway. She was blinded by flashlights and the pulse of red and blue beacons lit up the night. Two dozen people swarmed the car, all screaming orders to her at the same time.

Tuesday couldn't understand them but their guns conveyed the message. That and the blue windbreakers with *DEA* in bright yellow lettering. She threw her hands up and yelled a warning that there was a child in the car.

Danielle woke up to the sound of the ruckus. She cried as she watched Tuesday being dragged from her seat and thrown roughly to the ground.

As Tuesday lay there facedown on the cold hard cement with a knee in her back, she wasn't even concerned with her own well-being. All she thought was *Damn, this little girl is having a real fucked-up day!*

Tuesday was cuffed, thrown in the back of a Yukon, then driven to a nearby precinct where she was photographed, fingerprinted, and detained. She spent the first two hours in a holding cell with a fat Mexican prostitute who had no business charging anybody for sex. After that she was taken to a small interrogation room that had nothing but a table and chairs, insanely harsh light, and a huge two-way mirror.

She was grilled for almost eighteen hours straight.

They would take Tuesday in shifts: two agents would come in to question her for three hours, then they would leave to be replaced by two more. She wasn't read her Miranda rights, wasn't allowed a phone call, and had to threaten to piss on the floor just to get a bathroom break. They tried good cop/bad cop and all the other psychological tactics in the book—one agent would threaten her with jail time, the other would offer something while trying to convince her it was in her best interest to cooperate. They would leave her alone and cuffed to her chair for long stretches trying to make her go stir-crazy. They used sleep deprivation because during those alone times, the moment she would start to nod, another agent would show up with more of the same questions.

They asked her about the guns on the backseat and Tuesday claimed to know nothing about them. She also knew nothing about the two and a half million dollars in the trunk. They had a bunch of questions about a shooting that happened at a condominium downtown and she knew absolutely nothing about that either.

However those were all just warm-ups, because Tuesday soon realized that she wasn't really their focus. From the door most of their questions were concerned with the little girl she was with and the man who called himself Marcus King.

This was why Tuesday dummied up immediately. Tuesday claimed she didn't know a Marcus King, even though she was arrested in front of his house while driving a car registered to that name. Even when they showed her surveillance photos taken of their first date eating together at Gaucho's, she still played ignorant.

It was about the twentieth hour of interrogation when they sent in a black female agent, probably thinking she would have better luck, with Tuesday being the same race and sex. She was brown-skinned, early forties, wearing a gray pantsuit and black heels that Tuesday instantly peeped as low-budget. She came in all friendly and apologetic, offering to get her food and promising to be brief. Tuesday knew they were trying to use her fatigue against her so she asked for a six-pack of 5 Hour Energy but never got it.

She slid a picture of Marcus in front of Tuesday. "You might think you know this man, you might even think you love him. You might think he's just this handsome single parent who's struggling to get by and raise his young daughter, but you don't know the half of it. Girl, you don't have the slightest idea of who you're really dealing with."

The agent tried to take a casual tone as if she were talking to a girlfriend. Tuesday just glanced at the photo then looked back up at her like she was speaking a different language.

"Do you even know what the man does for a living?" she asked. "Have you ever heard of Abel Incorporated?"

Tuesday knew that was the company Marcus worked for and his father owned, but she just shook her head.

The woman explained: "Abel Incorporated is a very large multinational import/export company owned by your boyfriend. Now on the surface they're squeaky clean: they're on the *Forbes* list, they pay their taxes, they even give away millions each year to charity.

"But that's just the face they show to the public. Secretly we believe it's a front for a drug distribution network so vast that it spans from Thailand to Mexico, from Cuba to Canada. It's one of the largest operations in the U.S. and has been for years."

Tuesday asked, "And why are you telling me all of this?"

"Because the man had gotten away with the shit right up under our noses for twenty years, but he's finally about to go down. And if you're not careful, you're about to go done with him."

"I already told you that I don't know nothing about this man or what he does."

"Do you know why he's been able to operate for so long without being on the radar? He does nothing in person; all his deals are done through other people. He even uses front men for the legitimate side of his operation. Plus he doesn't leave loose ends—he'll eliminate anybody who he even thinks knows his secret. Have you ever heard the name Sebastian Caine?"

Tuesday shook her head.

"They don't just call him the Invisible Man because nobody ever really seen him. It's also because he can make other people disappear. He is a cold-blooded murderer who's suspected in more open homicides and missing person cases than I can count."

Tuesday just shrugged. "Sounds like a real bad guy. Good thing I don't know him."

The agent smiled at Tuesday, then leaned back in her chair to get comfortable. "Let me tell you a story. About five or six years back your boyfriend here had a different woman. He was even engaged to her."

Tuesday remembered the conversation they had where he did admit to once having a fiancée but Marcus never went in depth about what happened to her, other than a brief comment about her cheating. Tuesday stayed quiet and continued to listen.

"Your boy is very much in love but he finds out his woman is creeping on him, and with his best friend at that. This was in early

February, so he waits until Valentine's Day, then you know what he does?"

Tuesday was curious but had to play it off. "What? Buys her a lovely charm bracelet and teddy bear?"

The woman's frown revealed that she was getting tired of Tuesday's flippant attitude. "He took her out for a nice dinner then brought her back to a hotel room where some of his men had her lover waiting. He made her watch as they cut off the man's head then did the same thing to her. That's the man you think you know!"

Tuesday thought back to when he said his best friend had died on February 14, because she found it odd that he would remember that date so specifically. Alarm bells were going off in her mind but she played it cool.

"Then to add insult to injury," the agent said, continuing the story, "he takes his best friend's then three-month-old daughter and keeps her. Just changed her name and started raising her like she was his.

"Now the bodies were never found so we can't officially prove any of this, but let me ask you something. The little girl you had in the car with you, she stays with him, right? And isn't she about five?" She gave Tuesday a facetious smile.

Tuesday looked at her, trying not to give up anything with her eyes. "I don't know. I babysit from time to time but I don't know how old she is."

The agent took the photo of Marcus and slid it back into a folder. "You think this little routine is cute, but you're really just being stupid, Ms. Knight, Ms. Green, or whatever else you want to call yourself. We caught you with thirteen illegal assault rifles and two point five million in undeclared cash. Who's to say you're not planning a terrorist attack? Under the Homeland Security Act you have no Constitutional rights; which means we can pretty much detain you indefinitely."

She leaned forward and gave Tuesday a glare that was meant to intimidate. "If you don't start talking right now, you're going to do so many years that little Danielle will be collecting a retirement pension before you get out."

Tuesday kept her game face on but inside she was shaking like stripper ass. She was having visions of being locked up in Guantanamo Bay being water-boarded and whipped by the military police until she was ninety.

Just then an older white man came in and Tuesday thought they were about to double-team her again. To her it seemed like the walls were starting to close in and the air was starting to get thin. She didn't know how much more of this she could take.

Neither woman could believe it when he went behind Tuesday's back to undo the handcuffs then said that she was free to go.

Tuesday looked even more surprised than the black DEA agent, who screamed: "Free to go?! She's a material witness in a pending federal investigation and a wanted suspect in a local homicide! On whose goddamned authority is she being released?!"

"Agent Jackson!" the old man barked in a way that meant she should watch her tone. It also let Tuesday know that he was her boss.

"It's not like I want this either but there ain't crap we can do about it! This came down from the top. The agency director himself called the section chief and the chief called me personally to order her release."

He glared at Tuesday with some combination of animosity and fear. "I don't know who the hell she is, but she's got to have some powerful friends in high places to pull that off!"

When Tuesday walked out the front of the station, she was still massaging wrists that were sore from almost a whole day of being handcuffed. There were moments trapped in that little room when she felt like she would never see outside again, so she took a couple of deep breaths of the crisp night air.

Tuesday didn't know where Marcus was and hadn't seen Danielle since her arrest. Agents pulled Danielle out of the Audi and drove her away in a different Yukon. When Tuesday inquired about her at the front desk, she was only told that the little girl had already been picked up by a guardian.

Tuesday hardly knew where she was. She looked up and down the street, then scanned the surrounding neighborhood and saw nothing familiar. Tuesday figured she was somewhere close to Romulus but had no car, no purse, no phone, and no money. She came down the steps of the precinct and just stood there for a moment looking lost. She checked her watch and saw that it was close to midnight.

She had nowhere to go and no way to get there but didn't just want to stand in front of the police station. She feared they would change their mind or find some reason to re-arrest her so Tuesday started walking east.

She was halfway up the block when a black sixty-two-inch Maybach pulled up next to her with the rear curtains closed. The same chauffeur who drove the Rolls Royce for them in California jumped out and held open the door for her.

Tuesday beamed a smile and sprinted to the car, but when she climbed in the backseat, it surprised her to see that the person sitting next to her was not Marcus. It was the handsome older gentleman who had been introduced as his father, Brandon King. He was G'd up in a suit with a cashmere overcoat and scarf.

"I guess I'm not who you were hoping for," he said, reading the disappointment on her face. Once the driver closed the door for Tuesday, he slipped back behind the wheel and they pulled off.

She said, "So I guess you're the powerful friend in high places that got me outta there."

He shook his head. "It wasn't me. We both have a powerful friend. There are a few senators for whom Abel Incorporated is a major campaign contributor and he called in a favor. Of all the things a company can invest in, nothing beats a politician."

"You're not really his father, are you?"

"And you're not really a nurse," he said, smiling at Tuesday. "I'm just a humble employee. I'm on the board of Abel Incorporated and oversee the daily operations of his many businesses, but this is because he wants it that way. As you can guess, my boss likes to keep an extremely low profile. He's a man who enjoys his anonymity."

"Where is he? And where is Danielle?"

"Danielle is safe. And for obvious reasons he couldn't be here. Certain things have come up that require him to leave the country for a little while."

"Why?" she asked, confused. "Why is all this shit coming down now?"

He explained: "Ms. Knight, Abel Incorporated is a hundred percent legitimate and has been for several years, but before that my boss's primary interest was not. There are certain people within the government who believe he's still involved with his previous business. They can't accept that he's a changed man."

He opened up the small refrigerator where a bottle of Cristal Rosay was being chilled. He offered her a drink but Tuesday refused.

As he was putting the bottle away Tuesday noticed his stylish leather gloves. She knew it was the same hand that held the pistol that killed Slim and had most likely killed Brianna and Baby Doll.

"So I guess I owe you thanks for that little assist at the club?"

"Of course we were keeping a close eye on that situation," he said, brushing a piece of lint from his fine cashmere overcoat. "I stopped by earlier that day looking for Dani. At the time she wasn't there but two of the co-conspirators were. My apologies for ruining the ambiance of your lovely establishment."

Behind his articulate speech and white-collar swag, the old man was a killer. This made Tuesday reflect back on what Agent Jackson said about them not leaving loose ends.

"I didn't tell them anything!" she blurted out nervously. "I don't know shit and didn't tell 'em shit."

He smiled at her. "He already knows. Our sources inside the DEA said that you were being less than cooperative."

Tuesday stared the old man directly in the eye. "So is this the part where I die?"

He laughed. "Nobody's going to kill you, Ms. Knight. In fact, we've taken steps to make sure no charges will be filed against you for that little incident that happened at your building nor the situation that transpired at the club."

Then a realization dawned on Tuesday that made her mouth sag open. "He knew who I was from the jump, didn't he?"

He now gave her a serious look. "Ms. Knight, there's nobody or nothing my boss doesn't see coming from a mile away. It's this unique ability that has kept him ahead of the game."

"Then why did he go along with it?" she asked, confused. "If he had me smoked out, then why did he keep seeing me?"

"Maybe it was just to play the game." He gave her another smile. "Or maybe he saw something special in you."

"But why would he just let me take the money? How did I know I would do the right thing and get Danielle back?"

He shook his head. "Do yourself a favor and don't waste your time trying to figure out his thinking. Not only will you never be able to do it, the effort will most likely drive you crazy."

She said, "I'm sorry they took the money."

He waved it off. "Don't worry about that. We've already reclaimed our property. The DEA was kind enough to return the five million dollars they illegally confiscated from us."

"But it was only three," Tuesday said, puzzled. "Actually it was two and a half, because I spent a little."

"Well, our records indicate that it was five million." He winked at her. "It was his idea to make them pay for inconveniencing you."

He inquired about how Tuesday was treated during her detainment and when she confessed they hadn't fed her, he ordered the driver to the nearest fast food restaurant. They swung through a Wendy's and got her a double with bacon and fries. Tuesday smashed it as soon as the driver passed her the bag.

Then from the surface streets they ultimately found the freeway. The driver took them to the far lane and pushed the Maybach up to ninety-five. Tuesday sat back in the plush leather re-cliner silently admiring the luxurious interior and smooth ride.

Now that she knew she wasn't about to die, Tuesday felt re-laxed enough to accept that drink. He passed her a champagne flute and filled it before pouring one for himself.

"So what happens now? I just go back home to my normal life? My friends are dead and I'm done with the game. I don't even want the club anymore."

"I'm afraid we can't allow you to do that anyway."

She looked at him confused, and started to get a little nervous again.

He smiled when he read the fear in her eye. "No, it's not like that. I think it's best if he explains this part to you himself."

He reached down for a thin laptop that was on the floor. He opened it, typed a couple keystrokes, then passed it to Tuesday.

Marcus's face was on the screen via Skype. She could tell by the background noise that he was on the private jet, the one he had lied and said was his father's.

"How you doing . . . Sebastian?"

He gave her a half smile. "Actually I prefer Marcus . . . Tuesday."

She smiled back. "I guess we both just a couple of lying mutha-fuckas, huh?"

"Artists use lies to tell the truth," he said. "Besides our names and the characters we were playing, everything else was totally real between us. Wouldn't you agree?"

Still smiling, Tuesday nodded. "I would. Do you hate me now for stickin' you up?"

"I know what it's like to be trapped in a game you're trying to get out of. Plus, I love you for what you did afterward."

"I promised you I would get her back and I meant that. So where are you going?"

"I'm afraid I can't say out loud, but a smart girl like you will probably figure it out."

Tuesday understood why he couldn't tell her, but wasn't sure what he meant about her figuring it out.

"I'll bet they said some pretty nasty things about me in that little room."

Tuesday nodded. "They did."

He looked at her, his dark eyes just as penetrating on screen as they were in real life. "Does that change how you feel about me?"

"It scared me a little bit," she confessed. "But it didn't change anything.

"We both have a past. It's our past that shaped us into the people we are today. I love the man you are right now, so as a result, I must love everything that happened to make you this man. The good decisions, the bad decisions, and the lessons learned from those mistakes."

His facial expression revealed how impressed he was with her response. "Once again you prove that your beauty is only surpassed by your wisdom."

Tuesday beamed another smile. "And once again you remember that I run on compliments. Next time just make sure you sprinkle in something about my fly style and good sex."

He laughed but then was quiet for a moment, just staring at her. When he spoke again there was a much more serious tone to his voice. "Remember that little game we played at Chuck E. Cheese with the five questions? Now I gotta call in that favor you owe me."

Tuesday knew this was about to be important. She leaned forward in her seat and adopted the same tone. "You know I'll do anything for you, babe."

"I knew for a while now that I would have to make this move and been preparing for it. I knew when they were going to be coming for me, almost down to the hour and minute.

"I've always tried to give Danielle as close to a normal life as I could. Because of what I've taken from her, I felt I owed her that. Until I can get this situation fixed, I have to disappear for a while and I can't take her with me."

Tuesday knew what he was hinting at. She also realized that

he'd been planning this the whole time. "How long do you want me to keep her?"

Marcus used no words but gave the answer with his eyes. He intended for this to be a permanent arrangement.

He explained, "The problem is that she only knows you as Tabitha Green. So that's who you have to be from this day on."

Marcus's associate pulled out a manila folder and passed it to Tuesday. "Everything is in there. New driver's license, Social Security card, birth certificate, voter's registration card, medical and dental records. The IRS has tax records for Tabitha Green that go back fifteen years. She even has a Facebook page."

Tuesday switched on the interior light to inspect the documents. Percy, the person who usually did her fake ID's, had nothing on their people.

Marcus continued. "I don't care what you used to do or how you used to do it. Your old life is done! Danielle is your number one priority now and I'm counting on you to do right by her."

Tuesday had never heard him boss up on her before but liked it. "I'll give my life for her."

"I have to go now but my father will tell you everything else you need to know."

Before he signed off, Tuesday said, "Wait! When will I get to see you again?"

He smiled. "Not soon enough, but before too long."

Tuesday kissed her fingers and touched the screen right where his lips were. He did the same and then he was off-line.

She gave the computer back to the man Marcus called his father. She asked, "So where are we going from here?"

"To the airport," he explained. "Considering what she's been through, he figured that Danielle could use a change of scenery. She and her new mother are about to move to California with her grandfather."

Tuesday couldn't believe it. "You mean me and Dani are moving to your mansion in Beverly Hills?"

"Well, yeah, but technically it's not my mansion. My boss is an extremely wealthy man; he just preferred to live modestly."

"Goddamn, is anything what it seems with you people? Is Brandon King even your real name?"

The old man just smiled. "It is now."

This whole thing had been dropped on her fast, but Tuesday was down for it all: raising Danielle, the move, and the new life. She only had to tend to a few pieces of unfinished business before she left.

She put all her new documents back in the folder and cut off the light. "Two things," Tuesday said, holding up her fingers. "First we need to swing by my condo and find my cat."

Brandon just smiled at her again. "We've already been by your apartment." He nodded to the driver, who reached to grab something from the floor of the passenger seat. It was a small travel kennel, and when he passed it to Tuesday, she saw that Nicholas was sleeping inside. The fluffy white Persian woke up just long enough to glimpse his mistress, then went back out.

He said, "Eventually you're gonna learn that he thinks of everything."

She sat the kennel between her legs, then turned back to him. "Second, we gotta find a hardware store and I'll need to borrow a little bit more of the cash." She looked at his long cashmere overcoat and stroked his sleeve to admire the fabric. "I'll need to borrow this too."

"My coat?" the old man asked, puzzled. "What are you up to?"

"Nothing," she said with a mischievous smile. "I just wanna say good-bye to an old friend."

Chapter Twenty-seven

It was two in the morning when Dresden arrived at the motel on Telegraph. Tuesday had left an urgent message for him to meet her in their room. All she said was that she had something for him and this would be his only chance to get it before she left town.

Dresden stepped into Room 304 and found a pile of cash waiting for him on the bed. There were seventeen of those 50K bundles totaling $850 thousand. Tuesday was sitting next to it with a smile.

"Didn't I tell you that the next time you saw me I was gone have enough money for you to retire on? Did I come through or did I come through?"

Dresden wore the face of a kid on Christmas morning. He closed the door, then rushed over and scooped up two arms full of the cash bricks.

"You beautiful black bitch!" he gasped, staring at it, mesmerized. "You did it! You really did it! I knew you would."

"You can finally start treating that pretty li'l wife of yours the way she deserves to be treated."

Tuesday gave him a garbage bag that he began to load up. It wasn't until he filled it that Dresden even really noticed her.

"What's with that?" he said, looking skeptically at the long black overcoat she was wearing.

"No disrespect to your wife but—" Tuesday opened her coat to show him that she was totally naked underneath. "I was thinking since we probably not gone ever see each other again. What's up?"

If Dresden was leery, it was only for a split second. The sight of those round hips, smooth thighs, and pretty shaved pussy instantly made his tiny dick swell with desire.

"All this time you're pretending like you didn't want it!" He snorted. "You never had me fooled."

She teased, "Well, you know what they say: once you go white!"

He took two steps toward Tuesday, but froze when he heard the hammer click and felt the cold steel of a barrel on the back of his head. It was then that he knew he'd fallen for the okie-doke.

"You stupid bitch!" he roared at Tuesday. He instinctively reached for his holster, then thought better of it. Instead he put his hands in the air.

"Don't let this bitch get you killed!" Dresden said, speaking to the unseen gunman standing behind him. "She probably didn't tell you this, but I'm a lieutenant with the Detroit PD and I've got some very powerful friends."

Brandon King stepped into view with the silenced pistol still aimed at his head. "I already know who you are, Lieutenant Kyle Dresden. And I'm willing to bet that all of your so-called powerful friends probably take orders from mine."

There was a knock at the door and Tuesday let the driver in. He was carrying a bag of tools and supplies they picked up at the hardware store.

Tuesday ushered Dresden to the door of the bathroom so he could glimpse what was in the bathtub. He frowned when he saw Tank's bloated, naked corpse. Tuesday had offered Face an extra hundred grand to store him on ice then have him delivered here. Face had honored his agreement just hours before trying to rob and kill her.

Dresden looked confused. "Is that Humphries from the last one?"

She said, "No, that's the lover you set up to be robbed and killed in a jealous fit."

Dresden let out a dry laugh. "Is that what this is supposed to be? Do you really think you can frame me for murder? Nobody's gonna believe this shit!"

"I think they will." Tuesday pulled out the recorder she used on their last lick. Dresden just smirked when she pressed play and he heard his own gravelly voice ordering Tank to open his safe and give up the money.

"That doesn't prove anything. I'm a highly decorated officer with an impeccable service record. Do you really think they'll believe a black whore thief like you over me?"

"It's not about them believing me; they will believe the evidence." Tuesday made him look closer until he noticed the condom hanging out of Tank's ass. "That's one of yours, baby, and your DNA's still all in it. That's a little souvenir I kept from the last time we was here."

"It's still not gonna work," he said, but with less conviction. "I'll tell them it's a set-up. I'll say you're a prostitute I used it with and you put it there. At worst I only come out looking like a cheating husband. You'll never get me pinned on a murder rap or linked to some faggot shit."

"It will work," Tuesday said confidently. "Especially since nobody's gonna ever get your side of the story."

Dresden was forced back into the anterior room. They stripped his clothes then tied him up on the bed facedown with his arms and legs tethered to the posts.

He looked up at Tuesday but it was fear and not the usual contempt in his pale blue eyes. "Tuesday, don't kill me. I know I've treated you like shit; I know I've been a bastard, but I don't deserve to die."

Tuesday crossed her arms. "You're right, you don't deserve to die. For a long time I did want to kill you, but listening to a friend of mine today made me realize that there are things much worse than dying."

Dresden's eyes went wide when he saw the driver pull a sledge-hammer from the bag along with an assortment of other tools.

Tuesday covered his mouth with duct tape then whispered into his ear, "This is one room you're definitely not walking out of."

The thump from the sledgehammer making contact with Dresden's back could be heard over his muffled screams. The sound of his spine cracking made Tuesday shudder but she still planned on taking his eyes out personally.

Epilogue

During the next year Tuesday quickly adapted to her new surroundings and new role as Tabitha Green.

At first she was intimidated by the big white house with its Greek statues, spacious rooms, high ceilings, and marble floors. For the first few months Tuesday didn't feel like she belonged in Beverly Hills—she felt like a commoner trying to pass for royalty. The house was fully staffed but Tuesday was uncomfortable with asking the butlers and maids for anything. Even while out shopping on Rodeo Drive, she didn't walk with the same swag that all the other rich bitches had. She was new to the money life and Tuesday feared that everybody she passed could smell it on her like a stench.

However, time and actually having money slowly cured those insecurities. Tuesday was given a fake job as a consultant for Abel Inc., so on top of receiving a ridiculous salary for doing absolutely nothing, she also drew a huge monthly allowance from a multi-million-dollar trust account Marcus set up for her and Danielle. Between the two she wanted for nothing. Her walk-in closets were overflowing with brand names and her bag and shoe game was insane. She eventually bought herself another white sedan but upgraded from the Caddy to an S-class Benz.

Adapting to wealth was not as challenging as adapting to motherhood. Danielle was a sweet, bright, and loving child but it took a while for her to adjust to Tuesday as her parent. She was a good kid but still a kid, and there were times when Tuesday was forced to punish her when she got out of line. These times were seldom and Dani's violations were never extreme, just her testing the limits of their new relationship.

Still, their bond was strong and grew stronger with each passing day. Even though the driver offered to do it, Tuesday made sure to drop her off and pick her up every day from her new school and continued the tradition of stopping for ice cream afterward. The Gulfstream was always on standby so the girls were well traveled; they vacationed together in places like Spain, Paris, Brazil, and of course Disney World, where Danielle finally got to meet Princess Jasmine. The two of them were inseparable because if Danielle wasn't in school, she was usually with Tuesday.

It was in the tenth month during a trip to the L.A. zoo that Danielle and Tuesday had a major breakthrough in their relationship. Danielle was excited to see the monkeys, so without thinking she grabbed Tuesday's hand and pointed, saying, "Mommy, look!" Up until that day she'd only called her "Tabitha." Tuesday blamed it on an allergy when Danielle asked why her eyes had started to tear up.

Despite their connection, Danielle still missed Marcus. The line Tuesday and "Grandpa" Brandon gave was that he was away on important business. Danielle naturally had a lot of questions about this important business that was keeping him away, but they had no good answers.

Brandon did share with Tuesday that the politicians they owned and some of their friends within the Justice Department were working to quash the indictment. He would have to stay hidden until they did. It was a long, slow process but the proper people were being bribed, intimidated, and even murdered if necessary.

Every so often the old man would pass Tuesday a message from his boss and pretend son. It was usually just greetings and well wishes but nothing concerning where he was. Tuesday occasionally used Brandon to pass messages back to him because she was told that it wasn't safe for him to call or contact her in any way.

Tuesday pretended not to know where Marcus was but eventually she figured it out just like he said she would. She thought back to their trip to the Virgin Islands and how interested he was in that small private island right next to the resort. She remembered it was called Dead Chest Island and was willing to bet that's where he was laying low until the heat died down. Tuesday was also willing to bet that the dinner he had with his attorney, where they were discussing all the money moves, had actually been about buying the island and maybe setting up that trust fund for her and Danielle. Brandon was right, the nigga did think of everything.

Tuesday wasn't required to do any work but did enough digging to learn that Abel Incorporated was totally legal now. In fact, among the Fortune 500 companies, it ranked at the top in terms of philanthropy. Included with all its charitable contributions were its scholarship program for minorities and the tens of millions spent each year to empower the inner cities around the country. Tuesday understood that Marcus was trying to rebuild the very same communities that he'd destroyed with drugs. After reopening the Bible, she finally peeped the science behind a man who did evil under the name of Caine now doing good under the name of Abel.

In time Tuesday also peeped that Danielle was the real reason why Marcus had put on this elaborate front. He gave her a home, a father figure, even a grandfather, and finally a mother. He knew that with all his money and power, the most important thing he could give her was a loving family. Tabitha, Brandon, Danielle, Marcus; the names were fake but the love was real. Nicholas the cat was the only one not using a pseudonym.

A few months back Tuesday added to their family. Shortly after leaving Detroit, Tuesday learned that she was pregnant. Despite using birth control, this little girl refused to be denied life, so four days before Thanksgiving she gave birth to Destiny Tanisha (after Tushie) King. She was seven pounds and eight ounces with Marcus's face and hands but her complexion and gray-green eyes. Unfortunately, he couldn't be there but his father got the news to him along with some pictures.

While the new baby was demanding, Tuesday always made sure she had time for Danielle. She didn't want the girl to think she was now irrelevant, and Dani wasn't jealous but instead excited about her new role as big sister.

Then after a while they got into a routine the way families typically do. Grandpa Brandon went to work every day overseeing the empire, Danielle went to school, and Tuesday stayed home with baby Destiny.

Sometimes she thought about her old life in Detroit: The Bounce, the girls, and being in the game. She heard through the grapevine that DelRay and the club were doing well while Dresden's useless body was wasting away in a prison hospital. A.D. was still locked up too, and while Tuesday didn't write, she kept his inmate account swollen.

Tuesday thought back on that life but didn't miss it at all. In her mind Boss Lady had died right along with Tushie, Jaye, Brianna, and Baby Doll. Tuesday was so different from the person she was then that her OCD didn't even affect her anymore: she was still neat, just not compulsive. She was a mother now and had a family. Even without the money, her life was richer than she could have ever imagined.

Then one day, out of the blue, Tuesday came home from picking up Danielle and found a man with a big, bushy beard sitting in the nursery bottle-feeding Destiny. Dani ran to him but Tuesday just stood there in disbelief trying to fight back tears.

"I told you I would be back before too long," Marcus said, holding both of his daughters.

Smiling, Tuesday said: "Yeah. But not soon enough."

Cheaper to Keep Her

by Kiki Swinson

The night Duke Carrington walked into the Magic City strip club, Lynise Carter was working her usual bartending shift. But there was nothing routine about Duke. Wealthy, charming, and persuasive, he soon swept her off her feet. He convinced her to quit her job, and the future was looking bright. But just as Lynise was getting used to VIP treatment, Duke was getting ready to replace her with a rival she didn't even know she had . . .

Now available!

Prologue

"Bitch! You better open this fucking door!"

When I heard his voice, the banging and then the kicking on the door, my heart sank into the pit of my stomach. A hot flash came over my body at the sound of his deep baritone voice. I could tell he was more than livid. I immediately started rushing through the luxury high-rise condominium I had been living in for the past six months. Duke owned it. It was time to put my Plan B into motion. Quick, fast, and in a hurry.

"Damn, damn, shit!" I cursed as I gathered shit up. I didn't know how I had let myself get caught slipping. I planned to be the fuck out of Dodge before Duke could get wind of my bad deeds. I had definitely not planned my escape correctly.

"Lynise!" Duke's voice boomed again with additional angry urgency. He started banging even harder and jiggling the doorknob. I was scared to death, but I wasn't shocked. I knew sooner or later he would come. After all the shit I had done to him, I would've come after my ass too.

"Lynise! Open this fucking door now!" Duke continued to bark from the other side of the door. He didn't sound like the man I had met and fell in love with. He damn sure didn't sound like he was about to shower me with cash and gifts like he used to. Not after all the shit I had done . . . or undone, I should say.

"Open the fucking door!" he screamed again.

I was shaking all over now. From the sound of his voice I could tell he wasn't fucking around.

"Shit!" I whispered as I slung my bag of money over my shoulder and thought about my escape. I whirled around aimlessly but soon realized that my Plan B didn't include Duke being at the front door of his fifth-floor condo. There was nowhere for me to go. It was only one way in and one way out and I damn sure wasn't jumping off the balcony. If it was the second floor, maybe I would've taken a chance, but I wasn't trying to die.

"Fuck! Fuck! Fuck!" I cursed as I saw my time running out. Duke was a six-foot-tall hunk of solid muscle. I knew I had no wins.

"Bitch! I'm about to take this fucking door down!" Duke screamed. This time I could hear him hitting the door hard. I couldn't tell if he was kicking the door or putting his shoulder into it. Although it was his condo, I had changed the locks to keep his ass out.

I spun around and around repeatedly, trying to get my thoughts together before the hinges gave in to his brute power. Hiding the money I had stolen was paramount. My mind kept beating that thought in my head. I raced into the master bedroom and rushed into the walk-in closet. I began frantically snatching clothes off the hangers. I needed to use them to hide my bag of cash.

Wham!

"Oh, my God!" I blurted out when I heard the front door slam open with a clang. I threw the bag onto the floor and covered it with piles of designer clothes. Things Duke and I had shopped for together when shit was good between us.

"Bitch, you thought I was playing with you?" Duke's powerful voice roared. "Didn't I tell you, you had to get the fuck out of my crib?"

He was up on me within seconds. I stood defenseless as he advanced on me so fast I didn't even have time to react. I threw my hands up, trying to shield myself from what I expected to come when he reached out for me. But I was too late. He grabbed me around my neck so hard and tight I could swear little pieces of my esophagus had crumbled.

"Duke, wait!" I said in a raspy voice as he squeezed my neck harder. I started scratching at his big hands trying to free myself so I could breathe.

"What, bitch? I told you if you ever fucked with me you wouldn't like it!" he snarled. Tears immediately rushed down my face as I fought for air. "Ain't no use in crying now. You should've thought 'bout that shit a long time ago."

Duke finally released me with a shove. I went stumbling back and fell on my ass so hard it started throbbing. I tried to scramble up off the floor, but before I could get my bearings I felt his hands on me again. His strong hand was winding into my long hair.

"Ouch!" I wailed, bending my head to try to relieve some of the pressure he was putting on my head.

Duke yanked me up by my hair. Sharp, stabbing pains shot through my scalp.

"Owww!" I cried out as he wrung me around by my hair. I tried to put my small hands on top of his huge, animal hands, but it was no use. Hands I had once loved I now despised and wished would just fall off.

"You thought it was all good, right! You a fucking trifling-ass bitch and I want you the fuck out of here!" Duke gritted. Then he lifted his free hand and slapped me across my face with all his might.

"Pl-pl-pl-please!" I begged him for mercy. But Duke hit me again.

I was crying hysterically. Partly from the pain of his abuse, but more so from our past. I would have never thought our relationship would come to this. It had been a long road and all I wanted to do was teach him a lesson when I did the shit I did. I never thought I would have been facing this type of torment.

"I want all your shit out of here, you scandalous bitch! And don't take nothing that I fucking bought!" Duke roared, then he hit me again. This time I felt blood trickle from my nose. My ears were still ringing from the previous blow to my head. He hit me again. I was sure he had knocked one of my teeth loose.

"Yo, Ak, get this bitch shit and throw it the fuck out," Duke called out to one of his boys. He never traveled anywhere alone. There were always two dudes with him at all times. The one I knew as Chris rushed into the closet and started scooping up my clothes and shoes.

"Wait!" I screamed, but it was for nothing.

"Shut the fuck up!" Duke screamed in response, slapping me again.

I could actually feel my eyes starting to swell. I finally gave up. My spirit was broken, my body was sore. I watched as Chris and another one of Duke's boys slid back the glass balcony doors and started tossing all my shit over. I doubled over crying. More and more shit went over and I was sure it was raining down on the beautifully manicured lawn below.

"Yeah . . . that's enough. Don't throw none of that jewelry or those furs outside. I got bitches I could give that shit to," Duke said maliciously. His words hurt. "A'ight, bitch . . . ya time is up."

I shrunk back, thinking he was going to hit me again. But he didn't. He grabbed me by the arm roughly. "Oww!" I cried out.

Duke was squeezing my arm so hard the pain was crazy. "Let's go," he said, pulling me toward the door.

"Nooooo!" I screamed and then I dropped my body weight down toward the floor so he couldn't pull me.

"Oh, bitch, you getting the fuck outta here," Duke roared. He bent down, hoisted me over his shoulder and started carrying me kicking and screaming toward the door.

"You can't do this to me! You will regret this, Duke Carrington!!" I hollered.

"Fuck you!" he spat in return, opening the condo door and tossing me out into the hallway like a piece of discarded trash. I can't even describe the feeling that came over me. It was a mixture of hurt, shame, and embarrassment all rolled into one.

Duke slammed the door in my face and I yelled for him to listen to me. My cries fell on deaf ears. My shoulders slumped down in defeat. Duke had left me in the hallway with no shoes, a short nightgown, and nothing but my belongings on the lawn outside. I didn't even have the key to my BMW X6.

"Aggghhh!" I grunted in anger and frustration as I raked my hands through my tangled hair. I vowed from that minute on that Duke Carrington would learn just what all men have been saying for years . . . *it's cheaper to keep her.*

As I limped down the hallway of the building, all of the memories of how I had gotten to this point came rushing back.